WHA

MW01088592

Katie Schuermann continues to delight readers with her latest book, *The Harvest Raise*! Her addition of characters with disabilities is done with dignity, respect, and humor! Katie carefully depicts the natural process many experience as they move from cautious welcome to acceptance, belonging, and mutual ministry. Would that more congregations follow this example and embrace people of all abilities, the gifts they bring, and the value they add to the Body of Christ!

**—Mona Fuerstenau, Director of Lutheran Ministry Partnerships, Bethesda Lutheran Communities Past chair, LCMS Disability Task Force**

Katie Schuermann's playful humor draws the reader into *The Harvest Raise* from its first page, and her insights make you want to continue reading to the end. The bare flaws in her characters reveal our own failings; yet her story wraps us with such forgiveness, we feel an ever-warming forbearance toward those around us. *The Harvest Raise* is an especially well-written, thoughtful conclusion to the rare series that lightens my heart, makes my daughter giggle, and touches us both deeply.

**—Cheryl Swope, MEd, author of *Simply Classical: A Beautiful Education for Any Child*, coauthor of *Eternal Treasures: Teaching Your Child at Home*, and creator of the Simply Classical Curriculum for Special Needs**

Katie Schuermann's latest book, *The Harvest Raise*, is another winner. You've heard of "comfort food." Katie's books read like "comfort books." The pages slip by like silk as we read again about the lives in Bradbury. These characters come to life as we cry and cheer with their struggles and successes, smiling as it brings to memory some loved ones we know in our own lives.

Not only do we see their struggles with some of today's moral dilemmas but we read solid theological foundations from the Bible in words that we can take into our day-to-day meetings with similar issues.

Thanks, Katie, for giving us some of life's lessons through such a wonderfully imperfect place like Bradbury, for showing us God's love and forgiveness through His servants, and creating the characters so near to our own lives in all of the books in Anthems of Zion.

**—Shelley Moeller LWML Vice President of Gospel Outreach 2013–17**

Schuermann is at her best, crafting a narrative that is joyful and heartbreaking, hilarious and touching. This book serves as a reminder for us all—Christ is constantly at work in our lives; often in ways we least expect. While the story is fiction, the message is real. Zion is every church and her struggles are ones that we all encounter. Throughout the pages of *The Harvest Raise*, Schuermann's characters bring us face-to-face with ourselves; reminding us that our triumphs, our sins, and our best efforts are all covered by a merciful Jesus. This is pleasure reading with a purpose!

**—Matthew Machemer**
**Associate Kantor, Concordia Theological Seminary, Fort Wayne, IN**
**Choir director, St. Paul's Lutheran Church, Fort Wayne, IN**

If you've read the first two books in CPH's Anthems of Zion series, you already know that Katie Schuermann has a way with words, one that paints the people of Bradbury so vividly that they seem more like movie than book characters. The same is true of *The Harvest Raise*, as all our beloved Bradburians are back—singing, praying, laughing, crying, and yes, sometimes yelling their way through the trilogy's final installment. The love that Mrs. Schuermann feels for her characters is folded into every word she writes about them, and her invitation to share in that love is one no good Lutheran reader can refuse. Yet the author neither sugarcoats nor offers pat answers to life's most vexing questions, acknowledging throughout her story that sin is real and the devil always lurking. *The Harvest Raise* contains both joy and sorrow in abundance, along with a quiet and ever-present assurance of Gospel hope and comfort. Upon reading the final page, you will feel as though you have come full circle from your first encounter with Mrs. Scheinberg in *House of Living Stones*. Don't be surprised when the tears flow! Thanks be to God for Zion in Bradbury, and for each of our Zions—past, present, and future. "O grant that each of us, Now met before Thee here, May meet together thus When Thou and Thine appear" (*LSB* 921).

**—Cheryl Magness**
**Blogger at roundunvarnishedtale.blogspot.com**

*The Harvest Raise* brings Katie Schuermann's trilogy about life in Bradbury, Illinois, to an end—too soon! Katie has a real affection for her characters. Before Bradbury slips away, she guides us to an understanding that "family" reaches far beyond bloodlines, and there is freedom in forgiving others and having a sense of humor about oneself. Where is Katie in all these characters and situations? She is, of course, in every poignant, forgiving, insightful, hilarious word.

—**Ardis Larvick**
**German/English Instructor (ret.)**
**Stewardson-Strasburg High School**

Unlike other Christian books that focus on the Law and what you must do, this trilogy has been blissful and abounding in grace. Katie Schuermann has once again made such wonderfully relatable characters as she focuses on a pastor's life and his struggle to balance family and church. I have lived through some of the things Emily has faced. That absolute truth and honesty Katie brings to the reader is refreshing. Living the life of a pastor's wife is hard. I just want to hold Emily tight as she shoulders such pain with determination and strength. The hardships, struggles, and yet so many blessings make this book something to reach for when there is a want to hear pure Gospel and still get lost in a beautifully rich, complex storyline. I never thought the second book could be topped, sucking me into such human emotions attached to everyday life. And yet Katie has succeeded in making something that balances growth and loss at the same time while leading you into a greater, more in-depth devotional life.

—**Allison Hull**
**Pastor's wife and keeper of a rambunctious household**

This book is a must-read for all professional church workers, students, and spouses! Katie blows apart the myth of the "perfect church" and the "perfect Christian" by deftly applying Law and Gospel and a generous dose of humor to the dilemmas generated by her well-developed characters as she exposes their sins against God and society. Throughout the book, she demonstrates God's unconditional love, forgiveness, and power to use cracked, flawed vessels, people of all abilities, as instruments of grace and healing in a broken world.

—**Brenda Scarbeary**
**Deaconess, Bethesda Ministry Consultant, and pastor's wife**

Other Books by Katie Schuermann

*He Remembers the Barren*
*Pew Sisters*

Anthems of Zion Series
*House of Living Stones*
*The Choir Immortal*

# The Harvest Raise

## KATIE SCHUERMANN

CONCORDIA PUBLISHING HOUSE • SAINT LOUIS

*For Lucy, Becca, Julia, Becky, Kristi, Eliza,*
*Emily, and Lauren, who joyfully celebrate the*
*gifts God gives to all of us, even books*

*And for Michelle, whose laughter inspires me*

Published by Concordia Publishing House
3558 S. Jefferson Avenue, St. Louis, MO 63118-3968
1-800-325-3040 · www.cph.org

*On what has now been sown*
*Thy blessing, Lord, bestow,*
*The pow'r is Thine alone*
*To make it sprout and grow.*
*Do Thou in grace the harvest raise,*
*And Thou alone shalt have the praise!*

(*LSB* 921:1)

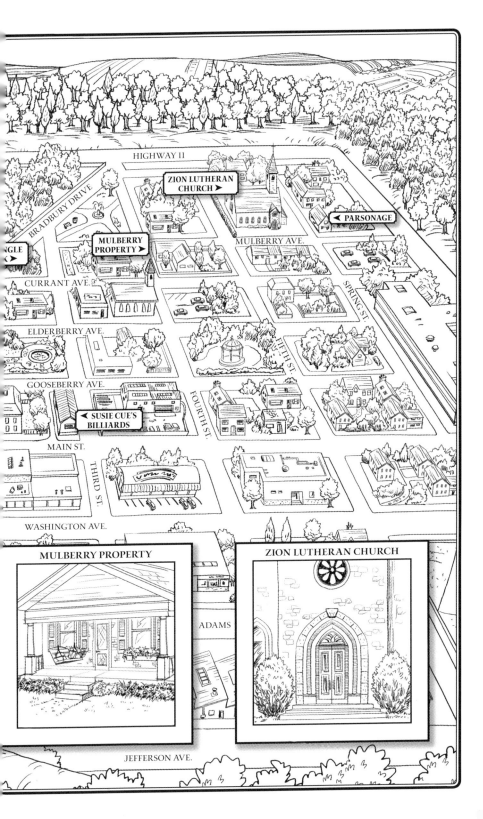

# Contents

# Character List

〰〰〰〰〰〰〰〰〰〰〰〰〰

**Pastor Michael Fletcher**—the good and right reverend of Zion Lutheran Church

**Mrs. Scheinberg**—Zion's secretary of forty-two years

**Emily Duke**—Bradbury's resident sweetheart and doctor of music

**Rebecca Jones**—Emily's best friend and local spitfire

**Robbie Jones**—Rebecca's middle, freckled son

**Beverly Davis**—lifelong member of Zion with the gift of gab

**Candice Bradbury**—wife of Thomas Edison Bradbury III and rightful queen of Bradbury

**Caroline Bradbury**—the heiress

**Ben Schmidt**—enterprising farm boy and gentleman extraordinaire

**Nettie Schmidt**—she may be there, but she's not all there

**Janet Koelster**—the fastest spatula in the Midwest

**Evan Ebner**—Zion's faithful, phlegmatic organist

**Blaine Maler**—voted best pianist (and hair) in Bradbury

**Mary Hopf**—Blaine's friend from Bradbury College

**Yvonne Roe**—the grouchiest beauty in all the land with a penchant for earthy piles of sand

**Anna Cecilia**—no one knows anything better than her, she's certain of it

**Marge Johnson**—best known for her Wurlitzer vibrato

**Lauren Basset**—head of Bradbury College's music department

**Zachary Brandt**—Bradbury College's ever dashing, always available literature professor

# CHAPTER ONE: THE BEGINNING OF THE END

|||||||||||||||||||||||||||||||||||||||||||||||||

The day of salvation had finally come, though it was Mrs. Arlene Compton Scheinberg—not the angel Gabriel—who sounded the proverbial trumpet.

"I've decided to retire," the stodgy secretary announced before the faithful remnant gathered in the front pews of Zion Lutheran Church.

Pastor Michael Fletcher's jaw fell into his lap. The good reverend had been praying for deliverance from the great tribulation for years—ten years, one month, and nine days, to be exact—ever since Zion's permed pontificate had first glared at him from her leather throne in the church office and pronounced, "I have barn cats older than you." But the man was surprised to find his blessed liberation coming on a Tuesday night of all things, for in his dreams—and he had indulged in such dreaming often—the eschatological event came at the end of a work week and in the quiet and privacy of his study. His secretary's sensitivities were eternally opposed to his own, however. Leave it to Mrs. Scheinberg, who was herself the very opposite of an angel in both stature and countenance, to choose the middle of a church voters' meeting to blow her horn and end life as everyone knew it in Bradbury.

"What?" Harold Schmidt hollered from his seat in the front pew, cupping an arthritic hand behind his right ear.

Mrs. Scheinberg leaned her heavy bosom forward and barked, "Retire, Hank! I've decided to *retire!*"

Harold was practically deaf, but he was the only member of the congregation yet to realize it. "New attire? I thought we came here to vote on repainting the parking lot."

Nettie, Harold's devoted bride of sixty years, diplomatically held up a finger to ward off the secretary's inevitable counterattack. She grabbed a Communion card from the front pew rack, penciled the appropriate verb across the top of the card, and handed the transcription to her impervious husband.

Harold squinted at the card for a long moment before attempting—and failing—to whisper under his breath, "Hallelujah!"

Mrs. Scheinberg's nostrils danced a flamenco.

Pastor Fletcher stood to intervene, but he fumbled his words. He honestly didn't know what to say. Now that the happy hour of emancipation had finally arrived, he found himself inflicted with a surprising sadness. Not a full-blown, flu-like melancholy, to be sure, but a twinge, an irritation, a sniffle of sorrow, for even the merry prospect of walking a new earth free of Mrs. Scheinberg and her withering ways did not fully quell his sentimental disposition toward his secretary. The woman was exasperating—that much was certain—but she was also loyal, resourceful, and too tightly woven into the fabric of the church's life to be yanked loose like some inconsequential thread. He opened his mouth to say as much, but Beverly Davis beat him to it.

"Oh, Arlene!" the cushy, gray-haired woman spouted, sniffing loudly in the fourth pew on the pulpit side and rummaging through her handbag for a tissue. "You can't leave us!"

"I'm retiring, Bev," Mrs. Scheinberg frowned, "not moving."

"You don't understand," Bev blubbered, her faucet now turned on full blast. "It just won't be the same without you sitting behind that desk. You're the only secretary our church has ever had. There's never been anyone but you in that office."

"Arlene is a constitution," Nettie nodded soberly.

Bev, open-mouthed, paused to consider this fact.

"She means *institution*, honey," Janet Koelster leaned over to murmur.

"Oh yes," Bev nodded, deftly picking up where she had left off. Verbal rambles were her specialty. "I simply can't stand the thought of someone else answering the phone whenever I call the church. It's just not right. You belong behind that desk, Arlene. You're irreplaceable, that's what. I don't care what Candice or Yvonne or anyone else says."

Mrs. Scheinberg's frown lines deepened into ravines. "And what, exactly, do Candice and Yvonne say?"

Candice Bradbury, the town's self-proclaimed first lady and the congregation's self-appointed authority in all matters of theology, sociology, psychology, kinesiology, and blame-ology, shrugged amicably from her seat next to Janet and ran a confident hand through her bobbed hair. "All I said was that it would be good to get some new blood in the office. Someone with a little more . . . mobility."

Everyone held their breath and looked down at their laps, no doubt afraid to make eye contact with the slighted secretary currently leaning heavily on an aluminum cane. Mrs. Scheinberg, in her earlier years, would have pawed at the ground and charged the smug woman like an angry bull, but as it was, she had eaten leftover ham loaf for both lunch and supper that day and her swollen hooves were now rooted to the ground like tree stumps. She settled for defiantly lifting her two chins in the air and declaring, "That is *precisely* why I am retiring, Candice."

"Well, it's too late. You can't retire now." This came from Yvonne Roe at the back of the crowd.

Mrs. Scheinberg squinted over her gold-rimmed glasses at the white-haired woman wearing pearls and a pressed, long-sleeved blouse to a casual meeting in June. "What do you mean, 'I can't retire *now*?' It's my decision, Yvonne. I can retire whenever I want, thank you very much."

"How can you be so selfish, Arlene?" Yvonne chirped. The woman's dark eyebrows arched in righteous condemnation like two fuzzy caterpillars flinching under the threat of a white storm cloud. "You know very well that there is no one else in this congregation available to cover the phones. You, at least, have time for such things."

"Oh, for heaven's sake!" Mrs. Scheinberg snorted through her nose. "There're plenty of people in this church capable of running an office."

"Like who?"

"Well, you, for one."

Yvonne smiled wanly. "I watch my grandchildren every weekday."

Mrs. Scheinberg's neck grew splotchy. She didn't have any children, let alone grandchildren, and Pastor Fletcher knew that fact embarrassed her. He silently willed one of his elders to speak up. Honestly, any man would do—any man other than Hank, that is—but every person growing facial hair or wearing a necktie or holding a corn seed hat in hand averted his eyes and busied himself picking at his fingernails. Pastor sighed. However faithful the men in his congregation were, they had fallen into a bad habit of remaining quiet whenever things got noisy in voters' meetings, especially if the noise was estrogenic in origin. He opened his mouth to say something, but Mrs. Scheinberg recovered enough to speak. She was used to fending for herself.

"Bev could do it," she said.

"Oh, I can't," Bev shook her head, still dabbing at her eyes. "Not with the county and state fairs just 'round the corner. And then it's harvest time. Ben Schmidt's off to college this fall, so Irv needs me to run the truck back and forth to the elevator this year. That, and Mother still needs me to help her take her meds every morning and evening. She won't swallow for the new nurse on duty. Oh, the girl's nice enough, but she's younger than the bushes in our front yard and Mother doesn't trust her. That reminds me! Did I tell you that her right foot is finally better? That new antifungal finally did the trick. Well, the left foot still has a bad spot on the underside of her pinky toe, but the doctor said there's no danger of losing it. At least, not now. But we still need to be careful, so I can't cover any office hours this summer. Besides, I wouldn't be very good on the phone. I never know what to say to people."

Every eye in the nave collectively blinked.

"What about Ida Greensborough?" Nettie suggested.

"Um," Pastor Fletcher stepped closer to Nettie, lowering his voice politely, "Ida's been dead for two months, Nettie."

"What?" Harold bellowed, cupping his hand behind his ear again.

Pastor's face blanched. He raised his voice a bit. "Ida Greensborough. She's dead."

"Fled?"

"*Dead*, Hank!" Mrs. Scheinberg spat, her entire face now covered with red splotches. "And the sainted woman's to be envied! At least she's spared the misery of having this *ridiculous* conversation with all of you."

"What about Mary Hopf?" Janet suggested cheerfully. As a lifelong member of the congregation and head cook on the line at Koelster's Kitchen on the town square, Janet was used to keeping calm under pressure. Positivity was the key. A squirt or two of whipped cream down the hatch every once in a while didn't hurt either. "Mary would be the perfect secretary for our church. Such a sweet voice! Why, I bet the church'll even start growing once we have someone young and pretty behind that front desk."

Pastor dropped his head into his hand, seriously reconsidering his theological qualms with the Rapture. Maybe the notion of Christians disappearing from the earth in the blink of an eye was not such a bad one.

"Mary would be ideal," Candice purred, "but she was hired full time at the public library last month. She's quite settled now. If only you had thought to retire earlier, Arlene."

"If only—?" Mrs. Scheinberg started, swinging her left hand out to the side in aggravation. The loose skin of her underarm flapped freely like a shirt on a clothesline in a summer breeze. Pastor pressed his lips together and waited for the secretary to sort the sheep from the goats—corporate judgment had always been one of her spiritual gifts—but she uncharacteristically let her sentiment fade into nothingness. It appeared as if her internal fire had petered out.

"Well, that settles it," Yvonne quipped. "You have to keep at it, Arlene. There's simply no one left to fill your chair."

Nope, the secretary's old fire was alive and well. It burst into majestic flame.

"First of all, no one's ever going to *fill* my chair," Mrs. Scheinberg clarified lest anyone be mistaken. "That's *my* chair. My brother gave it to me ten years ago for Christmas. It goes where I go. Second, I am retiring in two weeks, and that's final. And as for who is going to answer the phones after that," she began shuffling with her cane across the aisle, "I move that we outsource the phone line to India like every other idiot in America."

With that, Mrs. Scheinberg aimed her rear end toward the front pew on the lectern side and fell into her seat with a minor thud.

Bev sniffled into her soggy tissue, Yvonne rolled her eyes condescendingly, Pastor ran a weary hand through his hair, and Nettie, smiling winsomely, offered a hearty, "I second the motion."

# Chapter Two: Rooster Cogburn
## and the Lady

Mrs. Scheinberg was tired. Her feet hurt, her back hurt, her fingers hurt, and—as she tried to explain to her closest friend after the voters' meeting—her heart hurt.

"Angina?" Bev leaned in, concerned.

"No," Mrs. Scheinberg sighed. Her literal-minded friend was often deaf to imagery's subtle tune.

"Acid reflux, then?"

"I'm not talking about *that* kind of pain, Bev," Mrs. Scheinberg explained, keeping her voice low so as not to draw unwanted attention from the lipstick-wearing bloodhounds circling the parking lot. The last thing she needed was Candice or Yvonne sniffing out the details of her private life. "I'm talking about . . . oh, never mind."

Mrs. Scheinberg opened the back door of her Grand Marquis and jostled her cane into the empty spot behind the driver's seat. The last few months had been almost unbearable. Usually, it was wintertime when she warred against the blues, but June and all of its sunshine had proven ineffective in dissipating the heavy fog clouding her life. Maybe if her joints didn't hurt all of the time. Or maybe if everyone at church would listen to reason for once. Or maybe if—

"Blaine's not coming home, is he?" Not all of life's subtleties were lost on Bev.

Mrs. Scheinberg felt salty waves begin to roll under her eyes. Blaine Maler. How the mention of that troubled boy's name made her heart swell simultaneously with pride and pain! From the first moment he had sat down behind the piano to accompany the choir in the church balcony years ago, her usually begrudging affections had been stirred. He had needed a champion, and she had needed someone to love. They were a match made in heaven, and even though Blaine was all grown up now and making a good life for himself in graduate school, she couldn't help but feel that anywhere he lived outside of Bradbury County was simply too far to bear. "He can't come home."

"Not even for a weekend?"

"He's got school. A summer intensive course, I think he called it. He said he might be able to come for a few days before the fall quarter starts up."

Bev's voice grew tiny. "Are you really retiring, Arlene?"

"Of course I'm retiring. I'm a hundred years old." That last part wasn't exactly true, but Mrs. Scheinberg thought Bev needed some lightening up. Her friend was taking everything a little hard these days. It was the constant stress of taking care of her mother.

"Is it your knee?"

"No, my knee's fine. Today, at least." Mrs. Scheinberg carefully scooted alongside of the car, her right hand gripping the frame, and gingerly opened the driver's side door. "It's my feet that are trying to kill me."

"If you lost some weight, it would help."

This free tip came from Candice Bradbury, whose hot-pink Reeboks had silently coasted to a stop near the left rear tire of the Grand Marquis.

Mrs. Scheinberg looked up and glared at the woman dressed in purple activewear. "If you talked less, it would help."

Bev backed away slowly.

Mrs. Scheinberg pressed her lips together, instantly repenting. She shouldn't have said that last bit, she knew—it was harsh, and Candice never responded well to punitive measures—but it had been such a long day and some habits were so hard to break.

"Oh, Arlene," Candice sang, a note of condescension providing the perfect harmony to her sugary tone. "I'm serious. You'd feel a lot better if you exercised."

Mrs. Scheinberg was determined to be nice, but she had little patience for teenyboppers wearing spandex in public, let alone a grown woman well past her prime. And Candice rarely wore anything else these days. Ever since the woman had lost sixty pounds and opened Bradbury's one and only exercise facility—The Candi Box—she had been insufferable, making an embarrassing show of herself in tight clothes all across the county. Mrs. Scheinberg closed her eyes so as not to witness just how little Candice's leggings left for the imagination. She wanted to be able to fall asleep that night.

"Here. Take my card." Candice extended a purple piece of card stock cut into the shape of a piece of candy.

"I don't need your card, Candice."

"Take it."

"I've had your number memorized for twenty-two years."

"This one's different. It's the number for my gym."

Mrs. Scheinberg opened her eyes and gave Fitness Barbie a look of strained tolerance. This pet exercise campaign of Candice's was quickly moving beyond the realm of annoying and into the kingdom of unbearable. "I'm not calling your gym."

"It'll do you good, Arlene."

Mrs. Scheinberg's head felt remarkably like the regulator on a pressure cooker, and it took all of her resolve to keep it from jiggling. If she stayed in this ridiculous conversation any longer, she would most definitely blow her top. Measuredly, she lowered herself, backside first, into the driver's seat of her car and swung her concrete-block feet onto the mat. "Let it rest, Candice."

Unfortunately, Candice had never been very good at listening to others. She stepped forward, leaned her frame through the open door, and persisted, "You don't feel well, Arlene. Everyone can see that. I know how to help you."

This was exactly why she wanted to retire. Everyone in the congregation—not just Candice—had become a dictator of late, ordering her around and telling her what to do as if she didn't already know how to properly care for herself. "You need to take more breaks, Arlene," Pastor Fletcher said every time she mentioned her hands were aching from arthritis. "It's time to cut down on the carbohydrates and sugars," Bev bossed whenever she popped open a bottle of antacid after dessert. And then, of course, there was the corporate sentiment so lovingly delivered to her today: "You need to retire soon but not too soon!" Well, one thing was certain. She had managed just fine on her own as a widow for forty-three years, and the last thing she needed was anybody telling her what to do. She reached for the car door and pulled it shut. "Good-bye, Candice," she mouthed through the glass as she turned the key in the ignition. Then, she backed out of the parking lot, taking very little heed of any pink running shoes that might be in the way.

It took less than two minutes to maneuver the Grand Marquis out of Bradbury, but once she turned north on County Highway 63, Mrs. Scheinberg pushed on the accelerator and raced down the open road like a beast set free from bondage. The speed limit for unmarked roads in Illinois was fifty-five miles per hour, but she always felt more comfortable maneuvering the oiled roads at a hearty sixty-five. Sure, there were threatening potholes everywhere—Bradbury County was presently too short of funds to do any patching—but she knew every rise and fall of this road better than she knew the terrain of her own kitchen counter. She could probably drive it with her eyes shut, but she was much too old and sensible for such foolishness.

*Now, if only Candice would be sensible*, she thought, an involuntary sigh escaping from her lungs. Bradbury's purple princess was ridiculous in every single way, but the woman really couldn't help it. Some things were just genetic, Mrs. Scheinberg supposed. And then there was Yvonne. Mrs. Scheinberg's diaphragm unloaded another sigh. How on earth did that wrinkled raisin get off telling her—in public!—that she couldn't retire? As if it were anyone's choice but her own! She wrung the steering wheel between her aching hands like a wet dishrag. The real problem, of course, was that the congregation had grown lazy of late, behaving like entitled children, expecting everyone but themselves to do the work of the church. She shook her head in disgust. Well, they were all about to get the shock of their lives. Once she retired, they'd grow wise to just how much she had been doing all of these years. Mrs. Scheinberg relaxed against her seat, the thought of future justice a sweet salve on her presently injured pride, but no sooner had she turned west on 1000 North than all serotonin immediately fled her bloodstream.

"What in the—?" she cried, hard braking to a stop in the middle of the road. She sat staring, dismayed, at the absurd sight before her.

There, festering on the north side of the road like a pimple on the face of the earth, lay Max Mauer's farm. His property had always been an eyesore in the county—the man could never be bothered to paint his outbuildings or power wash the mold off of the siding of his double-wide—and in the forty-six years she had endured life as his neighbor, he had not once taken the trouble to build a shed in which to properly store his farming equipment. He was perfectly and maddeningly content to park his auger, disc, and old corn picker on the east side of a dilapidated, old barn, effectively turning his east pasture into a junkyard.

Years ago, Mrs. Scheinberg had reconciled herself to the fact that her beautiful 80 acres of tilled fields and pastureland butted up against his ugly 160 acres of tired dirt, but she had never made peace with that blight of a barn. Covered in sheets of rusting tin, it sat a mere twenty feet from the road, essentially blocking her front porch view of the summer sunrise. It was not the repulsive sight, however, which made all neighborly interactions between her and Max impossible. It was the barn's repugnant smell, for since the summer of '78, that churlish man had devoted the entire north stall of his derelict building to housing a couple dozen hogs, consequently turning every easterly breeze which fluttered the curtains hanging at her open kitchen window into an act of chemical warfare.

In all of her wildest nightmares, Mrs. Scheinberg had never been able to imagine a reality worse than the one they were already inhabiting, but apparently, she had never fully understood the depths of Max's indelicate nature. For there, casting a long shadow in the late evening sunlight, sat the sagging frame of her corroding nemesis—hideous as ever—but the roof was now painted the most garish shade of bright blue. Mrs. Scheinberg blinked twice, hoping her blood sugar was playing tricks on one of her optic nerves, but every time she opened her eyes afresh the Smurf-colored gable loomed before her as real as the marble marking Dean's grave. To make matters worse, giant white letters had been painted across the top, reading, "Cool down this summer at the Kuhl Whip Stand!" with an image of what she assumed to be a swirl of vanilla ice cream—only this one with a cartoonish pair of eyes—floating underneath.

"The fool!" she muttered, recovering her wits and gunning her engine toward home. She glared at the monstrosity as she drove by, unable to enjoy the quiet beauty of her own property glowing in the setting sun half a mile down the road. When she finally turned into the haven of her pristine gravel driveway, she was blind to the cascading loveliness of the bridal veil bushes encircling the metal grain bin. She didn't even notice the new day lilies that had opened near her front porch or the heathery sages maturing at the base of the stone silo. All she could see was the color red. She pulled straight into her single-car garage and parked the Grand Marquis.

Frenzied barking welcomed her from within the house.

"All right, now, Ceci," Mrs. Scheinberg called, pulling herself out of the vehicle and working her cane out of the backseat. "I hear you."

She hobbled ten feet across a covered breezeway, hoisted her frame up a concrete step, and opened a side door leading into the house. A red-and-brown-haired Shih Tzu landed her front paws fondly on her owner's knees. If the dog's incessant yapping had not been the mark of the highest affection, the sound of it would have driven Mrs. Scheinberg completely mad. But as it was, she leaned down to scratch Ceci behind her ears and returned the generous welcome with a few words of mutual respect. "Yes, yes, girl. I know. I know. I missed you too. Okay, now, let's settle down. I'm home."

Ceci licked Mrs. Scheinberg's right wrist and then hightailed it to the rear of the kitchen, leaning her dainty paws against the back door. She immediately tore into another round of barking.

"My goodness," Mrs. Scheinberg soothed, following at a much slower pace behind her companion. "One would think you've been stranded here all day long without a potty break, what with all of the racket you're making. I've been gone only a couple of hours, girl. Calm down."

Ceci did not calm down. She ran around in circles by the door, alternately jumping at the door handle and then looking back at Mrs. Scheinberg, barking frantically the entire time.

"Ceci!" Mrs. Scheinberg hollered, clapping her hands once. "That's enough. I said calm down."

Ceci quieted with a girlish whimper but failed to stand still. She continued circling the door mat but this time at a slightly slower pace.

"Do you need to go outside?"

A stream of unintelligible barks ensued.

"No!" Mrs. Scheinberg clapped again. "Sit. You need to ask me politely."

Ceci promptly ceased barking and looked up at Mrs. Scheinberg with dark, shiny eyes. She obediently sat her bottom on the floor and gave one short, polite bark.

"That's more like it," Mrs. Scheinberg said, unlocking the back door and opening it wide. "Go on, now."

But Ceci didn't budge. She did, however, resume her steady stream of barking at a fevered pitch, and when Mrs. Scheinberg stepped out into the backyard to try leading Ceci out herself, she finally understood what was causing her dog's breakdown.

There, bent low next to her south-facing chicken pen, digging furiously with his front paws at the base of the wire fence, was a mangy German shepherd whose drooling sights were set on her prized cock, Rooster Cogburn.

"Git!" she instinctively hollered, clapping her hands forcefully then wincing at the sudden surge of pain coursing through her fingers and wrists. "Git out of here, Dutch!"

Ceci joined her voice with her owner's, but Dutch didn't even flinch. He tossed one apathetic look toward the house and then returned to his digging.

*Oh, for a pair of feet that could run!* Mrs. Scheinberg tried banging her cane against the back stoop's black iron railing but to no avail. The dog would not be intimidated. She turned back into the house, shutting the door tightly behind her lest Ceci mistakenly decide she was big enough to take down that scruffy mess.

"Can't retire, huh?" she mumbled to herself, tottering down the hallway to her bedroom and opening the safe attached to the back wall of her closet. "Too old and fat to take care of myself?" She removed her dead husband's double-barrel shotgun, grabbed a box of ammo, and shuffled back to the kitchen. Well, this was one problem she could fix without anyone else's help, thank you very much.

Ceci watched her expectantly, sensing that the game was afoot.

"Stand back, girl," Mrs. Scheinberg said, pulling out a chair from the table and laying the gun on the nearby kitchen counter. She opened a north-facing window, removed the screen, and sat down in the chair. Loading the gun, she rested it on top of the windowsill and pulled out her cell phone. *First the barn and now this—enough was enough!* She knew that she should take a moment to calm down a bit before making the call, but this wretched day had been working toward a climax such as this. She dialed her neighbor's number.

"Yeah?" a perturbed voice answered on the other end.

"It's Arlene Scheinberg." Her own voice was as cold and thick as the whole milk chilling in her refrigerator.

There was a pause. "What d'you want?"

Mrs. Scheinberg tilted the shotgun sixty degrees in the air and unloaded both barrels at once into the twilit sky. The explosive sound caused Ceci to whimper and cower down the hall to hide in the bedroom.

"Hell, Arlene!" Max shouted into the phone. "Was that you shootin' just now, ya crazy woman?"

Mrs. Scheinberg opened both barrels with her right hand—what was a little arthritis?—and reloaded the gun. Clicking the barrels back in place, she carefully aimed at the dark shape still madly digging a hole in her yard. "That was a warning shot, Max. Now. Listen closely. I have my twelve-gauge pointed directly at your miserable beast's head, and you have exactly two minutes to retrieve him before I pull the trigger again."

## Chapter Three: Being Neighborly

⁙⁙⁙⁙⁙⁙⁙⁙⁙⁙⁙⁙⁙⁙⁙⁙⁙⁙⁙⁙⁙⁙

Mrs. Scheinberg stood on her front porch with the open shotgun draped conspicuously over her right forearm. She was carefully monitoring Dutch's incarceration. "That's the third time this month, Max."

Her neighbor, leading the convict by his collar to the back of an old, beat-up Ford pickup truck, whistled for Dutch to jump up into the truck bed. The dog immediately obeyed, and Max tethered him to the left tire well.

"Did you hear me, Max?" Mrs. Scheinberg called out. The exasperating man was either completely deaf or willfully ignoring her, and she'd bet her laying hens it was the latter. "I said, it's the third time this month."

Max shut the tailgate and walked around to the driver's side of the truck.

"I should call the police."

That got a reaction. Max looked up long enough to retort, "Dutch didn't do no harm."

"He dug a hole in my yard."

"It's jus' a little dirt."

"It's my dirt." Mrs. Scheinberg moved toward the front steps, though she had no intention of going down them unassisted. She had left her cane leaning against the kitchen table. "If I hadn't buried that new chicken wire a foot deep in the ground last fall, your dog would've made a meal of my rooster."

Ceci vehemently barked her agreement from behind the closed front door. Dutch, as apathetic as his owner, merely turned away from the scene and licked his right shoulder.

Max pulled off his seed corn hat, rubbed a hand over his balding pate, and put the hat back on with a decisive tug. His brown button-down shirt was stained and untucked, and his basketball-sized belly strained at a few of the middle buttons. "It's nature, Arlene. Dogs're always gonna go fer birds. Ain't nothin' I can do about it."

"You most certainly can. Keep him tied up."

"It don't work. He chews through rope."

"Then get a chain."

"I cain't be keepin' a dog from doin' 'is bus'ness day an' night."

"Well, your dog has absolutely *no business* on my property." Mrs. Scheinberg leaned against a railing post. She was missing her cane, but she wasn't about to let on as much to her neighbor. "Keep him tied up."

"Or what?"

"Or next time, I'll shoot first, call second."

Max shook his head, opened the door of his truck, and climbed up into the cab. "Yer crazy."

"Crazy? You think *I'm* crazy?"

Max shut the door and leaned his elbow out of the open window. "Yeah. I do. Dutch's harmless as a kitten. Ya could've jus' called 'im away from the pen yerself, but instead you've gotta go swingin' yer gun aroun' in the air like Annie Oakley."

"I tried calling your wretched dog, but he's just like you. He don't—*doesn't*—listen."

"Well, it wouldn't 'ave killed ya to walk ten feet and lead 'im away with yer own hands. Or do yer feet not work?"

Mrs. Scheinberg felt strangely caught. Her worthless feet were betraying her this very moment, but she fought hard to keep herself upright. A wild feeling of desperation gripped her around the throat. "You sold out, Max!"

"What?"

"That ridiculous barn of yours!"

Max stared at her for a long moment before flashing her a facetious grin. "Looks nice, don'cha think?"

Mrs. Scheinberg snorted.

"What's wrong, Arlene?" The mischief in his eyes was undeniable. "Got somethin' 'gainst art? Or is it the color blue?"

Mrs. Scheinberg utterly and completely loathed this man. Every time she tried to reason with him, he either laughed at her or ignored her completely. "You've made our road the laughingstock of the county with your cheap trick."

"Cheap, huh? I made a pretty penny wi' that sign."

"You sold out."

"I earned me a new trough for ma hogs, tha's what I did. What d'you care, anyway?"

"I care about the view out of my window."

"So look out a diff'rent window." The man looked more entertained than convicted, and she hated him for it.

Max started the truck and shifted into reverse.

That desperate feeling threatened to choke her again. She couldn't let the man drive away without fully understanding the gravity of the situation, but she was completely done in. If her feet didn't give out on her soon, her resolve most certainly would. The day had been too long and too hard. She gave it one last shot. "Your farm is a dump, Max, but it's still a farm. Or *was* a farm. Now, it's just a tacky billboard!"

"See, tha's the problem with you Christians," Max hollered over the sound of the engine. "Yer so high an' mighty an think ev'ryone else is yers to boss aroun'. I'm jus' mindin' my own bus'ness, tryin' ta make a livin', and yer over here makin' threats to poor animals and pollutin' the air with bullets. Well, as ya so helpfully pointed out earlier, my barn is *my* property, and ain't nobody got *no bus'ness* on my property 'cept me. So deal with it, Arlene. That, or keep yer crazy to yerself an' get some new curtains."

Having completed his speech, he backed the truck down her driveway and into the night.

Ceci let loose with a stream of infuriated barks from inside of the house.

"My thoughts exactly, girl," Mrs. Scheinberg muttered, turning her frozen feet toward the front door and letting herself back in the house. She limped through the living room to the kitchen, exchanging the shotgun for her cane. Then, removing the plastic wrap from a pie pan sitting on the counter and grabbing a fork, she settled herself and half of a cherry pie before the computer positioned on a corner desk in the room.

If Max refused to listen to her, then she'd find someone else who would.

## CHAPTER FOUR: PEANUTS AND A CRACKERJACK

Dusk in June was a happy occasion in Bradbury, a magical juncture in time when not one person wished it to be sooner or later in the day. Everyone lived in the moment, content to hover with the sun just above the western horizon. Children ran outside to chase lightning bugs, leaving open screened doors behind them to slam noisily in their wake. Fathers meandered to their property lines, chatting easily over fences about empty rain gauges, baseball lineups, and the price of corn. Mothers stood at open kitchen windows, scrubbing pots and pans in the sink, humming along with George Strait on the radio and dreaming of days gone by. And fans of the Lions Club summer baseball team reclined on metal bleachers, eating boiled hot dogs and Starbursts and cheering on their favorite players.

"C'mon, Robbie!" Rebecca Jones called out. "Eye on the ball, now, eye on the ball!"

Robbie, her giraffe of a son, dug the toe of his left cleat into the loose dirt next to home plate, steadily eyeing the pitcher while keeping his right foot safely out of the batter's box. The pitcher on the mound was waiting, already bent forward at the waist, holding the baseball in his glove behind his back.

"Hit a houserun, Robbie!"

Rebecca smiled involuntarily at the two curly golden pigtails bouncing directly in front of her. Little Julia had been speaking full sentences for at least a year, but she didn't always get her words quite right. Her twin brother, George, sat with a chubby hand buried deep in the recesses of a white paper bag, appearing more interested in hunting kernels of popcorn than watching any game.

"Robbie's too close to the plate," Evan Ebner observed, sitting perfectly upright on Rebecca's left. The elderly man's posture was impeccable even at the age of seventy, no doubt the effect of having served as Zion Lutheran Church's organist for almost half of his life. Evan wasn't much of a sportsman, but he was a quick study of any subject that involved the affections of his grandchildren.

"He's all right," Rebecca assured. "Left-handed batters are tricky for pitchers. Robbie's just trying to psych him out."

"I see."

Robbie landed his right foot in the box and swung his bat with both hands above his left shoulder, at the ready. The pitcher nodded at some mysterious sign made by the catcher and then wound the ball behind his head, using his arm like a slingshot. The ball made a crisp, snapping sound in the catcher's glove.

"Strr-IIIKE!" a padded umpire yelled from behind the plate.

Robbie stepped back and coolly swung his bat, keeping his long arms loose, focusing his gaze on the first-base coach flashing hand signals his way. He gave one curt nod of his chin and stepped back up to the plate.

"That pitch seemed low," Evan said.

"May have been, but Coach Keller makes the boys take a strike before swinging, regardless."

"Isn't that a waste?"

"It helps them learn to wait and be choosy. Not an easy lesson for teenagers to learn." Rebecca had a lot of respect for Coach

Keller. She cupped her hands around her mouth. "Make him pitch to you, Robbie!"

Robbie towered over the plate like a birch tree. He had grown five inches this year alone. At first, Rebecca had been afraid that her weed of a son would lose control of his hands and feet like most teenage boys undergoing a growth spurt, but Robbie's appendages ever remained his faithful servants. Even now, the bat appeared to be in complete submission to his steady hands, a natural extension of his limbs.

This time, the pitcher's fastball met Robbie's bat head-on. A loud cracking sound reverberated across the ballpark.

"Run, Robbie!" Rebecca shouted, jumping to her feet.

The ball shot like a bullet straight between the shortstop and third baseman, bouncing once on the ground before landing squarely in the left-fielder's glove. The boy quickly redirected the ball to the first baseman, but Robbie had already planted his left foot solidly on the base. The second the ball left the fielder's hands, the Lions' runner on third base made a break for home plate, sliding in a cloud of dust before a wildly gesturing catcher. One more run for the Lions! The crowd jumped to its feet in elation.

"Robbie has safety, George! Look!" Julia pointed at first base for the benefit of her brother. George sat unmoved, crunching on his popcorn.

"Did they just win?" Evan asked.

"No," Rebecca replied, still clapping and beaming at her son, "but they're up by one. And that was an RBI for Robbie!" She sat back down in satisfaction. Her middle son loved baseball with all of his heart, and baseball seemed to love him fully in return. Seeing Robbie happy made her happy. "It's the top of the last inning, so the Knights still have one more chance at bat after this. If the Lions can keep them from scoring, though, they'll win."

"More popcorn, pease?"

Rebecca looked down into George's serious brown eyes. "We'll have to wait and see what your father says when he gets here." Sympathetic at heart, however, she brushed her finger affectionately against his cheek and handed him her half-eaten bag in exchange for his empty one. George grinned and promptly returned to his digging and chomping.

Rebecca wished her other children could be there tonight—everyone in the Jones family loved baseball—but Davie and Frankie were both away at Camp CILCA for the week, the elder working as a dishwasher and the younger attending as a camper. Alison was at a birthday slumber party across town, and Emma—Rebecca felt a familiar tightening at the back of her throat—little Emma was buried in Bradbury Cemetery.

"Is Jeremy still at the voters' meeting?" Evan asked.

"Must be," Rebecca said, clearing her throat and looking at her phone for the time. It was getting late. Her husband was the chairman of the congregation at Zion, and while she appreciated his eagerness to serve, she hated it when meetings cut into family time. The kids were growing up so fast. Why, Davie was just two years away from going off to college, and Robbie wasn't far behind! Every moment spent with them was precious.

"I know I should be there, but I figure they all can get along without me for one night." Evan clapped his hands politely as the next batter struck out and the teams switched places on the field. Rebecca smiled to herself. Evan had no problem missing meetings that conflicted with his grandchildren's activities, but she knew that he drew the line at Sunday services. Only the flu or an act of God could ever keep him from the organ console. "We keep the Sabbath Day holy in this family," she had overheard him saying to the kids just last week.

Evan was not her father, but he had married her mother shortly before her mother died. His subsequent devotion to herself and to her children ran thicker than blood, and she rejoiced at the gift of family God had given them in each other. She felt her throat tightening again. Life on this earth was going to make her into a crier, one way or another.

The first batter for the Knights stepped up to the plate, and Robbie lowered his glove to the ground in anticipation of a hit coming his way between second and third base. His long limbs and quick reflexes made him an excellent shortstop. The batter struck out, however, much to the delight of everyone inhabiting Rebecca's bleacher, but their joy was short-lived. The second batter advanced to first after getting hit in the left ankle by a wild pitch.

"Clark must be getting tired," Rebecca mumbled, more to herself than to anyone else. Clark, the Lions' pitcher, was Coach Keller's son. He was a nice boy and a good friend to Robbie.

Out of the corner of her eye, Rebecca noticed that her husband and Pastor Fletcher were jaywalking across the corner of Washington Avenue and Fifth Street toward the ballpark. The voters' meeting must have finally adjourned. She waved at the men, directing them to their set of bleachers.

"Daddy, Daddy, Daddy!" Julia cried, seeing her father from afar. She waved both hands, setting both pigtails aflutter again. George looked up from his bag expectantly.

Before Jeremy and Pastor could make it to the bleachers, however, the telltale crack of a bat hitting a ball drew everyone's attention back to the field. The third batter had hit a fiery grounder, and it was burning a path straight to the left of second base. Robbie dove for the ball, stopping it in his glove in time to quickly flip it to Marty, the second baseman, who was already leaning firmly against the bag. Marty, in return, fired the ball straight at the first baseman, who caught it just before the batter reached the base.

"Out!" the umpire cried, and Rebecca and the crowd erupted in a frenzied symphony of hoots and hollers. The dusk had fully turned to night, and a double play had secured another win for the Lions. It was the perfect June evening, and even little George bore the jubilant marks of summer satisfaction, pinching his rosy cheeks into a smile and hugging his chubby arms around the second empty bag.

Robbie was slapping high fives to his teammates on the field as Coach Keller motioned for them all to huddle up.

"Daddy, Daddy, Daddy!" Julia called again, trotting to the end of her bleacher and jumping directly into Pastor Fletcher's arms.

"How was the game?" Pastor asked, balancing his daughter on his right arm while reaching out his left hand to tousle George's golden curls. "Did you two have fun?"

"Yes, yes, yes!" Julia sang. She liked to talk in threes. "Robbie is the winner!"

George, edging his way to the end of the bleacher, dropped his paper bag and wrapped his arms around his daddy's waist.

"Did you behave for Mrs. Jones?"

"They behaved beautifully," Rebecca assured, picking up the rejected bag with one hand while holding out the other to help Evan step to the ground. Jeremy came around to assist them both. "How was the meeting?"

Jeremy and Pastor exchanged significant looks.

"That good, huh?" Evan asked, ever insightful. He reached into his pants pocket for a handkerchief and blew his nose lightly. "Did the Ladies Aid Society finally decide to disband?"

"Not exactly," Jeremy answered. "Arlene announced that she is retiring."

"What?" Rebecca exclaimed, turning to look her husband full in the face. He didn't appear to be joking. "When?"

"In two weeks."

"Two weeks? That's kind of fast, isn't it?"

Evan began to chuckle slowly. "Well, we all knew that there would be no going quietly into the night with that woman."

"Does Emily know yet?" Rebecca asked, immediately thinking of her best friend. Emily Fletcher had a special place in her heart for Arlene Scheinberg. This news would rock her world, for sure.

Pastor shook his head. "I haven't been home yet to tell her."

As if on cue, Julia rested her tired head against her father's shoulder.

"I see that you had a snack," Pastor said, turning over her sticky hands to inspect them.

"I ate Skittles," Julia confessed, "and George ate two bags of popcorn."

"Two?" Pastor asked, looking down at his son.

George grinned, not a bit repentant.

"Well," Pastor smiled, taking George's hand and helping him jump down to the ground, "it's time to say good night to Mr. and Mrs. Jones and Mr. Ebner."

"Good night," both children sang.

"And thank you," Pastor modeled.

"Thank you," the little monkeys repeated.

"You're welcome," Rebecca smiled. "Tell your mother hello for me."

# CHAPTER FIVE: HAPPY HOUR

//////////////////////////////////////////////

"Honey, I'm home!"

Pastor Fletcher never tired of saying those words. For the first six years of his ministry, he had lived the life of a bachelor, coming home to an empty parsonage with only a wet newspaper, a half-empty jar of peanut butter, and a cold pot of coffee to greet him at the end of a long day. Now, whenever he stepped through the parsonage door, he was welcomed by the warm glow of lamplight, the savory smell of something simmering in the kitchen, and the stirring sight of the prettiest brown eyes in the county.

"How was the game?" Emily Fletcher asked, uncurling from an armchair in the living room and meeting him and the children in the entryway. She had an open book in her hand.

Those eyes! They got him every time.

"I made it just in time to see the Lions win. The kids had fun with Rebecca and Evan, I think." Pastor leaned down for a kiss before passing a sleeping George into his wife's extended arms. Julia was trailing groggily behind him.

"Long meeting, then?" Emily asked, turning toward the hallway at the back of the house.

"Eventful," Pastor said, pausing to admire his wife's figure in the lamplight. He liked it when she wore those red shorts.

"What did I miss?"

As a rule, Emily never attended church voters' meetings. Publicly, she hid behind the excuse of needing to care for their young children, but privately, they had both learned early on that some parishioners were impossible for her to love if she heard what they had to say about him in public. Staying home kept her at the Communion rail on Sunday mornings.

"I'll tell you about it in a minute." Pastor followed her down the hall, leading Julia by the hand and taking note of the closed nursery door. Little Becky must already be asleep in bed.

Emily entered an open door at the end of the hall and laid George on a toddler bed. She began removing her still-sleeping child's clothes and dressed him in pajama bottoms and a T-shirt. She nodded at Julia's nightgown resting on a nightstand, indicating that Pastor follow suit.

He carefully dressed Julia for bed, cleaning her sticky hands with a wipe before pulling her flowered sheet up to her dimples. Just like her mother! He smiled and leaned over his daughter to ask, "Who are you?"

"I'm a baptized child of God," the three-year-old answered, not missing a beat in their nightly litany.

"And whose are you?"

"I belong to Jesus."

Pastor nodded. "Do you want us to sing 'I Am Jesus' Little Lamb' or 'Built on the Rock the Church Shall Stand' tonight?"

"'I Am Jesus' Little Lamb.'"

Pastor wasn't surprised. Julia had been choosing the same hymn every night for the past two weeks. Usually, she was eager to sing along, but tonight her long lashes sank lower and lower with each stanza. George was already out cold, so Pastor and Emily moved on to praying the Lord's Prayer and Luther's Evening Prayer without him, trusting that their sleeping son was listening with ears of faith.

"I commend you into the hands of a loving God," Pastor spoke, making the sign of the cross upon his children's foreheads. Then, Emily turned out the light and Pastor closed the bedroom door behind them.

"Hot chocolate?" Emily asked, making her way to the kitchen. It could be a hundred degrees outside and his wife would still want hot chocolate at night.

"Sure."

"With brandy?"

"Of course." Pastor walked over to the front door and untied his shoes, leaving them on the multicolored rug Nettie Schmidt had bought for them at an auction last spring. He took off his clerical collar, setting it among an array of children's books, toys, and pacifiers on an end table. He picked up a plastic figurine of "Sleeping Booty," as George called her, and chuckled softly. All thoughts of church and retirement and disgruntled secretaries washed away like chalk art in a rainstorm, and his heart swelled with gratitude's high tide. Before, the parsonage had been just a building where he showered and slept. Now, it was his sanctum.

"Here you go," Emily said, holding out a steaming mug.

He took the hot chocolate from her hand and waited for her to make herself comfortable in her armchair before settling himself on the couch. It was a small gesture—this seeking his wife's comfort before his own—one he had learned from his father. He didn't know if Emily ever noticed it or not, but he made sure to do it all the same. At the least, he was daily reminding himself to respect and serve his wife.

Over the years, he had seen many a pastor's marriage end in divorce, no doubt the result of neglect and apathy, and he lived in fear of losing his family amidst the chaos of church life. It was so easy to do, what with the constant stream of needs flowing in and out of the parsonage that required his pastoral attention. That's what he was there for, after all—to help and serve this community of believers, to be the voice and hands and feet and face of Christ to this people—but he had made the mistake early on in his relationship with Emily of neglecting her in a big way, and he never wanted to do that again. God, help him!

"How was your day?" he asked, leaning back against an arm of the couch, sipping from his mug. Emily had put in more brandy than usual. She must have sensed that today had been a hard one. He loved this woman.

"Good," Emily murmured over her own mug. "Julia said the funniest thing."

"What?"

"Well, at lunch . . ." Emily launched into the telling of her story, her voice rising and falling melodiously in the most delicate music. Pastor listened, but he had trouble following her words. It wasn't that he didn't care about what his daughter had said earlier in the day or that he meant to ignore his wife. It was that this was his happy hour—the time of day that he looked forward to amidst the drudgery of church meetings and the stress of dealing with people's sin—and the very sound of his Emily's voice soothed and comforted him in a way that nothing else could. She was God's gift to him in this broken world—the love of his life, the alpha and omega of his family, the song in his home, the warmth in his bed—and he never tired of being near her. Maybe it was because it had taken thirty-three long years for him to find her in the first place.

" . . . and when I told her that eating her yogurt would help keep her gut healthy," Emily continued, "Julia said, 'I know what's in my gut, Mommy.' 'Oh, what's that?' I asked." Emily paused, her eyes sparkling over her mug. "Guess what your daughter said."

He shook his head. "I can't even imagine."

"'Intestentacles.'"

Pastor threw back his head and laughed.

"Seriously," Emily grinned, her dimples deepening. "I feel like I should write this stuff down and turn it into a book someday. Who wants to read about vampires and zombies when there are children to enjoy in this world?"

"How did your lesson with Caroline go?"

"It was good," Emily said, though her tone of voice immediately changed, betraying a note of discontent.

"But what?"

Emily shoved two books over on the end table to make room for her mug. "Oh, I don't know. I'm just not ready to say good-bye to her, that's all. She's made so much progress over the years. Do you remember how awful she sounded that first time she sang in public while her brother played his trombone at that dreadful party at Bradbury House? She's come so far in tone and range and musicality. High Cs are nothing for that girl now, and her phrases have a color and shape that is quite original. And it's not just her training. Her instincts are good."

"You're going to miss her." It was more of a statement than a question.

"I can't believe that she and Ben are off to college in a couple of months!"

Pastor listened. This is what he did for Emily. This is what she needed from him most. She gave him her heart, and he gave her his ear.

"I've never known a Bradbury without Ben Schmidt," Emily admitted. "That boy is . . . well, he's not a boy anymore—he's a man—but . . . well, he's special, you know?"

He did know. Ben Schmidt, even as a young boy, had given Emily his full trust and affection at a time when so many others in this town had refused. The boy was family to her, and she had lost so much of her family over the years. Moves and life transitions in general often triggered her many past griefs.

"Maybe we should have them over for supper this summer before they go?"

Emily's eyes lit up. "Do you think so? Do you think they would?"

"I know they would." That, and he knew his wife needed to give them a proper good-bye.

"I'll ask Caroline, then." Emily picked up her mug, settling back into her armchair, a smile playing at her lips. "Now, what happened at that meeting? Anything you can tell me about?"

Here came another one of those testy life transitions. Pastor set down his mug and folded his hands in his lap. "Arlene announced that she's going to retire."

Emily blinked. "What? When?"

She and Rebecca Jones sounded so much alike. "She said that she wants to be done in two weeks."

Emily was quiet for a moment. "Retire?"

"Retire."

"*Just* retire?"

"Just retire."

"Not move?"

"No. She's staying here, just retiring."

Emily looked at him thoughtfully. "Well, it makes sense, I guess. Her feet have really been bothering her the last few months. She can barely get in and out of her car, and I doubt she'll even be able to sing in the choir this fall. There's no way she can make it up and down the balcony stairs."

He hadn't even thought of that.

"Though it's odd that she never said anything to me about it." Emily stared into her hot chocolate for a long moment before looking up. "Did she say anything to you?"

Pastor shook his head.

"Huh. She's not usually impulsive, but maybe she just decided that the time is right. Yes, it makes sense," Emily confirmed, nodding her head as the news took a recognizable shape in her head. She was visibly relaxing, leaning back in her chair and pulling her legs up under her seat. He felt a wash of relief. This transition was going to be just fine. "I suppose we should have a party for her, don't you think? We can't tell her about it, of course, or she'd never come. Wait a minute—who's going to work in the office?"

Who, indeed? Pastor pressed his lips together in a straight line.

"Will the church be able to hire someone in two weeks' time?"

"Most likely not."

"Then who will cover the phones?" Emily frowned. "They're not asking you to do it, are they?"

"No, no." The idea had been brought up by Yvonne at the meeting, but Emily didn't need to know that. Besides, Jeremy Jones had nixed that one pretty fast from the floor.

"They want me to do it, don't they?" Emily's voice was as dull and as heavy as their cast-iron skillet.

Yvonne had also suggested as much, but again, Emily didn't need to know that. "You're not covering the phones, honey. You're already busy taking care of our children during the day."

The crow's-feet around Emily's eyes disappeared. "Who, then?"

"Well," Pastor cleared his throat, "we did have someone generously volunteer to help out until a proper replacement can be hired."

"Who?"

He knew that his face betrayed his exasperation. "Nettie Schmidt."

Emily blinked once and then exploded in a riotous laugh, spilling her hot chocolate all over her red shorts.

Those eyes again! Pastor stood to remove the mug from his hysterical wife's grip, setting it next to his own on the end table, and led her down the hall to the bathroom. Julia wasn't the only member of the Fletcher family who needed to be cleaned up before bed.

||||||||||||||||||||||||||||||||||||||||||||||

Across town, the Joneses were pulling into their garage.

"Are you hungry?" Rebecca asked.

"Yes," Jeremy answered.

"Not you," Rebecca smirked, unbuckling her seatbelt. "The other redhead."

Robbie was already out of the SUV, dropping his cleats by the door and making his way into the house. Rebecca frowned. Her son had been unusually quiet the entire ride home, especially considering the fact that it was his RBI and double play that had clinched tonight's victory. He hadn't said a single word on the drive out to his grandpa Evan's house in the country, and once they had turned back toward home, he had spoken only when his dad had asked him questions about the game.

"What do you think, Robbie?" Rebecca tried again, following him into the kitchen. "Care for a sandwich?"

"No, thanks."

This was definitely not normal behavior for their son. Typically, the starving fourteen-year-old downed two peanut butter and jelly sandwiches, an entire bag of Harvest Cheddar SunChips, and half a gallon of chocolate milk after every game. Robbie abstained from his usual fare, however, pouring himself only one glass of orange juice from a carton in the refrigerator and taking it with him upstairs. Rebecca looked meaningfully over her shoulder at her husband standing in the doorway, but Jeremy only shrugged.

The sudden gush of the upstairs shower could be heard.

"Did he say anything to you?" Rebecca asked.

"About what?"

"I don't know."

Robbie was their middle son, and while Rebecca didn't have favorites when it came to her children, she felt a special kinship with this freckled string bean. Maybe it was because Robbie's orange hair and long face were the spitting image of Jeremy's. Or maybe it was because his stubborn streak burned as brightly as her own. Or maybe—Rebecca's throat tightened again. She swallowed hard, willing her eyes to stay dry—maybe it was because his heart was as big and as generous and as sensitive and as kind as her sainted mother's. She swallowed again, fighting for composure. Whatever the reason, whenever Robbie hurt, she hurt.

As soon as she heard the shower turn off and the bathroom door open, Rebecca climbed the stairs and knocked on Robbie's bedroom door. He was lying on top of his covers, the *Treasury of Daily Prayer* open on his pillow.

"That was some play tonight," Rebecca started, pulling out his desk chair and helping herself to a seat. Years ago, she would have sat directly next to him on the bed, but things were different now. Robbie was older, and he preferred to govern his own personal space these days. "Nice RBI too."

"Thanks."

"Can I bring you a piece of pie? Mrs. Scheinberg dropped a whole pie off for you this afternoon. It's cherry. Your favorite."

"No."

"Did you put your socks down the laundry shoot?"

"Yes."

"Your shirt?"

Robbie stood up and left the room for a moment. She heard the closet door with the laundry chute being opened and closed, and then he came back to sit on the bed, leaning his back against the wall.

"How're your ribs feeling after that dive?"

"Fine."

Rebecca studied her son. "What did Coach have to say after the game? Did last week's rainout get rescheduled?"

Robbie didn't answer right away. He fingered the gold embossment on the edge of his book and furrowed his brow. "He said that Hamburg can only work in a makeup game this weekend."

"That's short notice." Rebecca felt a flash of irritation. Robbie couldn't drive yet, and it was expecting an awful lot of families to be able to rearrange their weekend schedules with only three days' notice. She immediately started thinking through how to make their driving schedule work. She'd have to drive up to Cantrall on Friday afternoon to pick up Frankie from camp—Davie would stay—and then they'd all have to turn around the next morning—

"The game's on Sunday."

Rebecca's stomach turned. Robbie's subdued behavior suddenly made perfect sense. She tried her best not to overreact—not to let her anger show on her face—but her immediate impulse was to jump up and call Coach Keller on the phone and give him a piece of her mind. Instead, she pressed her lips together and endeavored to give the man the benefit of the doubt. "Sunday afternoon, I suppose?"

Robbie's head was hanging so low, his chin almost touched his chest. "It starts at nine in the morning."

Rebecca felt her face fall. There it was. She knew she shouldn't be surprised. She and Jeremy had known this was coming for years. Why, by the time she herself had entered high school, the local school board had already been in full support of sports teams hosting practices and games on Wednesday evenings—a time that previously had been reserved for catechesis, church services, and the holy things in life. They had called it Wednesday Blackout, but by the time she was a senior in high school, Wednesday evenings were no more sacred to the community than Friday night lights.

Somehow, she and Jeremy had miraculously been able to get Davie through wrestling and marching band without any major kerfuffles, but with the way the world was going, they knew the assault on Sunday mornings was inevitable. She just had hoped it wouldn't happen this soon. And with Robbie's beloved baseball, of all things! The devil left nothing untouched.

Evan's voice began to replay in her head: "We keep the Sabbath Day holy in this family." She opened her mouth to remind her son of that, but the look on Robbie's face stopped her short. The struggle was real. But so was his faith, and she wanted to give him a chance to confess it. "What are you going to do, son?"

"I don't know."

Rebecca closed her eyes and prayed, *Lord, help him!*

"I mean, I can't miss church. It's one of the commandments and all, but . . ."

*Lord, help him!*

". . . Coach said I've got a real chance to make varsity this year. I just need to get in more time at bat."

*Lord, help him!*

"But Grandpa Evan said, well, you know. And Curt needs me. But if I miss a game, Coach said he'll bench me for the game after that."

*Lord, help* me! Rebecca opened her eyes, dismayed, her respect for that man plummeting to the first floor. Again, she fought the urge to call him and tell him what she thought of his ludicrous expectations for teenage boys and summer makeup games, but Robbie was a young man, a confirmed member of the church, and he knew right from wrong. He could handle this. She calmly repeated her question. "What are you going to do, son?"

Robbie looked up for the first time. He tried to smile, but she knew that his heart was breaking. "I guess I'm going to sit on the bench next Tuesday night."

Rebecca couldn't help herself. Teenager or not, her son was getting hugged. She crossed the room and squeezed her ruddy giraffe with all of her might, and when she finally stepped away, she cupped his freckled face in her hands and said, "No RBI or double play could ever make me so proud of you as I am right now."

## Chapter Six: God's Own Children

||||||||||||||||||||||||||||||||||||||||||||||||||||||

Robbie sat in the pew on Sunday morning between his younger sister and Curt. His heart ached to be with the rest of his team at the ballpark in Hamburg, but Curt's bear hug on the sidewalk outside of the Bethesda home earlier that morning had confirmed the rightness of his choice to be in church instead of out on any field.

"Iiiee yike-oo, Wob-bie Dones!" Curt had sung into his shoulder.

"I like you too, Curt."

"Iiiee meesed-oo, Wob-bie Dones!"

"I missed you too, Curt."

"We go tyurt?"

"Yes, we're going to church."

Robbie couldn't remember exactly when he and his family had begun picking up residents from the Bethesda home in Bradbury and taking them to church on Sunday mornings, but he knew that it had started sometime after Emma had died. It had been his mother's idea. She had come home from quilting circle one summer afternoon and announced, "Everyone get in the SUV. We're taking supper over to the Bethesda home tonight."

None of them had known what a Bethesda home was at the time, and Robbie would never forget how sitting across from Curt at the dinner table that first night had made his stomach uneasy. It wasn't that Curt had done anything wrong. He was always a very polite and friendly man. It was that he and the other residents had looked and sounded, well, weird. All of them were adults, but they acted and talked differently from any adult he knew. Some of their eyes were funny shapes and others had tongues that looked too big for their mouths. One of the lady residents even wore a towel for a bib during supper and used her fingers to eat her Jell-O. It all had made Robbie very uncomfortable.

His mom had explained on the way home that night that many of the Bethesda home residents had intellectual and developmental disabilities that required assistance to accomplish basic tasks in their daily lives.

"And two of the residents are Lutheran like you," she had said.

"Who?" Aly had asked, not even six at the time.

"Kathryn and Curt—Curt was the one sitting across from you, Robbie." His mom had eyed him meaningfully in the rearview mirror. "And Kathryn was the lady holding the baby doll during supper."

Two weeks later, Robbie had watched warily from the SUV as his parents walked Kathryn and Curt down the sloping driveway of the Bethesda home and drove them to church. At first, the whole ordeal had embarrassed Robbie terribly. Kathryn insisted on holding her baby doll through the entire service, and Curt sang so loudly that even people in the church nursery could hear him. His amens were practically hollers, and he prayed the Lord's Prayer so slowly that the congregation finished before he was even halfway done. Worst of all, Curt had melted down in the pew when it was time for them to leave the nave after the final hymn.

"Iiiee mit mamama!" he had wailed.

"What, Curt?" Robbie's mom asked, sitting by his side and putting an arm around his shoulders.

"Iiiee mit mamama!"

Rebecca looked up helplessly at Pastor and Emily Fletcher and the small crowd of concerned people gathering around their pew. "I can't understand what he is saying."

Everyone else shook their heads.

"He's saying that he misses his mom," Robbie murmured.

Davie and Frankie looked at him skeptically. Rebecca, hopeful, turned toward Curt and asked, "Do you miss your mom, Curt?"

"Yet," he cried, big tears rolling down his white cheeks. "Iiiee mit mamama!"

"Where is your mom, Curt?" Rebecca asked.

"Seeineven wit De-sah!"

Everyone looked at Robbie.

"She's in heaven with Jesus," he said.

Curt began to pull himself upright using the pew in front of him and bumbled toward Robbie with his arms outstretched. The tears on his cheeks made his big smile extra glossy. "Iiiee yik-oo. I Curt. Wah ter nem?"

"I'm Robbie."

Quite unexpectedly, Curt grabbed him around the middle and squeezed. The man was considerably shorter and stouter than he, so Robbie got an up close view of his white hair. It was buzzed short in a crew cut just like his own. Robbie looked around at everyone staring at him over Curt's head and, with more than a little reservation, began patting the older man awkwardly on the back.

Rebecca was looking at the two of them with her mouth hanging open and Davie, less awed but still curious, asked, "How can you understand him?"

Robbie felt an unexpected smile creeping about his lips. It seemed that he had suddenly become an authority of some kind. It was also kind of nice to be hugged. "I don't know. I just can."

And that was when the two became inseparable. Every Sunday, Curt sat by Robbie in church, followed him to the parish hall for doughnuts, sat by him through Sunday School, and even sang with him in the choir. Curt told Robbie everything, and Robbie interpreted everything Curt said. They were the best of buds, and even though Curt talked too much and sometimes drooled and often sat too close to Robbie for comfort, Robbie found that he didn't really mind any of it in the end. In fact, even though Curt was decades older than he, he couldn't help but fondly think of the sixty-five-year-old man as his younger brother.

"Yoo tad, Wob-bie Dones?" Curt asked him in the pew the morning of the game. He was wearing the Cardinals polo shirt Robbie had given him for his birthday.

"Yes."

"Waaiiee?"

"I'm missing a baseball game."

"Waaiiee?"

"Coach scheduled the game during church."

"Too-ring tyurt?"

"Yep."

"Waaiiee?"

"'Cause most people don't care about church, I guess."

"Tyurt ma fa-vwit."

"I like church too."

"De-sah ma fa-vwit."

Robbie nodded in agreement.

"Wob-bie Dones ma fa-vwit."

Robbie couldn't help but smile. Curt was the best. "You're my favorite too, Curt."

"De-sah tay, 'Cahm.'"

"Yes, He does, Curt. 'Come unto Me.'"

"De-sah in tyurt."

Robbie thought on this for a moment. Curt often surprised him with his theological insights. Whatever the man's disabilities, his faith remained unmuddied by any mental or physical limit. "You're right, Curt. Jesus is in church. He's in the Word. He's in the bread and wine."

Evan began playing the prelude to the opening hymn on the organ, and Curt leaned his head on Robbie's shoulder. "De-sah for-geeve Curt."

"Jesus forgives Curt," Robbie confirmed.

"De-sah for-geeve Wob-bie Dones."

"Yes."

"We in tyurt wit De-sah."

"Yes, Curt," Robbie smiled. "We are."

⁣⁣⁣⁣⁣⁣⁣⁣⁣⁣⁣⁣⁣⁣⁣⁣⁣⁣⁣⁣⁣

Further down the pew, Emily Fletcher could hear Curt singing the opening hymn with all of his might. The sincere man rarely sang any of the words written on the pages of the hymnal, but instead joyfully bawled along with the organ on whatever syllable felt most comfortable. And his gusto made quite an impression on her children. Just last month, she had caught the twins sitting at the piano in the parsonage living room, Julia running her fingers furiously over the keys and George shriek-singing "Ya-a-ah!" at her side.

"What are you two doing?"

"We're playing church, Mommy," Julia had answered, her brown eyes round with solemnity. "I am Mr. Ebner."

"I am Curt," George had blinked.

She smiled now at the memory. The twins were both quite fond of Curt. In fact, Julia and George didn't know much of church without him, for since the womb, they had been sitting in the same pew as the Jones family. (Well, most of the Jones family. Frankie liked to sit in the balcony with his grandpa.) Throughout every service, Julia could be found walking back and forth the entire length of the pew, alternately sharing a hymnal with Curt and helping Kathryn take care of her baby doll, and George liked to sneak Cheez-Its to Curt during the sermon. Emily let them, as long as they both continued to sit, stand, sing, and pray along with the rest of the congregation at the appropriate times.

Emily shifted Becky around to face forward on her lap as Evan resolved the final chord of the hymn. Her littlest always liked to see her daddy up front.

"In the name of the Father," Pastor said, facing the congregation and making the sign of the cross, "and of the Son and of the Holy Spirit."

"Spirit," Kathryn repeated, hugging her baby.

"Amen," the congregation confirmed.

"A-main!" Curt hollered.

"Beloved in the Lord," Pastor continued, "let us draw near with a true heart—"

"Heart," Kathryn hummed.

"—and confess our sins unto God our Father, beseeching Him in the name of our Lord Jesus Christ—"

"Christ."

"—to grant us forgiveness."

Kathryn rarely ever spoke full sentences to others, but she could recite entire sections of the liturgy word for word and with confidence, no doubt the good fruit of her parents' faithful teaching from an early age. Sometimes, on her more quiet days, Kathryn satisfied herself with simply repeating the last word of whatever pastor said. Her little interjections weren't intrusive, however. They functioned more like punctuation to his proclamation than actual interruptions.

Pastor turned toward the altar to lead the congregation in prayer. "Our help is in the name of the Lord."

"Lord."

Emily looked down in surprise. This time, the word echo hadn't come from Kathryn's mouth but from her little Becky's. Curt, it seemed, was not the only Bethesda resident to influence her children. Emily smiled. Kathryn was a fine role model for her daughter—kind and respectful—and there were worse things a child could repeat in church, that much was certain.

Julia tapped Emily's arm. "Mommy, when is Daddy going to baptize Miss Kathryn's baby?"

"Not now, Julia. Fold your hands."

"But Mommy—"

"Shh." Emily touched her finger to her daughter's lips. "It's time to pray."

Baptism had been on Julia's mind of late, especially since today was the twins' Baptism birthday. For at least a week, their nap time routine had included looking at and touching the baptismal banners hanging over their beds, enumerating what each of them remembered from their day of salvation.

"I wore Mommy's white baby gown," Julia recited, "and George wore Daddy's."

"I cwied," George recounted.

"During the flood prayer," Julia explained, "George flooded his pants."

"And I stopped cwying."

Neither of them could actually remember the details for themselves. They had been less than a week old at the time of their Baptisms, but their godmother had made each of them a scrapbook that detailed the events of their special day. Now, the two of them could remember more about their Baptisms than Emily.

Earlier that morning over breakfast, the twins had reminded their little sister over and over again about the fact that friends, godparents, and a chocolate cake with strawberry frosting were coming over to their house after Sunday School to commemorate the occasion. The Fletcher family had only just finished consuming the blueberry cream cake the twins had requested for their third birthday, and the last thing they all needed was another sugary goodie in the house. But their godmother insisted on it every year, and Julia could talk of little else.

"I'm having two pieces," she whispered loudly to George in the middle of her father's sermon. Her brother immediately started to cry, alarmed that he might somehow be short one piece of the coveted confection.

"You can have Becky's," Julia consoled, pointing to the pouting pile on Emily's lap. Becky, in return, showed her thankfulness for her big sister's generosity by grumpily pushing past knees and feet to the end of the pew, seeking sympathy and solace on the lap of the woman for whom she was named.

Everyone finally calmed down during the Lord's Prayer. Everyone but Curt.

"Owwa Fada," he hollered boisterously, "oo ah ineven. Allo-ee-i-ame . . ."

Emily found herself smiling again. Curt's joy was infectious, there was no denying it, but it was the congregation's measured pace of praying that presently gave her delight. A few years back, after Curt's emotional episode that first Sunday visiting Zion, everyone in the church began paying special attention to the needs of their new Bethesda members. Women brought blankets and bottles for Kathryn's baby doll, ushers forwent handshakes for hugs in the narthex whenever Curt was around, and—the part that made Emily's heart warm—adults and children alike instinctively slowed down whenever confessing the Apostles' Creed and praying the Lord's Prayer during the church service. No one told them to do it—no official announcement was put in the bulletin instructing them to do so—but the people of Zion naturally responded to Curt and Kathryn's slower pace. Emily's tender heart almost burst with appreciation and gratitude for the thoughtfulness of her fellow brothers and sisters in Christ. They weren't always so thoughtful of others, but this measure of kindness to Curt and Kathryn somehow earned them extra credit in Emily's mind.

After Sunday School, Julia and George practically bounced across the street, dragging Alison and Frankie Jones with them by the hands.

"Not so fast, you two," Emily hollered, carefully balancing a pink-frosted mountain on a cake plate before her. "I have the key, remember?"

It was a joyous celebration, though the luncheon resembled what one might expect at a school cafeteria rather than at Sunday dinner, but such was the present culinary palate of the twins. Julia had specifically requested corn dogs for lunch, and George wanted applesauce. Thankfully, Mrs. Scheinberg's strawberry-covered chocolate cake more than made up for what was lacking in the main course.

"Hold your horses, George," Pastor said, catching his son's chubby fingers before they could swipe at the mound of pink fluff. "First, we light your baptismal candles, remember? Then your godparents get to ask you any questions they want before we eat dessert."

"And then we sing!" Julia exclaimed.

Emily set out and lit the tall white candles that first had been lit from the Paschal candle three years ago to the day.

"Who did you put on in your Baptism, Julia?" Pastor asked.

"Christ."

"And who does God see when He looks at you, George?"

"Cwist."

"In your Baptism, Jesus gave you His righteousness. He made your scarlet sins white as . . ." Pastor prompted.

"Snow!" Julia grinned. "Jesus makes me Snow White!"

"Well—"

"And me a pwince!" George clarified.

Alison Jones giggled, but Frankie quickly elbowed her in the ribs.

Pastor smiled sheepishly. "Well, Christ *did* join you to Himself in your Baptism, so that *does* make you royalty, I guess. Yes. You're a brother and sister of the Son of God, and that makes you a prince and princess of the heavenly King!" He caught George's airborne hand one more time before it could land in the cake. Turning to the person sitting in a place of honor at the head of the table, he asked, "Is there anything you would like to ask your godchildren, Mrs. Scheinberg?"

The proud woman judiciously eyed her godson over her gold-rimmed glasses. "What's the First Commandment, George?"

George grinned. He seemed confident about this one. "You shall have no other dogs!"

Alison Jones tossed another giggle into the air but quickly caught it with her hand. Emily hid a smile of her own. Her son sometimes got his *g*s and *d*s mixed up.

"How about you, Jeremy and Rebecca?" Pastor looked to the Joneses. "Any questions for your goddaughter?"

"Can you recite a verse from the Bible about Baptism?" Jeremy asked.

"'Baptism now saves you!'" George shouted, still grinning.

"Hey." Julia crossed her arms, clearly put out. "It's *my* turn."

"Give your sister a turn, George," Pastor instructed, resting his hands on his son's shoulders. "Go ahead, Julia. There are plenty of verses to go around."

Julia took her time, looking at her captive audience with glee and holding her hands out to her side as she had seen her father do so many times when speaking from the chancel. "'Repent and be baptized,'" she recited, "'every one of you in the name of Jesus Christ for the forgiveness of your sins, and . . .'"

"'And you will receive,'" Pastor prodded.

"'. . . and you will receive the gift of the Holy Spirit.'"

"Go on."

Julia looked at her father with concerned eyes, not remembering.

"'For the promise . . .'" Pastor nodded.

"'For the promise,'" Julia repeated, "'is for you and for your children and for all who are far off, everyone whom . . .'" She trailed off again. Emily pressed her lips together in concentration, reciting the words in her own head as if that would somehow help her daughter. She had listened from the kitchen every morning for the past month as her husband and the twins practiced memorizing these verses from the Book of Acts after breakfast, but neither of them had been able to recite it all the way through without some help.

"'Everyone whom the Lord . . .'" Pastor prompted.

"'Everyone whom the Lord our God calls to Himself.'" Julia's dimples took flight.

"Amen," Pastor said.

"A-main!" Curt shouted. Everyone else in the room cheered.

"Now, blow out your candles," Pastor said.

Julia's eyebrows wrinkled. "No, no, no, Daddy! First, we sing."

"Oh, we do?" he asked innocently, pretending as if he didn't know any better.

"Yes, we sing!"

"What do we sing?"

"*Daddy.*" Julia's voice communicated complete exasperation. "Our special song!"

"We have a special song?" Pastor did his best impression of being confused.

George stepped in. "Ow Baptism song, Daddy."

"Do you know what they are talking about?" Pastor teased, looking at his wife. Emily shrugged, playing along.

"*Mommy!*" Julia cried.

Emily laughed and walked over to the piano, opening the lid. She sat down on the bench and played a short introduction. "Who's going to sing with me?"

Julia and George hollered an affirmative, Becky clapped merrily from the safety of Rebecca's arms, Kathryn hugged her baby doll, and Curt hugged Robbie. Everyone turned expectantly toward the piano as Pastor moved to stand behind his wife, and the eldest four in the Fletcher family sang from memory:

*What a wonder! Jesus loves me,*
*Cares for me the whole day through:*
*Morning, noon, and nighttime too.*
*When I rest, He sends His angels,*
*All my hopes and dreams to keep,*
*Granting me untroubled sleep.*

*What a wonder! Jesus shields me*
*Like a shepherd, wise and dear;*
*To my ev'ry pray'r gives ear.*
*He will never me abandon*
*Nor my sorrows cast aside.*
*I, for good, in Him abide.*

*What a wonder! Jesus saves me.*
*On the cross He bore my sin,*
*Endless life for me to win.*
*Now I rest in perfect gladness*
*With the Father reconciled,*
*Evermore His precious child.*

*What a wonder! Jesus cleans me,*
*Washes all my sins away.*
*On my blest baptismal day,*
*He secured me to His passion,*
*Put to death my guilt and shame,*
*Gave me His own holy name.*

Emily moved to close the piano lid, but Julia cried, "No, no, no!"

"What?" Emily asked.

"It's too soon."

"What's too soon?"

"The end."

"Well, that was the last stanza."

"No, it's not."

This time, Emily was the one to tease her children. "I don't know any more stanzas, do you?" She looked up at her husband.

George shrieked in wild anticipation. "It's ow Baptism birthday."

"What does that mean?" Pastor asked.

"We get new words, Daddy," Julia reminded him.

"Oh," he said, pulling a folded piece of paper out of his pocket. "Well, I guess I did find this earlier today."

Emily laughed as her children hollered and jumped up and down. She didn't know of any other father in the world who wrote hymns for his children, let alone a new stanza for every Baptism birthday, and she knew of no other children who got so excited about learning new rhyming words as her own.

"Here," Pastor said, setting the handwritten words in front of Emily. She played the familiar introduction again and began to sing,

> What a wonder! Jesus feeds me
> His own flesh and blood divine
> In and with the bread and wine,
> Granting me new life eternal.
> Hear me now this truth confess:
> Jesus is my righteousness!

"Again, again, again!" Julia cried when the music stopped.

"I'll sing it one more time," Emily said, "but then we'll save it to sing together at bedtime, okay?" She looked up at her husband and gave him a special smile. "It really is lovely, Michael."

He rested his hands on her shoulders and leaned down to lightly kiss her neck. "Thank you."

After the new hymn stanza had been sung once again, the candles rightfully blown out, and the magnificent cake devoured, the adults lingered around the table with glasses of iced tea.

"I'm going to start calling you the Fletcher Family Singers," Jeremy joked. "You do realize that all of this hymn-singing and memorization is putting the rest of us to shame?"

"It's all Michael," Emily said, blushing underneath her lashes as she admired her poet-husband.

"Oh, now," Pastor replied, "you're the great composer of the family!"

"Did you write the music for that song?" Rebecca asked and then immediately answered herself. "Of course you did! When are you going to write me a song, you two?"

Emily opened her mouth to answer, but a wild scream echoing down the parsonage hallway stole her air. She knocked over her chair in her hurry to find the scream's source, and Rebecca wasn't far behind her. Together, they discovered an inconsolable Kathryn standing outside of the bathroom.

"Kathryn, honey, what's wrong—" but Emily stopped short. There, standing on footstools next to the bathroom sink, were a couple of holy fools. Her holy fools. Julia, looking like the Virgin Mary with her blue blanket draped over her head, was holding Kathryn's baby doll under the running faucet, while George, decked out in one of his father's white undershirts and a green winter scarf, was splashing handfuls of water on the baby as well as his sister and the counter and the mirror and Kathryn and the floor.

"I baptize you," George shouted, "in the name of the Fodder and of the Son and of the Holy Spit."

Aghast, Emily rushed in to rescue the baby doll, wrapping her in a nearby towel and handing the sopping mess to her panicked mother, and Pastor, following closely on the heels of his wife, dove into the bathroom to turn off the faucet and mop up the flood zone with whatever dry material was within reach.

Emily felt her old temper flaring, but her husband, as always, rescued her from the worst of herself.

"Somehow," he said wryly, turning to his soaked children with the soberest of expressions, "I don't think 'spit' is what Jesus had in mind when He talked about us living by what comes from the mouth of God."

Emily tried her best to stay mad, but she found herself spontaneously spluttering, generously anointing the heads of her children with some holy spit of her own.

# CHAPTER SEVEN: THE IMPORTANCE
## OF BEING STERNEST

"Oh dear," Bev Davis murmured over her cup of coffee the next morning. "Arlene's finally gone mad."

"What?" Irv asked, looking up from the toast he was buttering.

"Here." Bev handed a copy of the *Bradbury Times* across the table to her husband and pointed to the fifth page. "In the editorial."

Irv set down his toast and pulled his eyeglasses out of the leather case sitting on top of the open *Portals of Prayer* and Bible in the middle of the kitchen table.

```
Dear Editor:

    For over sixty-six years, I have
proudly lived in this county, twenty of
which were spent over my father's store
in Bradbury and forty-six on my hus-
band's land straddling Cow Creek just
three miles north of town. I have always
seen it as my duty as a daughter and
as a wife and as a citizen of this fine
land to care for my property, knowing
that how I treat my acreage affects the
```

quality of everyone else's. Even though
it costs me extra in diesel and mainte-
nance every year, I make sure my ditches
are mown at least three times a growing season. I keep my pastures free of
trash and debris so as not to pollute
the water source flowing from my farm to
yours. I mend my fences and repair my
outbuildings regularly so my animals do
not become your burdens. I abide by road
weight limits and treat our bridges with
care, knowing that wear and tear ulti-
mately results in more money being taken
out of all of our pockets. I feel a responsibility to all of you, and I would
hope that you all feel a responsibility
toward me.

It has become evident over the years,
however, that not every citizen of this
county is equal, for sitting on the corner of County Highway 63 and 1000 North
is a property forsaken beyond all respectability. You all know that of which
I speak, and while many of you are not
daily confronted with the sights and
smells of what I shall hereafter call
The Offense, I hope that your conscienc-
es will at least be pricked in knowing
The Offense has grown monstrous under
your watch.

First, let us address the matter of
the land itself. For at least a decade,
The Offense has blinded us every year
during the months of May and June with
acre upon acre of butterweed. While The
Offense's proprietor may be saving money with his no-till farming methods, the
rest of us end up losing our pride for

the land. To quote the young gentleman who mows my lawn every summer, this is "farmin' ugly." And as to the additional pesticides being dumped into my helpless ditches and creek, God knows how much of it is ending up in my well and yours. Judging by the grotesque increase in this generation of children's unlikability, one can only assume the pesticides are already coursing through their veins and causing behavior disorders.

Second, let us address the issue of The Offense's smell. Pigs, by biblical nature, are unclean animals—which should not be held against them in light of the Gospel, for the apostle Peter has declared them now good for the plate—but even unclean animals should not be left to wallow in their own excrement for months at a time. Barns are not toilets, and farms are not sewers. If the proprietor of The Offense persists in manufacturing hog manure ad nauseam to use as fertilizer for his fields, then let him make certain his tractor wheels don't deposit the feces on public roads as well. Our garage floors should never be the final resting place of any part of any pig.

Third, while we are on the subject of animal neglect, let us address the issue of unrestrained pets. Any domesticated animal left to wander at will runs a high risk of contracting and carrying rabies from farm to farm and is a danger to others. And while The Offense's resident mutt presently appears docile toward humans, he is most certainly violent toward fowl of any kind, a fact which has been made most clear on three separate occasions in the last month alone. A mutt who continually strays to neighboring properties in search of food must be underfed at home. I hereby commend this issue to the county pound or, if left unchecked, to the nearest rifle.

Fourth and last, let us address what is the greatest and most recent violation made by The Offense: a blue ad for Bradbury's Kuhl Whip Stand painted on the barn's roof. While I do congratulate The Offense's proprietor for taking "farmin' ugly" to a whole new level, my commendation ends where whoring begins. I can never be in support of an enterprise which requires that farms service the needs of businesses like a brothel. I will be boycotting the Kuhl Whip Stand this summer, and it is my sincere hope that you will too.

Sincerely yours,
Mrs. Arlene Margaret Compton Scheinberg


Irv set the paper down and whistled slowly through his teeth. "Remind me never to paint our barn blue."

## Chapter Eight: Farmin' Uglier

Emily insisted that Mrs. Scheinberg's retirement party be kept a surprise.

"If Arlene finds out about it, she won't come," she reminded the small planning committee sitting around the parsonage dining room table.

"And we need to keep things light and bright and positive, okay?" Bev Davis added, more than a little concerned about the present state of her friend's mental health after that sniper letter published in the *Bradbury Times*.

"Where should we have it?" Emily asked.

"Triangle Park is pretty," Bev suggested.

"But it's also hot and has no pavilion," Candice Bradbury pointed out.

"The cemetery has a pavilion," Nettie Schmidt suggested, "and plenty of shade trees. And Dean is buried there! Oh yes, Arlene will like being next to him. We could spread out blankets and have a picnic."

Candice excelled at ignoring people, especially when it served her own purpose. She didn't even look at Nettie. "My house is clearly the best option. It's the only residence in town big enough to host the entire congregation, and I just bought the *perfect* plum-colored cloths on sale at Ben Franklin's last week. They'll look divine on my—"

"We can't have it at the church?" Rebecca interrupted, feeling a bit impatient. Robbie's game was starting in an hour, and even though her son was being unjustly benched for the night, she had every intention of sitting in the bleachers in support of him.

"That might be the easiest place to catch Arlene unawares," Emily acknowledged. But ever the peacemaker, she turned toward Candice and smiled. "It sure would be nice to use your new cloths to spiffy up the place a bit, though."

"I suppose that could be arranged." Candice's acquiescence sounded more like a sigh than a reply. "Though I must remind you that the fluorescent lighting in the parish hall will completely wash out the rich tone of the thread. They'll end up looking more purple than plum."

"Well, just as long as they don't look *too* purple," Rebecca teased.

Candice didn't look amused, so Emily moved the conversation quickly along. "What else should we use for decorations?"

"I have scores of my aunt Jessie's old glass vases just sitting in my basement," Bev offered.

"And I'm sure Evan would be happy to fill those vases with flowers from his gardens," Rebecca suggested, this time completely serious.

"And I can make a banner!" Nettie said. "Harold can help me hang it over the service window of the kitchen when I'm done."

Emily and Rebecca exchanged looks of concern. The last two people in the congregation who needed to be standing on any ladders were Hank and Nettie Schmidt.

"I will take care of the food," Candice said.

"Oh, that's too much," Bev asserted. She really did think that was too much work for any one person to take on, but her biggest concern was that Candice had been on a low-fat—meaning, low-flavor—kick these days.

"Now, don't worry." Candice flashed her signature I-know-what's-best smile around the table. "I won't make all of the food myself. I'm just offering to organize the spread."

"Oh, okay." As long as sensible people could contribute. Bev smiled brightly. "What can I bring?"

"How about a veggie tray with hummus?"

Bev's face fell. This was not a good start.

"Or kale chips? Those are crunchy and delicious *and* rich in vitamin K."

Bev bowed her head, suddenly grieved. She felt moved to observe a moment of respectful silence for the death of Candice's creamy cuisine. Gone were the days of towering twinkie cakes and buttered oatmeal rolls and rhubarb custard bars.

"I also have a recipe for brownies made with black beans instead of flour," Candice continued. "I can give it to you if you want to bring something sweet."

Bev drew the line at black bean brownies. She intervened on behalf of her friend. "I'll just bring some deviled eggs and ham salad and strawberry pretzel dessert. Arlene loves those."

Emily stepped in before Candice could call in the calorie cops. "And Pastor and I will organize some entertainment. Just some songs and silly things to keep things light, like you said, Bev. This is going to be great!"

⁣⁣⁣⁣⁣⁣⁣⁣⁣⁣⁣⁣⁣⁣⁣⁣⁣⁣⁣⁣⁣⁣⁣⁣

The evening of the party, Bev was all aflutter. She had successfully convinced Mrs. Scheinberg to join her and Irv at Koelster's Kitchen for Saturday supper—they'd pick her up on the way, of course—but she announced on the drive into town her dire need to pick up her manual for teaching Sunday School at the church.

"We can grab it on the way home after supper," Mrs. Scheinberg said.

"Oh, but it'll be dark then."

"What, you can't turn on a light switch?" Mrs. Scheinberg never liked delaying meals, especially for unexpected errands.

"It's not that," Bev hastily explained, giving Irv an entreating look. "It's just . . . well, I might forget about it then."

"I'll remember," Mrs. Scheinberg announced resolutely from her seat in the back of the Buick.

But Irv, ever the white knight in Bev's misadventures, turned east on Mulberry Avenue and pulled into the church parking lot.

"Oh, thank you, honey," Bev cooed, leaning over to kiss his cheek. She turned around in her seat and giggled. "I'm so embarrassed to have to ask this, but—well, can you both help me?"

"You need help carrying a teacher's manual?" Mrs. Scheinberg groused.

"It's actually not *just* the manual that I forgot to bring home. I also need some poster board and some construction paper and cotton balls and—"

"Oh, for heaven's sake!" Mrs. Scheinberg moved to open her door and began the laborious rocking process required to propel herself out of low vehicles. "Let's get this over with."

Irv gave Bev a quick wink and removed his cell phone from his pocket to text Pastor that the eagle had landed. Bev looked around, pleased to see that the parking lot was completely empty, just as it should be on a Saturday night. Everyone must have parked on side streets or near the school as instructed.

As soon as they entered the front office door, though, Mrs. Scheinberg's sheepdog instincts could tell something was different. She lifted her nose in the air. "What's that smell?"

"I don't know." Bev projected innocence.

"It smells like rotten trash in here."

It did stink. Bev sighed. It was probably Candice's wretched kale.

Mrs. Scheinberg and her cane were already moving down the main hallway leading to the sanctuary and into the parish hall. "And there's a light on! Good grief, I haven't been retired for even a week and the entire place is falling apart! I told Pastor Fletcher to make sure and check every light in this place before locking up at night, but that man's attention span is shorter than a squirrel's. And Lance Finley's even worse. You'd think the janitor of our church could be expected to remember which day of the week the trash gets picked up, but no! The man has to be called every Thursday night or the kitchen cans get left and end up fermenting into a full-bodied sludge by Sunday morning. I bet the back door's still unlocked too. If someone would just—"

"Surprise!"

Mrs. Scheinberg stopped dead in her tracks at the sight of the eighty people lined up in front of the kitchen service window along the far side of the parish hall. Everyone, Evan and the Joneses and the Kulls and the Plueths and the Holleys and the—oh, there were her precious godchildren!—and the Fletchers and the Rinckers and the Bradburys and the Schmidts and the Koelsters and Curt and Kathryn and, well, everyone was there. Even Yvonne Roe stood at the back with her nose lifted a haughty forty-five degrees in the air. Cloth-covered tables decked with fresh flowers filled the room, and a round table leaning in the southwest corner of the parish hall looked like it might collapse from the weight of too many gifts. In front of the crowd of people, a three-table-long buffet stood at the ready, and the old fifty-cup percolator was spitting and spewing like the little engine that could on a nearby beverage cart.

"We're not going to Koelster's, are we?" Mrs. Scheinberg asked, her voice extra gruff from the strain of holding back emotion.

"No," Bev answered, already crying into a tissue.

Mrs. Scheinberg looked at the mass of people assembled just for her, her heart filling with something akin to affection, but just as a lone tear threatened to crest her lower eyelid, she beheld the giant banner hanging directly over their heads. Her lone tear instantly retreated to the duct from which it came.

---

## RIP, Mrs. Scheinberg!

---

"Oh, Arlene," Bev blubbered, already alert to the fire growing within her friend. She seemed determined to put it out with her own tears. "I'm so, so sorry. None of us saw the banner until this afternoon, and then it was too late. Nettie made it."

Of course. "This is to be my funeral, then?"

"No, no, no!" Bev suddenly sounded like Julia Fletcher, and her face looked as if it were being squeezed like a lemon. "Nettie, well, you know how she gets confused. When we asked her about it, she said . . . well . . . apparently, she's always thought that RIP meant 'Retire in Peace.'"

Mrs. Scheinberg leaned forward on her cane, her countenance immovable. But then her shoulders fluttered. And then her bosom convulsed. And then her throat involuntarily hummed. Bev reached out a steadying hand, assuming her friend was about to be sick on the carpet, but when Mrs. Scheinberg finally opened her lips, a torrent of laughter poured forth with the volume and velocity of an avalanche. Irv immediately joined in, his low rumble the perfect bass line to Mrs. Scheinberg's trumpet blowing, and soon, even Bev was laughing hysterically.

Emily Fletcher rushed forward with Becky in her arms, ushering Mrs. Scheinberg to the front of the buffet line as Pastor Fletcher led the assembly in giving thanks.

"Lord God, heavenly Father," he prayed, "we give You thanks for Arlene, Your faithful servant in the church."

Bev sniveled loudly.

"We rejoice with her in her retirement, and in thankfulness we remember the good gifts You have given to her even as we eagerly anticipate the good gifts yet to come. We ask that You would continue to bless her with a sincere faith, an expectant hope, and a contented heart, trusting that in You, none of her labor is in vain. Thank You for adopting all of us as Your children in Baptism, and we ask that You would daily remind us of the life everlasting that is ours in Your Son. Please bless this food to the nourishment of her body and ours. In Jesus' name."

"Amen," the congregation prayed.

"A-main!" Curt shouted.

Mrs. Scheinberg wiped away an obstinate tear with a swollen finger before anyone could notice. Pastor Fletcher's prayers had improved significantly ever since the young man's sideburns had begun to gray.

Bev grabbed a plate for her friend and indicated that she go first down the buffet. Everyone else quickly fell in line behind them.

"What are these?" Mrs. Scheinberg asked, pointing to a tray of assorted crackers and cheeses.

"Those are flaxseed and zucchini crackers with a vegan cheese spread," Bev murmured.

Mrs. Scheinberg kept moving.

"And these?"

"Cashew sushi."

She raised her eyebrows in question, but Bev's only answer was a defeated shrug.

"And this?" Mrs. Scheinberg was looking down into a Crock-Pot filled with a creamy green substance. "Cream of broccoli soup?"

"Seaweed chowder," Bev mumbled shamefully.

"What?"

"Seaweed chowder."

"Our entire lives are spent eradicating weeds from this cursed earth. Why would someone put them in a soup?" Mrs. Scheinberg suddenly turned toward Bev and accused, "You left Candice in charge of my retirement party menu, didn't you?"

"I-it wasn't my decision" was Bev's meek reply.

She shook her head reproachfully and reached for a serving spoon stuck in a bowl of good old-fashioned coleslaw.

"Wait!" Bev whisper-shrieked. "Don't!"

"What? Why?"

"Penny Holley made that."

She dropped the spoon like a hot potato and reached into her bag for her antibacterial gel. Penny Holley was the nicest lady in the world, but friends didn't let friends eat her salads. Not, at least, since the ladies of the congregation had witnessed her method of making them. The sweet woman had hosted a Pampered Chef party in her own kitchen, slaving for an hour in front of them, cooking while they all stood around and watched, sipping leisurely on glasses of Gewürztraminer. She had done her best to use each and every pan and fancy utensil featured in the company's catalog, and she had spoiled them all by using only the freshest of ingredients—organic broccoli for the broccoli-raisin salad and pastured chicken for the tetrazzini. However, Penny had also spoiled their appetites for years to come by grabbing the unwashed knife she had used to cut her raw chicken and using it to chop the vegetables for her broccoli-raisin salad. No one had been able to eat her cooking since.

"Is there anything at this party suitable for consumption?"

Bev pointed down the table to a mound of ham salad surrounded by a ring of Ritz crackers. "I also made you deviled eggs and strawberry pretzel dessert, and Emily made your cinnamon rolls. She put cream cheese frosting on them too. They're at the end."

Mrs. Scheinberg breathed a sigh of relief. There was balm in Gilead, after all.

After everyone had filled up on weeds and seeds and nuts and ham salad, Emily Fletcher sat at the parish hall piano and motioned for the twins to come forward. Caroline Bradbury, Ben Schmidt, and the three youngest Jones children joined them as well, all of them lining up shoulder to shoulder at the west end of the parish hall from tallest to George. As soon as Emily started playing chime-like chords on the keys, Mrs. Scheinberg recognized "So Long, Farewell" from her favorite musical, *The Sound of Music*. She laughed heartily when Caroline Bradbury asked to taste her first champagne, and she cheered along with everyone else when Frankie Jones hit Kurt von Trapp's iconic high note. It was her precious godchildren who moved her to tears, however, singing in unison about the sun setting and it being time to sleep. They ended the song by walking over to her and laying their curly heads in her lap.

Thankfully, Pastor Fletcher stepped in to save her from a public show of weeping.

"Many of you don't know," he announced to the crowd as everyone settled back into chairs and pulled children onto laps, "that Arlene gave *me* a gift upon her retirement." He held up a homemade wall calendar for everyone to see. "Now, I know what many of you are thinking, 'Who uses a wall calendar anymore?' Well, Arlene knows that I do. I like to hang one near my desk in my study for quick referencing during my planning of the services, and she was so thoughtful as to make me one on her computer that includes all of the liturgical seasons and holy days. She even printed it in color, coordinating the ink choices to match the appropriate colors of the Church Year."

Everyone clapped politely in appreciation.

"What you may not be able to see from where you are sitting is that Arlene, ever thoughtful, also took the time to handwrite in— using red ink, mind you—the dates and times that she anticipates my needing a haircut—"

The crowd burst out laughing, though Mrs. Scheinberg couldn't imagine why. It was a completely sensible thing to do. The man was notorious for looking like a poodle every sixth week.

"—along with a brand-new set of hair clippers!"

Mrs. Scheinberg sat unmoved while everyone else around her hooted and hollered and clapped.

"Well, Arlene," Pastor said, lifting a large, square package from the gift table and walking it over to her, "we wanted to give a gift to you as well, one from all of us, which shows our appreciation for all of the hard work you have put in over the years. Our days—mine especially—would have been much harder without you, and our lives would have been a thousand laughs short."

Mrs. Scheinberg broke the bonds of the Scotch tape one by one and meticulously lifted the heavy silver paper from the gift. It was a framed photo of Zion Lutheran Church, and everyone had signed the white matting surrounding it with messages of love and goodwill. Down at the bottom right-hand corner, Pastor Fletcher's recognizable scrawl read, "Man blessings in your retirement, Mrs. Scheinberg!"

Oh no, he didn't! Her memory flashed back to a bulletin an-nouncement about Pastor Douglas's retirement so many years ago. That annoying tickle started at the base of her shoulders again, traveling up to her head, causing her nostrils to twitch.

"We thank God for the gift of you, and we all hope that you 'retire in peace,' Arlene," Pastor smiled.

That did it. Mrs. Scheinberg threw her head back so that the pressure built up behind her belly button could be released. She was a geyser of laughter, an unending stream of hot shrieks and fizzy cackles, and all she had to do was glance at Nettie's morbid banner or see a child trying to find something to eat off of Candice's bird-feeder buffet for the laughter to start all over again. These people! These ridiculous, predictable, wonderful people! They were such—well, they were her people, that's what they were, and she loved every one of them, poodle hair and all.

She was still laughing when Irv and Bev dropped her home that night, but the moment Mrs. Scheinberg sat down at the kitchen table with her nightly piece of pie to read the weekend edition of the *Bradbury Times*, her geyser immediately dried up.

Dear Editor:

1. No-till keeps my fields from eroding into your ditches. And you're welcome.

2. Y'all can thank me for that bacon on your plate.

3. Any fool who shoots my dog on my land gets to share his bullet.

4. The day Arlene Scheinberg starts paying taxes on my property is the day she can choose the color of my barn.

5. All of us are thankful to have more room at the Kuhl Whip Stand this summer.

Max A. Mauer

## CHAPTER NINE: PILLOW TALK

iiiiiiiiiiiiiiiiiiiiiiiiiiiiiiiiiiiiiiiiiiiiiiiiiii

"You never wear red anymore," Rebecca lightly accused, reaching for her pineapple martini and taking a luxurious sip.

"I can't." Emily nursed a pink-colored beverage of her own. The two friends were sitting in lawn chairs under the shade of a large maple tree in the backyard of the parsonage, their bare feet soaking in a yellow and green kiddie pool. Becky splashed cheerfully in front of them. "Not in public, at least."

"Why not? It's your best color."

"It's a hussy color. Didn't you know? Yvonne Roe told me so herself."

Rebecca snorted. "You've got to be kidding me."

"Oh no. I'm being perfectly serious. Red is on the list."

"The list?"

"Mmhm." Emily took another sip from her tumbler and set it on a nearby iron table that had at one time been painted red. The old paint was now chipping and peeling after years of rainstorms and freezes and outdoor tea parties conducted by the twins. "We have a list hanging in our closet of all of the helpful suggestions the women of Zion have made to me over the years. You know, of what a pastor's wife *shouldn't* wear."

"And what, pray you, is on this list?"

"Nail polish that sparkles, of course."

"Of course," Rebecca grinned, closing her eyes and leaning her head against the back of her chair, settling in for a good time.

"Skirts that hit above the knees."

"Naturally."

"Low-cut shirts."

"A given."

"Synthetic materials."

"Really?" Rebecca turned, her eyes dancing. "Who told you that?"

Emily smiled secretively, shaking her head.

"What else?"

"White tights—too childish. And open-toed shoes—too risqué."

Rebecca furrowed her brow in serious consideration. "Toes are alluring? I missed that memo in life, apparently."

"Apparently. And metallic belts."

"Oh, now, that sounds like someone is jealous of your waistline."

Emily leaned down to pick up the teething ring Becky had just thrown out of the pool and tossed it back toward her daughter. "Also, fashion jewelry."

"Seriously?"

"Oh yes. The pastor's family shouldn't have enough money for such frivolities. It's a sign that the pastor is being paid too much."

"Too much? Oh, come on! Somebody actually said that to you? What's wrong with people?" Rebecca looked a little less amused and a little more perturbed. She had grown up in a parsonage and knew a thing or two about the unrealistic expectations put upon a pastor's children, but she had not been privy to the puritan dress code imposed upon a pastor's wife. She pulled her Cubs hat low over her eyes. "I wonder what they used to say to my mom . . ."

Emily watched as her friend's blue eyes momentarily dimmed and then grew bright again like sunlight behind a fast-moving cloud. Alice Gardner-Ebner, Rebecca's mother, had been a pastor's wife in Bradbury for thirty years, and the gentle, kind, wise woman had, no doubt, heard an unhelpful opinion or two from Zion's fairer sex during her tenure. Alice would know exactly how to advise them in this matter, but she was no longer available to help. She had been dead for four and a half years, and her absence never failed to sting.

Emily tried moving the conversation into a less personal arena. "Look at George."

Rebecca turned her head to the left toward the yard's northern fence. The Fletchers' vegetable garden ran the entire length of the fence, the eastern end of which was devoted to the noble, messy endeavor of cultivating the twins' little green thumbs. Presently, Julia was digging fastidiously along her plat of dirt with a plastic trowel, but George was sprawled out lazily on his belly in a nearby patch of grass, nose to nose with the Fletchers' equally idle house rabbit, Carrots.

Rebecca smiled. "Is George still insisting that Carrots is pregnant?"

"Yes . . ." Emily sipped at her tumbler. "No matter how many times I try explaining to him that his rabbit doesn't have a womb."

"Maybe it's time to talk to him about what his bunny *does* have."

"Oh, we've tried that too. It's just that George has it in his mind that girls come from girls and boys come from boys." Emily shook her head. "I think it's the younger sister thing that's got him all confused. He remembers Becky coming out of me, and he's got it in his mind that only girls come out of girls."

"He needs a baby brother, then," Rebecca decreed.

"Yes, thank you," Emily nodded, feeling a blush blooming on her cheeks. "I'll get right on that."

Rebecca's tone held a note of accusation. "I know that you're pregnant, Em."

Emily froze, her eyes unable to look any direction other than straight ahead. "How can you—?"

"Em. I know you."

The two sat silent for a moment, each tending to her own thoughts. This was a conversation Emily always dreaded, not because the news of her child was joyless or because she didn't want to share it with her dearest friend. It was because, for the third time in a row, it was her news to tell and not Rebecca's. Her heart broke for her friend's silent womb. "I'm about a couple of months along."

"Does Pastor know?"

Emily shook her head, still facing forward. "I was planning on telling him tonight."

"It's all right, Em. This is a good thing. The best thing."

Emily wiped at her wet face with both hands. Why couldn't Rebecca have the best thing as well? Ever since Emma Jones had died in utero, Rebecca had been pregnant only once, but the pregnancy had ended in miscarriage.

"Don't be ashamed," Rebecca assured, facing forward herself. Eye contact was impossible for the moment. "This is how it should be. Thanks be to God."

Emily nodded, but tears streamed down her face. She reached for her friend's hand and squeezed it. Rebecca squeezed back. Such was their life together: laughing and crying, laughing and crying.

"How can you always tell?" Emily was thinking back to a time a couple of years ago when Rebecca had suggested that she take a pregnancy test. Her milk had dried up, and she was upset beyond consolation. When she had followed Rebecca's advice, she ended up finding Becky and everything was all right. "Sometimes, I think you know I'm pregnant before I do."

Rebecca's voice slipped on her tears. "You grow content when you're pregnant. Something restless in you quiets down."

Emily vacillated between the sweet comfort of being known and the bitter ache of wanting her friend to have another child. She was no stranger to such pain herself. It had not been too long ago that she had feared she would never have children of her own. Her first husband had died of a heart aneurism a couple of years into their marriage, and eleven long, childless years passed before she finally married Michael.

"Honestly, I think it's a special foreknowledge God gives me when you're pregnant," Rebecca ruminated. "A mercy He shows me. He gives me little warnings to soften the blow."

Emily winced. Her child was a gift, but a club-bearing gift, apparently.

"That, and," Rebecca nodded toward Emily's tumbler of pink lemonade, "I noticed that you made your lemonade a little more pink and a little less hard this time around."

George suddenly appeared before them holding an armful of brown-and-white fur. "Ca-wots needs a bath."

Emily withdrew her hand from Rebecca's and wiped the salty evidence from her cheeks. "No, he doesn't. Carrots keeps himself quite clean all on his own."

George opened his cherub lips to present a follow-up request, but his mother was one step ahead of him.

"He doesn't need to be baptized either. It's only people who need their sins washed away. Go on, put him inside, George. It's getting too hot for Carrots out here. You can give him an apple treat if you want, but only one. George, did you hear me?"

Her son was almost through the back door.

"How many treats?" she repeated.

"One," his treble voice traveled through the screen.

Emily nodded and sat back in her chair but instantly recoiled at the smell of cigarette smoke. She turned to look across the north fence. Charlene, their neighbor woman, had slipped out of her house unnoticed and taken up residence on a plastic chair at the northwest corner of her single-car garage. She sat wearing only a hot pink bikini top and white knit skirt, sunning her shoulders and picking at her toenail polish with one hand while dragging on a Marlboro with the other.

"Neighbors are the ones who need dress codes." Rebecca had noticed Charlene too. "Every backyard in town should have a shirts-only policy, don't you think?"

They were just as bad as the women at church. Emily sighed. She liked Charlene, and to keep it that way, she tried her best never to notice what her neighbor was—or wasn't—wearing. The smoke, however, was another matter. Emily loathed cigarette smoke.

"Julia!" she called, standing and rubbing at the stinging indentations pressed into the back of her legs by the lawn chair. "Let's go inside and get supper started for Daddy."

Charlene looked up then and waved.

Emily waved back.

"What does she do, again?" Rebecca asked, her voice low as she reached for both beverages and carried them toward the house.

Emily picked up Becky and wrapped her in a nearby towel. "She's a nurse's assistant at Bradbury Regency."

"Tough job," Rebecca admitted.

"Yes," Emily confirmed, casting one more glance at Charlene's half-naked frame before ushering her children into the smoke-free house. "Tough life."

||||||||||||||||||||||||||||||||||||||||||||

Pastor sighed into his pillow.

Emily set down her book and looked over at her husband. They had just finished putting the kids to bed, and though George could still be heard singing "Built on the Wock" from the twins' darkened bedroom at the end of the hall, both girls seemed to be asleep. Her husband, on the other hand, was wide awake but quiet and brooding as a storm cloud.

"Stressed?" Emily asked.

"Yes."

"Life stressed or church stressed?" There was a difference, and every pastor's wife knew it. One could be talked about, the other could not.

"Church stressed."

Emily let out a sigh of her own. Church Stress was her nemesis. It stole her husband's thoughts and robbed her of his time and attention. It was an invisible thief, and she felt so helpless against its advances. Other than offering up prayers to God for mercy, all she could do was watch from the sidelines as it paralyzed her husband and ate him alive from the inside out.

She turned on her side to better study his profile in the lamplight. He was a handsome man. His dark eyes, especially, could make her cheeks burn with the intensity of their stare. That, and he had boyish black curls that were now attractively outlined with stately silver threads.

"I'm going gray," he had said to her in the bathroom mirror one morning a few months ago.

"It's not gray, honey," she had assured him. "It's *gravitas*."

That had made him smile. In fact, his lips always seemed to be playing with a smile, even when Church Stress was on the attack. She liked that about her husband. Her own lips were way too serious most of the time, but he never seemed to hold it against her.

"Anything you can talk about?"

"I shouldn't."

"Okay." Emily fought the nasty, familiar urge to probe beyond salutary ministerial boundaries. Instead, she closed her eyes and prayed for a yoke that was easy and a burden that was light.

"How about you?" Pastor eventually asked.

"Hm?" Emily opened her eyes to find that he had turned on his side to face her. He was studying her with that penetrating look of his. She felt her cheeks grow warm.

"How are you?"

"Oh," Emily cleared her throat, "a little tired."

"Yeah? Not sleeping well?"

"No, it's just . . . a lot of work."

"The kids?"

"And the house and the laundry and the church and—well, you get it."

Pastor sighed again.

Emily instantly regretted making a list. She was adding to his unseen burden, and that was not what she wanted. But she *was* tired.

"I don't help you out enough at home."

"Yes, you do."

"No, I've been at church too much the past couple of weeks."

Well, that much was true, but Emily tried to be generous. "I bet it's been tough trying to get things done without Mrs. Scheinberg there."

Pastor scooted closer to her appreciatively, their noses almost touching. "How was your day?"

Emily smiled. She liked it when he gave her his full attention. "All of Rebecca's kids were out and about this afternoon, so she came over for a visit."

"That's nice."

"And Julia planted—or over-planted—her zinnia seeds from Evan. Some of them are buried at least a foot in the ground, I'm sure."

Pastor chuckled. "She's an over-achiever like you. Speaking of which, I've been thinking. You should get out more. You know, go do something fun every week. Like go out for a movie or something."

Emily wrinkled her nose. "I don't like movie theaters. They turn the volume up way too loud."

"You could go get one of those pedi-foot-things."

"A pedicure?" Emily smiled at his misclassification. "I don't like breathing in all of those chemicals. It burns my lungs and makes my voice feel tight."

"Diva!" Pastor teased. "Take a dance class, then."

"With whom? You?"

"Oh. No, I don't think I can get away in the afternoons. At least, not until we hire a new secretary."

Emily fought against another sigh. Afternoons weren't the only time slots currently unavailable to her husband. He never could get away, not as long as it was morning, noon, or night. Emily's mind flashed back to the many times Don Kull had teased her husband in the narthex that pastors only work one day a week. If only!

"What about joining the altar guild?"

"What?"

"The altar guild."

"Now?"

"Sure. The sacristy could use some new blood—"

"No pun intended," Emily winked.

The good reverend stopped for a moment to think about it and then, finally understanding, gave her a wry chuckle. "Funny."

"I thought so," Emily grinned.

"Yes, well," he quickly moved on, "what I mean is, the ladies could always use some more help, and it would be a chance for you to spend some time with other adults. Get away from home a little. Maybe Rebecca could join with you, and then you'd get to do it together."

Emily almost laughed. What pathetic season of life had they entered that the altar guild now seemed like a good social opportunity? Was bingo next on the list? Honestly, it did kind of sound like fun, though. The quiet. The solitude. And maybe the congregation wouldn't hold it against her husband if he stepped across the street to watch the kids so his wife could do some church work of her own. And if Rebecca joined, well . . . the idea held some promise. "I'll think about it."

"Good." Pastor reached behind his head to turn off the lamp.

"I'm worried about Charlene." The words came out of Emily's mouth before she could stop them.

Pastor paused with his hand midair. "Why?"

Emily groaned inwardly, wishing she hadn't brought the matter up. The last thing her husband needed was to hear about more people's problems.

"Did something happen?" Pastor tried again.

"No," Emily said. "It's just that she's been home a lot more in the afternoons."

"Did she lose her job again?"

"I hope not."

Pastor was watching her closely. "Something else is worrying you."

Emily knew that she couldn't hide anything from her husband, and she both loved and hated that fact. "I've seen a guy come in and out of her house several times."

"Who?"

"I don't know."

"Have you seen him before?"

"No."

"What does he look like?"

"He's in his twenties or thirties, I think. Pale face, dark facial hair. Always wears a hat. Low-hanging pants. You get the idea."

Pastor sighed again, and Emily felt pained.

"For how long?"

"At least a couple of weeks."

"Does he talk to you and the children?"

"No. He usually parks his truck in the drive and walks straight into her house. He doesn't ever knock. He just goes right in."

Pastor thought on this a moment. "What time of day?"

"Different times, I think. Sometimes morning, sometimes afternoon. I've heard his truck in the middle of the night once or twice."

"Why haven't I seen or heard him? Or his truck?"

Emily immediately thought of a thousand reasons—*You sleep like a hibernating bear; you were gone most of last week for the Synod's convention; when you are home, you're out of the house from sunup to sundown; your head is constantly filled with Church Stress, so you don't notice anything else*—but she didn't voice a single one.

"Do you think it's drugs again?"

"Maybe." Emily's heart sank. She didn't want to think the worst of Charlene, but it wouldn't be the first time their neighbor had been targeted by the slime of Bradbury's cesspool.

"Okay. I'll try to keep a better eye on things. In the meantime, don't let the kids play outside by themselves."

Emily felt a sudden flash of irritation. The threat of drugs aside, when did she ever let their toddler children play outside unattended? What did he think she did all day long? There were moments when her husband—dreamy eyes and all—didn't seem so pleasant and charming.

"I'm sorry," he immediately apologized, apparently reading her expression well. He reached out and folded her into his arms. "You are a wonderful mother, Emily. I'm just ashamed that I haven't noticed this guy around the neighborhood before. You and the kids are my life." He sighed against her hair. "I've got to figure out a way to balance everything better. I've got to find a way to be home more."

And then there were moments—like this one—when her husband was the most pleasant and charming man in the world! Emily smiled against his shoulder. Church Stress would always try to get the best of him, but she had one more winsome trick up her sleeve.

"Michael?"

"Hm?"

"I'm glad you think I'm a wonderful mother."

"Why's that?"

"Because I'm pregnant with your child."

## Chapter Ten: Mr. Hyde

,,,,,,,,,,,,,,,,,,,,,,,,,,,,,,,,,,,,,,,,,,,,,,,,,,,,,,,,,,

The next morning, Pastor stopped short before stepping out onto the front porch. There, hanging above the parsonage doorframe, was a small chalkboard that had not been there the day before. It was inconsequential in appearance except that on it, written in white chalk, were the words, "'Joy comes in the morning.'"

Emily's handwriting was unmistakable. His thoughtful—and sneaky—wife must have hung the short missive sometime after he had fallen asleep last night, and since he was the only other Fletcher in the house who could read, the reminder of God's promise must have been intended just for him. Pastor felt warm all over. He turned on his heel and let the front door swing shut behind him.

"Hey, Fletcher," he said, sticking his head around the kitchen door. His wife was standing at the stove, spatula in hand.

"Yes?"

He stopped to admire her wild nest of bedhead curls. He had never seen such a beautiful sight. "Be ready by eleven."

"What? Why?"

"I'm taking you out for lunch." It had been months since they had eaten at The Corner Coffee Shop. The little café on the corner of First and Main had been their favorite getaway spot before the twins were born, but somehow, they had fallen out of the habit of lunch dates in general. It was time to remedy that.

"What about the kids?"

"I'll take care of everything. You just be ready by eleven."

As he left the parsonage and walked across the street, he could feel his wife's dimples radiating through the walls of the house.

And Pastor didn't stop with lunch. He took his whole family to the Lions game that night as well.

"More popcorn, pease?"

Pastor looked down into George's seraphic eyes and dumped the rest of his own popcorn into his son's empty bag. "This is it, so pace yourself, Pac-Man."

"His name is George," Julia clarified.

"Yes, thank you, Julia." Pastor grinned at his blue-stained daughter. What a mess! Her lips and tongue and hands and shirt were the same unnatural color as her slushy. He chuckled, thinking of what she had said in line at the food stand just a few minutes before.

"What do you want to eat?" he had asked.

"Slushy, slushy, slushy!"

"What flavor?"

She had pointed to the giant pump bottle of blue-raspberry syrup sitting on a back counter. "Elsa!"

Everything in Julia's world—even colors—was classified as princesses.

"How's your slushy?" he asked her now.

"Good," Julia said, her mouth around her spoon. She turned to look at Curt sitting to her left. "Last time, when I was small, I liked Aurora. But now I like Elsa. You're eating Belle."

Curt looked down at his banana-flavored slushy. "Iiiee yike Beh-ya."

Pastor turned to share an amused smile with Emily, but his wife was wrestling with a hot and fussy Becky on her lap.

"We're going to pay for this," she said.

"For what?"

"For pushing back Miss Grouchy's bedtime."

"It's just one night," Pastor reasoned. "It'll be okay."

Becky wasn't the only fussy girl on the bleachers. Rebecca, sitting to Emily's right, looked red in the face under her Cubs hat, and it wasn't just because of the sticky, sauna-like air.

"I don't understand," she was whispering to Emily. "He's been to every practice and every game since that awful Sunday. He shows up early and stays late, and he's been logging extra hours in the batting cage. Why is Coach benching him *again*?"

Pastor looked toward the home team's dugout. The Lions had just taken the field, and Robbie was sitting on the bench alone with his elbows on his knees, his glove between his hands. He looked a bit defeated but ready to jump up at the sound of the call. *God, help Robbie*, Pastor prayed.

"Who's that man playing smallstop?" Julia asked.

Rebecca's already flushed cheeks deepened to a scary crimson. "That's Clark Keller."

"The coach's son?" Emily asked.

"Yes," Rebecca answered brightly. Too brightly.

"Hiiiee, Wob-bie Dones!" Curt hollered, waving his spoon hand in the air.

Robbie looked over his shoulder and quickly waved back before returning his attention to the field.

*God, bless Curt*, Pastor prayed.

"I don't think we're going to have a game," Evan commented from the lowest bleacher, pointing toward the southwest horizon beyond right field. "Those clouds don't look too good."

"Clouds always look darker when the sun gets low." This came from Mrs. Scheinberg, who was sitting in a lawn chair to the side of the bleachers and sipping on a fountain drink.

"I don't know," Ben Schmidt said, looking down at his phone instead of the game. The tall, broad-shouldered young man stood behind Mrs. Scheinberg, his face hidden by the brim of his Cardinals hat. "Radar's not lookin' too good."

Pastor liked Ben Schmidt. He was a hardworking boy, and he was a good friend to Robbie. In years past, Ben would have been standing out on that pitcher's mound along with the rest of the Bradbury Lions, but he was spending his last summer before college working three jobs to put some money in the bank. Pastor had seen Ben discing the ground for Irv Davis in the mornings, mowing lawns during the day, and working the register at Casey's at night. He didn't know of too many teenage boys these days who would choose work over leisure, and he knew of even fewer who would forgo summer baseball to save money for college. The Schmidts were doing something right.

Emily looked warily at the yellow-gray sky. "Do you think we should take the kids home?"

"There's no lightning or wind or anything," Rebecca said.

"That's what concerns me."

Pastor wasn't concerned—not about the weather, anyway. He was more concerned about Robbie. The boy's morale had taken quite a few hits over the last few weeks. This Coach Keller fellow seemed intent on treating summer baseball like the major leagues and church like a dumped date. At least all of Robbie's nearest and dearest had turned out for the game. That was nice.

"Oh!" Eagle-Eye Evan called, pointing toward the horizon. "I just saw some lightning."

The ump behind home plate had seen it too. He started calling both teams off the field.

"Michael, I really do think we should take the kids home," Emily murmured, trying not to alarm the twins. She got nervous in storms, and they had walked the six blocks to the ballpark. It would take them at least fifteen minutes to get home. "I don't want to get stuck in the rain."

"We all should head home," Ben announced, putting his phone in his back pocket and moving to help Mrs. Scheinberg stand. "Radar's showin' a tail at the back of the storm. County's issued a tornado watch."

That got everyone moving. Rebecca helped Evan to his feet, Ben escorted Mrs. Scheinberg to her car, and Emily started buckling a resistant Becky into the stroller.

"Forget that nonsense," Rebecca said. "We'll give you all a ride home. C'mon, George. Julia. Step down now. Everyone in the SUV."

"You don't have room," Emily said, nodding meaningfully at Curt.

"I can take Curt and Evan home," Mrs. Scheinberg hollered from across the street, waving for the men to walk her way.

"But you still don't have enough car seats for the kids," Emily persisted, staring at Rebecca, confused.

Rebecca gripped Emily's arm and pulled her and the stroller toward the SUV. Pastor grabbed the twins and followed suit.

"What are you doing? We can't ride with you, there's not enough room. We'd be breaking the law, Rebecca!"

Thunder rumbled in the background. Whatever was behind that storm cloud, it was coming. And fast. Rebecca opened the front passenger door and pushed Emily inside. "It's only six blocks, Em."

"But it's illegal!"

Rebecca ignored her friend and started buckling the twins into the middle row of seats.

Robbie ran to the vehicle and helped her while Pastor folded the stroller and put it in the back of the SUV. He then ran around and climbed inside, sitting between the twins and pulling Becky onto his lap. Robbie, cleats and all, squeezed behind the four of them to sit in the back row.

"Mommy?" Julia asked, her voice thin and wavy.

"Yes, sweetheart?" Emily turned around in her seat, her own voice anything but stable.

"If I die, will you please bury me with my blankie? I want to be with my blankie."

Emily started to whimper along with her daughter.

"No one's going to die!" Rebecca hollered.

The wind picked up just then. It felt strangely cool and refreshing after the sickly stagnant air, but it also felt freakishly unnatural for mid-July. That only fueled Emily's panic.

"We can't do this!" she kept protesting, her voice now hysterical. "It's against the law! We're breaking the law!"

"Yes, we are," Rebecca answered coolly, jumping in the driver's seat and turning on the ignition. "Now, do you want me to drive you home or to the police station?"

Rebecca drove them to neither. She made an executive decision as she backed out onto the road to take them home with her. The parsonage didn't have a basement, and the oncoming storm looked stronger than that old house's ancient plumbing. No godchild of hers was waiting out a tornado in a bathtub.

Ben Schmidt ended up taking Curt to the Bethesda home himself. It was more on his way out of town than anyone else's, and Mrs. Scheinberg hadn't argued with the sensible boy. Instead, she ushered Evan into her Grand Marquis and turned north onto the Fancy Creek blacktop. And just in time, too, for Bradbury's emergency sirens had begun to scream. She raced to Evan's, pulling into his drive just as the clouds began to spit.

|||||||||||||||||||||||||||||||||||||||||||||

"You'd better come in," Evan advised, staring southward as he exited the car.

"Nope." Mrs. Scheinberg looked straight forward, refusing to follow his gaze, however ominous. It didn't matter how close or how bad the storm was. Her dog was alone. She was going home.

"It's too dangerous, Arlene."

"Good-bye, Evan. Stay safe." She motioned for him to shut the door, and then she gunned the car down the drive.

Dr. Jekyll officially turned into Mr. Hyde at the Fancy Creek blacktop. The monstrous storm howled against her tires, rocking the Grand Marquis as it sprinted one mile north and another east to the Scheinberg acres, almost succeeding in lifting the heavy maiden off of the pavement at one precarious point. A tantrum of raindrops blocked Mrs. Scheinberg's view of the driveway, but she didn't really need to see to find the garage.

"I'm coming, Ceci!" she hollered over the rage, not even bothering to close the garage door. She forgot her cane, her urgency to protect her dog was so immediate.

"Ceci?"

The little pooch wasn't waiting at the door to greet her as usual. Mrs. Scheinberg staggered back to her bedroom and found the crazed dog running in circles on her bed.

"C'mon, girl." Mrs. Scheinberg lunged forward to catch her beloved companion midcircle. "Come with me."

Her ears were popping now, and it sounded like a train was going to come through her bedroom wall. She hugged Ceci to her chest and carried her to the closet, pulling on a loop of rope that was tied to a handle screwed directly into the floor. A three-by-three piece of the closet floor magically lifted, revealing a hole leading directly to the crawl space beneath the house. She threw her dog into the hole.

"I'm coming, girl! Hold on!"

Mrs. Scheinberg winced in pain as she lowered herself onto her worthless knees and swung her legs onto the packed dirt beneath the house. Ceci was barking madly, but all Mrs. Scheinberg could hear was the sound of glass shattering somewhere behind her and what sounded like the firing of a cannonball through the air. She fell down into the hole, crying out in pain, and pulled the trapdoor over them both.

And then there was only darkness and Mr. Hyde clamoring on the other side of the door.

## Chapter Eleven: Twisted

"Our Father who art in heaven . . ."

*Am I dead?*

". . . hallowed be Thy name."

*I can't be dead. I can still feel my wretched knees.*

"Thy kingdom come . . ."

*And Ceci's licking my—ack, doggie breath!*

"Thy will be done on earth—"

*If there's any earth left after that storm.*

"—as it is in heaven."

*Yes, heaven! Take me home now, Lord. I'm ready. I want to see You. And Dean.*

"Give us this day our daily bread . . ."

*Mm, pie.*

". . . and forgive us our trespasses—"

*I left the pie on the counter!*

"—as we forgive those who trespass against us . . ."

*I need to check if the pie's still there. Also, the counter.*

"And lead us not into temptation . . ."

*What's that noise?*

"But deliver us from evil."

"Arlene?"

*Yes, Lord?* "For Thine is the kingdom—"

"Arlene, ken ya hear me?"

*I'm in here, Lord.* "And the power and the glory—"

"Arlene, keep talkin' ta me."

*I already am!* "Forever and ever—"

"Arlene, I'm gonna lift this here door now. Tha's it."

*Wait. Jesus is a redneck?*

Mrs. Scheinberg opened her eyes to see the crawl space door folding back above her head, but it was Max Mauer's whiskered face—not the Son of God's—that was staring down at her through the opening.

"Amen," she mumbled.

"Amen, what?" Max leaned in. "What'd you say? Was you prayin'?"

Mrs. Scheinberg closed her eyes again, choosing death. Anything was better than being rescued by Max Mauer. Ceci, however, barked a cheerful welcome.

"C'mon, now. We've gotta get you outta here." Max was reaching down a hand. "Are ya hurt?"

Mrs. Scheinberg, eyes still closed, took mental stock of each of her limbs, inch by inch. Arms? Fine. Hands? Swollen and achy, same as before. Hips? Stiff, but that was nothing new. Legs? Too thick for her pants, but otherwise mobile. Knees? She skipped those. Feet? Better skip those too. All in all, she hurt, but nothing hurt out of the ordinary. She tried sitting up.

"Slow 'n' steady, now. Tha's it. Now, give me yer hand."

Mrs. Scheinberg gave him a prolonged look of utter disgust.

"Either yer gonna let me help ya, or I'm gonna have ta bring in a crane. 'S yer call."

Mrs. Scheinberg scowled at the loathsome man and extended both of her hands. "Watch the fingers. I have arthritis."

"Don' we all?" Max grabbed ahold of her wrists and leaned back against his rear to pull her upright. Mrs. Scheinberg winced as her feet bore her entire weight for the first time since jumping into the crawl space. When was the last time she had jumped? Primary school? She leaned her elbows against the closet floor. "I can manage on my own from here."

Max wasn't the eye-rolling type, but he never hesitated when it came to head-shaking. He wagged his stubbled chin from east to west and stepped outside of the closet, opening up Mrs. Scheinberg's view to the bedroom. Everything looked in order. All four of her bedroom walls were still standing, at least. She tried lifting her right leg up to floor level, but she couldn't quite clear the carpet. She tried the other leg but to no avail. Ceci leapt out of the hole with a single bound.

"Show off."

Mrs. Scheinberg tried the stomach-first approach next, reaching for a nearby step stool to use as leverage to pull herself out, but all she succeeded in doing was pulling the step stool closer to the hole.

"Don't watch," she spat at Max's boots, refusing to look him in the eye. The yokel was tracking mud all over her floors!

"Hurry up, then."

Mrs. Scheinberg put a hand on either side of the opening and tried lifting her seat up onto the floor's edge, but she had trouble clearing the ground floor of her three-story rump. She tried once more, this time aiming her right hip toward the sky, but her arms gave out. She sighed in frustration, her pride throwing a petulant fit within her chest. She crossed her arms in an effort to hide it. She hated what was coming next.

"Max?"

"Yeah?"

"I need help."

"Yeah, ya do."

"Then don't just stand there! Help me!"

"Crazy woman," he mumbled under his breath, stepping behind her to thread his forearms under her armpits.

"What are you doing?" Mrs. Scheinberg repelled from his touch as if violated.

"I'm gettin' my elbows 'neath yer pits."

"What for?"

"To lift ya."

"With your arms?"

"They's stronger than ma hands."

"But I thought we'd—"

Max put his arms where he needed them most and didn't apologize for it. "Ya want ma help? Then abide by me, Arlene. *Crawfish*, woman! Yer worse than one o' ma hogs!"

*Crawfish?* Mrs. Scheinberg was too stunned by the ridiculousness of the situation to think up a stinging reply.

"Now, put yer hands on the floor agin—I cain't lift ye from down under by myself, Arlene. Tha's it. Now, on the count o' three, lift and lean, 'kay? Backward, now, not forward. One, two, three!"

Mrs. Scheinberg closed her eyes and ignored the incredibly insulting fact that Max grunted while lifting her frame out of the crawl space, and once safely lying on the carpet, she refused to admit to her rescuer that her ground floor had lost a few layers of skin in the extraction. Instead, she sat up proudly on the edge of the closet floor, offered him a pert, "Thank you," and then proceeded to roll over onto her hands and knees as if it were the most natural thing to be on all fours like Dutch. Only, her knees refused to help any further. She sighed.

"Here." Max's hand was hanging near her face.

She took hold of his arm—"Mind the arthritis"—and let him help her to her feet.

"Ya need a cane."

*Yes, yes.*

"And ya need ta lose some weight."

Mrs. Scheinberg stood as tall as her knees would allow and looked her neighbor in the eye. He was shorter than her, and that gave her a grand feeling of satisfaction. "And *you* need to brush your teeth. And take a bath!"

Any feeling of superiority and strength soon left her, however, as she turned down the hallway toward her living room—or what used to be her living room.

"Dear God!" she cried, almost falling to the floor, but Max's arms were already under her own, holding her upright as if he had known this would happen.

"Steady, now," he murmured near her ear.

Mrs. Scheinberg began to whimper, "My home, my home, my beautiful home . . ."

"Here, now," Max returned, word for word. "Yer alive. Tha's wha's important."

"My home, my home, my home . . ."

He let her sink to the floor, bearing her weight the entire time. He knelt behind her, still offering support. "Yer alive, Arlene. You an' yer dog. Tha's wha's important."

Mrs. Scheinberg was openly weeping now, Max at her back and Ceci at her front, her dog licking at the tears falling down her cheeks. Her eyes and ears and nose and heart couldn't quite take in the violent scene before her. It was too savage and absurd. Max seemed to sense her need to have the situation defined.

"The twister ripped 'er right outta the groun' and dropped her not twenty feet from where's you an' yer dog was lyin'."

So that's what had happened, then. There, angled upward from the floorboards of her front porch to the ceiling beams of the upstairs guest bedroom, making a suspension bridge across her living room, lay the oak tree from her front yard. A garish gash in the roof let in the ironically soft, sympathetic gleam of twilight. It was all so ludicrous.

"Tis a mir'cle, I think."

Mrs. Scheinberg thought on that truth for a moment. Max didn't mean the gaping wound in her house. He meant the intact bedroom. The two lives spared by a measly twenty feet. *Deliver us from evil*, she had prayed in the deafening darkness, and now, sitting on the floor of her decimated house, she shivered as she stared her prayer's answer in the face.

"Ken ya git up?"

Mrs. Scheinberg nodded, gently scooting Ceci to the side. She didn't even protest when Max slipped his forearms under her armpits again to help her stand. He led her along the north wall of the living room, navigating sloped floors and splintered boards and curtains and glass and branches, and quickly ushered her under the fallen tree, through the breezeway, and into the safety of the garage.

Amazingly, her car was still there, unharmed, but as she turned to look at the hole in her front yard where the oak used to be, a suffocating sight claimed what little air was left in her lungs. The grain bin near the road—the one Dean had watered with his own blood—was gone. Utterly, completely gone. She moaned, and Max's arms, which had never left her, tightened their hold.

"Yer alive," Max said over and over, "tha's all tha' matters."

A few minutes later, after she had recovered somewhat from the initial shock of it all, Max sat her down on the front porch steps next to the uprooted tree and went to check on the other outbuildings and animals. She stared numbly at the circular pad of concrete where her husband's grain bin had stood just that very afternoon. Dean had been so proud of it. He had ordered it himself shortly after they were married, an early investment on his dream to slowly convert half of their eighty acres of pastureland into fields for crop farming. Their house and outbuildings and land were already a part of the Scheinberg family's fully functioning dairy, but Dean had always liked working with tractors more than animals. Forty-two years later, Mrs. Scheinberg had all but achieved her husband's dream. Out of necessity, she had closed the dairy and switched to raising beef cattle several years ago—widowhood had its limitations, after all—but at least half of Dean's original eighty acres were now devoted to the yearly cycle of growing and harvesting corn and beans.

"All's good," Max announced, rounding the corner of the house. "Jus' one winder busted on the south side o' yer shed. Twister made a mis-sile out o' yer feed bucket."

*And the tree*, she thought miserably, feeling rather than seeing the wounded house behind her. She continued to stare at the empty concrete slab across the lawn. Strangely, all of the bridal veil bushes she had planted around the plot were still in the ground. "How long were Ceci and I under the house?"

"Don' know, 'xactly." Max stayed on his feet, feeling around at one of the bigger tree roots. It really was a magnificent sight. "I came soon as the storm passed. Ten minutes, maybe?"

"That's all?" Mrs. Scheinberg felt incredibly tired. She looked to her right toward the peaceful horizon. Mr. Hyde had come barreling in from the southwest, but the western hemisphere now looked as placid as a pond. All hostility was gone from the sky. It had been chased away by the evening star and replaced with a gentle dusk, and now the field corn tucked its sleepy chin under a blanket of luminous orange as if to go to sleep.

"Why did you come?"

Max threw his prickly chin toward the northeast. "Thought there might be trouble for ya."

Mrs. Scheinberg followed his gaze and shivered. The blue-black wall of Mr. Hyde's backside could still be seen, even from miles away. Lightning flashed in the distance. To think that the sky had a split personality, one side quiet and inviting while the other a thunderous death threat on all of life. She inhaled the washed-clean tranquility of her little corner of the world and tried to dispel all thoughts of atmospheric terror.

"Where's Dutch?"

"He an' Ceci are in the back."

"What?"

"They's jus' fine."

Mrs. Scheinberg moved as if to stand, but her arms were shaking with fatigue.

"Let 'er be," Max placated. "They's fine."

"If your mutt—"

Ceci came bounding around the garage just then with Dutch hot on her tail.

"Ceci!" Mrs. Scheinberg hollered. "Come here!"

But Ceci ignored her mistress. Instead, she stopped, dropped, and rolled on the front lawn, landing on her back with her paws in the air. Dutch play-pounced on top of her, but Ceci deftly rolled to the side and took off again around the house.

"Ceci, come back here!" Her voice was hoarse.

"They's jus' playin', Arlene—"

"Ceci, come here at once!" Mrs. Scheinberg was growing hysterical again. Max moved as if to intervene, but Ceci came tearing around the opposite side of the house like a meteoric dust mop. She threw herself at Mrs. Scheinberg's feet, spreading her hot belly flat on the damp, cool sidewalk, her sides expanding and contracting frantically with every happy pant. Dutch, just a few feet behind in the chase, fell in a pile on Ceci's right and immediately began licking the smaller dog's backside. Mrs. Scheinberg stared at the pair, bewildered, her mouth hanging open.

"He's groomin' her."

"Yes, thank you," Mrs. Scheinberg said. "I have eyes. I can see what's going on."

"Ceci been fixed?"

"Has she been—?" Mrs. Scheinberg couldn't even finish the thought let alone the sentence. "Are you implying—?"

"I'm jus' askin' if'n she's been fixed." Max took off his hat and reapplied it firmly. "Fer the record, Dutch hasn't."

Mrs. Scheinberg's mouth couldn't drop any further, but her eyes still had room to grow. "Max Mauer, if you are suggesting that Dutch might *violate* my dog at any moment, then I *insist* you restrain him at once!"

Max whistled, and Dutch immediately moved to his master's side.

"See?" Max gave her a look as if to communicate some fact that had been obvious from the beginning. "Contrary to pop'lar opinion, alls you need do is whistle, an' he comes." As he led Dutch to the pickup truck, he looked back toward the house and smugly tossed over his shoulder, "An' gentle as a kitten!"

Mrs. Scheinberg frowned as Max shut the tailgate behind his docile dog and then made his way back up to the porch. Why the arrogant man didn't just get in his truck and drive on home already was a mystery to her, but as soon as he leaned himself against a gnarly tree root, she remembered her present predicament.

"Ya cain't stay here," Max pointed out the obvious.

"Well, I'm not staying with you, if that's what you're implying," she snapped.

Max narrowed his eyes at her, but he looked more confused than offended. "I weren't off'rin. But ya still cain't stay here."

Mrs. Scheinberg closed her eyes and squeezed her aching hands together in her lap. She felt dizzy. Her world literally had crashed in on her just minutes before, and she was having trouble sorting through all of the emotional debris. Bev's bubbly smile suddenly came to mind. "I'll call the Davises."

"Already did."

Mrs. Scheinberg opened her eyes. "What? When?"

"When I's checkin' on the shed, I called 'em."

"With what?"

"What d'ya mean, 'Wi' what?'" Max looked at her like she was nuts. He pulled a camo-covered smartphone the size of his forearm out of his back pocket. "Wi' ma phone. Don' you know 'bout cellular phones?"

Max Mauer owned a smartphone. Mrs. Scheinberg's overtaxed brain couldn't process the anomaly.

"Should be 'ere any minute." Max turned and looked toward the road expectantly, and Mrs. Scheinberg followed his gaze. Her eyes rested once more upon the lonely ring of bridal veil bushes. She sighed.

"I always hated that bin."

"Then why'd ya keep it?"

Her face pinched uncomfortably. "Because I also loved it."

And then she started to cry. She didn't want to, but she couldn't help it. Her shoulders rolled back and forth with sobs like waves crashing upon a shoreline. Time with its incessant tide was pounding her against life's jagged rocks, abrading her of every comfort she knew and loved—first her husband, then her health, then her job, and now her home—and there was nothing she could do about it.

"I hate growing old!" she wailed.

Max nodded, still facing the road. He said nothing else while she cried, but he didn't go anywhere either.

Slowly, Mrs. Scheinberg's tearful waves abated to meager ripples and then ceased altogether, leaving behind islands of wet splotches on her soiled shirt. She didn't bother with a tissue. What was the point?

"God took my husband," she sniffed, feeling sorry for herself. "Why did He have to take my husband's bin too?"

Max wasn't the sort to feel compelled to answer anything he didn't already know for sure.

"Well, I suppose it's for the best," she answered for herself, some of her old spirit returning. She sat up straight—as straight as her aching hips would allow—and breathed deeply of the tranquil twilight. "God knows, it was hard enough looking at that thing day in and day out. Maybe *not* looking at it will be better."

Max leaned his back against a root. Behind him, the western sky had diminished to a thin line of dying embers, and all she could make out of him was the outline of his hat.

"I's here the day Dean died, ya know."

"What?"

"I's here the day Dean died," he repeated.

"No, you weren't."

"I was. You jus' don' remember."

Mrs. Scheinberg sat silent, stunned by this turn in the conversation. Her spirited self retreated a bit.

"I's patchin' that piece o' fence on my southwest forty—that strip 'long the road—when I hear'd his screamin'. An' yers."

Mrs. Scheinberg winced and closed her eyes. She didn't want to hear this, but she also did.

"I ran. Ma truck was field side, so I dropped ma ax an' ran. You's talkin' to Dean when I got there, but he's already gone."

Mrs. Scheinberg's memory grabbed her by the neck and whipped her back to that horrible spot near the bin. She was kneeling. The sun was hot. The grass was red. An engine roared in her ears. Dean was on the ground. His eyes looked at her but didn't see her.

"The driveshaft was still spinnin' like mad, so I climbed on the ol' redbelly Ford an' turned her off. You's still talkin' ta Dean."

She looked up with her mind's eye and saw blood splattered on the side of the bin and her husband's mutilated leg wrapped around the auger, but no Max. He wasn't there.

"I wen' up to the house ta call an ambulance."

"No," she shook her head, emphatic, "that was Pastor Gardner."

"Gardner weren't there. Not yet."

He wasn't? Then who sat with her?

"I called Gardner, too, while I's at it. When I came back, you's no longer talkin' so I sat wi' you an' Dean till ever'body come."

That was Max? Mrs. Scheinberg stared down at the sidewalk, her paradigm awhirl. All of those years ago, it was Max? She looked up to try to make sense of it all, but darkness had completely swallowed her neighbor's face both in the present and in the past.

"I saw 'is head, Arlene."

She winced again. She had seen it too. She could still see it.

"He didn' feel no pain when 'e lost 'is leg. The auger'd whipped 'im into the tractor and bashed in 'is head. He didn' feel no pain."

Headlights turned into her driveway just then, and Mrs. Scheinberg felt herself crumbling at the familiar sight of the blessed cavalry: Irv Davis's white truck. Bev poured out of the passenger seat before Irv could even put the vehicle in park, and Mrs. Scheinberg was instantly swept away in an oral current of magnanimous concern. She didn't even notice Max getting into his truck and driving away.

Half an hour later, Bev loaded Mrs. Scheinberg, Ceci, an overnight bag, an aluminum cane, and the pie into the cab of the truck and climbed up into the driver's seat. She leaned through the open window to give her husband a kiss. "Call me when you're ready for me to pick you up."

Irv nodded and then stepped back to make room for the women's departure. It had been decided that he would stay behind to chore the animals and take stock of any damaged gas and electrical lines. Someone also needed to be there to meet the rural electric workers when they arrived.

Bev turned east toward the Davis farm, but as soon as they caught sight of the Mauer property, Mrs. Scheinberg gasped. "Where's Max's double-wide?"

"What? Didn't he tell you?" Bev's voice was painfully cheerful. She pulled to a stop on the side of the road, so they could get a better view of the damage. Max's truck was parked in the gravel drive, but her neighbor was nowhere in sight. "The tornado blew it off his property."

"Dear God!" Mrs. Scheinberg exclaimed, mortified. Max hadn't said a thing. But then, she hadn't bothered to ask. "Where did it land? How did he—?"

"He told Irv on the phone that he and Dutch waited out the storm in that cellar underneath his smokehouse. Said he'd look after his trailer once you were taken care of. It's a shame, isn't it? To think that the tornado was just a few feet from both you and—"

"The roof!" Mrs. Scheinberg loudly interrupted, pointing out of the windshield in disbelief. There, standing—or sagging—as if nothing had happened, was The Offense, but its hideous blue roof was missing.

Bev actually giggled. "Tornado ripped it clean off! Isn't that crazy? And after that letter you wrote to the paper, I bet this'll make the news. See? Something good came from the storm, after all!"

Mrs. Scheinberg's shame was bigger and mightier than Mr. Hyde. Only when Bev had pulled the truck back out onto the road and turned north on Highway 63 did she dare to speak.

"Where is Max staying tonight?"

"I don't know," Bev shrugged. "Motel, I guess."

Mrs. Scheinberg couldn't possibly sink any lower, but there was something she had to know. "Bev?"

"Hm?"

"Did Max Mauer help me with Dean?"

"What do you mean?"

"I mean," she felt sick to her stomach, "was he the first one to get there after the accident?"

"Oh. No, Pastor Gardner was the one who got there first."

Mrs. Schcinberg relaxed, somewhat comforted. That's what she remembered too. That must be right.

"At least, that's what you told me."

Her stomach knotted again.

"I'll tell you what I do remember, though," Bev said, her eyes lighting up in that special way of hers whenever she had a story to tell. "Max was the one who washed Dean's blood off of the side of the grain bin. He cleaned the auger too. He'll never admit it, of course, but Irv saw him wiping down the bin when he came to move the tractor later that afternoon. But both it and the auger had already been moved. Irv said it had to've been Max, because he was the only one who . . ."

*Lord God in heaven*, Mrs. Scheinberg prayed, unable to listen to another word, *forgive me!*

## CHAPTER TWELVE: BEST CONSTRUCTION

The morning light did Mrs. Scheinberg's house no favors.

"There's no repairing it," Irv explained. "Main support beams have been compromised. We're going to have to tear it down and rebuild."

Mrs. Scheinberg nodded. She had assumed as much the night before, but the verdict still fell on her like, well, an oak tree. She stared at the two-story farmhouse that had been her home since she'd taken her husband's name. The dew-covered aluminum siding glinted in the sunshine like refined sugar on a wedding cake. Mock orange bushes and day lilies blooming along the foundation provided its decorous trim, and a rooster-shaped weather vane tilted and twirled on the roof's peak like an ornamental cake topper. The scene would have been idyllic except for the oak tree slicing it clean through like a knife.

She closed her eyes on the incongruous sight and defiantly pursed her lips. Today was not a crying day. Today was a work day, and generous men and boys were already applying themselves to the task of removing the giant tree from her house. Ben Schmidt and his dad were manning chain saws they had brought from home, and Robbie and Frankie Jones were dragging severed oak limbs to a bonfire that was being maintained by their grandpa Evan. Pastor Fletcher was wrapping a large chain around the girth of the oak's trunk, the other end of which Irv had already hooked to the back of his 4020. The plan was to pull the monstrous log out onto the front yard for its final phase of disassembly.

Bev, Candice, and Rebecca and Alison Jones were buzzing in and out of the house as well, taking down curtains and unloading drawers and packing dishes. Most of the living room furniture— Mrs. Scheinberg's mother's delicate hutch included—had been damaged beyond repair, but the kitchen and ground-level bedrooms had passed the night untouched by storm, tree, or critter. All of their contents needed to be sorted, packed, and moved to a corner of the Davises' large machine shed by nightfall.

Mrs. Scheinberg, despite a monumental show of resistance, had been relegated to a lawn chair that Bev had set out in the shade of a nearby crab apple tree.

"You're to oversee the going's on," Irv had instructed.

It killed her to sit and watch while everyone else labored for her sake, but her knees were no good for this kind of work. She could barely get from here to there on an even floor let alone a busted one. She glanced humbly at the large moving truck presently parked in her gravel drive. The Bradburys had rented it themselves for the occasion. How would she ever repay these people?

"*Yer alive.*" Max's mantra from the night before played on repeat in her mind. "*Tha's all tha' matters.*"

Mrs. Scheinberg sighed. Her being alive was creating an awful lot of work for her kind church family.

"Who's helping Max?" she asked when everyone stopped for lunch. Emily and the kids had brought in fried chicken, homemade biscuits, and cold lemonade for the hardworking crew.

"The Kulls," Bev said, biting into a drumstick. "Irv checked on him early this morning, and Don was already helping him pull debris out of his fields."

Mrs. Scheinberg ambled down to the road for a peek when everyone else got back to work. She passed the bin-less concrete slab, shuddering, and looked east across Cow Creek along the stretch of field where Max's corn once had stood tall. Now, a half-mile strip of flatlined stalks ran like a green canal through high banks of yellow tassels from her front yard to Max's half-empty lot. In the distance, she could see Don Kull's Massey Ferguson dragging something blue and metallic and twisted across Max's north forty. Her heart fell a foot closer to the ground. The Offense's decapitation should have given her cause for victorious celebration, but instead the whole ordeal made her feel sick to her stomach. She wished she hadn't written that stupid editorial.

Her phone rang just then. She wrestled it out of her polyester pocket with her aching hand and almost cried out at the sight of the name displayed on the screen. "Hello?"

"Arlene! Are you okay?"

Mrs. Scheinberg fought back tears of relief at the sweet sound of concern in the voice on the other end. "Yes. I'm okay."

"You don't sound okay."

She smiled in spite of herself. It felt so good to be remembered. And known. "I'm okay, Blaine. I promise."

"I'm sorry I didn't call sooner. I just heard the news. Emily texted me, so I stepped out of class for a minute to call."

*Dear, sweet boy!*

"What happened?"

Mrs. Scheinberg sighed, turning back around and staring at the ridiculous gash running vertically up the side of her home. "You know that oak tree out front?"

"Yeah."

"Well, the tornado picked it right up out of the ground and dropped it on the house. We're going to have to tear it down and rebuild."

"Lord, have mercy."

Mrs. Scheinberg bit her lip in silent thankfulness, not only because of God's abundant mercy to her and to Max and to everyone, but also because she never got tired of hearing Blaine call upon the name of the Lord. She had taught him that very prayer herself. Well, the liturgy had taught him that prayer by rote Sunday after Sunday, but she was the one who pointed out its usefulness outside of church.

"Were you home when this happened?"

"In the crawl space. With Ceci."

"Is Ceci all right?"

"Noisy as ever."

Blaine laughed at that, but he sobered quickly. "Any fatalities?"

"None in the entire county. Not even livestock. Isn't that amazing?"

"It is. God be praised."

Her heart warmed again. "I hope this isn't going to keep you from visiting me at the end of the summer."

"I'm still coming, don't worry. Should I bring my sleeping bag? Are we going to tent it in the yard next to Cogburn?"

Mrs. Scheinberg laughed. "No, I'm going to order one of those prefab houses. It should go up quickly. In fact, if everything goes right, it'll be ready by the time you come home."

"A prefab house? Are those safe?"

"Safe as any other house. Maybe even safer. Honestly, I think I'm going to like it better than the farmhouse. It'll be a ranch-style home with no more stairs. Not any going up, at least, but you'd better believe I'll have some going down!"

"Digging a basement?"

"I am quite done with crawl spaces, thank you very much."

"Listen, I'd better get back to class. Can I call you later tonight?"

"Yes." Her voice teared up again. "Thank you for calling, Blaine. I needed to hear your voice today."

"I needed to hear yours too."

Around one o'clock in the afternoon, a news crew from WIBN drove up in a white van and took some footage of the demolition. They interviewed each of the boys in turn and then spent a few minutes talking to Irv and Bev. Candice made herself available for questioning as well, choosing the arrival of the news crew as the perfect time to deadhead the lilies in the front flower bed, but no amount of posturing on her part resulted in a coveted spot before the camera.

Eventually, the two-person crew turned toward the lawn chair.

"Are you Mrs. Arlene Scheinberg?" a slight, young woman in a gray-and-pink plaid blazer asked. Her hair was a corporate color of blond, and her painted eyes and pink cheeks looked about as natural as a geisha's.

"Yes."

The anchorwoman immediately stuck a WIBN microphone in her face. "What happened last night?"

"Excuse me?"

"Will you tell our viewers what it was like to live through the biggest tornado to hit Bradbury County since 1922?"

A cameraman pushed his lens twelve inches from her face.

"Oh. Well—"

"Don't look at the camera, please!" Ms. Pink-and-Gray barked. "Look at me. That's right. Never look at the camera. Now, tell us about the storm."

Mrs. Scheinberg frowned, irritated. The petite woman looked and sounded an awful lot like Ceci's namesake, but the hair color was wrong. "It was loud."

"Where were you when Abigail hit?"

"Abigail?"

"Yes, that's the name of the storm."

"The tornado has a name?"

"I thought it appropriate to give it a name."

"*You* named the tornado?" This had to be Anna Cecilia.

"Yes. A name personifies the disaster for the average viewer."

"The average viewer?" Mrs. Scheinberg looked up from her chair at the National Weather Service's imposter and squinted. Nope, the eyes were the wrong color too. Anna Cecilia's were blue. Or were they hazel? She couldn't remember. She tried her best to forget unpleasant memories. "What about the folks who lost their homes and farms in this storm—excuse me, in *Abigail*?"

"Well, most viewers want—"

"Move on, Hope," the cameraman instructed.

*Hope? How ironic.*

Hope's reinforced eyebrows stretched tightly across her forehead like rubber bands. "Where were you when Abigail hit?"

"The crawl space under my house."

"Talk in full sentences, please."

"I'm sorry," Mrs. Scheinberg put up a hand to stop the inquisition, "but do you have a sister named Anna Cecilia?"

"Huh?"

"Can we try standing?" the cameraman interrupted, lowering his lens and flashing a toothy smile at his seated muse. "Are you able to stand, Mrs. Shineburger? This angle is not the most flattering."

"Young man, when you reach my age, no angle is flattering." Still, she obediently pushed herself up to a standing position and leaned on her cane. The mic and camera immediately crowded in.

"Now," Hope sighed, "let's try that last one again. Where were you when Abigail hit?"

"My dog and I waited out the worst of the storm in the crawl space under the house."

"Did you feel the impact of the tree?"

"No."

Hope pursed her Pink Flamingo lips. "Could you *please* answer the questions in full sentences?"

"Could you *please* ask questions that require more than a yes or no answer?"

If Bev hadn't told her just this morning that she'd seen a rainbow on Mr. Hyde's backside the evening before, she'd be tempted to think that God was going to send another flood to wipe out this impertinent generation.

The cameraman seemed to sense another natural disaster developing under the crab apple tree and took over the questioning. "How did you get out of the crawl space, Mrs. Shineburger?"

"My name is Mrs. *Scheinberg*. And I climbed out."

"Did anyone help you?"

"My neighbor helped me."

"Who's your neighbor?"

"Max Mauer."

"How did Max Mauer help you?"

"He helped me climb—"

"Use his name, please."

She sighed. For the love of pie! "*Max Mauer* helped me out of the house after the storm passed!"

"Got it." The cameraman suddenly lowered his lens.

"Got what?"

"What we need." He flashed her another smile. "Thanks again, Mrs. Shineburger. Tune in at ten o'clock for the full story."

And then they were gone.

The Davises normally avoided eating past seven o'clock in the evening—Bev's acid reflux kept her up at night, otherwise—but tonight was a special occasion.

"I can't believe we're going to be on *television!*" Bev sang, handing bowls of popcorn to both occupied armchairs in the living room. She settled herself in the corner of their floral-print couch. "I went ahead and added melted butter to everyone's, but if you want Parmesan cheese as well, Arlene, just let me know. I like Parmesan on my popcorn, but Irv says he doesn't like his corn to taste like spaghetti. I've tried that orange cheese powder—you know, that stuff in the spice aisle at IGA?—but it makes my fingers swell. I also think it colors my urine, but Irv said that's just a coincidence, you know, like I probably didn't drink enough water the same day I used the powder. Anyway, the Parmesan gives it a nice, tasty flavor without so much of the sodium. And it's more satisfying than just Mrs. Dash, you know? Oo, have you ever tried—"

"It's starting," Irv said, unmuting the television.

Mrs. Scheinberg's facial muscles immediately relaxed as the lead music for the nightly news came on. She had been the Davises' houseguest for only twenty-four hours, but already Bev's unrestrained tongue had chased her sanity into a corner at three separate times. She loved the woman, but the way things were going, the Davises would need to move her into a sanitarium at the end of her stay instead of her new prefab home.

"This is WIBN, News Channel 42, your dedicated source for local news. I'm Jeb Mason." WIBN's longtime anchor nodded his gray head respectfully toward all of them.

"Yesterday evening," Gloria Smart, Mason's younger and prettier co-anchor, smoothly transitioned, "an F3 tornado with winds clocking up to 183 miles per hour was spotted just west of Fancy Creek in Bradbury County and tracked fifteen miles northeast to the Grant Parker Memorial Cemetery, obliterating homes and crops along the way. WIBN's Hope Braumstead has the story."

"It was an ordinary Tuesday night for the residents of Bradbury," Hope narrated as she walked toward the camera, her pink-and-gray plaid blazer looking out of place next to the Lions' dusty dugout. "Fourteen-year-old Robbie Jones and the Bradbury Lions were preparing to take on the Bonneville Hornets when their game was suddenly cut short."

"We saw lightning over right field," Robbie Jones explained, his freckled face suddenly filling the screen. Mrs. Scheinberg smiled. Oh, that boy! He had grown so tall and handsome. Where had the time gone? It felt like just yesterday that he had called her 'Mrs. Shinebug,' and truth be told, she missed it. "The ump called the game, and everyone got home as fast as they could. The tornado hit shortly after that."

"Tornado Abigail," Hope continued to narrate over what was most likely some storm tracker's smartphone footage of the twister, "is the largest storm system to hit Bradbury County since 1922."

"Tornado what?" Irv asked.

"Abigail," Mrs. Scheinberg smirked, her mouth around a handful of popcorn. "Ms. Braumstead named the tornado herself. To 'personify it,' she said."

Irv's slow, affable chuckle rose in inviting tendrils from his armchair like pipe smoke. He was no fool, but he was also too much of a gentleman to call out those who were.

". . . ripping one man's home clear off its foundation."

Max Mauer appeared on the screen. He looked small standing next to the ghostly rectangle of cinder blocks outlining where his double-wide used to stand. "I's in the storm cellar when it hit. Abigail ripped the roof right offa ma barn an' blew ma trailer to the middle a that there north'ly field."

Mrs. Scheinberg silently lauded Max for having the guts to use that ridiculous name on camera—no doubt coerced by the colors pink and gray—but her admiration, as always, came out sounding more like criticism. "Someone needs to tell that man to tuck in his shirt."

"Just one mile west of Mauer's home," Hope continued, "Abigail uprooted an ancient oak tree and dropped it directly on top of Arlene Scheinberg's farmhouse."

"It's really only about a half a mile," Mrs. Scheinberg mumbled.

"Oh, look, Irv!" Bev cried, pointing at the screen. "There you are! And there's Pastor Fletcher! Oh, good grief, there's me. Do I really look like that in person? I mean, I know that I tend to carry a little weight around my middle and all, but do I really—"

"Arlene Scheinberg waited out Abigail in the crawl space under the house, just *feet* from where the tree landed."

Mrs. Scheinberg shivered as a close-up of the oak tree sticking out of her beloved home moved across the screen. They must have gotten that shot early in the morning before any of them had arrived. She suddenly felt invaded and exposed.

"It was loud," Mrs. Scheinberg spoke from her lawn chair on the screen.

Bev clapped her hands merrily at the sight, and Ceci, scavenging stray popcorn kernels from around Irv's generous feet, let out a welcoming yelp. Mrs. Scheinberg, however, froze with a handful of popcorn inches from her open mouth. Her stomach and legs were so . . . large.

"My neighbor helped me." The montage had moved on to the part of the interview where she was standing, and she almost lost her eyeballs. When had she grown so *old?* and heavy? What kind of body type did she have, anyway? An apple? Or a pear? The way her bosom drooped over her middle and her belly fat hung about her hips, she looked more like a hot fudge sundae than any piece of fruit. "Max Mauer helped me out of the house after the storm passed."

"*I'm gonna have ta bring in a crane.*" Max's words from the night before replayed in her mind. The man wasn't kidding, apparently.

"Just days before," Hope was now walking along Max's eastern pasture, picking her way through metal debris that littered the ground, "Arlene Scheinberg had this to say about her neighbor, Max Mauer, in an editorial published in the *Bradbury Times.*"

Bev gasped into her hands from her seat on the couch. Irv moved the remote in his hand as if to turn off the television, but Mrs. Scheinberg stopped him.

"Nope," she said, lifting her hand. She was resolved to hear what the witless waif had to say. She had been too quick to dish out unpleasantries to Max in public—she knew that now—and she was going to eat her humble pie like a big girl.

"'It has become evident over the years,'" Hope read from a folded paper in her hand, "'that not every citizen of this county is equal, for sitting on the corner of County Highway 63 and 1000 North is a property forsaken beyond all respectability.'" Hope looked up from the paper. "And what does Arlene Scheinberg determine to be the greatest offense made by her neighbor-turned-rescuer?" Still looking unwaveringly at the camera, Hope pointed to a twisted sheet of blue metal that rested in rigor mortis beside her pink pumps. "'A blue ad for Bradbury's Kuhl Whip Stand painted on the barn's roof,' the one that is now lying demolished at my feet."

Mrs. Scheinberg saw Bev peeking timidly at her over her hands.

"What can we learn from Abigail and all that lies ruined in her wake?" Hope stepped closer to the camera, her painted face melting into what Mrs. Scheinberg assumed was supposed to be some kind of smile. "Be careful what you wish for. The cost might be more than you want to pay."

Mrs. Scheinberg rolled her eyes, but she dutifully swallowed down the last bitter bite.

"And thanks to Max Mauer," Hope nodded coyly at the viewers, "chivalry is not dead in Bradbury County. This is Hope Braumstead."

Well, two things were certain. No, three.

One, there was a kind of pie that she didn't like to eat after all.

Two, she no longer liked the name Hope.

And three—she sighed and pushed away the bowl of buttery popcorn—it was time to lose some weight.

# CHAPTER THIRTEEN: ON THE FENCE

Emily gave Carrot's fuzzy face one last snuggle before gently prodding him off of her lap. He hopped down to the living room floor, stretched lazily from head to tail on the rug in front of his cage, and then hopped into his tub to chomp on some Timothy hay.

"You're getting chubby," she said fondly to the brown-and-white splotched rabbit as she fastened his cage door shut with a metal clip. It was true. Her faithful furry companion of five years had grown quite rotund, but he wore his weight well. In fact, it seemed only to increase his charm.

"Lucky buck," she smiled.

The kids were all down for a nap, and now was her one chance in the day to dig some potatoes and pull some carrots out of the garden unattended. Normally, she would try sneaking in a nap at the same time as the children, but gardening—especially gardening in the sun free of Julia-sized interruptions—was too good for her to pass up. She grabbed an old newspaper from the pantry and a shovel from the garage, immediately dropping it in a noisy clatter on the concrete floor. She stood for a confused moment, staring at her empty right hand before suddenly remembering: pregnancy-induced carpal tunnel syndrome. How could she forget? Emily sighed in defeat and shook out her numb hand, trying to do the math in her head. It seemed a bit early in the first trimester for her to be losing her grip already, but then, she wasn't exactly a spring chicken anymore. This was also her third pregnancy. Resigned to her painful fate, she tucked the newspaper under her left arm, gently pulled on a pair of worn gloves, balanced the shovel between both hands, and pushed open the back door with her hip.

*Oh, snap!*

Charlene had already set up shop smoking near the garage. As much as Emily wanted to enjoy the afternoon sunshine, she didn't want Baby to breathe in any secondhand smoke. She moved as if to go back inside, but Charlene had already seen her. Her neighbor quickly snuffed out her cigarette in a nearby flowerpot full of sand and waved Emily over to the fence that separated their yards.

"Hi, Charlene," Emily said, keeping her voice low so as not to wake the twins. Their bedroom window faced the backyard, and if Julia even suspected that her mommy was digging in the dirt, she'd wake up and demand participation rights at the top of her voice.

"Hey," Charlene said, leaning her arms on the top of the fence. "Harvesting?"

"Potatoes and carrots. Want some?"

"Sure."

Emily dropped the newspaper on the ground and gingerly pushed her shovel into the dirt, letting her right foot do most of the work. Ben Schmidt had taught her years ago how to loosen the soil around the potatoes before pulling at the leafy plant. "How are you, Charlene?"

Her neighbor shrugged her bare shoulders. A strapless tube dress was her only adornment. "Fine."

"How's work?"

"I quit."

"How come?"

"Head nurse kept scheduling me every time I turned around. A girl needs a break, ya know? Good thing I quit when I did too, 'cause that storm near blew Regency off the map."

Emily held the shovel handle with her left hand and pulled on a loosened potato plant with her right. No pain, thankfully, and the plant lifted easily from the ground, eight or so round red potatoes dangling from its roots. She let the shovel drop to the ground, pulled the potatoes from the plant, wrapped them in a sheet of newspaper, and walked them over to the fence. "Here. Scrub them good in some water and put them in the oven with some olive oil and rosemary. It'll make your whole house smell good."

Charlene took the package and smiled. "Thanks."

Emily brushed the dirt from her gloves, taking the opportunity to better study her neighbor. Charlene was such a pretty woman, though years of smoking had started to gray her skin and roughen her voice. Emily hated how that happened. The voice was such a precious, delicate instrument, and smoke was its sworn enemy. "What are you going to do now?"

Charlene shrugged again. "Look somewhere else, I guess. They're hiring over in Hamburg. Thought I'd take a break for a while, first. Mom loaned me some money for a bit."

Emily bit her tongue. Charlene was a grown woman. Her choices were her own, and she hadn't asked for advice. Still, she wished her neighbor's mother would stop enabling her. "Who's your friend?"

"What?"

"That man. With the hat." Emily wondered if she shouldn't be pushing the issue, but her concern overloaded any sense of caution. "I sometimes see him coming over to visit."

"Oh. That's, uh, Mark."

"Is he your boyfriend?"

"Sure. Yeah."

"Is he nice?"

"Yeah."

"How'd you meet him?"

Charlene changed the subject. "You're pregnant, aren't you?"

Emily's eyes grew wide. *How did everyone always know?* She looked down at her stomach, but Charlene laughed.

"Don't worry! You're not showing."

"How can you tell, then?"

"I just can." Charlene suddenly looked uncharacteristically bashful. "I'm pregnant too."

"You are?" Emily's brain was living in a constant happy hour these days, imbibing continually of different hormonal cocktails, and she was having trouble registering the simplest of details, let alone the fullness of this news. Charlene, pregnant? But her neighbor had just smoked a cigarette. And quit her job. And she wasn't married. Children are always a blessing—a gift from the Lord, Emily knew—but where was this child's father? She glanced at her neighbor's house. The curtains were drawn shut even though it was the middle of the day, and the thought of Mark peeking out at them from the interior darkness made her shiver. She focused her eyes on Charlene instead. Her neighbor's tube dress revealed a stomach as flat as a book. "Is this your first child?"

"Nope. My third."

Emily held back a frown. In the four years she had lived in the parsonage, she had never once seen any children coming in or out of Charlene's house. "Are they with your mother?"

Charlene snorted. "Are you kidding? Mom hates kids." She shrugged. "I aborted them."

All oxygen immediately left Emily's backyard.

"Had to finish school the first time, of course," Charlene explained, her tone as detached as if she were talking about the inanimate potatoes in her hand. "Mom made me. She was right. Never would have graduated changing diapers."

Emily had to grip the fence to keep from sinking to the ground. To think that this young mother had aborted her own child out of obedience to, of all things, her *mother*. The younger generation slain to appease the older. It was backwards—a complete turning around of natural order—and the irony was beyond tragic. Emily stared into Charlene's green eyes, her own brown ones watering with compassion. What kind of hellish hold did Charlene's devil of a mother have on her to convince her of such a horrible thing?

"Was in rehab the second time. Bad time to be pregnant, you know?" Charlene actually laughed. "Can you imagine?"

Emily could imagine, and she thought she might vomit. "Who's the father?"

"Of which one?" The impropriety of the question was sadly lost on Charlene. "Oh, you mean this one? Mark."

That shady man. *Lord, have mercy!* "Is he happy about the baby?"

"Haven't told him yet. He'll be happy, though. Just have to find the right moment, you know? Does the Reverend know about your bun in the oven?"

Charlene was a master at changing subjects.

Emily nodded, still trying not to faint from her airlessness. A telltale blush was creeping across her cheeks, though. She could feel it.

"How far along are you?" Charlene asked.

"A couple of months."

"Hey, me too!" Charlene smiled. "We're twinsies!"

Under the attentive, congenial eye of Charlene, Emily somehow managed to harvest enough potatoes and carrots for her family's supper and deliver them safely to her kitchen counter before crumbling onto the linoleum floor in a weeping heap.

## Chapter Fourteen: Trash Talk

‖‖‖‖‖‖‖‖‖‖‖‖‖‖‖‖‖‖‖‖‖‖‖‖‖‖‖‖‖‖‖‖‖‖‖‖‖‖‖‖‖

Emily told her husband all about her conversation with Charlene after supper that night, and after hugging and listening to her for an extended period of time, he gently shooed her out the door for her first altar guild meeting.

"Stay out as long as you like," Pastor called after her as she crossed the street. "The kids and I'll be fine. See if Rebecca can go out afterwards for hot chocolate or something. Don't come back until you've laughed at least five times."

Despite the day's sorrows, she was actually a little excited about tonight's induction. Altar guild was one of those mysterious, coveted societies—a sorority of sorts—whose elite membership seemed attainable only after years of pious service in the church kitchen, nursery, and Sunday School. Not just anyone could join the altar guild, after all. To follow in the holy footsteps of Mary Magdalene, Mary the mother of James, and Salome in tending to the body and blood of Christ was no light matter, and consequently, one didn't just show up at the sacristy door uninvited. No, one was to be apprenticed into proper service by senior members whose venerable devotion to the keeping of the chancel was evident to all by their shining crown of silver hair. At least, that's how the situation appeared from the pew.

Whatever initiation was deemed necessary, Emily was willing to do it. She had always wanted to join the altar guild. Her introverted self was drawn to quiet servitude, and the sacristy seemed the perfect place to rest with Mary in the presence of Christ Himself and to wash His dishes alongside of Martha. Other than mothering, Emily could think of no other way she'd rather serve than to set her Lord's Table and to care for His body and blood.

Rebecca met her in the nave. "I feel like I'm walking on holy ground," her friend whispered as they stepped up to the chancel and bowed respectfully before the altar.

"Well, it *is* a sacred space."

"I made sure not to wear any red tonight, and I took off my metallic belt and fashion jewelry before I came."

Emily jabbed Rebecca in the ribs. "Behave. Or you'll get us kicked out before we've even started."

The Sunday before, Mrs. Scheinberg had warned both of them over the percolator in the parish hall, "Watch out for Irene. That old gal is golden to the core, but she can't hear a word and she refuses to wear hearing aids. I finally got so frustrated that I gave up and dropped the group. That, and I always make a point of spending as little time with Yvonne as possible."

"But you're supposed to love everyone, Arlene," Bev had lightly scolded as she poured powdered creamer in her coffee.

"Oh, I love Yvonne," Mrs. Scheinberg had assured. "I just love her best from afar."

Rebecca wiggled her eyebrows in anticipation as they approached the sacristy door hidden in the wall to the left of the chancel, but both of them stopped short of the threshold at the sound of Yvonne's sovereign voice.

"Well, *I* think she hasn't been a member long enough."

"Hasn't she?" That was definitely Nettie Schmidt.

"Six years is all. Rebecca, at least, has been a member of Zion most of her life."

"But Emily is Pastor's wife. That has to count for something."

"Exactly." Yvonne sounded triumphant. "She's taking advantage of her position to get in the sacristy. Pastor's sending her here as a spy, I'm certain of it."

"He needs a spy?"

"Oh yes. First, it was the balcony. Now, it's the sacristy."

Emily felt as if she had been slapped across the face and punched in the gut at the same time. So much for finding Mary and Martha in the sacristy.

"And to make matters worse," Yvonne continued, "Pastor's sending in a spy that is in *no condition* to be helping."

"What do you mean?"

"She's pregnant."

"A vagrant?" That was Irene's distinctive tenor voice.

"No, pregnant."

"Malignant? As in, cancer?"

"No, I said," Yvonne overarticulated, "*preg-nant.*"

"Who's pregnant?" Nettie Schmidt sounded confused.

"Emily."

"How wonderful!" Nettie clapped.

"No, you don't get it. She's pregnant *again.*"

"But she doesn't look pregnant. How do you know?"

"Lance"—that was Yvonne's son-in-law and current janitor of the church—"saw a pregnancy test in the parsonage trash when he took it to the church dumpster last Saturday, and it was positive."

"They look through my trash?" Emily whispered aloud, horrified. She immediately turned to flee, but Rebecca grabbed her arm and held her to the spot. Her friend gave her an I-don't-care-if-we-do-get-kicked-out look and dragged her into the uncomfortable glare of the sacristy's fluorescent light. Rebecca smiled suddenly, almost wickedly. "Why, Yvonne, congratulations!"

Yvonne stood stock-still, her eyes frozen. Nettie smiled welcomingly, but Irene had busied herself working at the counter lining the far wall. Her back was to the women, and her deaf ears were unaware that anyone else had entered the room.

"Are you having a boy or a girl?" Rebecca asked brightly. The question was absurd. Yvonne was at least a decade beyond fecundity.

Yvonne blinked once but refused to speak. Emily, mortified, stood silent and florid in the doorway. This was not happening.

"Oh, Yvonne's not pregnant," Nettie explained.

"Oh, no?" Rebecca asked, still staring at Yvonne like a madwoman. "One of your daughters, then? To whom should I extend my congratulations? I thought I heard you mentioning that Lance had told you someone is pregnant."

"It's Emily!" Nettie clapped, beaming gayly. "Isn't that wonderful news?"

Emily closed her eyes, resolving to strangle Rebecca later. Or hug and kiss her. She couldn't decide.

"Emily's pregnant?" Rebecca asked, her mouth agape in pretend shock. "However do you know? Did she tell you so herself? Or did I miss an announcement in the church bulletin or something?"

Emily thought she was going to die, but Yvonne's mouth twisted into a defiant pucker.

"Well, Emily," Rebecca turned to her and wrapped her in a bear hug, "congratulations are in order, I guess. What a blessing! And how kind of you to share the happy news with Yvonne and her son-in-law before even telling your own family. Talk about putting the needs of your church family before your own!"

Irene turned around then, visibly startled to see the younger two hugging in the doorway. "Good heavens! What's going on here? Are we in the sacristy or a dance hall?"

Rebecca instantly let go and straightened up. Irene had been Rebecca's Sunday School teacher in years gone by, and the sound of the woman's voice seemed to transport her immediately back to the second grade.

"Yes, well." Irene folded her hands in front of her waist and looked around the room. "Now that we are all here, we should get started. Rebecca Anne and Emily, we will start by familiarizing you with the paraments first and the vessels second. Nettie and I will show you the sacristy closet and cupboards, while you," she pointed to Yvonne, "set up the altar as we would for any Sunday morning."

Yvonne, her face a tomb, dutifully got to work at the counter. Nettie, gesturing her hand in the air toward the closet like a hostess on a game show, slid back the wooden pocket doors attached to the wall on the right, exposing folds upon folds of rich brocade hanging over wooden dowels attached to the back wall. She immediately began fingering the vibrant colors.

"Hands!" Irene warned.

"Yes," Nettie said, her hands snapping back to her sides and her eyes turning downcast in perfect servitude. She did sneak a peek at the younger women, though, and smile. "I just can't help myself," she giggled.

"Yes, well." Irene stepped forward, all business. She picked up a nearby yardstick leaning against the wall and pointed to the individual dowels, each in their turn. Emily thought the gray-haired woman looked like a sergeant inspecting her soldiers' barracks. "James and Harriet York bequeathed money to the congregation back in the late 1940s which was then used to purchase these paraments, and thanks to the guild's impeccable care shown over the years, they are still in excellent shape. You'll see that each colored set has a superfrontal for the altar, a veil for the chalice, and two antependia: one band for the lectern and one square for the pulpit. We switch out these paraments in accordance with the appropriate season of the Church Year. Violet is for Advent and Lent, you already know, I'm sure; red is for Pentecost; white is for Christ's feast days of Christmas, Epiphany, Maundy Thursday, Easter, Ascension, and Trinity Sunday—"

Nettie raised her eyebrows up and down at the ladies, clearly impressed by Irene's encyclopedic prowess when it came to liturgical seasons and their corresponding colors.

"—and green—the ones we have out now in the sanctuary— are for the season of Trinity, of course. Now these," Irene pointed to a set of rose-colored paraments, "are newer. Evan Ebner donated them in memory of Alice after she died."

Rebecca involuntarily reached out to touch the silky fabric that had been given in remembrance of her sainted mother, and Irene, showing herself to be more than just a drill sergeant, sensitively let the action go unchecked.

"These are set out on Gaudete and Laetare Sundays in Advent and Lent."

"They are my favorite," Nettie leaned over to whisper to Emily. "They're for breast awareness."

Emily coughed spastically into her hand.

"And here," Irene continued, blissfully ignorant of Nettie's grave misclassification, set down her yardstick and pulled out a long, low drawer from a cabinet that had been built into the closet just below the hanging paraments, "is where we keep our fair linens. *Some* guilds outsource the cleaning of their linens, but we see that as a misuse of our funds. We are not above taking the linens home to wash ourselves, are we, ladies? Besides, I don't remember reading in the Bible that a dry-cleaner came to the tomb on Easter morning. It was the women of faith who came to care for the body of the Lord."

"How do we properly wash them?" Emily asked.

Irene didn't hear Emily's question, so she didn't know to answer it.

Nettie, who was quite accustomed to compensating for Hank's impaired hearing at home, handed each inductee an altar guild manual. "This will tell you everything you need to know."

"I remember hearing that we need to be respectful when handling stains. Is there something in here about how to do that?"

Nettie smiled and nodded. "Oh yes. It has all kinds of helpful ideas. I've written in a few ideas of my own, as well. For example, one Sunday, one of the elders spilled the chalice onto the altar and wiped it all up with the purificator. That's the hankie, you know? Well, I tried rinsing it out and poured salt on it and everything, but it still had a pink hue at the end of Sunday School. So I brought it home and added it to the bucket of Hank's briefs—I like to soak his undergarments in OxiClean before laundering them—and the purificator came out looking whiter than ever!"

Emily blanched, suddenly picturing the cloth used to wipe the chalice soaking next to a pair of Hank's underwear.

Nettie clapped her hands, still talking. "Oh, it's going to be so wonderful to have your fresh faces helping out on the guild! We've been short-staffed ever since Arlene and Bev quit last year."

"Why did Bev quit?" Rebecca asked, already privy to the details of Mrs. Scheinberg's exit.

Nettie leaned forward and whispered, "She said it was a personable issue."

Irene, who was shutting the drawer and closing the closet doors, suddenly turned around. "Yes, well. I think we should move on to the vessels. Rebecca Anne, how about you help Nettie carry the paten and chalice out to the altar? Don't forget the corporal, now. And Emily. You stay behind to help Yvonne with the host."

Emily, alarmed, grabbed Rebecca's arm and held her in place. There was no way she was staying behind alone with Cruella de Vil. The woman would skin her alive.

"Um, how about I stay in here and help Emily with the—" Rebecca began to suggest, but Nettie draped a green chalice veil over Rebecca's right arm and escorted her out the door before she could even finish her sentence.

Irene stayed behind, but that was no comfort. The woman could no more protect her from Yvonne's tongue than Beethoven could protect an audience from an out-of-tune orchestra. Emily stood rooted to the spot, her heart racing.

"Come on over and join me, Emily," Yvonne invited.

Emily fought the childish urge to shake her head.

"Why, you look flushed, my dear." Yvonne's voice was missing the warmth that came with caring. "Do you need to sit down? It's the baby, isn't it? You must be exhausted. Here, come, sit down on this stool."

Emily managed to lift her eyes to meet Yvonne's. They were hot to the glance, but the silver-haired woman was smiling—quite pleasantly, actually—and proffering her a seat.

"Come, sit. You'll feel better once you do."

Emily looked sideways at Irene who was busy plugging in an iron and draping white cloth napkins over an ironing board. She turned back to Yvonne and succeeded in putting one foot in front of the other until she made it to the counter. Yvonne lightly touched her burgundy-painted nails to a covered chalice and chatted easily. "Now, this is the ciborium. It holds the host and it is our job to count out one hundred of them from this package. Of course, we used to have to count out two hundred, even more, on a Sunday, but attendance has dwindled quite a bit over the last decade."

That tiny dig was meant for her husband, and Emily knew it. She pressed her lips tightly together.

"How about you count the individual hosts while I dry the pyx?"

She nodded and took a seat.

"So tell me, Emily," Yvonne said, a dish towel in one hand and the lid of the pyx in the other. "When did you decide to join the altar guild?"

Emily proceeded with caution, fully aware that she, most likely, was being led into a trap. "I've always wanted to join the altar guild."

"Oh. How pious." Yvonne set down the lid and began drying the pyx itself. "And when are you going to get a real job?"

"I-I'm sorry?" The sudden switch in direction took her by surprise.

"When are you going to get a real job?"

Emily glanced an SOS toward Irene's back, but the elderly woman couldn't hear a word Yvonne was saying, of course. Resigning herself to the certain torture that lay ahead, Emily looked back down at the hosts she was sorting into the ciborium and pretended that she hadn't already lost count of them. She would come back later and recount once Yvonne was good and gone. "I'm raising my children."

"Everyone has to raise children in this life, Emily. That's a given, and there is always someone to help out with that. I watch my grandchildren for my daughter, of course, so that she can help put bread on the table and money in the bank for their education. I'm sure Arlene in her retirement or Bev or someone else in the congregation would *love* to care for your little crew."

Emily felt her face burning hot, embarrassed that her inner shame was on display for Yvonne to see. Her cheeks always told on her. She tried to will the blood back down to her heart.

"What there is *not* in this congregation," Yvonne continued, mistaking Emily's horrified silence as reverent awe for the wisdom she was imparting, "is someone else to earn money for your family, to help shoulder the financial burden that a pastor is on a congregation."

Emily blinked back tears. Her eyes were traitors too.

"We originally called a single pastor, of course, but now he has taken on you and multiplied. I think I can speak for the congregation when I tell you that we all assumed you would keep working at the college or at least bring in an income of some sort. I'm simply asking what you are going to do to help with the situation." Yvonne's voice was sickeningly calm and kind.

"I-I teach a few voice lessons each week," Emily stuttered, ashamed of her immediate need to defend herself. Why did she always cave under persecution? This was persecution, right? She felt unsure of even that.

"Oh, honey," Yvonne whispered, as if speaking any louder would somehow further shame the ignorant, "that's not what I mean. I'm talking about an income, insurance, something that would actually help."

A renegade tear slipped onto Emily's left cheek, and she reached up quickly to swipe it away.

"Oh dear," Yvonne tut-tutted. "You'll need to wash your hands again before you touch the hosts now."

Emily didn't wash her hands. Instead, she stood up and, against her husband's wishes, walked back to the parsonage before she had laughed even once.

## Chapter Fifteen: Mrs. Crybaby

Pastor had just made it to the second chapter of his new book when Emily walked through the door. She was crying. Still.

"What's wrong?" He jumped up from the couch, sending an unsuspecting Carrots skittering to his cage. The sleepy buck had been snuggled up between his feet on the floor.

Emily threw herself onto her favorite armchair, sniffing and snuffing and huffing and puffing in wet microbursts. Pastor slowly lowered himself back down onto the couch, silently assessing his wife's disheveled state. Her face was red, but otherwise she seemed fine. She didn't appear to be injured, at least. Could she be ill with morning sickness or whatever it was they called it when nausea hit in the evenings? She didn't usually get sick like that when pregnant. No, it was usually her hands that bothered her, but—Pastor frowned. Surely this didn't have to do with the altar guild.

Cautiously, "Do you want to tell me about it?"

Emily boohooed into her arm.

Pastor held his breath and waited. Once, he had mistakenly tried touching Emily during a fit like this, but that hadn't ended well. The result had been his being locked out of the bathroom for at least an hour. He also knew better than to say anything too pastoral in the first inning of the game. Nope, an early swing would most definitely result in a foul ball and an irreversible call made from his ump of a bride: "I need you to be my husband, not my pastor!" Trial and error had taught him that the best thing to do whenever Emily cried was to sit and wait for her to talk first.

Eventually, his soggy wife lifted her head from the bog of her arm and moaned, "I can't do it."

"You can't do what?"

"I can't . . . be in that building."

"What? You mean the church?"

"Yes."

"What happened?"

"They look through our trash, Michael!" Her eyes were crazed.

"What?"

"They look through our trash! Lance, Yvonne, all of them! And then they *talk* about it."

"Slow down. What are you talking about?"

Emily sat up and gave him her fiery prosecutor look. "Lance Finley dug through our trash before he emptied it on Saturday, and he saw my positive pregnancy test. And then he told Yvonne about it. And guess who Yvonne told?"

Pastor thought he knew the answer to this question, but to speak at the wrong time was to lose bathroom privileges for the rest of the night. And come to think of it, he kind of had to go. He kept his mouth shut tight.

"*Everyone* in the sacristy, that's who!"

Pastor furrowed his brow. This was awful. Terrible, in fact. The nerve of some people! To look through their trash and then talk about it—about his unborn child!—in public as if the news had been published in the paper. But at the same time—Pastor bit his lip— the situation was also kind of funny. Annoyingly, nonsensically, ridiculously funny. He sucked on the insides of his cheeks to try to keep from laughing.

"Well?"

"Well what?" he managed, a bit strained.

"What are we going to do?"

"About what?"

"About the fact that they are digging like moles through our trash! Our *trash*, Michael!"

And all of it was suddenly more than he could handle. The ludicrous antics of Yvonne and her raving family, Emily's feverish eyes framed by her wild hair, and the Church Stress—the omnipresent, omnifarious Church Stress. Pastor could hold it in no longer. He snorted through his nose and fell back against the couch in a helpless guffaw, recovering only in time to hear his wife barricading herself in the bathroom.

He wiped his eyes and reached for his shoes. It was to be the men's restroom at church, then.

‖‖‖‖‖‖‖‖‖‖‖‖‖‖‖‖‖‖‖‖‖‖‖‖‖‖‖‖‖‖‖‖‖‖‖‖

By the next morning, Emily had stopped crying, but her brown eyes looked like pathetic pools of melted chocolate. "I'm thinking about calling Basset to see if she needs any help covering the music history load next semester."

"What? Why?"

Emily sorrowfully mixed peanut butter into George's oatmeal and topped it with a spoonful of strawberry jam.

"More pease?" their son asked.

Emily, completely out of character, spooned more jam into his bowl. George, ever his poet-father's son, immediately erupted into an impromptu rhyme set to the tune of Ode to Joy. "Yum, yum, yum, yum, yum, yum, yum, yum, yum, yum, yum, yum, yum, YUM-YUM!"

"What's making you think about teaching again?" Pastor asked, careful to keep his tone light and his face neutral. He didn't want to set off his hypersensitive wife. That, and the children were watching.

Emily shrugged. "I don't know. I just thought it might be helpful."

"You're already helpful here."

"No, I mean financially helpful."

He frowned. Where was this sudden concern for their finances coming from? They weren't wealthy by any means, but they weren't poor either. Thanks to the generous provision of the church, they could pay their bills and then some. He studied Emily quietly, treading lightly. He sensed that Crazyland might be just over the horizon. "Are you sure that *now* is the best time to be taking on more responsibilities?"

"What does that mean?"

"Nothing. Just that we have children."

"Yes?"

"Well. If you teach at the college, who will care for the children?"

"How about you?"

"I'm at the church during the day."

Emily's cheeks lit up. "Yes, well, we wouldn't want you to neglect the *church*, now, would we?"

"What does that mean?"

Emily only shook her head.

Was she feeling neglected or something? Is that what this was all about? He had thought that she felt happy and valued at home, but maybe he was mistaken. He tried again. "Who will watch the kids?"

"I thought Arlene might like to watch them a bit more now that she's retired."

"Did she tell you that?"

"No. But I'm sure she'd love to."

"Arlene has been through an awful lot recently."

"Yes, thank you, Michael. I know what she's been through. I'm her friend, remember? And I've been here the whole time, same as you."

"I'm just saying that this might not be the best season of life for her to be taking on more responsibility either. I'm pretty sure she retired so that she could do less, not more."

"Did she tell you that?" Emily's voice held a faint note of mockery as she repeated his own phrase back to him.

"Yes, actually, she did." He immediately regretted his words. Being right was one of those no-no's in Crazyland, and he was almost certain they had crossed its border some moments before. Emily's temper was never something to be trifled with in reality, let alone in Crazyland.

His wife surprised him, though. She smiled brightly and poured another handful of Toasty O's on Becky's highchair. She even tickled their daughter's cheek. Pastor held his breath. Emily seemed all right. She wasn't crying or anything. She had taken the truth quite well, actually. Maybe they weren't in Crazyland after all. He relaxed a bit. "Even if Arlene could watch the kids, there's still the concern of you."

"What about me?"

"Well, you've been pretty tired lately."

"Everyone's tired."

"Yes, but not everyone who is tired cries all day long."

Emily's face fell. "Well, not everyone lives with *you*!" She jumped up and pretended to fill her glass with water from the sink.

Nope. They were definitely in Crazyland. "Honey, all I'm saying is that I'm concerned about you and—"

"Yes," her voice was shaking, "thank you *very much*, Michael. I can tell that you are *very* concerned about me."

"I am! I'm concerned about you and the baby!"

"What baby?" Julia asked, her clear, treble voice cutting through the chaotic symphony of adult emotion like a silvery chime.

Emily ran for the bathroom, and Pastor buried his head in his hands. It seemed that he and his bladder had been banished for the rest of the morning.

⸻

After he had washed up Becky and the twins and managed to coax Emily out of the bathroom, Pastor walked wearily across the street for work. Nettie was outside bending over one of the boxwoods flanking the front office door.

"Can I help you with something, Nettie?"

"Oh, good morning, Pastor!" Nettie turned and smiled. She had an electric kitchen knife in her hand. It was plugged into an orange extension cord that snaked back into the office through the cracked-open front door.

"What are you doing?"

"I'm trimming the bushes."

"Isn't that Irv's job?"

"Oh, well, Oprah told me to do it."

From Crazyland straight to Cuckooland. Pastor wasn't sure he had the fortitude to get through a day such as this. "Oprah told you to do it?"

"Yes, you see, it's called paying it forward. Irv's been so busy helping Arlene with her house this week. I thought I'd help him out for a change."

He simply nodded, choosing to ignore the absurdity of the electric knife's wimpy hum, and walked through the office door.

"I put your messages on your desk for you!" Nettie hollered after him as the door closed.

He walked into his study, dropped his bag on the floor, and fell into his chair. Nettie's list sat on the desk in front of him.

*Yvonne Roe left a message last night. She thinks Evan Ebner has been playing the hymns too slow. Suggests it is time for him to retire. She would like to remind you that Lance plays the guitar.*

Pastor closed his eyes and ran his hands through his hair. This was nothing new. Yvonne had tried to win her deadbeat son-in-law the choir director position a few years back when Emily had retired on account of the twins, but Lance hadn't taken a music lesson in his life let alone degreed in it. The man was the least qualified musician in the church, not that qualifications were of any concern to Yvonne when it came to the matter of her family. She would have Lance replace even himself in the pulpit, Pastor was certain of it, if the church bylaws allowed for such things.

*Karl Rincker called first thing this morning. He thought the hymns were played too fast on Sunday.*

Of course.

*Arlene Scheinberg called around 9:00. She says to nix the beard. It looks "unkempt."*

Pastor subconsciously reached for his whiskery chin. He didn't usually grow a beard, but he thought Emily might like it. She had once told him that she admired the graying hair on his temples— called it dignified or something like that—so he thought she might find a beard attractive as well. Most of his gray was on his chin, after all.

*Oh, Emily.* He sighed. He honestly didn't know what to do about her crying. It seemed out of control these days. Was it the pregnancy hormones? Most likely, but what if it were something else? Like what if she were unhappy? What if she no longer wanted to take care of him and the kids? Or worse, what if she no longer felt cared for by him?

He stood up and walked right back out of the church.

"Keep up the good work, Nettie," he nodded, walking toward the parsonage. "I'll be back in a bit."

Pastor found Emily and the kids in the backyard. Julia and George were busy digging in the garden, and Becky was walking around the lawn, pushing a plastic mower. He sat down in the chair opposite Emily at the red table.

"Remember when I gave this to you?" he asked, tapping an index finger on the peeling tabletop. He really should repaint it for her.

Emily nodded, staring at her lap. She looked so sad.

He reached across the table for her hand. "I'd give you anything, Emily. All you have to do is ask."

A tear slipped out of the corner of her eye.

"What is it? What's wrong?"

She started to cry, but this time it was less hysterical. This kind of crying seemed more real, somehow.

"Daddy, Daddy, Daddy!" Julia exclaimed, noticing him for the first time. She dropped her trowel and ran over to the table to give him a hug. "Is it time for lunch?"

"No, honeybee. I'm just here for a quick visit. I want to talk to Mommy."

"She's sad," Julia pointed out the obvious.

"Yes, I think she is. Why don't you give her a big hug and then go back to help George for a few minutes, all right?"

Julia dutifully complied, but then Becky started pulling at his pant legs. He picked her up onto his lap and then reached for Emily's hand again. Privacy during conversations was so three years ago.

"Did I do something wrong?"

Emily shook her head.

"What's wrong?"

She took a shuddery breath. "I'm embarrassed."

"About what?"

"About . . . doing nothing all day."

"What do you mean, 'nothing'? You do so much every day, more than me. You keep four people—no, five, now—alive and healthy and happy!"

"But anyone can do that."

Pastor frowned. This was new talk for Emily. It didn't sound like her. It sounded more like . . . He suddenly had a sneaking suspicion that this whole thing was about the altar guild after all. "What happened last night?"

It took a bit of prodding, but Emily eventually opened up and told him what had happened in the sacristy. When she finished, he sat quietly for a minute, trying his best to tame the angry lion that was rearing its head inside of his chest. It seemed that Church Stress wasn't satisfied with having just him as its slave. It wanted his family too.

"Emily," he started, rubbing her small hand with both of his. Becky had already slid off his lap, bored with mere conversation. "I'm so sorry. I'm sorry to have brought you into . . . all of this."

Emily wept silently.

"Maybe it was selfish, asking you to marry me."

Emily shook her head. "I want to be married to you."

His lion shook its majestic mane and roared. "I'll have a talk with Yvonne."

"No!" she exclaimed.

"Why not?"

"Because . . . I think that's what she wants." Emily's motherly intuition benefited more than just their children. "I don't think it'll help anything. I think it will make things worse."

He knew Emily was right. Every time he engaged Yvonne about any issue of contention, it seemed only to feed her eternal fire and make it burn all the brighter.

"I'll just drop out of the altar guild."

"No!" This time he was the one to exclaim. "Don't you think that's what Yvonne wants too?"

"Probably," she sighed, "but I can't do it, Michael."

He squeezed her hand. "I think you can."

"I can't be in the same room with her."

He fully empathized, but this was the special cross that pastors and, consequently, their families carried through all of life. Every time they walked into the church, they had to share space with people who hated them and blamed them and despised them and criticized them and hurt them. It was the very essence of Church Stress, this constant bearing of people's scorn. The world mocked and spit upon Christ Himself. It most certainly would do the same to His servants.

"Yvonne may never change her tune, and I can't promise that she won't keep lashing out at you in the sacristy. But the altar guild would still benefit from your service. And I think, maybe, you want to serve in that way."

Emily remained quiet.

"Can you serve with joy even though Yvonne is in the room with you?"

"Why does she hate me?"

Pastor's lion bowed its head. "Because she hates me."

Emily looked up. "Why?"

"I don't know exactly. It might have something to do with the fact that I came to Zion around the same time her husband died.

And I'm not Pastor Gardner, and she really loved Pastor Gardner. And I'm younger than her. And she's had a hard life."

"But so has everyone."

"But not everyone believes the Gospel, Emily." He probably had said too much, but his wife's rose-colored glasses sometimes kept her from seeing true colors. "I'm not saying that Yvonne doesn't believe. I'm just saying that not everyone is comforted by Christ's message of forgiveness and love like you are."

Emily's shoulders visibly sagged as, maybe for the first time ever, she fully bore the weight of Church Stress's cross. The sight grieved him more than he could say.

"I'm sorry I was short with you," she whimpered.

"Oh, Emily." He kissed her hand. "I forgive you. Please, forgive me for bringing you into this mess in the first place."

Emily got up and walked around the table to sit on his lap. "Are you apologizing for marrying me? Because there's no way you're getting out of it now, Pastor Fletcher."

||||||||||||||||||||||||||||||||||||||||||||

Later that afternoon, after he had returned to the church from making hospital calls, Pastor knelt at the Communion rail in the darkened chancel and prayed. He confessed sins that were too dark to be published, and he asked for the strength to serve the people who, out of their own pain and confusion, hurt him and his family. "'Forgive them, Lord, for they know not what they do.'"

Then, he stood and walked into the sacristy, flipping on the light. His thoughtful wife had encouraged him amidst Church Stress's relentless advance by writing notes on that little chalkboard above the parsonage door. It was time he returned the favor.

# CHAPTER SIXTEEN: MR. FORGETFUL

"My mommy's a loser," Julia announced to the librarian of the Bradbury Public Library.

Emily, who was pushing a sleeping Becky in a stroller up and down the novelty book aisle, stopped with her hand on the spine of an old edition of John Donne poems to listen to her daughter's latest theorem.

"Your mommy seems like a winner to me," the librarian replied. Emily smiled. Leave it to sweet Mary Hopf to put the best construction on everything.

"No. She's a loser," Julia declared. "She lost Go Fish and the Care Bears Game and—"

"Memo-wy."

"Geo-orge! *I* was telling the story."

Emily pushed the book back onto the shelf and peeked her head around the aisle. Her two eldest were standing at the front desk, their curly heads at least a foot below the countertop, staring up into Mary's kind face. "Julia. George. Stop pestering Miss Hopf while she's working."

"But Mommy—"

"No buts, Julia."

George giggled. "Mommy said butts."

"George Gregory." Emily stepped out of the aisle to better meet her son's eye. He had picked up a few base expressions from a play-date with Willie Plueth last month, and his boyish brain had yet to move on from the exposure. "That's enough. I did not say . . . *that* word. I said a different word that sounds the same. We say 'bottom' or 'seat' in our family, remember?"

"But you said—"

"No buts, George."

Julia started to giggle, and Mary hid a smile behind her hand.

Emily sighed in defeat. The entire morning had gone like this, and she held very little hope for the afternoon. It must be a full moon or something, not that she would know. She hadn't stepped outside of the house past suppertime for days. Her husband had needed to be at the church every evening for the past six nights in a row. First, it was the Wednesday night service, as usual, and then it was a meeting with the board of trustees and then an emergency hospital call and then a youth board meeting or something or other and after that she honestly couldn't remember. Everything on the church calendar ran together after a while.

"Okay, you two," Emily said, turning back toward the novelty aisle to retrieve Becky and the one book of poetry she had already pulled from the shelves. She liked to treat her poet-husband with surprise books every now and then. "Tell Miss Hopf good-bye. We need to go home and get lunch ready for Daddy."

"Daddy, Daddy, Daddy!" Julia cheered, clapping and jumping up and down. George ran a complete circle in the lobby of the library in celebration. Normally, Emily would attempt to corral her rambunctious children in public, but they were the only family currently in the library. That, and she understood their need to let off some steam. The kids missed their father too, and lunch was the only time they were going to get to see him today.

When she came back to the front desk with Becky and the stroller, Julia was busy telling Mary another story. "And George pushed me off the couch. The floor hit my beforehead."

"Yeah," George confirmed, too eager to be a part of the story to notice that he had just confessed to being its villain.

"Mommy said I almost had a percussion."

Mary was smiling down at the children, her black-rimmed glasses outlining her almond-shaped eyes. Emily watched as the young woman tucked a chin-length lock of dark hair behind an ear. Mary's face was distinct in its loveliness, all of the angles and lines and curves drawn bold as on a dogwood blossom. She was born in Korea but raised by adoptive parents in Hamburg, and even though she could sing better than any student Emily had ever taught at Bradbury College, Mary had chosen to earn a degree in library science instead.

A couple of years before, Lobelia Alwardt—Bradbury's former larger-than-life librarian—had met a cowboy online and moved to Wyoming to marry him, and Mary applied for the job. When she got it, she relocated to Bradbury, a big step in life considering that her ongoing struggle with epilepsy kept her from being able to drive. Thankfully, the Jones family's rental property on Mulberry Avenue had been vacant at the time, and Mary was able to rent a house within walking distance of the library. Emily smiled to herself. She liked knowing that Mary lived in the cute, red-brick bungalow she herself had called home her first two years in Bradbury. It all seemed so perfect.

"How is Blaine, Mary?"

Mary's smile was organic. "He's well. He has about a month left of his summer intensive before he can come home to visit."

"Well, we sure do miss him." Emily passed the slim volume of poetry across the counter. "I'd like to check this out, please."

Mary glanced at the white cover outlined in a pleasant shade of blue. "Oh yes. This was donated by a homeschooling family last month. I've been meaning to read it but simply haven't had the chance. The author lives not too far from here, I think."

"Really?" Perfect. Her husband would love that. She turned to the kids. "Okay, grab your books, Julia. George, don't forget Clifford. Good-bye, Miss Hopf. We'll see you on Sunday!"

When they got home, Pastor was already eating a sandwich.

"I'm sorry to eat without you," he apologized, "but Bev called. Oscar was transferred to Memorial in Springfield, and Helen needs a ride. I'm supposed to pick her up in ten minutes."

Of course.

Emily simply nodded and started mechanically strapping Becky into her high chair. "Will you be home for supper?"

"Not tonight. The elders are meeting at six thirty."

That's right. This earlier meeting time was a new thing. It was all Karl Rincker's doing. The head elder had suggested that meeting earlier might give the men a little more sunlight in which to do chores post-assembly, but Emily suspected the arrangement had more to do with catching the final innings of the Cardinals game at the end of each night.

"I have altar guild at seven," she reminded him.

"That's right. What about the—"

"Don't worry," she stopped him with a tired hand. It irritated her how he always double-checked her scheduling. "I'm planning on putting the kids down before I go, and Robbie and Alison are coming over to watch a movie here while Rebecca and I are at the church. Everything's covered."

"Good. Okay, then. See you after?" Pastor picked up his plate from the table and kissed Emily on the cheek. She winced. His whiskers felt like a bristle brush, poking her flesh like a thousand little wires.

"What? What's wrong?"

"Nothing."

"You made a face."

"Did I? Sorry. It's just a little whisker burn, I guess."

"Whisker burn?" Pastor reached up and touched his beard. "Does my beard hurt you?"

"It's fine, Michael. Really. It's like having my own personal exfoliator." She tried to smile and make her voice light, but it was impossible to tease so long as her stomach was empty. Baby was sucking her very lifeblood dry, and all she could think about was peanut butter. And bananas. And cheese and potato chips and ice cream. She moved toward the refrigerator.

"I've been meaning to tell you . . ." Pastor followed her with his plate. "Nettie can't use the computer."

"What do you mean?" Emily grabbed the milk and bread from the refrigerator and turned to set them on the counter, but she never made it. She walked straight into an open cabinet door, banging her forehead.

"Oh, honey!" Pastor cried, rushing over to take the items from her hands and setting them on the counter. He immediately returned to her, examining her forehead. "I'm so sorry. I must have left it open after grabbing a plate for lunch. I'm so, so sorry."

"It's fine, Michael." She raised her hand defensively to her head. All she wanted was food.

"No, now, let me look at it." He effectively blocked her path to anything edible and leaned down to further inspect the site of impact.

"Really. It's fine. I can barely feel it."

"I should have closed the cabinet."

*Yes, you should have.*

Pastor leaned down to plant a lingering kiss on her forehead, his whiskers clawing at her tender skin. Emily screwed up her face, silently enduring the torture. Why did the man have to grow a beard in summer, anyway? It was the hottest time of year. "What were you saying about Nettie?"

"Oh." Pastor stuck his hands in his pocket, walking across the room to look curiously out the back door, forgetting, once again, to close the cabinet door. Emily sighed and closed the door herself. "She can't figure out how to work any of the programs. The whole word-processing thing confuses her . . ."

Her gut sounded a warning bell. She knew what was coming next, and she coped the only way she knew how. She pulled a jar of peanut butter from the corner cabinet, swallowed a cry at the sting of pain in her thumb as she unscrewed the lid, stuck a spoon directly in the jar, and shoved the peanuty goodness in her mouth.

". . . I was wondering if you could get the Sunday bulletin ready for me this week? Just this once, of course. Until I find someone to help Nettie learn her way around a PC."

She left the spoon in her mouth to better hide her cranky face. The last thing she wanted to do this afternoon was coax her aching fingers into typing up a bulletin, but she nodded her head.

"Thank you, honey!" Pastor crossed the room in three happy steps to bristle-brush her bulging cheek. Then, he easily made his way around the table to hug each of the kids. "I already moved the bulletin file over to our shared drive. It's waiting for you on your laptop. Okay, I've got to run. Good-bye, kids. Listen to your mother."

"Daddy?"

"Yes, Julia?"

"Mommy is a loser."

Emily rolled her eyes at the ceiling and grabbed a clean knife to slather peanut butter on the bread. This day was stuck on repeat.

After she had put the kids down for a nap, Emily trudged down the hall to their bedroom to retrieve her laptop. She had been looking forward to taking a nap this afternoon, but duty called. Her shoulders shook out a dry, silent laugh. "Mommy said doody!" she could almost hear George saying. She shook her head, partly in amusement and partly in irritation, and moved to turn off the overhead light her husband had left on in the room. That's when she saw it.

*That man!*

There, sitting in a pile on the floor next to the laundry hamper, was the clergy shirt her husband had been wearing earlier that morning. He must have changed shirts before going to the hospital. He often did that in the heat of summer. Emily glared at the black offense and fumed. She could deal with her husband's annoying habit of forgetting to turn off the lights. She could stomach his new penchant for facial hair. She could forgive an open cabinet door or two, and she could even, after four years of marriage, tolerate his being gone six nights in a row—that last one not being entirely his own fault. What she could *not* endure, however, was a dirty shirt pile on the floor lying directly next to an *open* hamper.

Emily wasn't sure whether to scream or cry. She considered trying both, but waking the children would do her no good. She bit her lip instead and decided to take a good, long, quiet shower. Nettie's bulletin could wait.

Her plan was a good one—the streams of hot water effectively coaxing all tension from her shoulders and back—but she had neglected to bring a change of clothes with her into the bathroom. She wrapped a towel around her body and tiptoed to the bedroom.

"Oh, snap!" she grumbled, remembering midway that she was out of undergarments. She turned back down the hallway toward the kitchen, where a load of clean whites was waiting in the dryer, but she never made it past the living room. There, standing in her way on a footstool in the kitchen doorway, was Lance Finley.

Emily stifled a scream.

"I-I knocked," Lance quickly explained, stepping—almost falling—off of the footstool. He fumbled with the screwdriver in his hand and stared at the floor. A deep burgundy color sprouted above his shaggy beard.

Emily was mortified. She felt she should say something, but she couldn't get her lips to move. Nor her feet. Only her arms responded, so she hugged them around her towel and did her best to ignore the water dripping down her exposed shoulders and legs.

"Irv tol' me to ch-change the batteries in the smoke detectors. This's the only afternoon I have free to do it." Lance was hurriedly packing up his toolbox and stool and moving toward the front door. "I called your husband this morning, but he never called me back—"

*That man!*

"—an' no one answered the door when I knocked. An' the door weren't dead bolted or nothin'. I assumed y'all weren't home, honest! And well, I guess . . ."

Lance had made it safely through the screened door, and he unabashedly abandoned his words for his truck. Emily ran to close the door behind him and dead bolted it at least four separate times. When she was finally satisfied that no one else could come in without taking an ax to the door, she leaned her forehead—*Ouch!*—against the door and cried.

Well, at least Yvonne would have something else to tell the ladies in the sacristy that night.

ıllıllıllıllıllıllıllıllıllıllıllıllıllıllıllıllı

Emily's nerves were still on edge later that evening.

"Now, try it one more time." Nettie smiled encouragingly.

Emily spread the square corporal on the altar and smoothed it out with her fingertips, careful to keep the side with the tiny embroidered cross toward the front of the altar. The material was a brilliant white, and even though she had just washed her hands, she still feared soiling it. Rebecca leaned in to set the silver chalice in the center of the material and draped it with the white purificator, Nettie's "hankie."

Emily glanced sideways at her friend. She still hadn't told Rebecca what had happened in the sacristy that awful night, let alone in the parsonage this afternoon. Thankfully, the pastor's kid in Rebecca knew to stop asking questions beyond a certain point, though she was keeping to Emily's side this evening like a hired watchdog. Emily balanced the paten, a silver plate holding the sacramental bread, on top of the draped chalice, and Rebecca unfolded the chalice veil to cover the entire setup.

"The pall before the veil, now, Rebecca Anne," Irene corrected from behind.

Rebecca blushed and nodded, halting with the veil held midair. She whispered into Emily's ear, "Why do I feel like I am being examined for confirmation all over again?"

Emily fought a wild urge to giggle. She pressed her lips together and concentrated on laying the pall, a square-shaped, linen-covered plate of glass, on top of the paten. The pall wasn't heavy, but she didn't trust her renegade hands to do what she told them. Then, she stood back for Rebecca to drape the veil.

"Now, remember, Emily," Irene instructed, "even though the Wednesday night crowd is smaller, we still don't pour the wine directly into the chalice before the service."

"Yvonne tried that once," Nettie confided, "but an edge of the napkin must have been drooping down into the chalice. It soaked up all of the wine before the service had even started. Boy, it made a mess—"

"Use the cruet on Wednesday nights just like on Sunday mornings."

Emily nodded at Irene. It had been decided that she would handle the setup and cleanup for Wednesday night services all by herself. It was a less attended service, so the work was perfectly manageable for just one person. That, and she could easily pop over to the church during supper on Wednesdays while Pastor watched the kids. Then, she could head back over to the church to clean up once he had returned home from leading the service. Emily didn't say as much to anyone else, but this arrangement also handily ensured that she would never have to work alongside Yvonne in the sacristy.

"What do I do with the leftover consecrated wine in the cruet after the service?" Emily asked.

"There won't be any," Nettie assured her. "You'll start with less in the cruet for a smaller number of people—"

Emily nodded. Of course.

"—and Pastor likes to consummate after the service."

Emily's eyes grew round in shock, and Rebecca snorted into her hand.

"I think she means *consume*," Emily whispered. "He'll *consume* whatever is left."

The two friends fell against each other in a fit of giggles.

"Rebecca Anne!" Irene clipped.

Rebecca immediately sobered and stood up straight. "Yes, Mrs. Rincker. I'm sorry. I'm better now. Sorry."

"What's so funny?" Yvonne asked, walking out of the sacristy with the ciborium in one hand and the cruet in the other.

Emily panicked and her mind went blank.

"Nettie was just telling us," Rebecca saved her, "how Pastor consumes whatever is left of the consecrated bread and wine."

Yvonne's dark eyebrows rose in sharp reprimand. "Yes, well, Pastor Gardner never consumed the leftover elements. He instructed us to pour them out respectfully onto the ground. Still, I suppose we should put the best construction on the situation and not assume Pastor Fletcher to be a . . . a . . . what's the word?"

Rebecca's eyebrows gave a reprimand of their own. "A lush?"

"Well," Yvonne smiled evenly, setting the ciborium to the back and left of the vested chalice. "*I* didn't say it."

Emily felt her cheeks burning.

"Consummation is a faithful practice too," Nettie said.

Rebecca unsuccessfully stifled another snort, but Yvonne merely shook her head and closed her eyes as if the very sight of Nettie were an indecency better avoided.

"Jesus said so Himself," Nettie continued, blissfully impervious to Yvonne's silent condemnations. "Take and eat, take and drink."

The three women looked at Nettie in surprise. The spacey woman was not usually known for her theological prowess.

"Okay," Irene spoke up, seeing that everything was finally in its proper place. She was not aware that she was interrupting any discussion of any kind. "That's how it will appear. Do you have any questions, Emily? You are up for Wednesday."

As Emily carried the ciborium and cruet back to the sacristy, she willed her cheeks to stop flushing. They, of course, did not comply—at least, not as long as Yvonne's stare of hate kept searing her mind's eye.

"Where's the altar guild schedule?" Irene barked, gazing at the bulletin board hanging above the sacristy sink.

"It looks like someone pinned this over it." Rebecca removed a piece of paper from the board. Emily peeked over her friend's shoulder and silently read,

*Whatever is true, whatever is honorable, whatever is just, whatever is pure, whatever is lovely, whatever is commendable, if there is any excellence, if there is anything worthy of praise, think about these things.*

Emily's cheeks flushed again, only this time, the rush of warmth was welcome. She recognized her husband's handwriting, and she had a delightful suspicion that this Scripture passage from Philippians was intended just for her. Yvonne's look of hatred faded into the distance. "May I have this?"

Rebecca handed her the paper.

Emily quietly pinned it to the top left corner of the corkboard—out of the way but where she could still see it—and moved to put away the ciborium. She smiled. Maybe her husband's tendency to forget shirts and lights and cabinet doors wasn't so bad after all. It seemed that he had no trouble remembering the most important things, and she loved him for it.

*That man!*

## Chapter Seventeen: Mourning and Evening

Caroline Bradbury opened the front door of her family's historic home to find Ben Schmidt standing on the grand front porch, all smiles. He was wearing a crisp button-down shirt, tan slacks, and the watch she had given him for Christmas. She reached out to brush back a stray lock of his golden-brown hair—still damp from his recent shower—but he caught her hand midair and pulled her outside for a more private greeting.

"Sorry I'm late." He leaned his nose against hers. "Someone dumped a truckload of aluminum siding in one of the ditches I was mowin'. Took me an' Irv a bit to get it all cleared."

Caroline didn't mind. She'd wait her whole life for Ben Schmidt if need be. She'd been in love with him since the sixth grade, and she didn't see herself stopping anytime soon. She turned to call a quick good-bye to her mother inside of the house, shut the door behind them, and allowed Ben to help her climb up into the passenger seat of his old Chevy truck.

"Pretty dress," he complimented.

Caroline smiled. She had hoped he would notice. She and her mother had found the orange gingham—exactly the shade of the vibrant petals on a tiger lily, Ben's favorite flower—at JoAnn's in

Springfield last week, and she had slaved all morning and afternoon before her sewing machine to finish the sundress for tonight.

The drive to the parsonage was short, and Ben chatted easily the whole way.

" . . . just one more week at Casey's. The sixth's my last day, can you believe it? I think I've fin'lly got enough saved up for first semester, and—oh, I haven't even told you the best of it!" Ben turned his brown eyes excitedly her way. "Dad told me last night they're gonna match my savings penny for penny. That means I've got the whole year covered!"

Caroline smiled, proud of Ben's hard work, but she also felt a small pang of shame. Her own parents were paying for her college education in its entirety.

"Know what this means?" Ben reached over with his right hand to take hold of her left one. "Means I won't have to take out loans, least not this first year. An' it means I'm one step closer."

"To what?"

He squeezed her hand. "To bein' able to take care of you myself."

Caroline's heart sprouted roses that bloomed pink on her cheeks. There was nothing in the world she wanted more than to be cared for by Ben Schmidt, though her mother had expressed a very different desire for her future just that morning over breakfast.

"It's not too late."

"For what?"

"For you to apply to Juilliard."

Caroline had needed to stare hard at her yogurt to keep her eyes from rolling back into her head. "Mom. It's the end of July."

"Oh, now, I know all of the scholarships will be taken, but your father and I can swing one year's full tuition, I think. You'll surely win a scholarship for the next year."

"I've already been accepted to U of I. I want to study design."

"You want to be close to Ben Schmidt."

Caroline hadn't argued. There was no point. Whatever she wanted, her mother kept insisting that she go off to New York in the fall and study vocal performance and enter the Miss America pageant and audition for Broadway and make a name for herself in some ridiculously public way.

"You have so much talent, honey. I just don't want to see it go to waste."

"Design isn't a waste."

"That's not what I'm talking about."

"What *are* you talking about?"

Her mother had smiled in that artificial way of hers. "I'm talking about marriage."

"I'm not married. You are the one who's married."

"And I don't regret it for a moment, darling. Marrying your father was the best decision I ever made—"

"But getting married would be my worst decision?"

"Now, honey"—that saccharine smile—"I'm simply saying that it's good to get a degree before you tie the knot. Besides, you have more musical talent than I ever had, and your father is keen to see you use it."

Caroline was pretty sure that her father had never said any such thing in his life, not about music, at least. All he had told her year after year was to "be sensible," and she knew what that meant: study law in Iowa like he did and then move back home to join the family practice in Bradbury. Thankfully, her older brother was well on his way to making that family dream come true, but their mother's crazy expectations of celebrity remained hers alone to fulfill. She threw her final card on the table.

"You couldn't wait for Dr. Duke to get married."

"Well. That was different."

"How?"

"She already had her degrees. She was sensible and waited to marry until she was done with school."

"No, Mom. She earned her graduate degrees after her first husband *died*."

That last trick had won Caroline some quiet and peace for the remainder of her breakfast, but she didn't feel any better for it. Why couldn't her mother see that her ambitions for fame and fortune were, well, *her* ambitions? All Caroline really wanted in life was to be called Mrs. Schmidt, and if she got to sit before a sewing machine and make curtains and grow a garden and sing songs to her children someday, well, that would be nice too.

Ben pulled up in front of the parsonage and parked under a tree. In three seconds flat, he was on her side of the truck, opening her door and helping her down from the tall seat.

"After you, ma'am," he grinned, indicating that she should walk up the front porch steps ahead of him. The Fletcher twins—George with his nose pressed flat against the pane of glass—were waving madly through the front picture window.

"Come on in, you two," Pastor Fletcher invited, holding Becky in one arm and opening the front door with the other. He ushered them into the living room and proffered them seats. "Emily just about has dinner ready. Can I get you something to drink? Lemonade? Iced tea?"

Ben waited for Caroline to respond.

"Just water, please."

"Lemonade, sir," Ben nodded.

As Pastor disappeared into the kitchen to fill beverage orders, George maneuvered himself directly in front of Ben's armchair. "Do you have baby teef?"

"Not anymore."

"You have parent teef."

"I do?"

George nodded. "When yo' baby teef fall out, then yo' parent teef come in."

"But nothing comes in after that," Julia expounded, pushing her way into the conversation and Ben's line of sight. "Nobody has grandparent teeth. They're just pretend."

"I see."

As Ben discussed serious dental matters with the twins, Caroline picked up a photo album from the coffee table and opened the front cover. She smiled. These were pictures from Dr. Duke and Pastor's wedding.

"Mommy wore white," Julia said, not missing a thing. Her little-girl wedding radar was apparently as sharp as any woman's. She climbed up onto the cushion directly beside Caroline and snuggled against her arm to better see the pictures.

"Yes, I know," Caroline said, turning the page. "I sewed her dress."

"I want to see!" George called out, abandoning his conversation with Ben and claiming for himself the cushion on the other side of Caroline. "Daddy may-weed Mommy."

"Yes. I was there."

"I was too."

"No, you weren't, George." Julia leaned over the album to better reprove her brother. "We weren't born yet."

"Daddy was the pastor." George looked up at Caroline, ignoring his sister.

"No, George," Julia sighed. "Daddy was the *groom*."

"Daddy was the gwoom," George nodded.

Caroline smiled down into the two big eyes rising like moons above a pair of boyish cheeks. She had always had a soft spot for George.

"Were you a flower girl?" Julia asked.

"No. There was no flower girl. Only a matron of honor."

"Auntie Rebecca," Julia confirmed.

Caroline nodded and lightly fingered one of the pictures. It was a snapshot taken from the church balcony. Dr. Duke and Pastor were facing each other, hands joined, and Jeremy and Rebecca Jones flanked them on either side. The ancient Pastor Weaver from Grace Lutheran in Fancy Grove stood on the top step of the chancel, officiating.

Even from afar and through a lens, Dr. Duke looked radiant in her gown. She had picked out a rather plain pattern—a waisted A-line dress with a portrait collar and quarter-length sleeves—but Caroline had talked her into using a shimmery satin fabric that gleamed whenever she turned in the light. Caroline also, of her own volition, had added darts to the bodice and just enough pleats to the tea-length skirt to make it flare and billow attractively whenever Dr. Duke walked. The result, especially when paired with Alice Ebner's gloves and Rebecca Jones's veil, was pure perfection.

In fact, the entire wedding ceremony had been perfect. It was simple and noble and beautiful, just like Dr. Duke's dress—all straight lines and elegant angles and classic cuts. No grand pageant of satin-wrapped bridesmaids shimmied up the aisle. No unity candle or sand art or knotted rope embellished the chancel. No brass quintet or celebrated soprano fringed the balcony. There was only a veiled bride on the arm of her father, walking up the aisle behind a processional cross as the small congregation sang "Gracious Savior, Grant Your Blessing."

And Caroline would never forget the look on Pastor's face when he first beheld Dr. Duke in the nave! It was the look of Adam, for sure, one of wonder and gratitude and delight. Caroline sighed happily at the memory. She hoped a man would look at her that way someday. Well, not just any man. She glanced up at Ben and blushed to find him already studying her.

"Ben was the crucifer," she suddenly announced, trying to change the subject from her feelings, not that her feelings had ever been the subject.

"Caroline sang at the wedding," Ben counteroffered.

"What did you sing?" Julia asked.

"I just sang in the choir with everyone else." Caroline cleared her throat, feeling strangely vulnerable. She could still feel Ben's eyes on her. "We sang Duruflé's 'Ubi Caritas et Amor.'"

"That's a song about cars," George explained.

Caroline caught the laugh with her lips before it could escape her mouth. "It's a song about love. The love of Christ."

"And cars," George added.

"I'm going to marry George," Julia declared. "Who are you going to marry, Miss Caroline?"

The question hung suspended in the air, vibrating noisily throughout the small room like a copper gong. She dared not look up at Ben, even through her lashes. Instead, she focused her eyes on Carrots, who, lying prostrate across the entrance of his open cage, miraculously appeared oblivious to any cosmic noise. "I-I don't know. No one has asked me yet."

"George asked me last night." Julia's voice was pragmatic.

George nodded.

"Who's hungry?" Pastor asked, setting Becky in the high chair pulled up next to the dining table. "George, would you please escort Miss Caroline to her seat? Julia, Mr. Ben is going to sit next to you."

"Yay, yay, yay!" Julia cheered, hopping onto the floor and bouncing toward the table like a bunny.

Dr. Duke entered the room, balancing a large, heavy platter piled high with croquettes. She looked like she was trying hard not to drop it, and her cheeks were rosy from the concentration.

"Here, Miss Emily." Ben immediately jumped up from his own chair to help her with it. "I'll take that."

Caroline smiled. Even though their hostess had been married for four years, Ben still called her "Miss." Not that Caroline had any room to talk. She still called her beloved voice teacher "Dr. Duke." Strangely—and sweetly—the Fletchers never bothered correcting either of them.

"You were pretty when you were young, Mommy," Julia said, climbing into her chair at the table.

"Was I, now?" Dr. Duke laughed, good-naturedly accepting the half-compliment. She leaned down to kiss the top of her precocious daughter's head. "Thank you, Jules."

Caroline thought Dr. Duke was still pretty. She risked a quick glance at the woman's tiny middle, marveling that a baby was growing in there. She sighed wistfully, hoping that she looked as beautiful someday when she was pregnant. She felt her face grow warm at the thought.

Once everyone had been seated, Pastor opened his hands and bowed his head. "The eyes of all look to You, O Lord, and You give them their food at the proper time. You open Your hand and satisfy the desires of every living thing. Lord God, heavenly Father . . ."

"Bless us and these Your gifts," everyone responded in unison, "which we receive from Your bountiful goodness through Jesus Christ our Lord."

"Amen!" George shouted, imitating Curt.

Dr. Duke had prepared a feast. The chicken croquettes, Ben's favorite, were piping hot, the roasted carrots from the Fletcher garden were tossed in a vinaigrette made from Caroline's own recipe, and the fingerling potatoes were purple.

"We thought we'd try a new variety this year," Dr. Duke smiled. "They're kind of fun, don't you think?"

"I don't like them," Julia pronounced.

"You haven't tasted them," Pastor corrected. "Besides, they're purple. What's not to like?"

"How is work going, Ben?" Dr. Duke redirected.

"Fine, Miss Emily," his mouth around one of those potatoes. "I'm almost done workin' night shifts at Casey's."

"I'm glad to hear it. I bet Irv is going to miss you at harvest time."

"Yes, ma'am. But Davie Jones's helpin' him."

"Is he?" Dr. Duke smiled. "Yes, I suppose he's that age, now, isn't he? And how about you, Caroline? Have you decided on a major yet?"

"Art and design with a concentration in printmaking."

"Interesting. What is printmaking, exactly?"

"I'll get to design and print fabrics."

"Ah, yes," Dr. Duke nodded. "That sounds perfect."

Caroline smiled happily. Dr. Duke had always understood her.

"And you are studying engineering, Ben?" Pastor asked.

Ben paused to lift another croquette onto his plate. "Mechanical engineering, sir."

"Hoping to get a job with Caterpillar someday?"

"Or John Deere," Ben grinned.

"And how about church? Did you call Pastor Henshaw like I suggested?"

"Yes, sir. He's expectin' both of us in the pews come late August."

"I'm glad to hear it. College is a busy time, and many of your professors are going to try to teach you away from the faith. You need to gather regularly with other Christians in church to hear God's Word and receive Christ's gifts for the strengthening of your faith." Pastor nodded his head at the two of them. "It helps that you have each other. I expect you both to hold each other accountable in the years ahead."

"Yes, sir."

Caroline nodded her head and swept her eyes around the table, catching Dr. Duke's soft, brown gaze. The older woman's eyes were tearing up, and Caroline felt her own doing the same. Pastor's words were sobering, but they were also comforting. It felt good to be cared for like this. She had always felt safe under the Fletchers' watch, but it suddenly hit her that she and Ben, for the first time in their lives, were moving beyond the sight line of this family she loved and admired so much.

||||||||||||||||||||||||||||||||||||||||||||||

Before they left the Fletcher home, Dr. Duke handed them each a wrapped gift.

"Should we open them now?" Caroline asked.

"If you like."

Ben tore open the paper on his package and held up a framed pressed flower.

"It's one of the tiger lilies you gave me so many years ago," Dr. Duke explained, already crying.

Ben's cheeks colored under his tan. He seemed to be having trouble looking at their hostess.

"I don't think," Dr. Duke blubbered, her breath shuddering around her words, "I'll ever be able to tell you just how much you and your family's kindness meant to me when I first moved to Bradbury."

Pastor put a supportive arm around his wife's shoulders.

Ben finally looked up, his lips tight. "I think you just did, Miss Emily." He reached down to hug her and then stepped back to wipe at his eyes.

Everyone turned expectantly to Caroline. She looked down at the package in her hands and broke the bonds of the Scotch tape, pulling back the paper to reveal a leather-bound copy of *Lutheran*

*Service Book.* Her eyes strayed to the bottom right-hand corner of the burgundy cover, where her name was embossed in gold letters.

"These are the best songs you will ever sing."

Caroline looked up at her favorite teacher and whispered, "Thank you."

"Thank *you*, dear girl." Dr. Duke hugged her around the neck for a full five seconds and then released her to the world. At least, that's what it felt like.

iiiiiiiiiiiiiiiiiiiiiiiiiiiiiiiiiiiiiiiiiii

When Ben dropped her back at Bradbury House, he walked her to the darkened side yard instead of the front door.

"Where are we going?" Caroline asked.

"You'll see."

He led her by the hand through the stand of tall pin oak trees, stopping only when they had reached a short decorative table holding a candle flickering within a glass hurricane. The purple doily underneath the burning light bore the unmistakable mark of her mother.

"What's going on?"

Ben stopped and set both of their packages on the table. The locusts were making a wild ruckus in the branches overhead, and fireflies flirted all around them. Caroline glanced nervously about, discovering the silhouettes of her parents standing at a window in the game room at the back of the house. They appeared to be watching them. Was this a—?

"Do you remember the first time we talked under this tree?"

Caroline looked back at Ben, wide-eyed. He had taken both of her hands in his and was studying her intently, the exact same way he had in the Fletchers' living room.

"You brought me a glass of water while I was mowin', remember?"

179

Caroline nodded, her head suddenly feeling very light. "And you gave me an orange maple leaf."

Ben kissed her hands before lowering himself down on one knee. "I knew that I was goin' to marry you, even then."

Caroline gasped. This *was* a proposal!

"I know that I'm not much to look at right now, but I'm gonna work hard for you, Caroline. I'm gonna study hard and get good grades and get a job that can support you and our family. I'm gonna do you proud."

She could only stand there, open-mouthed and mute. Dreams, as it turns out, steal all of your breath when they come true.

"Now, I already asked your father's permission last night—"

*So that's why her mother—*

"—an' he agreed, so long as we wait till next summer to get married. An' your mother made me promise that we'd both come home all next summer long leadin' up to the weddin'."

Caroline started to cry and laugh at the same time. Well, if her stubborn, opinionated, exasperating, strong, wonderful mother could compromise, so could she.

Ben fumbled in his pocket, pulling out a white gold band lined with glittering stones. "School's not the only thing I've been savin' for all these years."

Caroline's tears won out over her laughs.

"Will you marry me, Caroline Francine Bradbury? Please?"

She looked toward the dark silhouettes in the nearby window and caught her mother wiping at her face. Her dad nodded his head and waved. With a heart full of gratitude for parents who loved and supported her, simple dreams and all, she turned back to the farm boy with the rusty lawnmower who had stolen her heart once and forever and said, "Yes."

# Chapter Eighteen: Mea Culpa

||||||||||||||||||||||||||||||||||||||||||||||||||||||

Bev silently handed Irv the Friday morning editorial in the *Bradbury Times* and tapped her finger on the third column. She was keeping as quiet as she could. Mrs. Scheinberg was still asleep in the guest room down the hall.

Irv set down his coffee and donned his reading glasses.

Dear Editor,

I would like to offer my condolences to every citizen of Bradbury County whose property was damaged in the recent tornado. I find it especially troubling that Mr. Max Mauer lost his home and barn roof in the storm. I have set out a jar on the counter of the Kuhl Whip Stand, and both I and the sensible owners of that fine establishment have pledged to match, dollar for dollar, the money that all of you donate on Mr. Mauer's behalf. Thank you for helping us restore what has been tragically lost.

Sincerely,
Mrs. Arlene Margaret Compton Scheinberg

Irv let out a low chuckle, soft as a whisper but energizing as a bumblebee's buzz, and returned his eyeglasses to the leather case resting on top of the family Bible. "Atta girl, Arlene."

Well, that decided it. Bev reached for the box of Raisin Bran and returned it to the top of the refrigerator. Cereal was no longer fitting for a new dawn such as this. Arlene was getting pancakes for breakfast.

## Chapter Nineteen: Dumbbells and Dumb Belles

‎‎‎‎‎‎‎‎‎‎‎‎‎‎‎‎‎‎‎‎‎‎‎‎‎‎‎‎‎‎‎‎‎‎‎‎‎‎‎‎‎‎‎‎‎‎

"We're going to the gym, Bev, not the prom!"

Mrs. Scheinberg eyed her watch for the eleventh time that morning. Bev had disappeared into her bedroom shortly after breakfast, announcing a need "to change clothes," but that had been a good thirty-five minutes ago. Houdini could have changed in and out of a dozen straitjackets by now.

"Here I am!" Bev finally called, scurrying breathlessly into the living room.

"You forgot your pants."

"I am wearing pants."

"No, you're wearing tights."

Bev tugged self-consciously at the bottom of her red-and-white polka-dot T-shirt, ineffectually covering her matronly curves. "They're called leggings."

"They look like tights."

"But these are thicker."

"Are they? I can still see your underwear line."

Bev's open palms hovered defensively near her rear. "Well, this is what the lady at the store said everyone wears to the gym these days."

"You bought new clothes? For exercising?" Mrs. Scheinberg shook her head in open judgment. "You do realize that you just spent money on clothes for *sweating*?"

She, of course, had been sensible and pulled on her oldest pair of polyester pants—the powder blue ones that were fraying at the ankles—and the cotton plaid shirt with the snaps she wore whenever working in the garden. They both breathed in all of the right places and had proven on more than one occasion to be roomy in the areas that counted. She scooted her prudently packaged rear to the edge of the armchair and leaned forward to better pour the rest of her body onto her feet.

"They're really comfortable, Arlene," Bev defended, talking nonstop the entire way to the garage. "You should try them. Why, I can almost touch my toes when I bend over in these, and I can *never* touch my toes in my other pants. Now, they were a bit tricky to get on, I'll admit, but once I had them in place I felt real secure-like. Like being hugged. And I know this sounds vain, but I feel skinny in them. Black is slimming, right? Well, I felt so skinny when I put them on that I stepped on my scale in the bathroom just to see. I still weighed the same, but I don't *feel* the same, you know what I mean?"

Mrs. Scheinberg closed her eyes, praying for a mute button. Living with Bev was like being stuck in a perpetual documentary where every thought, word, and deed—and piece of clothing, evidently—was narrated in its mundane entirety.

"Though you should wait to put your socks on *after* you've got the leggings on. I made that mistake the first time, but they really came on much better once my feet were bare. In fact, the lady at the store said that some women don't even bother wearing—"

"Bev. Please."

"Oh, now, you know me better than that, Arlene," Bev tittered as she climbed into the passenger side of the Grand Marquis. "The lady *also* pointed out that black hides sweat marks. Isn't that handy? And the fabric is wicking too, did I tell you? The lady said these leggings'll wick away the sweat from, well, from everywhere. Though I wonder where it goes. Huh. I forgot to ask her that. Maybe it just evaporates or something like that? Anyway, I'm thinking about wearing these to quilting circle."

"Please, don't."

"But they're so comfortable—"

"And indecent."

"But—"

"Ah-ah," Mrs. Scheinberg held up a finger to stave off what was sure to be Bev's next unremarkable observation. "Remember our special little rule we made for the summer?"

Bev blinked and nodded. "No talking in the car while it's running?"

Mrs. Scheinberg proceeded with quiet joy to turn on the car's ignition.

||||||||||||||||||||||||||||||||||||||||||||||

Curt greeted them at the gym door.

"Wwway-kah to dah Can-dee Bah!"

Bev stared at the man for an uncomfortable moment before admitting, "I'm sorry, I didn't catch that. What did you say?"

"He said," Candice smiled wanly, stepping alongside of Curt and putting her arm around his shoulders, "welcome to The Candi Box!"

"Oh, of course," Bev nodded, smiling at their friendly greeter. "Thank you, Curt."

"Curt started working for us at the beginning of the summer," Candice explained. "He wipes down equipment and folds towels and greets members as they come through the door. His friendly smile is a bright spot in this box."

"Iiiee Can-deese fren."

"Yes, you are, Curt. Yes, you are."

Mrs. Scheinberg watched as Candice smiled sincerely at Curt. It was the most real expression she had ever witnessed on that counterfeit woman's face. Why, she looked quite pretty when she smiled like that, though her purple leggings and white tank top quickly leveled Mrs. Scheinberg's admiration. Was there no woman left in Bradbury who finished dressing before going out in public?

"Oo wahn-a ta-wahl?"

Bev looked pained in her ignorance.

"Do you want a towel?" Mrs. Scheinberg repeated.

"Oh. Yes, please." Bev gladly accepted a white hand towel from Curt and let loose with a mouthful of fluttery giggles. "I'm so sorry. I don't have the slightest idea what to do in here. I've never been to a gym before."

"Well, we call this a box, not a gym," Candice corrected, ushering Bev toward the front desk, "and you have nothing to be nervous about. We're a CrossFit affiliate, so we specialize in functional fitness. You're going to feel so good and strong when we are done with you. And don't you look *adorable* in your new workout clothes!" She glanced back at Mrs. Scheinberg. "The bathroom is just ahead and to the left, Arlene."

"I went before we came."

"No, I mean for changing clothes. We don't have actual locker rooms here, but the bathroom will do."

"I don't need to change."

Candice stopped and gave her a quick once-over. "Are you here to work out?"

"Well, I'm not here to quilt."

Something like amusement passed over Candice's features. The woman had been aggravatingly cheerful ever since she had met up with endorphins. "I see. Well, then, let's get you two signed up and ready to go. Class begins in just four minutes. Anna Cecilia here will take care of you."

Mrs. Scheinberg nearly dropped her cane. Surely not! But there, hovering behind the counter like a nightmare come true, was the most fearsome mop of red curls in the county. Mrs. Scheinberg immediately closed her eyes to protect them from the sight. She had meant to drive to the gym that morning but had somehow ended up in hell.

"Arlene, honey, what a surprise! Are you here to get some exercise? Well, good for you! I am so proud of you—both of you—for coming here today. It's the right decision." Anna Cecilia's patronizing tone had remarkable healing powers. Mrs. Scheinberg felt as if she could run all the way to the Davises' home, right then and there.

"Today is what matters. Yesterday is gone, and tomorrow is not promised, but today, well, today you can make a difference in how you feel tomorrow. We'll get you set up on the right vitamin supplements and talk through a whole foods meal plan and—"

"Actually," Candice interrupted, "today we'll just get them signed up for the next class before it starts. These two are my guests today, so no charge, okay?"

Candice gave a quick, authoritative nod of her head and then turned and walked out to the middle of the room, chatting easily with a pack of spandex-clad individuals currently gripping PVC pipes and stretching with them behind their backs. Mrs. Scheinberg followed Candice with her eyes, eager to look anywhere but at Anna Cecilia. The oddly sparse room really did look like a box with its black, padded floor and gray walls. There wasn't a single mirror in the whole place—peculiar for a gym, let alone one owned by Candice Bradbury—and the only equipment she could see in the entire space was a tall, jungle gym-type structure lining the far wall, a few thick ropes and rings hanging from the ceiling, and some plywood boxes and leather-covered balls clustered nearby.

"Please sign and date these waivers," Anna Cecilia was saying, passing two pieces of paper over the counter, "and you can hang your purses on the pegs by the door. We don't have any lockers."

"What about chairs?" Mrs. Scheinberg had noticed that one of her orthopedics was untied.

"We don't have any."

"What do you mean?"

"We don't have any chairs. Most of us just sit on the floor if we need to rest, but," Anna Cecilia crossed the room and dragged one of the wooden boxes over to the counter, "Curt sometimes sits on one of these. Will this work?"

No locker rooms? No chairs? What kind of uncivilized place was this? Mrs. Scheinberg sighed and sat on the high box, leaning forward to try to reach her shoe. She came up a good fourteen inches short.

"Oh, honey, let me help you with that."

Anna Cecilia was at her side in an instant, pityingly bending over her shoe before Mrs. Scheinberg could do any redirecting. Bev watched with wide eyes, one hand clamped tightly over her mouth. Mrs. Scheinberg gave her a look that threatened immediate decapitation should any laugh escape.

"Oo wahn-a ta-wahl?"

"No, thank you, Curt," Mrs. Scheinberg shook her head. She tried smiling at the kind man, but she couldn't loosen her cheeks from misery's vise grip.

"All right, everyone," Candice called, clapping her hands in that royal way of hers and walking over to a sound system built into the wall. She turned a knob, and some unidentifiable electronic junk with a strong downbeat immediately flooded the air. "Time to get started. Everyone line up against the wall. We'll warm up with some soldier kicks down the length of the floor and then high knees back. Arlene and Bev, come when you're ready."

"I can't do that," Bev murmured in Mrs. Scheinberg's ear, staring at the line of thirty-somethings kicking their legs almost up to their ears.

"Everything can be modified," Anna Cecilia assured, her imperious smile radiating self-importance. "Don't worry, I'll help you."

"Oh, that won't be necessary," Mrs. Scheinberg assured, but Anna Cecilia just kept on talking.

"Walk to the far wall and back, and try lifting your knees as high as you can." Bev immediately did as told. "Arlene, I want you to try it without your cane. I'll be beside you, so don't be afraid."

Mrs. Scheinberg did not do as told. The last thing she wanted was Anna Cecilia for a personal trainer. She had come to this wretched box in hopes of bettering her health, but what good was staying and exercising if the hired help kept causing her blood pressure to spike? She turned toward the door, ready to shuffle-bolt, but Candice stopped her with a whispered promise.

"If you do what Anna Cecilia says this one time, I'll make sure she's nowhere near you for the rest of the class."

Mrs. Scheinberg turned to look the mistress of the box in the eye, slightly in awe of the understanding she found there. When had Candice learned compassion? She felt a small smile play at her lips and gave a curt nod of the head.

Five minutes later, Bev and Mrs. Scheinberg were leaning against the wall, panting, while Candice sent Anna Cecilia on an errand to purchase more bottles of water.

"Now," Candice said, winking at Mrs. Scheinberg, "we're doing squat cleans today. Everyone load up a bar and build up to seventy-five percent of your one-rep max. Bev and Arlene, come with me."

"Oo wahn-a ta-wahl?" Curt asked, dangling another white swatch of terry cloth in front of Mrs. Scheinberg's face.

"Not now, Curt; thank you."

Candice led them over to a pair of rings hanging from the ceiling. "A good squat is nothing more than letting your bottom sink down toward the ground while keeping your knees bent and behind your toes. Any of us who have tried going to the bathroom in the women's restroom at Walmart instinctively know good squat form."

Bev grinned and nodded, fully understanding.

"Now," Candice rolled one of the large leather balls behind the rings while she talked, "I want you to squat until your backside hits the leather ball, and then stand right back up. It can be a bit tricky keeping your balance in the beginning, so I want you holding onto these rings the entire time, okay? You try it first, Arlene."

Mrs. Scheinberg maneuvered herself in front of the ball and gripped the rings.

"You can do it, Arlene!" Bev cheered.

"Yes, thank you, Bev. I know I can do it." Mrs. Scheinberg squeezed the rings tightly as she lowered her rear toward the ball, her arms shaking significantly.

"Good, now lift back up," Candice coached. "Use more of your legs than your arms if you can."

Mrs. Scheinberg pushed into the floor with her orthopedics and somehow managed to stand upright without falling over. Bev clapped excitedly like a schoolgirl, and Mrs. Scheinberg, in spite of herself, felt her lips turning upward into a smile.

"Good," Candice commended. "Now do it again."

Mrs. Scheinberg set her jaw in concentration and regripped the rings. She sank more enthusiastically this time, hitting her bottom squarely on the ball and then pushing straight back up.

"Again."

With each repetition, Mrs. Scheinberg gained in confidence. It wasn't so hard, really, and while her legs burned a bit, the burning felt strangely good. The whole experience was quite thrilling, really.

"That's it," Candice encouraged. "Now, squeeze more with your glutes this time."

"My what?"

"Your bottom."

Mrs. Scheinberg nodded, dropping toward the ball and then obediently squeezing her bottom on the upswing. Midway to the top, however, she stopped.

"What is it?" Candice asked, reaching out to support her at the arms.

Mrs. Scheinberg, panicked, remained silent.

"Arlene, what's wrong?" Bev asked. "Can't you speak? Oh no, she's stroked! I knew this was going to happen. Can you hear me, Arlene? Stay still. I'm going to call an ambulance."

"Not yet, Bev," Candice soothed, still looking Mrs. Scheinberg in the eye. "Can you say something, Arlene?"

Mrs. Scheinberg could say something, but she didn't want to. Bev's outburst had drawn the attention of a few of their classmates, and they were throwing furtive glances her way over their loaded bars.

"Try sitting down," Candice instructed.

"I can't."

"Why not? Are you hurt?"

Mrs. Scheinberg closed her eyes and shook her head.

"What is it, then?"

"I . . ." Mrs. Scheinberg whispered, weighing her options and settling for the truth. There was no way she could hide it in the end, anyway. Not, at least, while it was literally collected at her end. "I defecated."

"You . . . what?"

Mrs. Scheinberg opened her eyes and gave Candice a convincing look. "I evacuated. In my pants."

"You mean you wet them?"

*For the love of peace!* "Not my bladder, Candice. My bowels."

Bev gasped. Candice simply stood there, stunned, with her mouth hanging open.

"Oh no!" Mrs. Scheinberg whimpered, a horrifying warm sensation traveling down her left leg. The off-brand disposable briefs she had purchased in Hamburg last week weren't seaworthy, apparently. She gritted her teeth. Never again would she be tempted by a seventy-percent markdown to stray from the tried-and-true in life. Well, there was no stopping it now. All she could do was wait for the source to run out and pray her shoes kept the majority of it contained. One thing was certain: growing old was the absolute worst part of life.

"Do you need a tissue? You know, to . . . uh . . ."

Mrs. Scheinberg looked up at Bev. The woman's lips were twitching. "Don't you *dare* laugh at this, Beverly Davis! This is all your fault, I hope you know. You kept *smothering* my pancakes in that fake butter spread that you and Irv insist on digesting. It goes right through a girl before she has a chance to build up any kind of a defense."

Candice snorted into her hand.

"And *you*," Mrs. Scheinberg turned on the preposterous pair of purple pants. "You're the one who told me to squeeze!"

Bev couldn't hold it in any longer. In a dramatic show of no core strength whatsoever, she fell straight to the floor.

"Oh, great. That's really nice, Bev. Thanks a lot. It's nice to know I can count on you in a pinch."

That was too much for Candice. She dropped to the floor next to Bev.

"Oh, for the love of decency!" Mrs. Scheinberg hissed, catching the eye of more than one curious onlooker from across the room. She proudly pulled herself to her full height and let go of the rings. At least any stains would be on the backside and inseam of her pants. If she kept her front toward everyone else, maybe she could steal sideways to the bathroom without any of them noticing. She was suddenly, painfully aware of the efficacy of Bev's black leggings. Her own powder blue pants were telling on her this very moment. Well, she may have soiled her pants, but she still might be able to save her reputation from being smeared. If she could just get across the room without making a mess on the floor.

"Don't just stand there, you villains," she fumed. "Help me!"

Candice nodded an affirmative, making a valiant attempt to push herself up from the floor with her hands, but Bev's hums of laughter cut her feet right out from under her all over again. Mrs. Scheinberg rolled her eyes.

Thankfully, there was at least one sane soul left in the box.

"Oo wahn-a ta-wahl?"

Mrs. Scheinberg looked up to find Curt holding out a simple cotton lifeline to dignity. She beamed at the dear man, resolving to bake him a pie that very afternoon.

"Why, thank you, Curt. I wonder, though, would it be possible to have two?"

## Chapter Twenty: Casablanca

⁜⁜⁜⁜⁜⁜⁜⁜⁜⁜⁜⁜⁜⁜⁜⁜⁜⁜⁜⁜⁜⁜⁜⁜⁜⁜⁜⁜⁜⁜⁜

The next morning, Mrs. Scheinberg rolled her legs out of bed, dropped her swollen feet to the floor, and leaned forward to stand up.

"Ahh!" she cried out in pain as lightning bolts shot down the front of her legs. She gripped a nearby lamp stand to keep from toppling. What in the world was that? She blinked several times to clear morning's fog, not remembering what injury she had incurred in the night. Or was it restless legs again? Was she finally getting the nerve damage her father had endured toward the end of his life? Had fibromyalgia taken her hostage at last?

Candice's purple leggings suddenly sauntered across her memory.

Oh, yes. Candi's Miserable Box. How could she forget?

A few seconds later, Mrs. Scheinberg attempted a second launching, grimacing as a fierce electrical storm crackled across her legs and hips. Surprisingly, the pain dissipated the second she was standing, and she felt a sunny burst of optimism brighten her world as she shuffled quite easily across the hall and into the bathroom. The fickle sunshine disappeared, however, the moment she tried sitting down on the toilet.

"Ouch!" she hollered, salty tears smarting her eyes. Her "glutes," as Candice liked to call them, failed in the descent, and her tender rear hit the hard seat with an agonizing thump. Her backside felt bruised from the inside out, and no amount of twisting or leaning or rocking offered relief from the constant pressure of her own weight. She did her best to finish her business in a respectable fashion, but the worst, she soon learned, was yet to come.

"C'mon," she mumbled, rocking front to back and then side to side in order to achieve liftoff. Her sore leg muscles and tender backside, however, proved unable to support her frame. She rolled her eyes at the ceiling, sighed mightily, and called out into the bleak, hostile world, "Beverly!"

No one came.

"Bev!" she tried again, thinking through what to do if her hostess had already gone outside to do chores. Maybe she should throw a toothbrush at the window.

"Everything all right in there?"

The sound of Bev's voice brought a wash of salty relief to Mrs. Scheinberg's eyes. "I need some help."

"Did you run out of toilet paper?"

"No. I just . . . Will you come in here?"

"Should I open the door?"

"Unless you want to come in through the window." Mrs. Scheinberg bit her traitorous tongue. Sarcasm would leave her friendless in the end, she was certain of it.

Bev turned the knob and peeked her head around the door. "Can I open my eyes?"

Mrs. Scheinberg sighed. "Yes. But prepare yourself. And shut the door behind you."

Bev stepped all the way into the bathroom and obediently shut the door. When she opened her eyes, she didn't seem a bit surprised. "You can't get up, can you?"

Mrs. Scheinberg, painfully aware that she was blooming, half-naked, out of the toilet bowl, kept it simple. "Yes."

"I couldn't either!" Bev exclaimed, smiling conspiratorially and leaning against the counter. "I had to call Irv in to help me in the middle of the night. And if you think it feels bad now, just wait till you try putting on your pants. I think it's those squat-things Candice had us do. Every time I try to sit down, it feels like fire is coming out of—"

"Bev."

"Oh yes," Bev jolted, shutting her mouth and planting herself, feet staggered, in front of the toilet.

Mrs. Scheinberg took Bev's extended hands and closed her eyes, submitting to what was, perhaps, her greatest humiliation to date. Colonoscopies, at least, were performed under sedation and with a gown that opened in the back. This toilet extraction was going down in the clear light of dawn and with her undergarments at her ankles. Oh well. If she had to choose one other person in the world with whom to trust such ignominy, it would be faithful, loyal, trustworthy Bev. The girl was gabby but only about unimportant things.

Mrs. Scheinberg felt dangerously close to hysterics. "I was in the porcelain prison," she semi-quoted, her voice trembling with nervous energy, "and you came to visit me."

"Don't make me laugh, Arlene," Bev warned, squeezing her arthritic hands until they hurt, "or I'll fall to the floor and then we'll both be in real trouble. Now, on the count of three, okay?"

Seconds later, they were both standing on their feet and washing their hands.

"Bev?"

"Hm?"

"Thank you."

"Of course."

"No, I mean for more than just helping me this morning."

Bev looked at her curiously in the mirror.

"Thank you for not making a big deal out of, you know, my accident yesterday. Well, you could have showed a little more self-restraint in the box—let's be honest—but you were really nice to me in the car. After the hard time I gave you about your leggings, you could have teased me mercilessly about my pants. But you didn't."

"Well," Bev turned off the water and eyed her seriously in the mirror. "I'm not supposed to talk in the car."

Mrs. Scheinberg held her friend's gaze for one moment before throwing back her head and laughing. But that didn't last for long. Her abdominal muscles hurt too much to stand it.

〰〰〰〰〰〰〰〰〰〰〰〰〰〰

Candice arrived midmorning with a tupperware container full of suet cakes. At least, they looked like suet cakes.

"These are called energy bites," she crowed. "You're going to *love* them. They've got peanut butter and oats and chia seeds and honey and all kinds of nutritious energy."

"They're for birds, right?" Mrs. Scheinberg frowned.

"Oh, Arlene," Candice sighed. "They're for *you*. You should try eating them in place of pie. Maybe then you'd be able to touch your toes."

Everyone was prone to judgments, but Candice was one of those people who gave herself permission to pronounce them—all for the benefit of others, of course.

"Oo, yummy," Bev murmured, nibbling at an energy bite and wiggling her eyebrows in a grand show of appreciation. She was used to serving as the alkali to Candice's acid.

"Bev, I'd like to steal Arlene for a minute."

"Of course," Bev nodded, avoiding all eye contact.

"Um, excuse me," Mrs. Scheinberg waved her hands from across the kitchen table. "I am my own keeper over here, thank you very much."

"How about we go outside, then?"

"Why?"

"I'd like to talk."

"We can talk right here."

Candice smiled horizontally. "Please?"

After considerable effort, Mrs. Scheinberg extracted herself from her chair and wobble-jerked through the front door and down the Davises' front steps. "The swing?" she asked, heading straight for the two-seater hanging from a green metal frame in the front yard.

"Let's walk," Candice redirected, hiking down the Davises' sidewalk toward the gravel drive. She was wearing red leggings today.

"What do you want, Candice?"

"I'm concerned about you, Arlene. You don't feel well."

"I haven't felt well in twenty years. Why do you suddenly care?"

"Because," Candice stopped in the driveway and turned around, waiting for Mrs. Scheinberg to catch up with her, "you can barely walk. If you don't do something about it now, you'll be in a wheelchair by the end of the year."

"I can't help my arthritis," Mrs. Scheinberg grumbled, shuffling past Candice and starting for the road. Barely walk? She'd show the impudent woman.

"I realize that, but there are things you *can* help. Like your eating."

Here it came: *Life by Candice*, an essay.

"If you simply cut your portions down by one-third, you'd lose inches and find yourself moving better and sleeping better and feeling better. Or there are other ways to do it. Some people prefer to lower their intake of carbohydrates and simple sugars—"

"I'm not giving up pie."

Candice's jawline grew firm. "Why not? What has pie ever done for you?"

"Well . . ." Mrs. Scheinberg frowned. She didn't like this conversation. It made her feel weak. Or made Candice feel too powerful, she wasn't sure which. "It makes my house smell good."

"So do flowers and candles and open windows."

"It keeps my wrists loose."

"So does crocheting."

Mrs. Scheinberg shook her head. "I can't crochet anymore. The arthritis in my fingers is too bad."

"Okay, then," Candice deftly redirected, "roll energy bites into balls. There are other treats you can make in the kitchen that'll loosen your wrists but won't kill you."

"Pies aren't terrorists, Candice."

"Well, they're not your allies either."

She wasn't so sure. She had seen a pie work peace between parties just as effectively as any treaty. "People smile when I give them a pie."

"They're smiling because *you* are behind the pie. People love *you*, Arlene, not the pie."

Mrs. Scheinberg's throat started feeling tight and uncomfortable. "Pie is what my mom used to make."

"But she made other things too. You once showed me her recipe for green bean salad. Pie isn't the only thing you can whip up in the kitchen that'll bring her memory to life."

Blasted tears! And blasted woman! Mrs. Scheinberg stopped in the middle of the road and faced her confronter full on. "Pie makes me happy, all right?"

Candice finally let silence reign. Her eyes softened in an irritatingly sensitive way.

"Stop looking at me like that!" Mrs. Scheinberg griped, wiping at her eyes. Why did fluids keep leaking out of every opening of her body? "You don't know what it's like to be in pain every single moment of every single day. Pie gives me something to look forward to. It's the only thing that feels good. I'm not giving it up."

"This has been a hard year, hasn't it?" Candice's voice was remarkably soft, like a caress. "First you lost your job, then your home. It probably feels like too much to lose pie as well, doesn't it?"

Mrs. Scheinberg sniffed and eyed Candice warily. The woman had recently begun displaying moments of thoughtfulness and considerateness, and it was downright alarming. It always caught her off guard. She liked it much better when Candice was her normal, egomaniacal self. She at least knew how to handle her then.

"The thing is, Arlene, I happen to know that pie isn't the only thing that makes you happy. I've seen you with your dog. And you look almost cheerful whenever Blaine is home."

She felt an odd jolting sensation around her cheeks and eyes. An involuntary smile often pulled at her stubborn lips and forehead whenever she thought of that wonderful boy.

"And I see the way you smile at the Fletcher children." Candice appeared to be taking careful aim for her final shot. "What's a piece of pie compared to your godchildren?"

Bull's-eye.

"Fine!" Mrs. Scheinberg threw up her hands and started down the road again. Standing still was killing her feet. That, and she knew when she was beat. "I hear you, all right?"

"Good," Candice grinned, falling easily in step at her side. She ran a confident hand through her hair. "Because I think you're going to find that you like being free of your addiction."

Mrs. Scheinberg rolled her eyes. Candice was nothing if not melodramatic. "I'm going to like being free of *you*."

"Oh, you're not going to be free of me, Arlene Scheinberg."

"Well, I'm not going back to that hellbox of yours."

"I know." Candice's smile was smug. "That's why I'm coming to you."

"What do you mean?"

"I'm coming here every day."

"Why?"

"To help you exercise."

Mrs. Scheinberg felt an odd mix of vexation, fear, and pleasure. She thought back to the way her muscles had thrilled yesterday, but then she had not appreciated being held hostage on the porcelain prison this morning. Everything came at a cost. "What kind of exercise?"

"Walking, for one." Candice pushed at a button on her wristband. "Well, would you look at that? We've walked six hundred steps already." She took off the band and handed it to Mrs. Scheinberg. "Here. Put it on."

"What is it?"

"It's a pedometer. It tracks your steps."

"How much does it cost?"

"Nothing. It's a gift."

Mrs. Scheinberg pushed the band away. She had never been good at receiving gifts, and this one looked expensive. "I can't take this from you."

"You're not taking it from me. I'm giving it to you."

"No, you're not."

Candice's eyes looked powerful again. "You helped me once, remember?"

Mrs. Scheinberg thought back to an evening, years ago, when she and Candice had shared a bowl of brownie batter between them. Alice Ebner had been close to death, and Candice's grief had proven to be more than she could bear alone. Mrs. Scheinberg had sat with her through the worst of it.

"Why won't you let me help you for once?" The exasperating woman was relentless. "Please, Arlene."

Mrs. Scheinberg felt that odd urge to cry again. She grabbed at the black band, fumbling with the strap. Candice leaned in to help, her self-satisfaction throwing off more heat than the sun overhead.

"What am I supposed to do with this thing, anyway?"

"Just wear it and walk. I want you to reach five thousand steps by the end of the day—"

"While starving myself!" Mrs. Scheinberg grumped.

"Only of pie," Candice smiled smugly.

They turned back toward the house just in time to see Bev and Ceci stepping out onto the porch in search of them.

"How long until your house is ready?" Candice asked.

Mrs. Scheinberg sighed wearily. "Three more weeks."

Candice nodded, seeming to require no further explanation. "Bev talks a lot."

"You have no idea."

"Well," Candice smirked, "if it helps, just remember that it could be worse."

Mrs. Scheinberg eyed her skeptically.

"You could work with Anna Cecilia."

Mrs. Scheinberg snorted. The queen of Bradbury, it appeared, had a sense of humor after all. Subsequent feelings of goodwill billowed around her heart and set sail down her arm toward the hand that pushed playfully at Candice's shoulder.

The miracle was twenty-two years in the making, but it seemed that today—pie prohibition and all—just might be the beginning of a beautiful friendship.

# CHAPTER TWENTY-ONE: ONE FOR HER NOB

Cribbage night in the Joneses' household was a time-honored tradition—one that extended far beyond the establishment of two Fletchers, let alone six—but the addition of little people to the party seemed only to elevate the festal mood of the monthly tournament.

"Alison, make sure you put a towel underneath the twins," Rebecca instructed, handing a giant bowl of popcorn to her daughter.

"And don't let George eat more than his fair share, okay?" Emily pleaded.

Alison nodded eagerly, her strawberry-blond hair—the exact shade of her mother's—falling prettily over her blue eyes. As the youngest member of the Jones family, the eight-year-old never shied away from the chance to have authority over others.

"Steel yourself against his charms," Rebecca winked, tucking a stack of paper napkins under her daughter's arm. "That boy's got dimples, and he's not afraid to use them."

Alison flashed a toothless grin and turned to deliver the bowl to the basement, where the minors were gearing up to watch *Swiss Family Robinson*.

"She looks just like my mother," Rebecca sighed wistfully, turning back toward the open kitchen cabinets.

"She looks just like *you*," Emily clarified, handing her friend another dripping plate. "Except you're penciling in your eyebrows all of a sudden. What is that about?"

"Well, I realize that this may be hard for you to understand, Mrs. Thirty-Something," Rebecca pontificated, earning an immediate, playful swat from Emily's wet dishrag, "but once you reach the wise, old age of forty-one, you'll learn that there comes a point in every woman's life when wearing makeup best serves her neighbor."

Emily rolled her eyes.

"I'm serious, Em," Rebecca insisted, drying and stacking the plate in a nearby cabinet. "Drawing my eyebrows onto my face every morning protects young children from being terrorized. Besides, it's fun. It's like coloring."

Emily carefully handed Rebecca a handful of wet silverware. Her friend's longstanding rule for cribbage night was to use only low-maintenance dishes that could be stuffed in the dishwasher or tossed in the trash, but her priorities had dramatically shifted over time. Maybe it was the death of Rebecca's mother or maybe it was the birth of the twins, but the friends found themselves using the dirty dishes as an excuse to escape to the kitchen by themselves to talk over the difficult and the profound and the simple things in life. "I'll wash if you dry" had replaced the feminine "powder my nose" call of old, and the men of the party didn't seem to mind one bit. In fact, Jeremy and Pastor usually took advantage of the opportunity to slip outside with tumblers of bourbon—two fingers each—for a "let me show you my new grill" summit of their own.

"Now," Rebecca continued, "enough about me. Tell me; how are you feeling? Wrists hurt yet?"

"Like the dickens."

"Veins?"

Emily groaned. "Absolutely, positively disgusting. My legs look like one of those maze puzzles in Julia's activity books." Varicose veins were another physical casualty resulting from her pregnancies. She looked down at her expanding belly, thankful that Baby was modestly and fashionably covered in a ruffled red maternity shirt—a gift from Auntie Rebecca—but she was even more thankful that her legs were properly hidden from view by the navy blue maternity capris her mother had mailed her just this week. She glanced facetiously over her shoulder and altered her voice to sound just like Rebecca's. "This may be hard for you to understand, Mrs. Glam Gams, but there comes a point in every woman's life when wearing pants in the summer best serves her neighbor."

Emily ducked as a dish towel flew over her head.

⁙⁙⁙⁙⁙⁙⁙⁙⁙⁙⁙⁙⁙⁙⁙⁙⁙⁙⁙⁙

Pastor Fletcher walked his empty tumbler back to the kitchen and made his way down the stairs to check on the kids. Frankie Jones had tucked himself into a corner of the couch, his eyes focused on the open book in his lap rather than the movie being projected on the wall. Julia sat snuggled up next to him, entranced, her brown eyes wide with wonder and a little bit of fear as a man in the movie wrestled a boa constrictor in the middle of a jungle river. Alison Jones lay sprawled out on her belly on the floor, and George, situated in the middle of a green bath towel beside her, two-fisted popcorn out of a giant bowl directly into his mouth.

Pastor chuckled and shook his head.

Robbie Jones was sitting at the back of the room on a barstool, his knobby elbows leaning on the polished wooden counter before him. The teenage boy appeared to be perusing a website on a tablet. Pastor ambled over to his side and claimed a neighboring stool.

"Checking baseball scores?"

Robbie glanced up. "Nah. Lawnmowers."

"Looking to buy a rider?"

"Pusher. Old Rusty finally gave out."

"Ah, I see."

Rusty was Ben Schmidt's old mower, the one the soon-to-be collegiate had given Robbie four years back when he first invited the red-haired boy to help him with his lawn care business. Now, between the two of them, the boys mowed the majority of the yards in Bradbury, including the parsonage's.

"What are you going to do now that Ben's going off to college?"

"Frankie's going to help me in the fall and spring, but Ben'll be back next summer." Robbie's freckles faded against a happy flush. "I'm keepin' his rider for him during the school year."

"Sounds like a good deal. Hey, speaking of deals," Pastor changed the subject, "I wanted to run an idea by you."

"Yeah?"

"I was wondering what you think of our making Curt and Kathryn greeters on Sunday mornings. Not every week, but maybe once a month or quarter or something like that?"

Robbie frowned thoughtfully. "I think that would scare Kathryn."

"Not a good idea, then?"

"Well, not for Kathryn. But Curt would love it."

"Do you think he could manage it by himself?"

"Probably. But maybe I should greet with him?"

Pastor smiled. He had hoped as much. "That would be perfect."

"Timing'll be the only thing. How early would we need to be there?"

"8:40 at the latest. But 8:30 would be ideal."

Robbie nodded. "I'll check with Mom. That's a bit earlier than the Bethesda home is used to us picking them up, but I doubt it'll be a problem." Robbie suddenly grinned. "In a couple of years, I'll be able to drive Curt myself."

Time was a straight-line wind, Pastor realized, and it persistently propelled everyone—freckle-faced boys included—ever forward. Pastor looked down at the lanky boy folded over the countertop and sighed. In just a couple of years, Robbie would be driving. And then in a couple of years after that, he would drive away from Bradbury, perhaps forever. That meant only three years remained to influence and teach and shape and encourage and serve this clever, compassionate boy. "How's baseball?"

Robbie shrugged.

"Is Coach Keller still benching you?"

"Not all of the time. But . . . " Robbie kept his head down.

"But what?"

"I don't know."

Pastor studied Robbie's bent head and stooped shoulders. This wasn't the posture of a confident shortstop. "Is he playing Clark instead?"

"Not always."

How to dig deeper without encouraging Robbie to put the worst construction on the matter? That was the question! "Has Coach suggested any areas for you to work on so that he will play you more?"

"See, that's the thing." Robbie's arms suddenly took flight. "Coach said I need to improve my batting in order to play varsity this year, but he's always having Clark or Austen DH for me—"

That didn't add up.

"—and he doesn't *say* it's because I missed that Sunday game, but he keeps saying over and over again to the whole team that commitment is the thing he values most in a player. Everyone knows he's talking about me."

"Now," Pastor treaded lightly, "we don't know for sure that he's talking about you alone," though he wasn't convinced, himself. Robbie's having chosen church over the makeup game seemed to have been the impetus for Coach Keller's sudden lineup shake-up. "Have you asked him if you can bat more in the games?"

"No."

"Maybe you should. That would show your commitment, I think."

"What's the point?" Robbie looked defeated. "Coach'll still expect me to play club ball on weekends during the school year. And even if I go to church on Wednesday nights instead of Sundays, I'll still have to miss practices."

It did seem a bit hopeless. Pastor felt a flash of anger toward his own generation. Misguided coaches and parents put such heavy burdens on children these days, and for what purpose? To chase after some elusive dream of fame and fortune? To earn a scholarship for college? What benefit was to be had for these precious children if they gained the whole world but lost their souls? For years, Pastor had suspected that the American dream was, in fact, a vision cast by Satan, but now he was certain of it.

"Did I ever tell you that I coached baseball?"

Robbie looked up. "You did?"

"Yep. Back when I taught high school English. Before I went to seminary."

Robbie looked wistful. "I wish you could be my coach."

"Well, maybe you do, but most people wouldn't stand for it."

"What do you mean?"

Pastor sighed, debating whether telling his own story would do Robbie any good. He often avoided talking about himself with his congregation. He wanted them to see and know Jesus in his life and ministry, not the man, Michael Fletcher.

"I enjoyed coaching, actually. I always loved baseball—played first base back in high school—but several of my players' parents went to the school board and complained about me."

"Why?"

"They said I wasn't competitive enough."

Robbie looked confused.

"I think they wanted their boys to have a coach who would push them more to win. You see, I focused on sportsmanship and team dynamics as a coach. And I never held practices on Wednesday nights."

"Lent," Robbie said, understanding.

"Exactly. I wasn't going to require my students to miss church for batting practice. And when I refused to sign the team up for weekend tournaments that spilled over onto Sunday mornings— well, let's just say the parents pushed for my resignation."

"What did you do?"

Pastor looked down into Robbie's wide eyes and smiled. "I became a pastor."

⁂

The Fletchers left the Joneses' after being properly double skunked.

"That was the worst hand I've ever had," Emily bemoaned, but her dimples still danced alongside of a smile. Loser or winner, cribbage night always left her feeling light and happy. What was Church Stress, again?

"Wow, it's ten o'clock!" Pastor exclaimed, looking at his watch.

"So late?" Jeremy asked, popping the last chocolate-covered orange into his mouth.

"We really should get home to relieve Arlene," Emily suggested, reaching to pick up the now-empty tray. Ever since Emily had weaned Becky, Mrs. Scheinberg kept insisting that she watch their youngest on cribbage nights, "so you can stay out later than a toddler's bedtime," she explained.

"God bless that woman," Rebecca invoked.

"Amen," Pastor confirmed, scooting back his chair from the table and gently prodding Julia off of his lap. The twins, their movie completed and popcorn consumed, had joined the adults in the dining room for the last hand of cards. George was already fast asleep against his godmother's shoulder. The Jones kids had snuck upstairs for dessert but then headed right back down to the basement to watch an episode of *American Ninja Warrior*.

"When does Arlene leave for Indiana to pick up Blaine?" Jeremy asked, opening the front door and following all of them out onto the front porch.

"Well, her basement's dug and her foundation's laid, finally," Pastor said. "All she's waiting on now is the halves of her prefab to be delivered and mated. Should be any day, I think."

"Are they putting up the siding as well?"

"Yep. Interior trim too. God willing, she should be moved in by the time she leaves."

"How's her Kuhl Whip drive going for Max?" Rebecca inquired, passing George's limp body over to Pastor.

"We took her there Monday night for an ice cream cone," Emily said, leading Julia down the porch steps with one hand and balancing the empty dessert plate in the other. "Well, she didn't actually eat hers—she fed the entire thing to Little Man, here—but she's emptied the fund jar three times, so far."

"Wonderful!"

"Okay, Fletchers," Pastor said, ushering his family to the van parked in the driveway. He turned back to give his friends a grateful nod over George's downy head. "Thank you, Jeremy. Rebecca. Tonight was just what we needed."

"So glad you could come!" Rebecca waved, leaning into Jeremy's open arm. "Thanks for bringing dessert."

"And thanks for the delicious macaroni and cheese," Emily returned, tossing a final smile over her shoulder. "I'm going to sleep like a baby tonight."

But she didn't.

When Pastor pulled the van up in front of the parsonage a few minutes later, Emily's adrenal glands emptied themselves into her bloodstream. There, just beyond the northwest corner of their house, illuminated by the glaring security light hooked to the peak of their neighbor's garage, lay Charlene, prostrate on the driveway. And a bearded man in a ball cap was straddling her back, smashing the side of her face into the concrete with his hand.

## CHAPTER TWENTY-TWO: SINGLE WHITE FEMALE

ⁿⁿⁿⁿⁿⁿⁿⁿⁿⁿⁿⁿⁿⁿⁿⁿⁿⁿⁿⁿⁿⁿⁿⁿ

"Emily," Pastor kept his voice low and calm. "Take the kids into the house. Now. Lock the door, and stay there with Arlene until I tell you it's all right to come out." He was already dialing 911 on his cellphone. "Don't answer the door for anyone else."

A loose whimper caught in Emily's throat, but his wife nodded her head in compliance. She quickly turned in her seat to unbuckle Julia and George, smiling as brightly as she could.

"Why are you crying, Mommy?" Julia asked.

"I'm just a bit tired, honey," Emily managed shakily, reaching to help Julia slide out of her seat and onto the floor of the van. She pulled at George's straps and immediately shushed his subsequent cries. Thankfully, the children's view of the violent scene was blocked by the front passenger seat.

An operator answered the phone. "What is your emergency?"

"I'd like to report a domestic disturbance on Spring Street." Pastor kept his eyes glued to the horrid scene in front of him.

"What is your name?"

"Michael Fletcher."

"What is the phone number you are calling from?"

Pastor answered the operator's questions one by one while simultaneously reaching behind his seat to help Emily with George's stubborn straps. He never took his eyes off of Charlene. He thought he saw her wriggle once under the man's hold, so she must be alive, at least. *Thank you, Lord!*

"Come, now," he heard Emily whisper behind him. She had climbed into the back of the van with the kids and was opening the sliding door from the inside. "I want you to be as quiet as you can. Let's pretend we're mice and scurry up the sidewalk. Maybe we can surprise Mrs. Scheinberg."

"Yes!" Julia whispered excitedly, always ready for a game. His wife was so smart.

"Okay, Michael," the operator spoke into his ear, "we'll send an officer right away."

George persisted in fussing, so Emily hastily picked him up, held his head against her shoulder, and ran him to the front door herself, Julia galloping just ahead of them. His daughter turned around in the doorway to wave triumphantly back at him before Emily pushed her through and shut the door.

Pastor knew that he should do something now that his family was safe inside of the parsonage. He killed the van's engine, turned off the headlights, and stepped out onto the street. Amazingly, Charlene's assailant didn't even look up.

Pastor was painfully aware that he had no weapon on him other than his wit. He found himself suddenly wishing that he had worn a clerical that night. He didn't fancy himself a superhero, but the clerical was the closest thing he had to a uniform. And it reminded him of the omnipotent God who cared for and protected him in all things. He took a deep breath and turned toward the back of the van, curling around the rear bumper and running straight for the parsonage. Then, he crept alongside the front porch, keeping to the shadows, and peeked around the northwest corner of the house.

Charlene was still facedown on the pavement, sobbing. He couldn't see her attacker's face for the ball cap pulled down over his eyes, but judging by the way Charlene kept crying out, the man must have been leaning his full weight onto the hand that was pushed up against her face.

"You're hurting me!" Charlene slurred.

"Shut up." The man's voice was hoarse and cruel. "Where is it?"

"I don't know—"

"Where is it?" he hollered again, spitting in her face. The man lifted his head just enough for Pastor to catch a brief glimpse of his sickly profile. He didn't look well. His gray-white skin was glistening with sweat, and the scraggly black beard outlining his bony cheeks served only to highlight his ghostly pallor. And his eyes. They looked soulless.

The man was high; Pastor was certain of it.

Charlene whimpered as the man laid his entire body on top of her own. He then leaned his cheek flat against hers and whispered a gritty, "Where is it, Lena?"

"I don't know, I don't know, I don't know," Charlene whimpered.

The man pushed up with a sneer and let loose with a stream of expletives, grabbing her cheek flesh afresh and pinching it in the palm of his hand, soliciting an ugly scream. "Try again."

Charlene was crying too hard to talk.

"Where is it?"

"I lost it."

"Where?"

"I don't know!" Charlene moaned. "I don't know, Mark! Stop it! Please. I'm sorry, I'm sorry, I'm sorry—"

The man let go with his hand long enough to make a fist and come down hard on Charlene's face. Pastor jumped. He couldn't wait any longer. The operator had urged him, with great caution, not to intervene before the police arrived, but he would not be the priest who passed by on the other side. He stepped into the driveway and declared, "Leave her alone!"

The man looked up and squinted, his fist raised midair for another strike. He appeared confused.

"Step back and release her."

"What?" The man stared for a second longer before flashing a vile grin full of eroding teeth. "Why, it's the padre! Didn't recognize you without your pretty collar. Come to have a turn with ol' Lena, have you? Tired of your prissy little wife? Why don't you tell Emily to come on out and—"

But the man didn't finish. Colored lights began flashing across the white siding of Charlene's house as a police car pulled up, blocking the driveway. He sprang up like a cat and sprinted into the black backyard.

"Stop!" Officer Plueth yelled, jumping out of his car and racing after the perpetrator.

Pastor barely noticed what happened next. Later, he remembered hearing some rattling sounds as Officer Plueth most likely met up with Charlene's chainlink fence in the darkness, but other than a few isolated shouts in the silent night, all he noticed in the moment was Charlene's evident distress.

"I'm sorry, I'm sorry, I'm sorry," she moaned over and over again.

Pastor knelt on the ground beside the pitiful woman and assessed the situation. No bones seemed to be sticking out of any limbs. Both elbows were bleeding—and her left eye was swelling at an alarming rate—but other than that, no injury was visibly apparent.

"Charlene, it's Pastor Fletcher," he spoke evenly, leaning close to her face so that she could better see him. "He's gone now. You're safe."

"I'm sorry, I'm sorry, I'm—"

"I know. Listen to me now. Can you sit up?

"—sorry, I'm sorry, I'm sorry—"

"Listen to me, Charlene. That man is gone. He's gone, do you hear me?"

Charlene's mumbling turned into soft whimpers.

"Take a deep breath for me. That's right. Now another one. It's just you and me. You're safe. Officer Plueth will be back in a minute, and we're going to take care of you, Charlene."

"Emily," Charlene murmured.

"Emily? You want to see Emily? She's inside the house. How about we go and see her? How does that sound? Shall we get up and go see her?"

Charlene hummed as she sighed. That was enough of an affirmative for Pastor.

"Okay. Let's go see Emily. But I need you to try to get up, first. Can you do that for me?"

Charlene took another deep, shuddery breath and then put both hands flat on the pavement. She slowly raised her cheek from the ground, her head hanging like a dead weight. She couldn't push herself all the way up, but she did manage to roll over onto her side. Pastor had to bite his lips to keep from wincing at the sight of her face. The skin on her right side was scraped raw, most likely from the immovable concrete. There was also an open gash on her chin, and the top of her cheekbone was swelling.

"C'mon, now," Pastor urged, offering both of his hands to help. "Let's get you inside."

As he helped her to her feet, Pastor felt stuck on one disturbing thought: that reprobate—Mark was his name?—had recognized him. Though they had never met in person, the man knew him well enough to call him "padre." He also knew—

Pastor's heart immediately stopped.

*Little wife*, he had said. *Emily*, he had called her.

That perp knew Emily by name! How in the world—? Had Charlene talked to him about her? Had that *degenerate*—? Pastor's eyes flew to the golden light emanating from the kitchen window overhead. The curtains were presently pulled tight, but they weren't always shut. Had that degenerate been watching his wife? Pastor almost tore at his clothes with his teeth. He glanced at Charlene's grated profile and shook his head. If this was how a rat like him treated women, then what would keep him from—?

Pastor wasn't normally a violent person, but he made a decision right then and there. Once Charlene was safe inside the parsonage, he was coming back out to hunt down that lowlife himself.

## Chapter Twenty-Three: Batter Up

Officer Plueth knocked on the parsonage door before Pastor could properly commence his solo manhunt.

"Got big plans for that thing?" the uniformed man asked, aiming a cocked eyebrow at the old baseball bat Pastor was white-knuckling.

Pastor looked down at his right hand and colored. He released his grip on the bat and, with as much dignity as possible, rested it against the nearby doorframe. He really needed to get a gun.

"Gonna beat him to a pulp, were you?"

Pastor wished his cheeks weren't so hot. "Yes. No. I don't know."

Plueth's gray mustache twitched. "If a rat like that had beaten a woman outside my kitchen window, I'd wanna eliminate him from the gene pool too. But I'd really rather arrest just one guy tonight, okay?"

Pastor nodded, looking at the floor like a repentant fourth-grader. Mrs. Scheinberg entered the living room just then.

"Kids are asleep," she said. The selfless woman had offered to take Charlene to the hospital so that Emily could stay home, but Charlene would have Emily or no one. "Did you get him?"

"No, ma'am," Plueth frowned. "Chased him to the edge of the property, but lost sight of him soon as he turned east. I think he looped back around the house and headed south across Mulberry. I've a hunch he's hiding out with one of his drug buddies in the neighborhood."

"In the neighborhood?" Pastor's hand itched to reach for the bat again. "You think he's still in the neighborhood?"

"Can't you search the houses?" Mrs. Scheinberg asked.

"Not without a warrant. And Dawson's no fool."

Mark Dawson was the perpetrator's name. They had finally gotten it out of Charlene before Emily took her to the hospital.

"He knows I'm looking for him," Plueth continued. "He's watching me, sure as rain, and soon as I come near his hideout with a warrant in hand, he'll be off to some other rathole down the street. This is the game these guys play."

"What now, then?"

"Now, we wait," Plueth advised, "and watch."

Pastor moved toward the doorway but stopped short at the sound of Officer Plueth's sharp reprimand.

"*Without* the bat."

ııııııııııııııııııııııııııııııııııııııı

"We should call your mom, Charlene."

"No." Charlene put out her hand as if to stop Emily. They were sitting side by side in the waiting area of Bradbury Regional's emergency room. "Please don't. I don't want to talk to her."

"But she's your emergency contact."

"Can't you be my emergency contact?"

Emily looked down at the registration form she was filling out for Charlene. Nothing was ever simple with her neighbor. She blinked her tired eyes and, against her better judgment, crossed out

Charlene's mother's name on the line and wrote down her own. She would explain the matter to Michael later.

"Charlene Nordheimer?" a nurse in blue scrubs called out from across the room.

"That's us," Emily said, standing and helping Charlene to her feet.

"Come with me," the nurse beckoned, taking the clipboard from Emily and ushering them both through a door and into a cold, sterile room with two empty hospital beds. She pulled a privacy curtain between the beds and indicated that Charlene take the nearest one. "Lie down here, please. We'll get your blood pressure and temperature checked real quick, and then we'll take a look at those scrapes. Motorcycle accident?"

Charlene shook her head, lifting her left leg up onto the bed. "I fell."

The nurse raised an inquisitive eyebrow at Emily.

"On my driveway," Charlene explained further.

"Oh." The nurse, whatever she really thought, was light and nimble in her reply. "Well, concrete's no good for a facial, that's for sure."

Charlene attempted to scoot her body to the center of the mattress. Emily noticed that she was avoiding using her right hand. The nurse noticed too.

"Right wrist bothering you?"

Charlene nodded.

"Can you move your fingers for me? Just the thumb and pointer, huh? How about your wrist?"

Charlene shook her head.

"Okay. Can you feel this?" The nurse gently touched the tips of Charlene's middle, ring, and pinky fingers.

"No."

"I'm going to go ahead and order an x-ray—"

"Oh," Emily interrupted, pointing toward the form on the clipboard, "we need to be careful about that. She's pregnant."

"Is she?" The nurse looked down at the form, squinting. "Oh yes."

"It's okay," Charlene said.

"No," Emily turned to Charlene. Her poor neighbor had been through a lot that night. "You have to be careful of radiation. It can hurt the baby."

"No, I mean," Charlene looked past Emily at the nurse, "I'm not pregnant."

Emily frowned, confused.

"But your form says—" The nurse was studying the clipboard.

"I had an abortion."

That last word punctured Emily's gut like a knife, and her stomach deflated and sank into a bottomless black pool. She closed her eyes. *Another child dead.* A deep sadness washed over her from head to toe. She was drowning as she stood there, silent and suffocating, but the other two women chatted easily about the purposeful, apparently inconsequential, taking of another life.

"When?" the nurse asked.

"Last Thursday."

"Well, we'll still run a quick pregnancy test, just to be sure."

Emily opened her eyes to see the nurse making a quick note on the form, setting down the clipboard, and reaching for a nearby blood pressure cuff. "Let's get those vitals checked and your face cleaned up, and then we'll wheel in an x-ray machine."

Emily could not move on from the devastating moment quite so easily. She somehow got herself seated in a nearby chair while an ER doctor came in to examine Charlene. Only when the doctor and nurse left to retrieve the x-ray cart did Charlene rouse her with a desperate plea.

"Don't be mad at me, Emily. Please."

Emily had to force herself to look her neighbor in the face, the right side of which now glistened with some kind of salve. She could think of nothing to say.

"I had to do it," Charlene explained.

Emily shook her head. "No, you didn't."

"I did," Charlene insisted.

"Why?"

"I don't know."

"Did Mark threaten you?"

"No."

"Then why?"

"I just . . . I didn't want . . . I can't have his child."

This was the part that always confused Emily when it came to Charlene's lifestyle. "Then why let the man into your home and into your bed?"

Charlene looked further wounded. "I don't know."

"I'm serious, Charlene. If you don't want to have a man's child, then you don't really want to have the man. Can't you see that?"

It was so exhausting caring for this woman. Charlene was nice enough—even thoughtful at times—but she was foolish and caught in a bad cycle of hurting herself and, subsequently, others. Especially her children, it seemed. Emily felt a strong urge to cry, but she fought it. Now was not the time for crying. Now was the time for speaking, except—she had to sit on her hands to keep from burying her head in them—she wasn't any good at this. She wasn't strong like Rebecca or witty like Mrs. Scheinberg or wise like dear, sainted Alice. She could never think of what to say when it really mattered. There was nothing in her personality that excelled at the extemporaneous, but she knew in her soul that this was one of those times that called for action beyond her own self. This was a time to trust in God's promise to give her the very words to say, for she had to say something. Too many children were being killed.

She closed her eyes and begged her heavenly Father for help, opening them to discover her earthly father smiling at her from across a table in her mind's eye. It was the memory of the time he had taken her out to supper the night before Peter proposed. She went with it.

"My dad once told me," she started, "that it's a man's duty to lay down his life for his bride."

Charlene looked up curiously. Emily had never met Charlene's father—she suspected her young neighbor had never met him either—and her heart flowered with immediate compassion. Where were all of the fathers in this wretched world? Didn't they know that their daughters needed protecting? Emily reached for this abandoned daughter's hand but, remembering her injury, settled for resting her palm awkwardly on the bed. The truth was going to be hard for Charlene to hear.

"I-I don't know if you've ever read the Bible," Emily stammered, "but that's how God instructs husbands to love their wives: to give up their lives for them 'as Christ loved the church and gave Himself up for her.'"

Charlene shook her head, clearly not understanding. Emily tried again.

"A man is to love his wife enough to die for her—like how Jesus died on the cross for His bride, the church. That's a husband's duty toward his wife, to give up his life for her." There was a point to be made here, and Emily decided to hold nothing back. "Mark didn't give up his life to love and protect you tonight, Charlene. In fact, he *hurt* you in order to protect himself."

Charlene's eyes filled with tears.

"And my dad says that there is only one time a woman is asked to risk her life for her husband. Do you know when that is?"

Charlene shook her head.

"When she's giving birth to his child."

Charlene seemed to be holding her breath.

"Every time you become one flesh with Mark," Emily explained, "you are risking your life for him." *And your children's lives,* she wanted to add, but she didn't. "It's a beautiful act of submission for a woman to receive her husband's seed, and this," Emily leaned forward to emphasize her point, "is why you should give your body *only* to your husband—to the man who promises to *die* for you."

"Mark hasn't promised to die for me."

"No, he hasn't."

"He's not my husband."

"No, he's not."

"What do I do?" Charlene asked, her voice tiny.

Emily wasn't exactly sure. "Well, for tonight, let's just make sure you're okay. Tomorrow, we'll talk to Pastor and figure out a plan."

"I'm afraid," Charlene suddenly disclosed.

"Of what?"

"Of being alone."

Emily's memory jerked backward toward a lonelier time in her own life. "I think I understand a bit of how you feel. I was alone when I was your age too. In fact, I lived on my own for ten years, and believe me, it wasn't always easy. But I can think of something far worse than being alone."

"What?"

"Being with a man who won't die for you."

Charlene's sad eyes radiated a definite knowing and—Emily was further pained to see—an unmistakable envy. "What else did he say?"

"Who?"

"Your dad."

"Oh." Emily wasn't even sure where to start. "Well. He said a lot of things."

"Nice things?"

"Some of them."

Charlene looked down at her swollen wrist, her tone miserable. "My mom says terrible things."

"Now, I'm sure she means well." Though Emily doubted it herself.

"She said I should do whatever it takes to keep Mark."

Emily winced.

"Said he might be my last chance to get married."

What was wrong with that woman? Emily swallowed the reproach on her tongue and focused on the present task at hand. "And how's that working out for you, 'keeping' Mark?"

"Not very well." Charlene's voice shook.

Emily watched as her neighbor's lower lip quivered. The battered woman looked so broken and vulnerable and trapped, like a butterfly caught in a spider web. Everything she did seemed only to worsen her plight. And Emily was beginning to suspect the mom—not Mark—was the spider. *Lord, help!*

Charlene's left eye was completely swollen shut at this point, but she managed a small half-smile. "I like watching you with Pastor Fletcher. You're perfect together."

"We're not, trust me," Emily insisted, but Charlene would have none of it.

"He always holds your hand and smiles at you. He watches you, even when you're not looking, and he does things for you. Nice things, like opening your car door. I once saw him carry you to the porch when your sidewalk flooded. You were laughing."

Emily blushed. Charlene watched them, apparently, and often.

"He would die for you, I know it."

Emily knew it too.

The nurse came back in with the x-ray cart then, and Emily politely excused herself to avoid exposing her baby to radiation. Her hand flew protectively to her abdomen as she stepped out of the room. She knew her child was safe, but the conversation had left her feeling shaky and concerned.

Officer Plueth was standing in the hall.

"How is she?"

"Alive," Emily sighed.

He nodded. "Do you think she'll talk?"

"Maybe."

When Charlene's x-ray was complete, Emily led Officer Plueth into the examination room.

"Hello there, Charlene," the balding man greeted her kindly, standing next to the bed. His mustache rippled with a smile. "How are you feeling?"

Charlene glanced wildly at Emily, who nodded encouragingly. "Fine."

"I'd like to ask you a few questions, if you don't mind."

Charlene wouldn't look at him, but she nodded.

"Pastor Fletcher said Mark Dawson was with you earlier this evening, that he held you to the ground against your will. Is that true?"

Charlene, still avoiding eye contact, nodded her head ever so slightly.

"Did he hit you in the eye?"

She bit her lower lip. "Yes."

"Pastor Fletcher said Dawson accused you of losing something."

"I didn't!" Charlene barked, her head snapping up to look at Officer Plueth. "I didn't lose anything!"

"Okay. Did Dawson lose something then?"

Charlene looked back down, making an obvious effort to calm herself. "I don't know."

Plueth lowered himself into the chair next to the bed to better look Charlene in the one eye that could see him. "Was it drugs?"

"I don't know."

"What was it that Dawson needed so badly?"

Charlene kept her head bent low. When she did speak, it was in a whisper. "I don't know."

Plueth nodded his head and stood up slowly, stretching his long legs. "Well, you've been through a lot tonight, so how about I let you rest for a bit? I'll come by sometime tomorrow to get your official statement." He reached into his pocket and pulled out a business card. "This is my number. I want to help you, Charlene. I'd like to keep you safe as best as I can, so if you think of any-thing—*anything*—that might help me be able to do that, call me. Day or night, all right?"

Charlene took the card and nodded.

"Do you need a place to stay?" he asked. "I'd rather you not be alone tonight. There's a home for women in Hamburg I can recom-mend. It's clean and safe and completely anonymous."

"That won't be necessary," Emily found herself saying. It was as if the words suddenly grew on her tongue, seedless, but the second she spoke them, she knew they had been planted there by God. She still felt hurt and betrayed by Charlene's selfish choices and actions, but the woman was her neighbor. "Charlene's going to stay with us tonight."

‌‌‌‌‌‌‌‌‌‌‌‌‌‌‌‌‌‌‌‌‌‌‌‌‌‌‌‌‌‌‌‌‌‌‌‌‌‌‌‌

It was close to three o'clock in the morning when Emily and Charlene finally made it back to the parsonage.

"We'll find a more private space for you in the morning," Emily said, shaking out a bedsheet and tucking it into the cushions of the living room couch. "For now, this will have to do."

"It's fine," Charlene said, nursing her wrapped wrist. "Thank you."

"I'm afraid that I won't be able to keep the kids from waking you in a few hours. They'll be so excited to find you here. They'll probably think it's Christmas and that you've been delivered just for them. I apologize ahead of time for the jumping and shrieking."

"Oh, I won't mind." Charlene shyly touched her face. Between the shiner on her left eye and the abrasions on her right cheek and chin, her face was almost completely immobile from the swelling. "Hope I don't scare them."

So did Emily, but she didn't say as much. "Blankets are on the chair. Please, use as many or as few as you want. I've put a glass of water on the end table if you need to take more ibuprofen. Otherwise, is there anything else I can get you?"

"No. Thank you. Please, go to bed."

"All right then." Emily reached out to hug her neighbor, suddenly feeling awkward and overexposed. Even after all of their talks over the fence, it felt peculiar to have Charlene in her living room. In many ways, her young neighbor was still a stranger to her.

Once safely behind the bedroom door, Emily clung to her husband and cried as quietly as she could.

"She aborted the baby, Michael."

She felt him sigh against her hair. "When?"

"Last week."

He held her close and said nothing.

"It's so awful, Michael. It makes no sense. She keeps killing her own children."

"It happens."

Emily pulled back in horror. Was that all he had to say?

"What I mean is, it's not uncommon for a woman to have more than one abortion. It can be a behavioral manifestation of post-abortion syndrome."

Emily knew her nose was running, but she didn't bother wiping at it. "What?"

"When a woman has an abortion, she sometimes has another and then another to prove to herself that it was okay to do it the first time."

Emily felt stunned. "That's so sad."

"Yes." Pastor pulled her close again. "It is."

## CHAPTER TWENTY-FOUR: A BEAUTIFUL DAY
## IN THE NEIGHBORHOOD

The next morning dawned way too soon, and true to Emily's word, the twins wasted no time in waking the entire household.

"Miss Charlene is here!" Julia hollered for all the world to hear. "She's dead!"

Emily groaned miserably from somewhere around her pillow and proceeded to pull the bedcovers over her head. Pastor blindly rolled out of bed and into the living room as fast as he could, his eldest children slowly coming into focus. They were standing two feet from the couch, staring at their guest with eyes as round and wide as full moons.

"Let Miss Charlene have some space," he urged, coming around the couch to retrieve his rude children.

"They're all right," Charlene said. She was already sitting up on the couch, a blanket tucked neatly around her legs. She really did look terrible.

"Your eye is missing," Julia pointed.

Pastor immediately swallowed his daughter's hand with his own and tucked it back at her side. "Come with me, Julia. George. Help me get breakfast ready."

"Did you have an accidental?" Julia asked.

"Julia, come. Now."

While he was at it, Pastor also grabbed George who was still standing beside the couch, openly staring. His son's silence didn't last forever, though. As soon as Pastor flipped on the kitchen light, George blinked and said, "Miss Chaw-lene looks like bacon."

The morning's improprieties didn't stop with his children. When Pastor finally made it over to the church two hours later, Nettie was wearing a silken half-slip over her head.

"I'm conducting an experience," she said, touching the sheeny fabric with her fingertips. The elastic waistband of the under-garment framed her face perfectly like a nun's wimple. "Harold's forbid me from seeing my hairdresser anymore. Misty's charging twenty-five dollars a sitting now, and Harold says that's robbery, seeing as how I have less hair now than I ever did before. He has a point, I guess, but I'm nervous, Pastor. Harold told me that sixty years of cutting *his* hair is plenty of practice for cutting my own, but perms are confusing. The print on those bottles is so tiny, and Harold and I don't agree on what they say. I decided just to let Harold figure out how long I should leave the chemicals in. He's always been better at numbers than me, anyway. I'm the one who balances our checkbook, but he's the one who writes the checks. I had to leave home before my time was up, but don't worry, Pastor. Harold set the kitchen timer for me. He's going to call me here when it goes off."

Pastor felt quite mute. All he could do was stare, speechless, at his interim secretary wearing an undergarment on her head. And today of all days.

"And would you believe it, Pastor—"

Oh, he would. He most definitely would. Nothing surprised him anymore when it came to the Schmidts. They were kind and generous people, to be sure, but age and hearing loss and, perhaps, some grief had ripened their eccentricities to the point of fermentation. To think that sensible, level-headed Ben came from such mercurial stock.

"—Harold up and used every last one of my head scarfs on the rag rug he made at the home extension office last week. All I could find to cover my rollers was this old slip." Nettie giggled into her hand. "Do you want to know a secret, Pastor? This slip is my *dust rag*, but you can hardly tell, can you? OxiClean is the most amazing powder! I've tried Borax and washing soda, but they don't have those magical blue crystals."

The office phone rang.

"I'll get it, Pastor," Nettie assured, setting her bag on the filing cabinet and lowering herself into the creaky metal folding chair situated behind the front desk. The church board had offered to buy her a more comfortable chair for her tenure, but Nettie insisted on using this tetanus-carrier from the third-grade Sunday School room—the one she had been sitting in every Sunday for the past forty-five years. "It's a beautiful day in the neighborhood! This is Zion Lutheran Church, and I'm Nettie Schmidt. How can I help you? Well, good morning, Candice! Why, yes, he's in. No, of course, I won't tell him you're on the line."

Pastor shook his head and walked toward his study.

"Well, I'm not exactly sure. I haven't asked him yet. I only just got my curlers in. Okay, hold for a minute, please." Nettie hugged the receiver to her chest. "Pastor, *someone* wants to know if your neighbor is still alive."

He turned in his doorway and looked at the clock on the far wall. 9:15. That sure didn't take long. "Yes, Charlene is alive."

Nettie put the receiver back to her ear. "Yes. Oh, I didn't ask him that." She hugged the receiver again. "Is her attacker in jail?"

Pastor debated the appropriateness of this conversation. One way or another, he supposed, it was all going to come out in the end. At least this way, the facts would be unexaggerated. "The police are still looking for him."

"They haven't found him yet," Nettie whispered into the phone. "Well, I don't know. I've never met her, but Emily has. You could call her—"

*No!*

"Nettie," Pastor interrupted, "would you please thank Candice for her concern and encourage her to pray for Charlene and the police? Otherwise, we probably should keep the line clear, don't you think? Just in case Harold is trying to get through?"

"Oh yes!" Nettie said, her eyes growing big with alarm. She impulsively touched her wimple. "Thank you, Pastor."

Just as Nettie hung up the phone, Yvonne walked into the office.

"Your slip is showing," the Abbess of Zion declared, eyeing the abstruse secretary as if she were an out-of-line postulant and dismissing her with one shake of the head. She turned toward Pastor. "Oh, good. The reverend is in. I was wondering if I might have a word with you, Pastor."

He highly doubted that she wanted just one word. "Of course."

Yvonne held her purse in front of her as a shield as she approached the study, and Pastor stepped aside to allow her to enter ahead of him. Then, he pulled at the door, being careful to leave it respectfully ajar an inch or two. "How may I help you, Yvonne?"

She sat in a chair and began to talk before he had seated himself behind his desk. "Today is the day you are interviewing candidates, am I correct?"

"Yes."

Yvonne pursed her lips. "I was told that no members of the congregation are being interviewed."

"That is correct."

"Why?"

This was not a secret. "The board decided to hire from outside of the congregation."

"Well, this is the first I've heard of it."

"But the board wrote as much in their report last week."

"I received no such report."

Pastor frowned. "Nettie put a copy of the report in everyone's mailbox last Friday."

"Well, there was *no* report in my box on Sunday."

"Oh dear," Pastor said. "I am so sorry. Perhaps—"

"Perhaps this congregation is being mismanaged?"

There was no slow build with Yvonne. It was always, *Off with his head!* Pastor was careful to rein in his sigh before it had a chance to get away from him. It was important that his body language communicate only respect and kindness. Anything short of that would be interpreted as insubordination, which was, whether real or imagined, simply insufferable for Yvonne. "I was going to say that perhaps there was a mixup. I am sure that Nettie did not mean to—"

"I am not blaming Nettie. I am blaming management."

Pastor knew that "management" was actually code for "the pastor."

"For what, exactly?"

"For not overseeing matters in an appropriate manner."

Pastor once tried explaining to Yvonne that the pastor of a congregation is not a business manager but a shepherd of souls—the board of directors were actually the ones in charge of managing the church—but that had not been well received. This time, he tried for defending the reputations of the men who volunteered their time for the good of Yvonne and everyone else. "The board is doing the best they can, considering the circumstances."

Yvonne opened her mouth—no doubt to speak to the contrary—but Nettie effectively shut it with a knock on the door.

"Excuse me, Pastor," she said, pushing open the door and peeking around it. "Don Kull left a message last night asking you to call him this morning. He has a question about," she squinted at the note in her hand, "whether or not it is a sin to vote Democrat in the next election."

One of Yvonne's affronted eyebrows shot up to her hairline. "You are now offering political counsel, are you?"

"No," Pastor shook his head, distracted by the fact that Nettie walked into his study without invitation and in the middle of a private consultation. He'd have to talk to her about that. Again. "I do, however, meet with anyone who wants pastoral counsel."

"Well, Harold and I aren't voting Republican or Democrat in November," Nettie assured. "We're Libertines."

Yvonne closed her eyes and lowered her head, touching a manicured pointer finger and thumb to her temple. "*Libertarians*, Nettie."

"Would you please excuse us, Nettie?" Pastor intervened. "I'll take my messages after Yvonne and I have finished talking."

"Oh yes! Of course, Pastor. I'll save these for later." She bowed her wimple and took the messages back to the front office desk.

"I'm sorry, Yvonne," Pastor apologized. "You were saying?"

"I was saying," Yvonne sighed, opening her eyes and returning her hand to her purse, "that it is foolish *not* to hire from within the congregation. It is *unchristian* to keep our own people from benefitting from such an opportunity. 'Feed My sheep,' Jesus commands. Not the goats."

Ah, so this was about Lance. He should have known. "Well, that is definitely something that you can take up with the board at the next—"

"There is not time to take it up with the board. The candidate interviews are today."

She had a certain point, though she was making it before the wrong person. "What is it that you would like for me to do, Yvonne?"

"For one . . ." Yvonne lit into her usual harangue of criticism—his deplorable time management skills, his evident favoritism of certain members of the congregation, his lack of proper biblical scholarship when it came to women's roles in the church—and Pastor sat and listened as attentively as his fatigued body would allow. It was hard for his mind not to wander over to the parsonage where the real drama was being played out. It wasn't that he didn't care about what Yvonne was saying. It was that he had heard it all before—many times. His ears perked up again, however, when she finally reached her closer. It was a bit different than usual.

". . . since you have been here, our attendance has consistently decreased every year by an average of 6.67 percent. That's an astronomical hit for a congregation of our size."

She was running actual percentages, now? That was alarming, not because there was anything scandalous to be revealed by such a report, but because it hinted at a trust in something other than Christ to build the church. Who were they to measure and discern God's holy plan by such human standards?

"God grows the church, Yvonne."

"And you are shrinking it."

Pastor strangled another sigh. He knew he shouldn't give in to the temptation to self-justify, but the woman was relentless in her attack. He caved and threw up a tiny man-made shield. "We have had many beloved members die over the years, and others have moved out of Bradbury County. And honestly, there aren't many people moving into Illinois, let alone Bradbury, these days. Did you factor in those variables when you ran your numbers?"

Yvonne gave him a look of contempt. She did not seem to appreciate having her methods called into question.

"Another factor to consider," Pastor continued, knowing that he should be encouraging Yvonne to look at Christ, not at numbers, "is that not as many children are being born these days."

"Yes, yes," Yvonne rolled her eyes. "Blame the low birth rate, just like everyone else, but what about new members?"

"What about them?"

"Where are they?"

"Well . . ." He ran a hand through his hair. He should stop. "Four of them are sitting across the street in the parsonage as we speak." *And I should be with them!*

"Family doesn't count."

"Doesn't it?"

Pastor willed his mouth shut. That was enough. How could he expect Yvonne to look beyond the temporal if he kept forcing her gaze to return to it? The woman needed a pastor, not a broker. *Lord, help me!* he prayed, bowing his head for a moment before looking back up to meet her disapproving eye. He tried to smile. The woman was irritating, for sure, but he had long outlived his anger toward Yvonne. Five years ago, he might have been in danger of exploding whenever she heretically named—and therefore mistakenly blamed—him as lord of the harvest, but now he mostly felt sad for her lack of understanding that God, not any man, was the great grower of the church. No wonder the woman had no peace in times of famine. No wonder she found little comfort in God's promises to preserve and sustain His church unto life everlasting. Perhaps she didn't believe those promises. Pastor tried to put the matter in terms she would understand.

"Pastor Gardner was such a wonderfully kind man and faithful pastor, wasn't he? I know you miss him, and Pastor Rogers and Pastor Peterson were both faithful shepherds here at Zion as well." While Pastor Gardner had served Zion for over thirty years, the two men following him had been chased out of town by a certain silver-haired matriarch of the congregation. Pastor Fletcher didn't dare make mention of that fact now. "The three of them planted the seed of the Gospel in this community for thirty-six years. It is my honor to water what they have planted."

"Are you really watering, though?"

Pastor bore the accusation.

"Our church membership thrived under Pastor Gardner. Under you, it is waning."

All Pastor knew to do in moments like this was to quote God's Word directly. "'Neither he who plants nor he who waters is anything, but only God who gives the growth. He who plants and he who waters are one, and each will receive his wages according to his labor. For we are God's fellow workers. You are God's field.' God help all of us."

Nettie suddenly knocked on the door again. "Pastor?"

Yvonne's eyebrows threatened to fly off of her face.

"Jeremy Jones is here for the interviews," Nettie peeked around the door, "and so is the first candidate. May I let them both in?"

"To my study?"

"To the church. I locked the front door to keep anyone from interrupting your consultation with Yvonne. Hello again, Yvonne," she smiled warmly.

Yvonne flared her nostrils like a mad cow and stuck an agitated arm through the strap of her purse. "Why do I ever bother trying to help? My words always fall on deaf ears."

Pastor knew exactly how she felt, but his ministerial yoke didn't allow for him to storm out of the church in a huff. "Yvonne, let's keep talking about this. I do need to conduct the interviews with Jeremy right now, but I hope you will be comforted in knowing that I do not make the final decision about who is and isn't qualified to be hired as secretary. The board does that."

Yvonne looked anything but comforted as she marched out of his study.

||||||||||||||||||||||||||||||||||||||||||||||

"What do you think?" Jeremy asked two hours later. Their fourth and final interviewee of the afternoon had just left the study.

"I don't know," Pastor shook his head.

"Any of them seem like they could work here?"

Pastor ran both of his hands through his hair. "Honestly? I don't think so."

"All right," Jeremy nodded, making some notes on his pad of paper. "I happen to agree with you, but for screening purposes, can you tell me why?"

Pastor thought about it for a long moment. The first two candidates were an easy out—neither had any experience dealing with the inner workings of a church—and the third candidate was asking for a higher starting salary than the congregation could ever afford. The last interviewee, Laura Price, had looked quite promising on paper, but the moment she had walked through the study door, Pastor realized there was an insurmountable problem.

"The problem is," Pastor smiled sheepishly at the chairman of his congregation, "none of them is Mrs. Scheinberg."

## Chapter Twenty-Five: No Small Feet

It wasn't just humid outside. It was corn humid. Acre upon acre of spindly stalks were tasseling under the sweltering August sun, their wide green leaves sweating moisture into the already saturated atmosphere. Mrs. Scheinberg felt certain the sum total of it was condensing upon her very own forehead.

"Keep going."

"I am," Mrs. Scheinberg barked, wiping at her face with an old dish towel.

"Then don't slow down."

"I'm not."

"You're mopping instead of stepping."

Mrs. Scheinberg dropped her towel on the sidewalk and gripped the iron railing of the Davises' back stoop. Up she stepped, down she stepped, over and over again per Candice's instructions, wheezing like Darth Vader without a helmet. Bev was panting to her right, leaning against the side of the house with both of her palms flat against the vinyl siding. She pushed her body away from the house in a modified version of a push-up.

"Five more seconds, ladies," Candice called out, hovering behind them with a stopwatch in hand. "Three . . . two . . . one . . .

stop! Only one more interval left now, and then you're done. Get ready to switch."

Bev groaned as she shook out her arms. "I don't know how you got eleven reps in that last set, Arlene. I only made it to nine this time, and my arms feel like they're going to fall off. It reminds me of the time I tried hanging a clothesline by myself the first year Irv and I were married. I held that thing over my head for at least—"

"Get ready," Candice warned.

Bev immediately shut her mouth and shuffled over to the stoop. Mrs. Scheinberg was already at the wall.

"And . . . go!"

Mrs. Scheinberg didn't mind these interval workouts so much. In fact, she kind of liked them. The variety of movements kept things interesting, and the shorter, more intense spurts of activity suited her personality. That, and Bev usually got so out of breath that she talked less.

"Get lower, Arlene," Candice coached. "Kiss the siding if you have to."

She most certainly was *not* kissing the barn side of the Davises' house, but she did lower her face closer to the wall. She rather enjoyed being challenged, though she would never dare admit as much to her spandex-clad trainer. Every time she pushed herself harder, her lungs tingled and burned with life.

"That's your lungs expanding," Candice had explained last week. "Feels good, doesn't it?"

It did. Well, at first it felt awful—all of the walking and squatting and crunching and whatevering made Mrs. Scheinberg feel so exhausted that Bev had to wake her up for supper every night— but a few days into it something miraculous happened. Her lethargy converted into energy—delicious, addictive energy—and she found herself looking forward to each workout.

"Embrace the burn, ladies," Candice cheered. "Five seconds left."

Mrs. Scheinberg put her head down and pushed, arms quivering, with all of her might. She was determined to reach twelve this set.

"And time!" Candice called, hitting a button on her stopwatch.

"Oh!" Bev huffed, lowering herself onto the bottom step of the stoop and leaning against the rail. "That was miserable! My right calf started cramping, and I thought I was going to have to stop midway through. But you kept going, Arlene, so of course, I had to keep going. I'm never getting up from this step again, though. When Irv comes home, just tell him to bury me here next to the asters. How many, Arlene?"

Mrs. Scheinberg couldn't keep the corners of her mouth from lifting. "Thirteen."

"*Thirteen*? You got more in your final set than you did in your first four? You're a machine, Arlene Scheinberg. You amaze me!"

Not all of Bev's talking was unwelcome.

"Heart rate check," Candice interrupted. "Ready? Start counting now."

Mrs. Scheinberg held two fingers to her jugular while shielding her face with her other hand. The sun glaring off of Candice's metallic gold leggings burned her eyes more than the sweat.

"Okay, stop. How many beats, Bev?"

"Nineteen."

"Not bad. Though I'd like to see you pushing harder next time. Arlene?"

"Twenty-one."

"Now that's what I like to hear!" Candice flashed her teeth like a satisfied cat. "One hundred twenty-six beats per minute. Keep it up, Arlene. All right, you two," she grabbed two mats from the patio and unrolled them onto the grass, "let's finish up with some abs. Sit-ups, leg lifts, bicycle crunches, and supermans—fifteen each."

Bev groaned as she pulled herself back up onto her feet and lumbered over to claim the red mat.

"Need help?" Candice asked, offering a hand to Mrs. Scheinberg as she lowered herself onto the blue one.

"Nah, I've got it."

"You know, Arlene," Candice leaned down on her knees to hold both sets of their feet to the ground, "I didn't hear you complain *once* about your knees or feet today."

"That's because," Mrs. Scheinberg grunted as she sat up, "I didn't."

"No pain?"

"None worth mentioning."

Candice grinned and nodded. "I told you this would work."

"I still have arthritis," Mrs. Scheinberg grumbled in irritation—it wasn't like exercise had miraculously healed her—but she did let her smug friend keep grinning. She didn't mind Candice being right about some things. Just not all things.

"I saw Caroline's ring before she left for Champaign," Bev sang, resting idly on her back with her hands behind her head. "She looks *so* happy, Candice. And everyone knows Ben Schmidt is the best catch in town—"

"Sit-ups, Bev," Candice drilled.

Bev obediently moved, but she was not so easily silenced. "You and Thomas must be so proud," she sighed wistfully, stopping at the top of her motion. "I always wanted to be a mother of the bride, but we only had Johnny, of course." She lowered her torso back to the ground and took her time, looking at the sky. "And honestly, I don't think he's ever going to get married, so I'm probably never going to be a mother of the groom either. Oh well. At least Irv and

I had a nice wedding. We were high school sweethearts too, you know."

"Have they set a date?" Mrs. Scheinberg asked.

"Next summer."

"Good for them."

Candice looked like she needed convincing. "They're a bit young."

"For marriage?" Mrs. Scheinberg put her hands under her backside in preparation for the leg lifts. She held her breath and pulled her feet off the ground simultaneously, pausing for a moment with them above her head. "They're old enough to drive and vote and work."

"They should wait."

"For what? When did waiting ever make marriage any easier or better?"

"Well, Arlene," Candice clucked defensively, "delay of gratification—as you have learned—is nothing to shirk."

Mrs. Scheinberg indulged in a luxurious eye roll. "Those kids've had their minds made up about each other since they were twelve. Seems to me, they've been waiting quite a long time already."

"They're immature."

"Ben Schmidt? Immature?" That was crazy talk. Candice must be taking heat about the matter from some choice women in town to be feeling insecure about that boy. Ben Schmidt was more mature than most men twice his age. Mrs. Scheinberg lifted her legs in the air and grunted emphatically, perfectly punctuating her feelings, but Candice was stubborn in all things.

"Caroline won't even be twenty next summer."

"I married Irv when I was nineteen," Bev offered, still lounging on the ground, "and I think everything turned out just fine."

There was no arguing with that, but Candice's penciled brow remained furrowed. "She should at least wait until she's out of college."

Mrs. Scheinberg felt too strongly about the subject to keep shadowboxing. She threw a punch straight at her trainer's gut. "If I had waited to finish college before marrying Dean, I would still be Miss Compton to this day."

It took a second for the truth to sink in—Mrs. Scheinberg had been made a widow so young—but when it did, Candice's stubborn countenance fell, the wind properly knocked out of her.

"Life is short, Candice. It really is."

Bev, her overactive sensitivity only amplified by the afternoon's physical exertion, sniveled loudly from her mat.

"God only knows how many days each of us has left. Let Caroline live hers out as Mrs. Schmidt."

Bev was full-on crying, now—*for the love of tissues!*—but Candice merely gave a resolute nod of her head. The woman had never been one to stay down for long. She lifted her chin and controlled what she could. "Feet together, Arlene. You're getting sloppy. And why are you just lying there, Bev? Unless your goal in life is to be a mattress, start moving."

Mrs. Scheinberg grinned. She couldn't have said it better herself. "Candice?"

"What?"

"Caroline's blessed to have you for a mother."

|||||||||||||||||||||||||||||||||||||||||||||

For some reason, Mrs. Scheinberg suddenly cared about how she looked. She checked her blouse twice to make sure every eyelet had a button before climbing up into her F-150. This wasn't a new shirt, but it felt like new. It hung comfortably about her hips, straight as can be, not a single inch gathering around her backside as it had the last time she had worn it.

"Up, girl," she said, patting the seat. Ceci, who had been passing the bulk of the hot summer days belly-down on the cool linoleum of the Davises' kitchen floor, seemed less than thrilled to be climbing into a sauna-like truck. She turned her sappy brown eyes toward her mistress and whimpered.

"Lazy mongrel," Mrs. Scheinberg muttered, reaching down and scooping the pooch up herself. "You're the one who wanted to come along." She pulled herself up into the truck, shut the door, and turned on the ignition. "That's more like it," she breathed, cranking the air. Ceci leaned her fluffy face appreciatively toward one of the blasting vents, her fur flying. "All right, girl. Here we go."

They bounced easily down the driveway and turned east onto 1200 North, braking for an intersection just ahead. The field corn now stood taller than the truck, and the mile-thick rows of razor-sharp, green foliage made an impenetrable rampart on either side of the road. Only fools raced through country intersections this time of year without first coming to a complete stop and looking for oncoming traffic. That's how people got killed, Mrs. Scheinberg's uncle Fred included. She still cringed at the memory. She had been only eight at the time, but she could still remember standing out in her grandmother's flower garden early one August morning. She was filling the concrete birdbath with water before breakfast when a terribly unnatural sound—a metallic shriek of sorts—cut through the gentle hum of bird calls and bumble bees. She dropped her bucket and soaked her dress—much to her grandmother's chagrin—and only later did she learn that her uncle Fred, just one mile over, had driven through a corn-blind intersection heading west at the same time as a salesman driving south from Decatur. Both of the men had died on impact.

Mrs. Scheinberg wondered if she would ever be able to drive the roads of Bradbury County without meeting up with a ghost or two from her past. Every corner she turned and creek she crossed brought back memories of family and friends and experiences long gone. There, to her right, was the ditch into which she, her mother, and the new Cadillac had slid during the ice storm of '61. That tree growing in the middle of the Semples' acreage was the one under which Gary and Meredith's only daughter was buried. The farmhouse across the way had been rebuilt two separate times in the last fifty years: once because of a house fire and then again after Rueben Brown crashed his crop duster into it the month before his wedding. Mrs. Scheinberg sighed. The world used to be an empty canvas and her life a loaded brush—each day a bold, new stroke made upon the wide, white vista—but somewhere along the line she found herself painting a little less and looking a little more. The sum of her years lay before her in vibrant, poignant images, and her heart pulled at the sight of every one.

"Mom, Dad, and Dean are gone, Ceci," Mrs. Scheinberg said. "The land is my longest acquaintance now, and it talks more than Bev. It always wants to reminisce when I'm driving."

Mrs. Scheinberg turned south on County Highway 63. In just a couple of days, she would be driving a moving truck down this road instead of her old Ford. It was too early to celebrate, of course. The walk-through of her new home wasn't scheduled for another day and a half yet, and even after that, she'd still need to wipe down all of the walls, trim, floors, and appliances. She didn't trust these construction workers to clean up after themselves. She knew their mothers. But she and Ceci would soon be back in their own space, and Blaine would soon follow. Her heart almost burst from the happy thought. There was still a bit of life's canvas left for her to paint after all.

She slowed down as she approached 1000 North. There it was—The Offense, ever slumped and leaning—but with a new, respectable metal roof. She turned onto the familiar road and made an immediate right. Max was exiting the closed-in portion of The Offense as they pulled up, Dutch following close behind. Ceci started barking before they had even parked.

"Calm down, girl. Didn't anyone ever tell you never to show a man your true feelings?"

Ceci ignored her mistress and planted both front paws on the passenger side door.

"Go ahead, then." Mrs. Scheinberg leaned over to open the door from the inside, and Ceci bounded over to Dutch. "*Now* you don't mind the heat."

As Dutch licked Ceci from nose to tail, Max ambled over to the truck. "Where's yer cane, Arlene?"

"In a closet." Mrs. Scheinberg climbed down from the truck and shut the door. The last thing she wanted was any of the dirty flies from Max's pigs setting up house in her clean cab.

"You's lookin' lean. Like a filly. Them Davises been workin' you?"

"I've been working myself, thank you very much."

"Well," Max nodded, "it suits ya."

Mrs. Scheinberg blushed with pleasure. "Here." She shoved a manila envelope toward him.

"What's this?" Max took the envelope and peeked inside.

"It's the money everyone donated at the Kuhl Whip Stand."

He shut it immediately.

"I hope it's all right with you," Mrs. Scheinberg kept talking, suddenly nervous, "but I went ahead and converted all of the cash. That's the cashier's check from the bank. The other two checks are from me and the Kuhl family, of course."

Max was silent.

"Those pictures in there were drawn by the Fletcher children, and a few people from my church wrote notes for you. I put them at the bottom."

Max kept his eyes downcast and rubbed self-consciously at his scraggly jaw. "Thank ya. All of ya." He lifted his seed corn hat off of his head only to immediately replace it. "I's don' know what else ta say. You's always been better at talkin' than me."

Mrs. Scheinberg silently agreed. "You're welcome. Thank you for taking care of me and Ceci in our hour of need." *And for sitting with me after Dean died,* she wanted to add, but her throat suddenly seized with emotion. She tried to swallow but to no avail. She finally managed to squeak, "That was real decent of you, Max."

Max shrugged. He saved her by changing the subject. "Movin' home soon?"

"Wednesday."

"Yer house's lookin' good. Think I like it better'n the las' one. Noticed yer sidin's blue." His eyes twinkled.

"Yes," Mrs. Scheinberg smirked, a bit recovered. "We all know how much you like that color."

"Well, now, I may 'ave ta write a letter to the paper 'bout that!" Max hooted and slapped his free hand against his knee.

Mrs. Scheinberg let him laugh. She supposed he deserved a good chuckle at her expense. He'd certainly been a good sport to her, all things considered. She turned good-naturedly toward the golden sun and squinted at the pop-up camper sagging in the middle of a plot of overgrown grass where Max's trailer used to sit. She pursed her lips. Would it kill the man to mow once in a while? She knew for a fact that his Troy-Bilt rider hadn't blown away in the storm. "The contents of that envelope should take a good chunk out of your next double-wide. It's time to get shopping, don't you think?"

Max followed her gaze with his own. "Well, now. I'm thinkin' 'bout sellin'."

"Selling what?"

"Ma land."

Mrs. Scheinberg's head snapped back toward her neighbor's profile. "What do you mean?"

"Don Kull's offerin' me a good price. Lettin' me borrow 'is camper while's I think it over."

"What about your hogs?"

"Whata 'bout 'em?"

"You love them."

Max shrugged. "Sometimes they's more trouble than they's worth."

This admission stung her for some reason. "But you've always lived here."

"Tha's jus' it. A've lived 'ere in this speck of a county ma whole life. A man wonders what he's been missin'."

Mrs. Scheinberg was struggling against her straitjacket of a throat again. "Where would you go?"

"Tha's the thing 'bout double-wides," Max said, finally turning her way. His eyes looked sad. "You's ken set 'em anywhere."

Mrs. Scheinberg pondered this news on her ride back to the Davises'. She had never considered the fact that Max might move someday. He had always been her neighbor and always would be— at least, that's what she'd assumed—and the thought of Don Kull buying his land filled her with a strange sense of panic. It wasn't that she didn't like the Kulls. They were decent people, and quite frankly, Don and Lois would take far better care of the property than Max ever did. Maybe they would even tear down The Offense and convert the land for crops. That would certainly improve the quality of her summer breezes, but none of this comforted Mrs. Scheinberg. Sure, she loathed that barn and its inhabitants with every fiber of her being, but—she was surprised to realize—she no longer felt the same about their proprietor. In fact—there went her throat again—she found that she rather liked him.

## Chapter Twenty-Six: Feed the Birds

꜖꜖꜖꜖꜖꜖꜖꜖꜖꜖꜖꜖꜖꜖꜖꜖꜖꜖꜖꜖꜖꜖꜖꜖꜖꜖꜖꜖꜖꜖꜖꜖

Bev was in worse shape than Mrs. Scheinberg when she got home.

"What's wrong? Is Irv all right?"

Bev nodded her curly gray head, clearly unable to talk. She was sitting on the big swing in the front yard, blubbering.

"What is it, then?"

"N-nothing."

"I don't believe you."

Bev blew her nose noisily into a tissue. Mrs. Scheinberg stood there for a moment, flummoxed, trying to think of what she possibly could have done to cause such distress. Was it something she had said? Probably. She looked beseechingly at Ceci, but the dog was no help.

"Give me something, Bev."

"I-I'm okay," Bev managed. "I'm just tired."

So it *was* because of her. Mrs. Scheinberg's cheeks grew warm, her conscience pricked. For weeks, Bev had tirelessly and joyfully cooked, cleaned, laundered, ironed, gardened, shopped, baked, walked, shoveled, and sweated, all for the good of her human and canine guests, and Mrs. Scheinberg hadn't always been the most gracious recipient. She lowered herself onto the swing next to her friend and inquired, with the most earnest intentions of actually listening this time, "What can I do to help?"

"Nothing."

Bev was being remarkably concise. Something must be terribly wrong. "Ceci and I have added too much to your workload this past—"

"No, no," Bev shook her head, wiping at her nose. She took a deep, percussive breath. "It's not you. It's," she boohooed afresh into her hands, "m-my mother!"

Of course. Adeline. She should have realized the truth earlier. Bev's mother always caused grand episodes of emotion like this.

"What about her?" Mrs. Scheinberg asked, settling back into the swing for what was bound to be another epic update on Adeline's chronic foot fungus.

"She's going to die!"

"What?" Mrs. Scheinberg's heart stopped in her chest. Adeline was nearing ninety and had been living in a home for several years, but other than her rotting toes, Mrs. Scheinberg had never heard of any other pressing ailment. "What happened?"

Bev blew her nose again and sniffed, trying to calm herself. "Harriet gave her Mr. Selzer's bird feeder."

Mrs. Scheinberg frowned, confused. "What?"

"Harriet Grit died last week, and she left Mother Mr. Selzer's bird feeder in her will. Now she's going to die!"

Mrs. Scheinberg closed her eyes for a moment, mentally fastening her seatbelt. She was about to take a ride on one of Bev's spiraling rollercoasters—she could feel it—and she preferred not to fall to her death. "Tell me again. Why exactly is Adeline going to die?"

"Because that feeder's cursed, Arlene!" Bev cracked, waving her tissue in the air for emphasis. "Doris Yokey owned it at first.

Her children gave it to her for Easter one year, but then she died the following week. The family didn't want it, so they left it for Doris's nurse, Petulia. Well, Petulia—remember her?—she died in a car accident that same month and left it to Lewell Hamley, who then died of a heart attack. And then—"

"What are you saying, Bev?"

"I'm saying," Bev's voice shook as she fought for composure, "that whoever gets the bird feeder ends up *dying!*"

*For the love of reason!* "And your mother now has it?"

"Yes!"

Mrs. Scheinberg sighed. Well, there was no getting around it, not after all that Bev had done for her this summer. She took her friend's hand and stood. "C'mon."

"What?"

"Let's go."

"Where?"

"To Bradbury Regency."

"Right now?" Bev looked confused. "But I already gave Mother her meds."

"We're not going there to give anyone any meds."

"What for, then?"

"To get the bird feeder."

Bev's eyes grew round. "You think it *is* cursed, then?"

"Of course not! But your mother'll give herself—and you!—a heart attack with these *ridiculous* superstitions."

It was true. Adeline could get her sensitive daughter riled up about the most asinine things. Last month it was the harmless glue on envelopes—"Mother said you can get worms on your tongue from licking the seal!"—and next month it would be something else. Well, next month was in the Lord's keeping, but today, God had given her and Bev to each other to bear each other's burdens, even the loony ones.

"But where will we put it?" Bev asked, still resisting somewhat.

"What do you mean?"

"We can't keep it, Arlene. It's cursed."

Mrs. Scheinberg glared at her crazy friend, appealing to the well-catechized Lutheran living somewhere deep down inside of those gray curls. "Don't make me go all Martin Luther on you, Beverly Davis."

Bev immediately closed her eyes and breathed deeply. She looked like she was exorcising herself. "You're right. I'm being silly, of course. I know it's not cursed," she opened her eyes, "but we still can't keep it. Mother will worry."

As if they could ever keep her from that. "We'll burn it, all right?"

"But it's metal."

*For the love of—!* "Then we'll bury it. Now, c'mon. I haven't got all evening."

She actually did, but that was beside the point.

Bev stood up, a little smile playing on her face. "We're really going to do this, aren't we? We're taking the feeder? We can do that, right? I mean, it's not wrong to take—"

"Bev."

"Yes," she nodded her head obediently. "Right. Let's go. It'll be kind of fun, really. We'll be like Cagney and Lacey on the hunt. I don't have dark hair anymore, but—oh, we're both gray. Hm. Well, we can pretend it's the reunion show." Bev was obviously feeling better at least. "Just watch out for Kathleen and Lucy Elaine."

"Who? Are they villains on the show or something?"

"No. Kathleen and Lucy Elaine are real people," Bev said. "They're sisters. They've been rooming together at Regency for years."

"And that matters because . . . ?"

"They sit in the lobby all day long and watch people come in and out of the entrance."

Mrs. Scheinberg still didn't see the problem.

"Just wait," Bev sobered, a bit of her twinkle dimming. "You'll see."

Mrs. Scheinberg did see—the sisters at least. As soon as she and Bev pushed through the entrance doors of Bradbury Regency, two blue-hairs looked up from their pink wingback perches along the lobby wall. One sister was taller than the other, stately and regal with knitting needles in hand. The other was shorter and stockier with a wattled chin that hung almost to her bosom.

The chin elbowed the needles. "Here comes Adeline's daughter."

Bev put her head down and picked up her pace.

"She looks older every time I see her."

"And heavier."

"It's those elastic pants she wears."

"She wouldn't wear them if she could see herself from behind."

Mrs. Scheinberg stopped in front of the sisters and gaped reprovingly at the two hens, but Bev grabbed her elbow and pulled her further down the hall.

"Is that other one a man or a woman, Kathleen? I can't tell."

Mrs. Scheinberg wrenched her elbow free, wheeled around—she could do that now that her legs were stronger—and marched back to the wingback chairs, towering over the idle sisters like a stern schoolmarm. "Listen here, Statler and Waldorf. You should be ashamed of yourselves!"

"It's definitely a man," Kathleen confirmed, talking as if the person in question weren't standing before her to hear for herself.

Mrs. Scheinberg's eyes grew large. Someone was definitely about to break a hip, that much was certain, but the question was who. Kathleen looked ripe for the picking, though she could definitely harvest both rotten apples at the same time.

Bev pulled at her with both hands this time. "C'mon, Arlene. It's not worth it."

"No, Bev, I have something to say!"

But Bev's muscles were none too shabby either, not at least since working out with Candice. She dug in her heels and succeeded in dragging Mrs. Scheinberg out of sight.

"That must be one of those transvestites," she heard Lucy Elaine clucking from somewhere behind them.

"Why, those two—" Mrs. Scheinberg growled.

"—are not in their right minds," Bev finished charitably.

"Oh, don't give me that. They are too in their right minds!"

"Just let it go, Arlene."

For Bev's sake, she tried to, but she resolved to exchange a choice word or two with those old vultures on the way out. Irritated, she pulled at the front of her shirt and tried to think of something pleasant. Pie. Yes, pie! Oh, how she missed pie!

They had reached Adeline's apartment, and Bev reached out to knock on the door but hesitated. "Wait. How are we going to do this?"

"What do you mean?"

"I mean, how are we going to take the bird feeder?"

"We simply take it."

"As in *you* take it, or *I* take it, or—"

"I will take it." Mrs. Scheinberg knocked aggressively on the door. "You deal with your mother."

Bev nodded, taking a deep breath.

They waited a few seconds more, and when no one answered, Bev knocked again. "Mother? It's Beverly." She turned the knob and opened the door just a crack. "Mother? Can I come in? Arlene Scheinberg is with me."

Still no answer.

"She must have her hearing aids out," Bev explained, pushing the door wide open. She stepped into the two-room apartment and, not finding her mother asleep in her recliner, peeked inside the bedroom. She turned back around, her eyebrows raised. "She's not here. Maybe she's playing cards in the dining room."

"This makes things easy." Mrs. Scheinberg crossed the room and opened the sliding door, stepping out onto Adeline's modest patio. The bird feeder was hanging just to the right of the concrete pad, dangling from an iron post that had been stuck into the ground. She dumped the bird seed on the grass and lifted the entire apparatus at once. "I'll walk this thing to the truck," she called over her shoulder to Bev. "You go find Adeline, and I'll meet you back in the lobby."

Bev nodded her head and shut the patio door behind her. Mrs. Scheinberg turned and carried the iron post in one hand and the feeder in the other, crossing a small grassy mall and then stepping onto the asphalt parking lot. She shook her head. This was all so ridiculous, but then—she couldn't help but smile a little—when was the last time she had been able to help anybody like this? A month ago, she couldn't have managed the walk to Adeline's apartment unassisted, let alone hiked across a lawn with a bird feeder and post in hand. She grinned. She didn't really miss pie all that much.

As soon as she lifted the feeder and post into the bed of her truck, Mrs. Scheinberg saw the obvious flaw in her plan. Meeting Bev in the lobby meant facing Kathleen and Lucy Elaine again. Well—she set her chin resolutely—this time, she was entering the war zone with her rifle aimed and ready. She marched across the parking lot and into the lobby, vengeance in her heart, but her guerrilla plans were thwarted by a slip of a woman in a wheelchair.

"I can't find my piece of paper," the woman mewled, grabbing at Mrs. Scheinberg's hand.

Mrs. Scheinberg dutifully stopped but glanced over the troubled woman's head at the sisters murmuring to each other against the wall. "What piece of paper?"

"The one that helps me remember. I'm going to forget."

Those old birds were talking about her, she just knew it. "Forget what?"

"I don't know."

Mrs. Scheinberg patted the woman's hand distractedly. "That's okay. There are many people here who will take care of you even if you forget."

"But my parents are going to be so upset."

Something in the woman's tortured tone tugged at Mrs. Scheinberg's heart. She dropped her sights and settled her gaze on the woman's gray eyes. They were cloudy with both cataracts and tears. There was no way this woman's parents could still be alive.

"They are going to be upset with me, I just know it."

Poor soul! Whatever neuron was misfiring in this woman's white head, it was burdening her conscience. Mrs. Scheinberg's knees still weren't the best, but she knelt down beside the wheelchair all the same. She'd worry about getting back up later. "Do you feel guilty?"

The woman nodded her head, tears slipping down her cheeks.

Mrs. Scheinberg didn't hesitate. Whether the woman was living in the past or present, the truth was still the same. "God sent His Son, Jesus, to die on the cross for your sins," she said. "Whatever you have done, you don't have to feel guilty any more. Jesus was punished in your place, and you are forgiven. He has made everything right, and your heavenly Father is no longer upset with you."

The woman stared back with discerning eyes.

"Would you like to pray?"

She nodded.

"Lord Jesus," Mrs. Scheinberg prayed aloud, folding both of her hands around the woman's cold, frail ones, "thank You for redeeming us. Thank You for taking our sins and giving us Your righteousness. Thank You for bearing our punishment, that we might have peace. Give us faith, which trusts in You, till the end of our days. In Your name we pray. Amen."

Mrs. Scheinberg somehow managed to get back onto her feet, but not before the woman wrapped her arms fiercely around Mrs. Scheinberg's middle.

Bev rounded the corner just then, her cheeks flushed. "Mother was in Ermina Mottel's room. They were bowling on her Wii. Apparently, Mother is the undefeated champion of her wing—Oh, hello there, Hester! I see you've met Arlene."

It took a bit of prying, but Bev finally managed to disentangle Mrs. Scheinberg from Hester's grip.

"She's forgotten almost everything, you know," Kathleen called out across the lobby.

Mrs. Scheinberg looked up, surprised. She had all but forgotten the sisters. Poor old gals. Living in this place was surely not what they had envisioned for their final days. Perhaps they needed to hear the truth as well. She beamed her brightest smile across the room.

"Thankfully, Jesus will never forget her. Nor you, Kathleen."

# CHAPTER TWENTY-SEVEN: UNHOLY WEEK

It had been way too long, and Emily knew it. Thankfully, Pastor knew it too, and he offered to take the kids to Triangle Park after their naps.

"You, Mrs. Fletcher, are going to stay home and sing." He smiled and pulled fondly at one of her curls. "*Really* sing."

Emily didn't argue with the man, and when the front door was finally shut and locked behind George's chubby wave, she wasted no time in pulling stacks of songbooks from her music cabinet: Jerome Kern, Hoagy Carmichael, Richard Rodgers, George Gershwin, all of the American greats. She even grabbed her old Ivor Novello songbook off the shelf and clutched it to her heart, remembering with a sweet sadness a special afternoon spent singing "I Can Give You the Starlight" to a beloved, sainted friend. Oh, how she missed Alice! Well, she would be sure to revive that song in memoriam today, but first, she needed to feel her ribs. She wasn't even sure that she remembered how anymore. She opened the cover of her piano, rolled a bright D-major chord, cheerfully ignored the consequential ache in her hand, sucked in a breath that inflated her very pinky toes, and took off. Scales, slides, sirens, arpeggios, and melismata—oh, they felt so good!—streamed from her mouth and splashed against the far dining room wall, painting the inside of the little house with dazzling, musical colors. Ah, there were her ribs again! She took in another revitalizing breath, enjoying the sensation of her intercostal muscles expanding, and floated up to a shimmering high E-flat.

"How'd you like that one, fuzzy love?" she asked, bending over to scratch behind both of Carrots's floppy ears. Her four-footed audience replied with an approving wiggle of his nose.

Maybe it was the increased intake of oxygen or maybe it was being alone for the first time in what felt like months or maybe it was the simple pleasure of doing something she truly loved. Whatever the reason, Emily couldn't wipe the happy grin off her face. She turned around and reached for Hoagy Carmichael, setting the songbook on the music rack and opening it to "Stardust."

"This is one of my favorites, Carrots."

It had been one of her first husband's favorites too. Peter had played it on her parents' old Baldwin the first night she had brought him home to meet her family. Her father had hummed along and danced with her mother in the kitchen, and Emily had been convinced that night that the world was full of goodwill toward her and all of mankind. That was long before she had learned anything about heart aneurysms and life insurance and burial plots. Now, twenty years the wiser, she struck the first chord and sang of love's refrain in purple, lonely tones. How strange—and cruel—for a song to outlive a man.

Emily grabbed Jerome Kern next. The book automatically fell open to "Why Was I Born?" and she tossed a "you'll love this one" to Carrots over her shoulder. She had always been a sucker for haunting melodies that hung above the clouds before floating back down to earth. They were such a pleasure to sing, and this particular song was the one on which Caroline Bradbury had cut her vocal teeth. How her young student's eyes had brightened when she finished the refrain with breath to spare! Somewhere between the start and the finish, Caroline had discovered that mysterious, invisible connection between a singer's diaphragm and musical phrasing, and the result was pure magic. Emily smiled now, remembering, and reinterpreted the song with indulgent fermatas above each high note, savoring the sensation of those sound waves spinning behind her own mask.

Richard Rodgers was another one of her favorite composers. He adorned his melodies with the most surprising harmonies that never failed to arouse a deep yearning within her soul. "Mister Snow" was her absolute favorite to sing, but today she turned to "If I Loved You," thinking of Charlene. Her neighbor was not unlike the quirky, vulnerable Julie Jordan, the female protagonist of the song's lyrics who falls prey to the passive aggressive charms of an abusive carny. Charlene was currently spending the week at her mother's in Fancy Grove—for better or for worse—and Emily wondered if her young friend would ever truly escape the abusive manipulations, both mental and physical, of those who held her heart captive. She sighed a prayer to the One who orders the universe and leaned in to the augmented, minor, and diminished chords climbing the treble clef. She opened her mouth to sing, but an unexpected motive of sharp, percussive knocks on the door stilled the breath in her lungs. Michael must have forgotten the kids' water bottles. *And apparently the house key*, she sighed, shaking her head. She walked over to the heavy door, unlocked it, and swung it wide open.

"Well, hello, beautiful."

Emily froze. Her husband was nowhere to be seen, but Mark Dawson—all six feet of his foul, clammy self—was leaning both of his forearms on either side of the doorframe, effectively blocking her nearest exit. His white T-shirt looked and smelled as if it had not left his skin for days, and the beltless jeans levitating at his hips appeared to be held on by sheer will alone. His beady black eyes feasted on her face, and the stubble around his cracked lips parted with a sadistic grin. He looked at her as if he owned her. She shivered.

"Why don't you let me in, sweetheart?"

Emily wasted no time in slamming the door shut, leaning all of her weight against the wood. Her hands were shaking with unspent adrenaline, but she somehow managed to work the dead bolt into place. She knew she should pull the curtains closed as well, but the thought of seeing—or being seen by—that awful man again struck terror in her heart. She hid behind the door.

"C'mon, Emily," Dawson hollered, banging his fist on the door and penetrating the wood with his hoarse, ugly voice. "I heard you singin'. Why don't you sing a song for me?"

Her phone! She needed her phone. Where in the world had she left her phone? She put her hands to her face, panicked. She could barely think, she was so scared. *Lord, help!* The phone was in the kitchen. That's right. She had left it in the kitchen.

"We could sing a duet," Dawson rasped, the very sound of his voice a violation. "Just you an' me. Before that goody-goody pastor comes back."

He knew she was alone! Emily shuddered, her entire body quivering like a plucked string. She pushed toward the kitchen, grabbing her phone off the counter and running for the only place where she felt safe in the entire house: the bathroom. She shut the door, locked it, and called the name at the top of the screen.

"Well, hello, beautiful," Pastor answered, the irony almost breaking Emily.

"Michael, I need you to come home," she whispered, her voice trembling. She could now hear Dawson banging on their front window. "*Now*, Michael. I need you to come home *now*. That man is here. Mark Dawson. He's on the porch, and he's trying to get in. Hurry, Michael. I need you here, *right now*."

Pastor's voice was tight. "Where are you?"

"In the bathroom."

"Listen to me. There's a baseball bat under our bed. I want you to go get it—"

"Hurry, Michael!"

"I'm coming, but I want you to go get the bat."

Emily nodded, not thinking that he couldn't see her. She heard him say something, but it sounded jumbled, as if his mouth were far away from the phone. "Emily? Are you there?"

"Yes."

"Stay on the phone with me, okay?" He sounded like he was running. "I'm on my way."

"The children?" she whimpered.

"They're staying at the park. Holleys are here too. Penny's watching them. She's calling 911."

"Hurry, Michael."

"I am. I'm coming. Did you get the bat?"

"No."

"Go get the bat."

She really didn't want to open the bathroom door. Everything had grown strangely quiet out there, and she was afraid Dawson had broken in. For all she knew, he might already be standing outside the bathroom listening to their conversation.

"I'm almost there, all right?" He was panting. "I can see the porch. Dawson's not there, and the door is shut. Windows are closed."

Emily closed her eyes, silently praying.

"All right, I'm on the porch. Hold tight, honey. I'm coming."

She heard the door shake, but it never opened. An unintelligible cry came through the phone.

"Michael? What is it? Are you all right?"

For an agonizing moment, she heard absolutely nothing, but then her husband's voice emerged from the quiet. "I—I'm so sorry, Emily."

"Michael, what's wrong?"

"Nothing's wrong. I mean, I'm okay, and Dawson seems to be gone. I think he fled."

"What is it, then?"

"Well . . ." His voice was meeker than a penitent child's. "I seem to have forgotten the house key. I think I left it in the stroller."

Emily closed her eyes and leaned the back of her head against the bathroom door. *That man!* She didn't know whether to be relieved or enraged. Thankfully, her body made a decision all on its own.

"Emily? Are you there?"

Her ribs expanded once again, only this time, it was a different kind of music that bubbled out of her mouth.

"Honey, can you hear me? I need you to come open the door."

She tried to answer, but she couldn't get out a single word. Her entire body was shaking with hysterical laughter, and it was all she could do to stay upright. Eventually, she gave up on even that and sank deliciously to the floor, the phone falling unheeded in her lap. She'd open the door in a minute.

‖‖‖‖‖‖‖‖‖‖‖‖‖‖‖‖‖‖‖‖‖‖‖‖‖‖‖‖‖‖‖‖‖‖‖‖‖‖‖

Officer Plueth stopped by that evening with some good news.

"Dawson's in a holding cell. We picked him up at Casey's about an hour ago."

Emily, who had run instinctively to the bathroom at the sound of the doorbell, stepped sheepishly back into the living room and settled herself under Pastor's extended arm.

"How'd you find him?" Pastor asked.

"Mel Burl called him in. He was pumping gas and saw Dawson run into the store. Recognized him right away. Vern got there first and caught him shooting up in the bathroom. It was meth."

Emily shivered. They had all suspected drugs from the beginning—Dawson was definitely high on something this afternoon—but she had secretly hoped it wasn't something so hard. Not around Charlene, at least. Their neighbor was already so vulnerable. She had fooled around with marijuana a couple of years ago, but after losing her job at the hospital over the matter, she had cleaned up fast and had been walking the line ever since. Or so they had thought.

"Is he a dealer?" Emily asked.

"Don't know. Doubt it, though. Dealers are usually more interested in making money than getting high."

She could barely get the next words out of her mouth. "Is Charlene a dealer?"

"I don't think so," Plueth shook his head. "Dawson's still the more likely candidate. He has a history in this county."

*So does Charlene*, she thought, looking beseechingly at Pastor. He squeezed her reassuringly.

"What happens now?" Pastor asked.

"We try Dawson on possession."

"Not battery?"

"Charlene's not pressing charges."

Pastor frowned. "What about me? I witnessed the attack. Can I press charges?"

"Technically, yes," Plueth ran a hand over his balding pate, "but I wouldn't recommend it. We'd have to convince the state's attorney's office to process the whole affair as a victimless crime, and I can tell you now, Jim won't go for it."

"What happens if Dawson's convicted?" Emily asked.

"Well, with his prior history, he'll get four to fifteen years."

That didn't sound like nearly long enough to Emily. She was worried about Charlene, but she was also worried about her children and herself.

Pastor kissed Emily's forehead, seeming to sense her unease. "At least we're done with Dawson for now."

But they weren't.

Two days later, Julia presented her mother with the strangest produce from the garden.

"Look, Mommy! We grew sugar!"

Emily gently kicked a soft rubber ball back to a grinning, toothy Becky in the grass before turning to inspect Julia's bounty. The twins had been elbow-deep in dirt all morning, harvesting everything from "gold" rocks to "sausage" sticks and now "sugar." She turned around with a smile on her face, fully expecting to see her daughter's dirty little hands cupped around an insignificant pile of sand, but Julia was proudly dangling a tiny plastic bag of sparkling crystals between her fingers. Emily nearly tripped over her own feet in her haste to grab the bag. "Julia, where did you get this?"

"In the garden, Mommy. We planted flowers, but we grew sugar! George is making a chocolate cake!"

Emily's head snapped up in time to see her son dumping the contents of another one of those sugar packets directly onto the dirt.

"George Gregory!" she screamed, running to the twins' garden plot and grabbing George's wrist in a fit of panic. She shook his arm aggressively until his little fingers opened and dropped the empty bag onto the ground. Distressed by both the noise and the shaking, he began to cry.

"Did you eat any of the sugar?" Emily hollered, equally as terrorized as the boy. "Answer me, son!"

"No-o-o-o-o!" George wailed, throwing his head back and bawling into the sky like an injured dog.

*Thank you, God!*

Emily picked him up and held him tightly in her arms, burying her face in his hair. "Okay, okay, okay," she murmured quietly, shedding a few tears of her own. She felt like her heart was going to jump out of her chest. She took in a few deep breaths to calm both herself and her son. "I'm sorry, Georgie," she sang, careful to keep her tone light. "I'm so, so sorry. Did I hurt you? I didn't mean to hurt you. Mommy was just afraid. That sugar is poison. We *never* eat sugar in the garden."

George continued to cry his displeasure into her neck, and she gladly bore his grief, rocking him back and forth and shushing him with hummed kisses and tender, grateful, prayerful touches. When she turned to look at Julia, her daughter was staring up at both of them with big, round, apprehensive eyes. Becky, blissfully ignorant of any sugar—poisoned or not—was smiling and shrieking and slapping the rubber ball with both palms of her hands. To her, the noise and motion was just a game.

"Come here, Julia," Emily smiled, extending her hand like an invitation. "Show me where you found the sugar. It's okay, honey. You didn't do anything wrong. I just want to see it."

Julia submissively took her mother's hand and led her to the far end of the garden. Sure enough, there, about a foot and a half down in the loose dirt, was a small stash of about ten sugar packets. Emily didn't know very much about such things, but she would bet her Hoagy Carmichael songbook that they were looking at crystal meth.

"Thank you, Julia," she said, turning back around and redirecting them all toward the house. She glanced up at her neighbor's kitchen window, certain she saw a flash of movement there. Charlene had moved back in yesterday morning after hearing of

Dawson's arrest. "Would you please be a big girl and take Becky's hand? Let's go inside and have a snack. Shall we pop some popcorn, George?" Her son, worn out from all the crying, sighed his approval against her shoulder. "Maybe we can even ask Daddy and Officer Plueth and Miss Charlene to join us."

ıııııııııııııııııııııııııııııııııııııı

"It's meth all right," Plueth confirmed an hour later, coming in from the backyard after questioning their neighbor. Pastor was walking her back to her house. "Charlene swears it's Dawson's, but she admits to burying it herself."

"Do you believe her?" Emily asked. She wasn't sure she'd believe anything Charlene said ever again.

"I do."

Emily shook her head, unconvinced. Charlene had put her children in danger with her foolishness, and she felt bitter and angry about it all. "She's lied in the past."

"But she shows no symptoms of using. Or selling, for that matter. And she's not exactly swimming in drug money, is she?" Plueth tucked his notepad and pen away in a pocket of his blue shirt. "I'm thinking the girl's just caught in the wake of a boatload of bad decisions."

Emily didn't argue with that.

"Regardless, Vern dusted the packets for fingerprints. We'll know for sure by this afternoon."

Emily thanked Bradbury's faithful civil servant and showed him to the door, her mind wandering across the driveway. "Is it okay for me to talk to Charlene?"

"Why, Mrs. Fletcher," Plueth smiled kindly, his eyes full of knowledge and wisdom beyond her own experience, "I have been hoping and praying for that very thing these last twenty minutes."

He touched his fingers respectfully to his forehead and was gone.

An hour later, after she had put the kids down for naps and promised her husband that she would keep to Charlene's backyard where he could safely see her from the parsonage kitchen window, Emily walked across the driveway to knock on their neighbor's back door. The rank smell of cigarette smoke threatened to choke her as she ascended the back stoop, but she determinedly set her chin and raised her knuckles to the storm door. It opened before she could knock, as if Charlene had been waiting for her, and the woman was crying.

"I'm sorry, Emily," she snuffled, her eyes red and puffy. "I saw what happened with George today, and I'm so sorry."

No Christian's spite can burn bright under the rain of true repentance, but Emily wasn't quite ready to concede her fury. Not just yet. She stoked her blaze of anger with thoughts of those insidious packets of meth in her sweet children's hands. To endanger her children like that! Charlene was a fool, and that was being charitable. Emily crossed her arms defiantly over her chest, shielding her smoldering heart from her neighbor's wet contrition like an umbrella. "George thought it was sugar. He almost ate it."

Charlene shuddered at the thought and buried her face in her hands.

"He could have died."

"*I* should die," Charlene confessed, her words spilling through her fingers like liquid remorse. Emily held her breath against the spate, but it swirled and pooled directly over her already dwindling fire. Black embers steamed noisily in her ears, and she stood for a long, sober moment—divinely doused—observing her neighbor's obvious distress. She let loose a harried sigh and turned, dropping her seat unceremoniously on the top step.

"'None is righteous,'" she muttered, "'no, not one.'"

"What?" Charlene asked, following her out onto the stoop and letting the storm door swing shut. She was still crying.

"We all deserve to die," Emily restated, preaching more to herself than to anyone else. She sat with her chin in her hands, still fuming, but she yielded a begrudging pat on the concrete step, indicating where Charlene should sit. Her neighbor was wearing a shirt with actual sleeves this time. Emily hadn't even realized that the woman owned clothes that extended beyond her undergarments. "Just answer one question for me."

Charlene sat down tentatively and nodded.

"Why'd you do it?"

Her neighbor shook her head and hugged her knees, staring straight ahead. "I was afraid."

"Of Mark?"

"Of myself."

Emily thought on this for a moment. Maybe Charlene wasn't as much of a fool as she had thought.

"It was dumb," Charlene said. "I see that now, but I needed it gone. Your yard is safe. *You* are safe. I knew the drugs couldn't touch me over there."

"But they touched my children."

Charlene shuddered again, burying her head in her arms. "I'm so sorry, Emily. I'll never forgive myself!"

Emily closed her eyes and rubbed her face with her hands. There was no getting around it. Either she believed in God's Word, or she didn't. She sighed—stubbornly resistant to the end—and stood to extend a hand to this woman for whom Christ died. "C'mon."

"What?" Charlene looked up, confused.

"Come with me."

"Where?"

"To real safety."

"I don't understand."

"Come on over to the church."

"Why?"

"Because God promises that 'if we confess our sins, He is faithful and just to forgive us our sins and cleanse us from all unrighteousness.'"

"What does that mean?"

"It means," she pulled Charlene to her feet, "that God is forgiving."

Charlene looked skeptical. "Even of me?"

"Even of *me*," Emily choked, her throat suddenly tightening. She gazed into her neighbor's eyes and saw the reflection of herself, an angry woman who hated and despised the vulnerable and the weak. *God, forgive me!* She quickly blinked her stinging eyes and smiled. It was easier than she had thought. The truth was setting her free. "You'll feel better once you've talked to Pastor Fletcher about all of this. That's what he's here for, you know. To listen and to talk and to help."

Charlene allowed herself to be led down the driveway.

"We'll grab Pastor from the parsonage first, and then you and he can go over to the church for a good, long chat." Emily grinned effortlessly now, her previous fire gone completely cold. "But come on back over to the parsonage when you're done. The twins want to make a chocolate cake after naps. But we'll use *real* sugar this time!"

## Chapter Twenty-Eight: Home on the Plain

||||||||||||||||||||||||||||||||||||||||||||||||||||||

It had rained the entire trip home, but Mrs. Scheinberg didn't care. Her smile dazzled like the sun behind the wheel of the Grand Marquis, for Blaine Maler—the son of her heart—was stretched out comfortably in the passenger seat beside her.

"You're not going to believe it when you see your bathroom."

"*My* bathroom?" Blaine asked, tossing back a white cheddar cheese curd. They had stopped at Amish Acres in Nappanee for some broasted country chicken and to pick up some necessary provisions for the drive home. "You mean I have my own now?"

"The new house has two bathrooms." She munched on a wasabi pea from the open bag in her lap. "Yours is in the hall, and mine's in my room."

"A master bath? You're moving up in the world, Arlene."

"Well, it's twice the cleaning," she reminded him, "but I like the exercise."

Blaine playfully held up the back of his hand to her forehead.

"Oh, stop it," she smirked, swatting at him, almost spilling her bag of peas. "Just wait and see. All kinds of things have changed on the home front."

Blaine's smile dimmed almost imperceptibly. "Change is over-rated sometimes."

Mrs. Scheinberg instantly regretted her words, wishing she had put the matter a different way. It wasn't that Blaine was oversensi-tive to change—the young man had proven to be quite resilient to life's painfully fickle personality over the years—but he had en-dured the most shattering of alterations to his home just six years before. His father, after twenty-plus years of marriage, abandoned his wife, son, and daughter for a homosexual lover, and Blaine alone was left behind to pick up the pieces of his broken family.

"You're staring."

"What?"

"You're staring at me," Blaine repeated.

"I am not!"

"Yes, you are. And you're psychoanalyzing me. I know you, Arlene."

Mrs. Scheinberg opened her mouth to deny it, but then she immediately closed her lips tight. She and Blaine had always been straight shooters with each other—that was part of their natural camaraderie—and anything less than the truth sat like foreign matter between them. She sighed, irritated, her voice resuming its familiar snark. "Well, what do you expect? I'm an old woman. I read nonverbal cues, even when they're not there."

Blaine threw back his head and laughed.

"And don't be so touchy," she growled. "Not all change is bad, and you know it. I'm telling you, you're going to love the new bath-room sink. It comes up to my ribs. I bet you won't even have to bend over to spit out your toothpaste."

"Well, that'll be a change, for sure." Blaine's voice was still light with laughter. "I never could see my forehead in that ancient bath-room mirror of yours. Though I'm going to miss the old footed bathtub with the rubber stopper."

"I kept the bathtub."

"You did?" Blaine was a world-weary twenty-six-year-old, but every once in a while, the eager glow of a schoolboy lit up his face. "In the guest bath?"

"No sense in paying for a new one when the old one works perfectly fine."

"Well, that's debatable, I think."

Mrs. Scheinberg frowned. "That tub still works!"

"If it works so 'fine,' why didn't you put it in your new, fancy master bath?"

"Because," she stared straight ahead, suddenly sheepish, "the master bath came with a jacuzzi."

"Oh, well, then." Blaine chuckled. "I see how it is."

Mrs. Scheinberg couldn't keep the smug, satisfied smile off of her face. Blaine's happiness did that to her. "And my new stove is gas. I can boil a pot of water in four minutes."

"As long as it has an oven for baking your cinnamon rolls, I'll be impressed."

"Well," Mrs. Scheinberg tilted her head, "I'm gluten-free now, didn't I tell you?"

"Only about eight times."

"I thought I'd try making you a new roll recipe while you're home. It uses tapioca flour and—"

"Nope," Blaine said, his mouth around another curd. "I haven't come all this way for some wimpy, pudding-flour substitute. I want the real thing. *With* cream cheese frosting."

"But I'm telling you, Blaine Maler, my knees don't hurt nearly as bad since I took out wheat! You should try it."

"Why? My knees feel fine."

Mrs. Scheinberg sighed, letting the matter rest. It didn't really matter anyway. The last thing Blaine needed in life was to restrict food of any kind. The boy was as thin as an electric line—she was convinced he only ever ate in her presence—but he could down an entire pan of her rolls in one sitting. She smiled proudly at the thought. Well, she would fatten him up over the next four days, even if she had to bake him a new pan of cinnamon rolls every morning. She turned on her blinker and veered west onto 1000 North.

"What's going on there?" Blaine asked, squinting through the wet windows at The Offense. The east pasture was almost unidentifiable without its trademark rusting machines.

"Oh, Max is selling."

"What? His tractors?"

"Among other things."

She gunned the car, emptying the road of its puddles. She was eager to show off the far western end of the mile. "Okay, now, close your eyes. I'm serious, Blaine. Close them. And no peeking! I don't want you to look until I've pulled into the driveway. The view of the house is best from—" She stopped short, both in word and in deed. Without even thinking, she braked hard in the middle of the road, throwing both her and Blaine's heads forward and then back against the headrests.

"Whoa!" Blaine called, stabilizing himself with his hands on the passenger door and dash. His eyes were still obediently closed. "Brakes a little touchy in the rain?"

She didn't answer. She couldn't.

"Can I open my eyes now?"

How would she ever—?

"Arlene?"

She was crying now, and the sound of her sniffling jolted Blaine's eyes open.

"What is it? What's wrong?"

She shook her head, unable to explain. She merely pointed a crooked finger out his window, and Blaine turned in his seat to follow her gaze. There, standing guard in the gentle rain around an empty concrete pad, were six tall support timbers holding up what appeared to be the top ring and roof of Dean's old grain bin. The corrugated metal was misshapen in a few places, as if someone had carefully hammered back into place the ugly twists and turns made by the tornado, but the roof's familiar weather-worn texture and rusted color were unmistakable.

"What is it?" Blaine asked.

"It's," Mrs. Scheinberg sobbed, strangely overwhelmed by both gratitude and grief at the same time, "a gazebo. I think."

The concrete pad looked reddish, as if it had been capped and stamped to look like a patio, and two washtubs filled with yellow and burgundy mums decorated the smaller, rectangular pad where the bin's fan had previously sat. Mrs. Scheinberg was thankful to see that the bridal veil bushes she had planted after Dean's death were still bordering the plot, but the part of the charming scene that touched her the most was the rough-hewn, two-seater swing hanging from a rafter in the middle of the homemade shelter.

"You didn't do this?" Blaine asked.

Mrs. Scheinberg shook her head.

"Then who?"

Her face scrunched up in another appreciative sob. The answer to that question had been apparent to her from the first moment her eyes beheld it. She mutely gestured eastward toward Max's property.

"Max?" Blaine was looking at her tenderly, curiously. He was not oblivious to the reasons her present emotion was running so high—she had told him years ago about Dean's death, and of course, he knew about the recent tornado—but he was not up-to-date on the significant part her neighbor played in either story. "Max did this?"

She nodded her head, sniveling.

"And you like it?"

She kept nodding.

"Well, then," Blaine smiled, leaning back in his seat as if ready for another trip, "we probably should turn around and tell him, don't you think?"

||||||||||||||||||||||||||||||||||||||||

Blaine waited in the car while she stepped out into the mud and waded across the yard. The rain had dwindled to a drizzle, but everything on the ground—dirt, gravel, and sod—was squishy and generous, sharing its brown abundance with her parched canvas shoes and cotton socks. She should have grabbed her boots from the house first, but no matter.

"Max?" she called, looking around the empty lot. Her neighbor's truck was in the drive, so she knew he was there. She highly doubted he was passing the gray afternoon in Don Kull's old camper, so she headed toward The Offense. One quick peek in the open pig pen revealed only a sloppy, snorting, shifting mess, so she moved on to the southwest corner of the barn and knocked on the wooden door. It was closed, but the top half, separated from the latched bottom, bounced precariously against the frame at her touch. She swung it open and stared, shocked into silence, at the tidy, pleasant workshop within. The rectangular stall smelled of shaved wood and was illuminated by three bare bulbs hanging from the ceiling. Brackets attached to the southernmost wall supported stacks of various cuts of wood, and a large pegboard hanging on the wall opposite of the door boasted more woodworking tools than Mrs. Scheinberg could call by name. To her left, a high counter topped with jars of screws and bolts and washers ran the entire length of the floor, and various electric-powered saws and planers were pushed neatly underneath. Dutch was lying comfortably in a pile of sawdust that had been swept into the southeast corner of the shop, and Max was down on one knee, screwing bolts into the seat of a picnic table sitting in the middle of the room. Both of them looked up in surprise at the door's opening. Mrs. Scheinberg stared back, confused and somewhat awed.

"You saved Dean's bin" was all she could think to say.

Max was quick to look back down at the table, effectively hiding his face under his cap, but the tops of his exposed ears grew red. The only sound Mrs. Scheinberg heard for the next few moments was the clicking of Max's ratchet, but when his hands had stalled, he pushed himself back up onto his feet and mumbled, "Well, you's said ya missed it."

As she watched Max walk across the room to put away his tool in a red Craftsman cabinet next to the pegboard, she was struck by the man's obvious embarrassment. She had always thought him to be proud and insensitive, but in this pine-scented room, he seemed so humble and thoughtful. Soulful, even. The gazebo definitely revealed a creative side to Max that she had not known existed, and his careful attentions to her physical needs over the past few months—no, years—were unparalleled. Sure, he wasn't good with words, but had she ever really given him a chance to speak past her own bitter accusations and rejections? Come to think of it, she was the one who usually instigated and perpetuated their squabbles. Maybe Max wasn't really mean and lazy like she thought. Maybe he was just reclusive and awkward and shy. Yes, he was like this barn—neglected and worn on the outside but warm and artistic on the inside—and she had terribly misjudged the both of them. She bent her head in shame.

"I came to say thank you, Max," she said, looking back up at the dear man, tears streaming down her face, "and I don't just mean for the beautiful gazebo you made out of the wreckage of my husband's bin." She was full-on crying now, but she persisted. There was something she needed to say. She'd been building up to saying it all summer long, and now was the time. "Thank you for coming to get me after the tornado. I needed you. And," her voice broke, "thank you for sitting with me and Dean by the bin. I'm so sorry I couldn't remember. I was numb and such a mess. I still am, apparently. I'm sorry, Max. Will you please forgive me for being such a wretch?"

Max looked genuinely alarmed at her bawling. "Crawfish, Arlene! Ya ain't gonna faint er nothin', are ya? You's skinnier now an' all, but my arthritis done froze ma hands, what wi' the rain an' workin' wood all day, and I ain't sure's I ken lift—"

Mrs. Scheinberg snorted a laugh through her tears. The man really was terrible with words. Thankfully, overcommunication was her spiritual gift. "I'm all right, man. Just penitent."

"Peni-what?"

"Penitent. Sorry. I'm *sorry*, Max." She wiped at her face with her hands, still dangerously close to weeping or laughing—she wasn't sure which. "I'm asking for your forgiveness."

His ears burned bright red again. He looked at the ground, lifting his cap only to immediately replace it on his head. "Tha's decent o' ya, Arlene."

She stared at him, waiting for his full pardon. He didn't say anything else, though, and as she watched him fumble nervously with his shirttail and then his left jeans pocket, she realized that— in his own heathen way—he had already given it. Well, she would work on the words thing with him later, and then she would tell him about sin and Christ's atonement and His promise of forgiveness, life, and salvation. Max would believe it all, of course. The man worked with wood. How could he deny the good work of a fellow Carpenter? Yes, Max would be sitting next to her in church before the month was out, she was certain of it. "Join us for supper?"

"What?"

"Join us for supper?" she repeated. "Me and Ceci. And Blaine. He's home from graduate school for a few days."

"Oh, well—"

"We're grilling burgers and sweet potato packets. And there will be fudgy babies."

"What?"

"Fudgy babies. It's my friend's recipe. Dates and walnuts ground up with—oh, never mind. Just be there at six. And bring Dutch. But on a chain. Chicken's not on the menu."

⁞⁞⁞⁞⁞⁞⁞⁞⁞⁞⁞⁞⁞⁞⁞⁞⁞⁞⁞⁞⁞⁞⁞⁞⁞

Supper was a simple affair, at least that's what she had originally planned. Selfishly, she wanted to keep Blaine all to herself—he was home for only four days, after all—but there was no way that she could keep sweet Mary from coming over to see him. And Emily had given her that quiet, beseeching look of hers when she'd heard Blaine would be home before dark. And Robbie missed his old piano teacher, of course, and she supposed the Davises should be invited as well, seeing as how they kept Ceci for her while she was gone. In the end, she decided to just go ahead and invite everyone over for a proper homecoming and be done with it. Then, she justified to herself, she could keep Blaine home every morning and afternoon for the rest of the week.

Max was the first to arrive. Blaine opened the red front door—Mrs. Scheinberg had chosen the cheerful color herself—and greeted him warmly like an old friend. The Davises pulled up next, Bev and Ceci yapping in perfect unison, and the Joneses spilled out of their SUV, all of them rushing Blaine to hug him at once. Evan followed his family a little more slowly, shaking Blaine's hand and extending a bouquet of fresh-cut flowers to the hostess. The Fletchers, having picked up Mary along the way, squeezed into the living room last. Emily started crying the moment she saw Blaine, and the wattage of Mary's smile threatened to overload Mrs. Scheinberg's new circuit breaker. The Fletchers' neighbor woman, Charlene, was with them too, and the thin woman hastily snuffed out a cigarette in the cement planter on the front step to take Blaine's extended hand. The twins trailed behind, all big-eyed and silent—they barely knew Blaine from a stranger—but it was Pastor Fletcher's greeting that filled Mrs. Scheinberg's heart to the point of bursting.

"Well, look who's here!" Pastor Fletcher grinned, reaching out his free hand for a hearty shake. Becky was holding tightly to his other. "Welcome home, Seminarian Maler!"

## Chapter Twenty-Nine: The Good, the Mad, and the Ugly

ıııııııııııııııııııııııııııııııııııııııııııııı

"Will you be preaching on Sunday, Blaine?" Bev smiled cheerfully over the top of her cheeseburger.

"Oh, not yet," Pastor Fletcher answered for him, lowering his fork and shaking his head. He leaned forward to better see Bev at the far end of the makeshift table. Mrs. Scheinberg and Blaine had laid a large piece of plywood over two sawhorses in the middle of her new attached garage and covered it with a flowered, cotton cloth. "Once he's had Homiletics I, he'll be ready. Maybe we can invite him down to preach over Thanksgiving break."

"More roasted sweet potatoes, anyone?" Mrs. Scheinberg asked, entering the garage from the house with a replenished platter in her hands. George raised his fork in the air.

"Finish what's on your plate first, son," Emily quietly monitored. George lowered his fork and attacked his potatoes.

"How was summer Greek, Blaine?" Evan asked, his eyes watching George with interest from across the table.

Blaine had just taken a bite of broccoli salad, but he politely covered his mouth, quickly chewed, and swallowed. "Good."

"Good?" Mrs. Scheinberg scoffed, setting the platter down in front of Irv. "More than good, I'd say! Blaine got the highest marks in his class, *and* the professor asked him to be the tutor for next year's students."

Evan tore his eyes from George's feasting and nodded approvingly. "I can't say that I'm surprised. Greek is a language of logic, and you've always been an ace at music theory. Hebrew may be a different story, however."

"Oh, Evan." Mrs. Scheinberg sat down in the empty seat next to Blaine. "Don't be such a sourpuss. He'll do great at Hebrew!"

"Evan's right," Pastor chimed in. "Rarely is a man good at reading both. I had an Old Testament professor once say that he had always been a doodler, and he was pretty sure he was good at reading Hebrew because it looked like someone had doodled backwards."

Blaine laughed appreciatively, a lock of his black hair breaking away from the pack and straying down his forehead. Mrs. Scheinberg liked this new cut of his. It was a bit long on top, but the hair just above and behind his ears was cropped extra short. It was a bit old-school—groomed but roguish—much like her father's hair in an old snapshot she had of him standing next to his plane in World War II.

"Do you get to play the piano very often?" Emily asked. She tore her burger and set the smaller portion on Becky's plate.

"Not much," he said.

"How about the organ?" Evan asked.

"Kantor has me playing every month in chapel."

Evan nodded his approval.

"What about you, Robbie?" Blaine suddenly turned to his left to look down the table at his former student. "Are you still playing?"

"Yes."

"Every day?"

"Grandpa makes him!" Alison reported.

"He does not!" Robbie threw his sister a hot look. "I practice all on my own."

"Grandpa *bribes* him, is more like it," Rebecca winked at her son.

Robbie's face burned. This embarrassed him for some reason.

Blaine raised his eyebrows questioningly at Evan. The elderly man took his time sipping his water.

"I told Robbie that studying and practicing are his primary jobs in high school," Evan shrugged. "I simply fund his employment."

"Can you be *my* grandpa?" Jeremy grinned.

"Would anyone like more quinoa?" Mrs. Scheinberg asked, rising from her seat to pass some of the heavier dishes around. "Sliced tomatoes?"

"Yes, pease," George said.

"Which one, honey? Tomatoes or quinoa?"

George stared up at his godmother with big, entreating eyes. "Yes."

"George," Emily intervened, "you've already had seconds. Does your tummy say stop?"

"George's tummy never says stop," Julia explained for the benefit of everyone at the table.

"Neither does mine," Bev sighed.

Emily leaned across the table toward her son. "Are you full?"

George shook his head.

"Then you can have one slice of tomato, but that's it."

George eagerly lifted up his plate, and Mrs. Scheinberg sneakily forked two slices onto it. Emily graciously pretended not to notice.

"Your new gazebo is lovely, Arlene," Rebecca admired.

"Oh yes!" Bev bubbled, coming alive. "It's darling! It looks like something from a magazine. And you did such a good job keeping it a secret too. I had *no idea* you were putting it in. You are such a tease, Arlene. Who was your contractor? Ronald? Hank?"

"Max built it."

Everyone looked up and gaped at Max. His ears grew red.

"Really?" Bev asked. "Why, Max Mauer, you've been holding out on us. Since when have you been making gazebos?"

"How'd you do it?" Irv asked.

Max looked up, setting his elbows comfortably on the edge of the plywood table. He seemed to have no trouble meeting another pair of eyes as long as it looked at him from under a seed corn hat. Mrs. Scheinberg took note of that. "I foun' Arlene's ol' bin in ma north forty, day after Abigail."

*Oh, for the love of wit! That* ridiculous *name!* Mrs. Scheinberg couldn't hold back a swift eye roll.

"Most of it were torn clean 'part," Max continued, unawares, "but the top piece were only twisted. Thought it'd make a nice shade spot." He gallantly didn't make any mention of Mrs. Scheinberg's agony over the bin's having been destroyed. She took careful note of that too. "That ol' concrete weren't bein' used fer nothin', so's I drug what I could o' tha bin to ma barn an' shaped it fer a shelter. The timbers're cemented in the groun'."

Irv nodded, understanding.

"Can you make us one, Max?" Bev asked.

"He makes picnic tables too," Mrs. Scheinberg added. She noticed Max's head turning her way out of the corner of her eye, but she was careful to keep her face forward and her voice neutral. No sense in giving the shy man a chance to refute, not when good business was about to be made. "And swings."

"Really?" Rebecca asked. "What kind of swings? I've been wanting to replace the one on our front porch. It rotted out this year." Her eyes brightened. "Hey, you don't by any chance make swings out of tree branches, do you? You know, with the bark still on? I love that rustic look!"

"If it's made of wood," Mrs. Scheinberg answered, "he can do it."

Max was staring openly at her now, baffled.

"Rebecca, I've got a cherry tree that needs to come out," Evan said. "You could have the wood."

"What do you think, Max?" Mrs. Scheinberg prodded, finally meeting his eyes and smiling. She couldn't help but toss him the tiniest of winks.

Max stared at her another long moment, clearly bewildered, before turning toward Rebecca and shrugging his shoulders. "S'pose so."

"That settles it then," Rebecca clapped, elbowing Jeremy playfully in the arm. "Happy anniversary to me!"

Jeremy pretended to look put out, but his dancing eyes gave him away. He leaned across his wife to say, "I'll catch you before we leave tonight, Max. You know, to settle the terms. Seems my wife has made up her mind."

Mrs. Scheinberg had made up her mind too. If Max was tired of farming, then he could very well make a living working with wood. He just didn't know it yet.

llllllllllllllllllllllllllllllllllllllllll

"Hey, where's Candice tonight?" Bev asked as everyone was getting ready to leave. "I thought she was coming."

Mrs. Scheinberg shook her head. "She's in Champaign, visiting Caroline."

"Again? Wasn't she just there last week?"

Mrs. Scheinberg gave Bev a knowing, exasperated look. "She's batting a thousand when it comes to weekend visits for the fall semester."

"Poor Caroline," Davie Jones mumbled, overhearing.

"Hey, now," Rebecca said, stepping alongside of her eldest son to wrap a motherly arm around his shoulders. "Poor Candice is more like it! I think I'll probably do the same thing once you move off to college."

"Please," Davie entreated, "don't."

The teenager, however, couldn't keep a small, pleased smile from playing at the corners of his mouth, and his mother saw it. She rewarded him with a kiss on his cheek before he could pull away.

"Well," Bev sang, stepping over to the guest of honor to give him a hug. "It's so good to see you, Blaine! Though I have to admit," she suddenly frowned, "I'm a little disappointed."

Mrs. Scheinberg looked up, alarmed. Bev was staring openly at Blaine's forehead. *Lord, help!* Surely the woman wouldn't make a scene about his eyebrow ring. Not tonight. Not in public.

"I had hoped you'd be wearing a clerical collar."

She sighed, relieved.

"Not until Liturgics," Blaine explained. "I'll start that fall quarter. Maybe I can wear a clerical over Thanksgiving, like Pastor said."

"But you can still wear Jesus!" Julia ran up and pointed toward the crucifix hanging around Blaine's neck. "Anyone can!"

Bev's face blanched, and Mrs. Scheinberg fought the urge to go run interference. She knew her friend. Bev, on principle, didn't like eyebrow rings, but she was positively averse to crucifixes. Jesus was to be worshiped, not worn.

"Daddy wears Jesus too!"

"I do," Pastor grinned and nodded.

Bev had to close her eyes and lean against Irv to cope.

"Can I see?" George asked, climbing up Blaine's leg to better see Christ's corpus.

"George," Emily gently admonished, "Mr. Maler is not a tree."

Blaine leaned down so that George could better see.

"Daddy sometimes puts Jesus in his pocket," Julia explained, "over his heart."

"Really, now," Bev clucked, her eyes popping open with a wild cackle. "All of this nonsense talk! Jesus is alive and sitting at the right hand of God. He's not in any pocket."

"He is too! He's in Daddy's pocket, right now!"

"Julia." Emily's voice was low, a certain warning. "Don't shout at Mrs. Davis."

Julia obediently lowered her voice to a whisper. "I like to see Jesus on my crosses."

"I do too," Blaine whispered back.

"Well," Bev was not whispering, and her cheeks were deepening in color to match the shade of Mrs. Scheinberg's front door. "I think crucifixes are disrespectful."

Blaine looked up from his young companions, surprised. "Why?"

"Because Jesus didn't stay dead on the cross."

"Actually, He did," Mrs. Scheinberg pointed out wearily. She really didn't want to do this. Not now. Not tonight. "In fact, He was so dead, Joseph of Arimathea had to take Him down, remember?"

"That's not what I mean," Bev frowned. "What I'm saying is, Jesus didn't *stay* dead, you see? He rose on Easter morning."

Mrs. Scheinberg sighed. They *were* going to do this, apparently, and just as all of her happy guests were leaving. Hell hath no fury—or persistence, it seemed—as a Lutheran scorned. "But an empty cross isn't a sign of the resurrection, Bev. It never has been. It's always been a sign of Jesus' death, just like a crucifix. And they're both perfectly fine pieces of art, so leave it"—*and Blaine*, she thought—"be!"

"But surely you don't think we should keep Jesus on the cross or on any chains or in any pockets when He didn't stay there?"

"Well," Mrs. Scheinberg countered, "Jesus didn't stay sleeping in the manger either, but you leave Him lying on the hay day after day in that nativity on your TV stand."

"That's different."

"How come?"

"The nativity reminds us that Jesus came to save us."

"And the crucifix doesn't?"

Bev was looking flustered. "It doesn't tell the whole story, Arlene!"

"Neither does an empty cross, yet you hang one on your living room wall!"

"Stop mixing up my words!" Bev cried, wringing her hands. She was beginning to look upset. Mrs. Scheinberg wondered if they shouldn't take this conversation outside, away from the children and Max and Charlene. This kind of talk was made up of too much meat and not enough milk for their stomachs. "You know I can't think as fast as you. I just don't like crucifixes, all right? They're Catholic, and I'm not Catholic! I'm Lutheran, and so is Blaine."

"Oh, for the love of Good Friday, Bev!" Mrs. Scheinberg clipped.

"Blaine," Pastor said, his voice a quiet gavel in the debate. He had been leaning against the kitchen doorway, listening. "Why do you wear a crucifix?"

Everyone in the room turned expectantly toward the new seminarian.

Blaine reached up to finger his eyebrow ring, almost sending Bev into a fit of shakes. Seeing her revulsion, he sensitively dropped his hand and said, "I wear a crucifix because an empty cross is a symbol of death. *My* death. I am the one who deserves to die on that cross, and the devil knows it."

Bev opened her mouth to speak, but Irv silenced her with his hand on her arm.

"Whenever I look at an empty cross, Satan whispers, 'You should be up there.'" Blaine's face darkened slightly. Mrs. Scheinberg recognized that shadow. It had passed over his face earlier in the car when she had mentioned change. "When I look at a crucifix, though, I see that there is no room for me on that cross. Jesus is already hanging there in my place. He bore the punishment for my sin, once and for all. He died my death, and I need never be afraid of Satan or sin or death or . . . *anything* ever again."

Pastor pushed away from the doorway and nodded. "He sounds Lutheran to me."

Then he moved toward the front door to leave, silently indicating that everyone else should too.

Bev was upset, but she was also kind and thoughtful and seasoned. She pulled herself together like the experienced church woman she was and smiled brightly for the good of Blaine and her hostess and everyone else in the room. "Well, I don't know about all of you, but I sure have missed choir! Summer break is wonderful—don't get me wrong—but I'm beginning to miss the balcony."

"We start up again a week from tonight, right?" Emily asked, quickly taking the bait and turning toward their director. "Seven fifteen?"

"Yes," Mary nodded.

"The boys and I can't wait!" Rebecca added, quickly scooting her crew out the door. "Davie's going to have to miss the first rehearsal because of a leadership camp, but he should be able to join us the week after that."

"Did you find an accompanist for this year?" Evan asked, stopping in the doorway.

"Yes," Mary said. "Henry Ball, a piano major at BC. He'll be a junior just like Blaine was when he first started playing at Zion."

"Hard shoes to fill," Evan said, patting Blaine's arm affectionately before stepping out the door.

"You know, Mary," Bev cheered, mostly recovered by now, "you should apply for the church secretary position. You're already our choir director. You might as well be our secretary too."

Mrs. Scheinberg grimaced. If anyone knew how hard choir directors and church secretaries worked, they would never wish this double plight on any sister in Christ. In fact, no human being should ever be expected to suffer such overexposure to the people of God. Well, except for pastors, and—Mrs. Scheinberg looked ruefully at Emily—maybe his saint of a wife.

"I like being a librarian," Mary said, effectively ending the discussion.

But Bev, however improved, was still off her game that night, and wisdom had failed to show up to coach. "Well, you might as well get used to being in the church office, Mary. You know what happened to our last choir director." She gave Mary and Blaine meaningful looks, each in their turn. "She ended up marrying a pastor!"

Mrs. Scheinberg had no choice. She face-planted directly into her palm. It was that or plant her palm directly in Bev's face.

*For the love of subtlety!*

## Chapter Thirty: The Hamburg Confession

||||||||||||||||||||||||||||||||||||||||||||||||||||||||||||

Blaine volunteered to drive Mary home in Mrs. Scheinberg's truck.

"I'm sorry about Bev's comment," he apologized, pulling into the driveway of the Mulberry property. He turned off the ignition, but Mary didn't say anything. She rarely did when it came to these things. Instead, she opened the passenger side door and silently climbed down from the truck.

"So," he hurried down from the driver's side and quickly shut the door, trotting to catch up with her on the sidewalk. "Are you upset?"

"No."

"How do you feel, then?"

Mary shrugged. "Fine. Should I not be?"

"I don't know. Do you feel all right?"

"You just asked me that."

"Well . . ." Blaine wished she would stop and look at him. "I'm concerned."

Mary stepped up onto the porch of the brick bungalow and fished for her key in her purse. "Look, I'm not going to have a seizure or anything, okay?"

He couldn't tell if she was teasing or not. "Have you had any seizures this month?"

Mary finally looked up at him, but it wasn't a look he necessarily savored. "Why are you asking?"

"I'm just curious. You and I haven't talked since you started the new medication. We're friends, remember? I care about you." He suddenly grinned. "You're my godmother."

She wasn't really, but Blaine liked to tease her about it whenever she looked like she was struggling. Four years ago, the Sunday before he had moved to Boston for his masters in piano performance, Mary had stood up in church to witness his Baptism. Mrs. Scheinberg had too, as well as his grandmother and Evan Ebner. Even his mother had made the trip to Bradbury for the service.

Mary's defense lowered just a centimeter.

"So? Have you had any seizures this month?"

She turned toward the door with her key. "None that I know of."

Blaine didn't miss the hint of cynicism in Mary's tone. She had suffered a very public tonic-clonic seizure at a New Year's Eve party last December—her first in years—but unless someone was with her to witness an impaired partial seizure, she could never be sure if she was having one. Doctors tried monitoring her brain activity through tests and sleep studies, but Mary didn't always want to know the results. She was stubborn in her determination to live on her own, and statistics and odds had always been a fluttering red cape in the face of what Blaine liked to call her "beautiful bullishness." Independent living came with risks for someone with epilepsy, but Mary would have it no other way. And Blaine admired her for it.

"What now?" he asked.

"Same ol', same ol' for me," she said, unlocking the door and stepping into the dark house. "Just the library and the church choir and my cat. Can we talk about you now? You're the one with the interesting life."

The second Mary flipped on the inside light, a thick, orange tabby immediately rubbed up against her left leg and mewed. She reached down to stroke the tomcat's arched back. "Well, hello there, Thomas. Did you miss me? I told you I would come back. And look. It's Blaine."

Blaine stepped into the house and reached down to scratch behind Thomas's ear. "He's gotten huge!"

Mary nodded and moved toward a nearby table, setting down her purse and immediately starting for the kitchen.

"Hey, Mary. Stop for a second, will you?"

She stopped, but she didn't turn around.

"What's going on?"

"Nothing." She crossed her arms. "Always nothing."

Blaine's heart sank. He thought he knew where this was going. "Look at me, please."

She wouldn't, so he walked up behind her and turned her around with his own hands. Mary fell against his chest, crying.

"Hey," he said, hugging her and leaning his chin against the top of her head. She was so short, she barely came up to his collarbone. "What is it?"

Mary could only weep softly, so he let her. He tightened his hold and prayed. She was such a tender heart, and he knew she barely let anyone else see her sadness. She had so few friends to actually take notice, and Blaine sometimes worried that she was too alone in life. Her parents loved her and checked in on her every day by phone, but they lived in Hamburg. They didn't see her every day.

"We've been friends for, what, five years, now? I can tell when you're hiding something."

Mary finally pulled away a bit and wiped at her face. She looked so sad.

"Is this about what Bev said?"

Mary still couldn't look at him. She stared down at her feet, tucking a stray lock of dark, shiny hair behind her ear.

"People will always talk," he said.

"That's just it," Mary finally spurted. "They talk, but they don't know."

"Don't know what?"

"Don't know," she moved her hands back and forth between them, "us."

Blaine frowned. "What do you mean?"

"I mean," she said, moving past him to sink into a nearby armchair, "everyone in Bradbury knows we've been friends forever."

"Yeah?"

"And they expect things."

"Like what?"

She finally looked up at him pointedly. "Like marriage."

"Whoa," Blaine raised his eyebrows. "Shouldn't you ask me out on a date or something first, before proposing to me?"

Mary looked away and shook her head, defeated. "Never mind."

"Hey, now," Blaine said, moving to sit in the chair opposite her. "You know I'm just kidding. But seriously, Mar, why do you care so much about what other people think?"

"You wouldn't understand," she sighed, crossing her arms and leaning back in the chair. "You've had it easy all of these years off in Boston and then Northwestern and now Fort Wayne, but I have to face these people *every day*. I have to stamp their books and shop in their stores and answer all of their questions about *you*."

"So?"

"Everyone thinks I have some kind of special connection with you or something."

"Well, you do. You're my best friend."

Mary shook her head. "No one believes that, Blaine."

"Why not?"

"Because you're a boy, and I'm a girl! We're both getting old—"

"Speak for yourself."

Mary's eyes flashed, and they never flashed. "Would you *please* be serious for one moment and listen to me?"

Blaine instantly shut his mouth and sobered. Mary really was hurting about all of this.

"Look," she said, "we're not kids anymore, right? And we're both still single, and every time you come home you're always hanging out with me. People think we should be getting married."

"I hang out with Mrs. Scheinberg too. Do they think I should marry her?"

"You're impossible." Mary looked away.

"No, I'm sensible. This is ridiculous, Mary, and it's not like you. People gossip. They're always going to gossip—if not about this, then about something else. What I don't get is why you suddenly care so much. Why do *they* care so much?"

"Because," she threw her hand toward the invisible people on the other side of the darkened picture window, "they *need* us to be married!"

Oh. Blaine looked at the floor. He thought he finally understood what Mary was trying to say. Bradbury, thanks to his father's public affair with another man, had always been abuzz with speculation about his own sexuality. But he had hoped that after all of these years, people would let the matter rest. It was none of their business anyway, and Mary certainly didn't deserve to be implicated in such talk. Yet, implicated she was, apparently. He looked back up at his friend, heart heavy. There she sat, burdened, and all because of him. She was already so alone in her condition. This gossip would most certainly push her toward complete isolation.

"Do you want to be married to me?" he asked.

"What?" Mary looked at him, surprised.

"Do you want to be married to me?"

"Are you serious?"

He shrugged. "Sure."

"Don't tease me."

"I'm not teasing. I'm sincerely asking."

"Well," she furrowed her brow, "I want to marry *someone*. Someday."

He nodded.

"What about you?" she asked carefully. "Do you want to be married to me?"

He stared beyond her black-rimmed eyeglasses into her almond eyes, truly loving her. She was the most beautiful woman, inside out, he had ever known, and her vulnerability always compelled him to tell the truth. "If I were to marry someone, it would be you."

Her eyes looked pained. "But?"

"I just . . . I don't . . . I'm not—"

"It's okay, Blaine," she waved her hand, quickly shutting down the conversation. "I understand."

Did she?

Mary stood suddenly, moving fast toward the kitchen again. "The thing is," she called over her shoulder, "it's not me who needs an explanation. It's Bev."

|||||||||||||||||||||||||||||||||||||||||||||

Blaine trusted Pastor Fletcher. The man was smart, and—in contrast to other modern ministers waving Bibles around on television and shouting object lessons across the airwaves—he was oddly quiet. He was not given to heated arguments or impulsive passions, but instead seemed to apply a measured thoughtfulness and ordered patience to all that he said and did. Perhaps it was his inherent calm that had drawn Blaine to Pastor Fletcher's study four years before, exactly one week after his senior recital at Bradbury College. His own insides had been anything but calm at the time, thanks to his father's licentious affair.

"Does God love homosexuals?" he had asked, barely able to look the collared man in the eye.

"He does."

"But my grandma says that God calls homosexuality an abomination."

"He does."

Blaine frowned, shaking his head. Christians were always making contradictions. "I don't understand."

"I suppose it would help if we define the word *love*, first," Pastor said, leaning easily back in his chair. "Think of it this way. The world likes to shout 'Love!' from the rooftops in response to all of society's ills—'Love is all you need,' for example—but what exactly does the word *love* mean, do you think?"

When Blaine didn't answer, Pastor continued.

"Now, we can't speak for every person, but from the context of society's present conversation on homosexuality, we can safely assume that most people think love means tolerance of others' sexual preferences and behaviors. Would you agree?"

Blaine nodded. "My dad keeps telling me that my family has to accept him—to *love* him—because the Bible says 'God is love.'"

"And he's right!" Pastor said. "Where your dad might be wrong, though, is in assuming that 'God is love' means 'God is tolerant of sexual deviancy.' Nowhere does God say in His Word that love is acceptance of homosexuality or adultery or sexual sin of any kind. In fact, He says that love is something quite different."

Pastor suddenly turned in his chair and pulled a Bible off of the shelf behind him. He shuffled quickly through some pages. "We would be poor scholars indeed if we ascribed a quote to someone out of context, and so many times people quote God apart from knowing His full counsel on a subject. If you'll permit me, I'll read to you what God actually says about love." He stopped on a page and ran his finger down a column of text. "Here in First Corinthians, chapter thirteen, God reveals to us through the apostle Paul that love 'does not insist on its own way; . . . it does not rejoice at wrongdoing, but rejoices with the truth.'"

Blaine couldn't think of a time in recent history when his father *hadn't* insisted on his own way, all in the name of "love."

Pastor shuffled through some more pages. "And here in John, chapter fifteen, Jesus proclaims that 'greater love has no one than this, that someone lay down his life for his friends.'" Pastor looked up at Blaine. "You see, God defines love as *sacrifice* of self, not *indulgence* of self."

Blaine stared at him, strangely electrified. He had never heard any of this before.

"In Romans, chapter five, Paul writes, 'But God shows His love for us in that while we were still sinners, Christ died for us.'" Pastor passed the Bible over for Blaine to read for himself. "You see? God's love is not *tolerance of* sin. It is *salvation from* sin. And that is another part of the conversation where people fail to properly characterize God's true nature and intent. God *is* love, and so He *can't* tolerate sin. Do you see? God is holy and righteous and, by nature, intolerant of sin. That's how we know that His love is so amazing. Because—despite our being sinners—He still lays down His own life to save us from the very sin that separates us from Him. *That* is love."

"And homosexuality is a sin, then?" Blaine asked, needing confirmation. His grandmother had said as much, but he wanted to hear it from a theologian.

"It is. God's Word is very clear on this. We read in the Book of Genesis how God destroyed the towns of Sodom and Gomorrah because of their sin—including the sin of homosexuality. And

the Book of Judges calls homosexuality 'outrageous' and 'wicked.'
Also, Levitical law condemns lying with someone of the same sex
and calls it an 'abomination.' And the books of First and Second
Kings condemn male prostitution at pagan religious sites."

Blaine furrowed his brow, thinking of something irksome his
father had said. "Yeah, but that's the Old Testament, right? Wasn't
there a new covenant or something with Jesus that made all of that
old stuff obsolete?"

"Not obsolete," Pastor corrected, "but forgiven."

"What does that mean?"

"Ah," Pastor drummed his fingers excitedly on the desk, "now
you're asking questions like a Lutheran. We know with certainty
from God's Word that Jesus came to fulfill God's command for
holiness and to mercifully offer Himself up as the atoning sacrifice for all of humanity. This includes murderers, cheats, liars,
gossips, gluttons, power-mongers, and—yes—homosexual fathers.
Jesus shed His blood on a cross that all of us gross sinners might
be washed clean of our sin and reconciled to the Father. You see,"
Pastor tilted his head, looking as if he were about to make a point,
"here is an important distinction that the world often gets wrong:
Jesus doesn't promote sin. He washes us clean of it."

Blaine nodded, trying to keep up. He wanted to pause and
dwell on everything Pastor was saying, yet at the same time, he
didn't want the man to stop.

"For example," Pastor grabbed a pad of paper and began writing down a list of citations, "when Jesus heals the paralytic in the
Bible, He makes sure to tell the man that his sins are forgiven—because that is the worst of his problems. That is the disease which
plagues his body *and* soul. And Jesus doesn't send him or anyone
else away saying, 'Now, go and sin some more.' No, to the adul-
terous woman He rescues from stoning, He says, 'Go and sin *no
more.*' Jesus is not a friend to sin. He is a friend to sinners."

"But my dad says that Jesus never condemns homosexuality as a sin."

"Your dad is mistaken. In His famous Sermon on the Mount in Matthew, chapter five, Jesus proclaims that He has come not 'to abolish' the Law and Prophets 'but to fulfill them.' If that's not an amen to the Old Testament, then I don't know what it is."

"But if it's a sin, why didn't Jesus say something outright about it?"

"Well, one could, in return, ask the question, 'Why would He?' At the time Jesus walked on this earth, the Jews clearly understood from the Old Testament that homosexuality is condemned by God. There was little to no confusion on the matter, but there was plenty of confusion on other things, like salvation, forgiveness, suffering, righteousness, the Messiah, and the kingdom of God. We can easily see in the Gospels that Jesus tends to preach on those things about which the Jews were confused. And look, all we can know of what Jesus said during His earthly ministry is what has been recorded in Scripture, but that doesn't mean Jesus didn't also say other things. Yet, as a pastor, I never think it's a good idea to base one's theology solely on an argument of silence. Nor should you base your theology solely on the words of any man, for that matter. So don't take my word for it." He smiled, handing Blaine the piece of paper and a new Bible from a drawer in his desk. "Take God's."

Blaine did. That very night, he dug into Pastor's list of suggested readings in the Bible, making it through the entire New Testament by the end of the week and finishing the Old Testament by the end of the month. And he kept revisiting Pastor Fletcher throughout the summer, knocking, seeking, and asking, his curiosity growing into a full-blown zeal for biblical truth. Always, he took home more and more books—Pastor's copies of Luther's Small Catechism, C. S. Lewis's *Mere Christianity*, history books by Josephus and Eusebius, and the Book of Concord—eventually returning them and buying copies of his own to mark up and inwardly digest. By the time he drove out to Boston for graduate school, he had been baptized into Christ through water and the Word and welcomed into full altar fellowship at Zion Lutheran Church. Now, four years later, Blaine was staring down four years of seminary education, and he found himself turning to Pastor Fletcher for advice once again.

"Do you think pastors should get married?"

They were eating at Happy Lotus Flower II, the Chinese restaurant in Hamburg, and Pastor Fletcher, biting into a crab rangoon, shrugged lightly. "It depends."

"On what?"

"On the man."

Blaine dunked an egg roll into a bowl of peanut sauce. "What is it about the man that matters?"

"Well," Pastor wiped his fingers on a napkin, "I would want to know if he burns."

"Burns?"

"With passion. Paul writes about it in his First Letter to the Corinthians. 'It is better to marry than to burn with passion,'" Pastor quoted. "But Paul also writes that it's good for a man not to have sexual relations with a woman. His argument is that an unmarried man is free to focus on how to please the Lord, but the married man—well, his focus is divided between pleasing the Lord and his wife."

Blaine nodded, understanding.

"When I met Emily," Pastor continued, "I burned, so I married her. And I'm glad I did. Marriage is not only a blessing to me personally, but as a pastor, I've benefitted from what Loehe calls the strict 'school of sanctification.'[1] Bachelorhood never did so much to improve me as living with a wife and children, that's for sure! And honestly, being married has made me wiser in premarital

---

1 *The Pastor* by J. K. Wilhelm Loehe, CPH, p. 124.

counseling and better at caring for the women in my congregation in general. And need I expound on the blessing that is the gift of children? But still. Paul concedes that it is better not to have your interests divided."

Blaine absently pushed another egg roll across his plate.

"Can I take this to mean you're contemplating marriage?"

Blaine looked up, taken aback. "Me? No. I mean, yes. I-I guess?"

"You guess?"

"Well . . ." Blaine felt embarrassed for some reason. "Shouldn't everyone contemplate marriage?"

Pastor was studying him. "Do you burn?"

"Do I burn?"

"Yes. Do you burn?"

Blaine thought about Mary with her sad eyes. He honestly didn't know what to say.

"Marriage is a blessing, Blaine, but chastity is also a gift from God. That's the thing. Celibacy and marriage are both permitted in Holy Scripture. You are free to choose which is better for you. And as a future pastor, I urge you to prayerfully consider which is better for your ministry."

"But what about . . ."

"Mary?"

Blaine's heart felt so heavy with her burden.

"I heard what Bev said last night," Pastor admitted. "I wondered how that might affect you both."

Blaine frowned. "Mary's hurting. She's alone a lot of the time, and people keep saying things to her about, you know, the two of us. And I think she wants to be married."

"And you want to take care of her."

Blaine nodded.

Pastor's voice was quiet but firm. "It is an honorable thing to want to take care of your friend, Blaine, but if you don't burn, marrying her won't serve her in the end. It will hurt her."

Blaine immediately thought of his dad. The man was a sexual addict who burned like no other, and in his weakness for passion and pleasure, he ended up burning everyone else around him. For years, Blaine had lived in fear that he, too, would someday wake up and burn with the sin of his father, but—God be praised!—that wretched morning had never come. Instead, his body, mind, and soul were occupied with music and books and conversation and the wonderful mystery of Christ's blessed exchange. He was almost embarrassed by his lack of interest in the benefits of marriage.

"I care about Mary," Blaine said, his voice thick.

"But?"

"But," he was having trouble admitting it, even to himself, "I don't burn."

Pastor didn't seem surprised at his words or even concerned. "It's okay, Blaine. In fact, I think it's wonderful! Chastity is a rare and special gift from God, and you can rejoice in it. Even if Mary can't."

"But what do I say to her?"

"Tell her the truth. Tell her what Jesus says: 'Not everyone can receive this saying, but only those to whom it is given. For there are eunuchs who have been so from birth, and there are eunuchs who have been made eunuchs by men, and there are eunuchs who have made themselves eunuchs for the sake of the kingdom of heaven. Let the one who is able to receive this receive it.'"[2]

"And when she never speaks to me again?"

"Then pray for her and 'remain in the condition in which you were called.'"[3]

---

2   Matthew 19:11–12
3   1 Corinthians 7:20

## CHAPTER THIRTY-ONE: SEE YOU LATER, ALLIGATOR!

iiiiiiiiiiiiiiiiiiiiiiiiiiiiiiiiiiiiiiiiiiiiiiiiiiiiiiiiiiiiiiii

For the first time in the history of Zion Lutheran Church, the Ladies Aid Society was entering a float in Bradbury's annual Labor Day parade.

"We can hand out catechisms instead of candy!" Bev suggested, her eyes alight with missional fervor.

"And make all of the children cry?" Mrs. Scheinberg countered. "That doesn't sound particularly evangelical to me."

"Bev's idea is a great one," Candice declared sullenly, patting at the right side of her head. Her alopecia was acting up again. It was the stress of her baby girl living in a coed dormitory. "Sugar is poison."

"Yes, thank you, Dr. Oz," Mrs. Scheinberg acknowledged, "but I think the town would rather be poisoned than proselytized, don't you?"

"What you distribute is inconsequential. It is the float that matters," Yvonne asserted. The prickly woman wasn't actually a member of the Ladies Aid Society, but since she had been awarded the title of grand marshal of this year's parade—her daughter, Kayla, was head of the planning committee—she thought it important to keep abreast of the ladies' plans. "Now, I can't be on the float, of course—I will be in the car at the head of the parade—"

Mrs. Scheinberg stretched her eyeballs from left to right in a long, obvious arc.

"—but I still care about my church's reputation."

"Well," Bev grinned, full of ideas, "I thought it would be fun to put folding chairs on Irv's flatbed and have the choir sing 'A Mighty Fortress' down Main Street!"

"Oo, with Dorothy's vertigo?" Emily pointed out, frantically fanning herself with an old church bulletin. Her face was still flushed from having crossed the asphalt parking lot in the late summer heat, and her red cheeks perfectly matched her ruffled maternity shirt from Rebecca. "I don't know if that's a good idea."

Mrs. Scheinberg snickered. "I can just see the headlines now: 'Koelster's Kitchen loses beloved sous-chef in holiday parade.'"

"What if," Rebecca redirected, "we turn one of Irv's wagons into Noah's ark?"

"Yes, yes!" Nettie clapped. "Harold would make the perfect Noah. He's already so old, and he knows how to drive a boat. I'll have him start growing a beard right now."

"We could dress up the Sunday School children as animals," Rebecca added.

"Oh, they would be so cute and fuzzy and scrumptious!"

"They wouldn't be for eating, Nettie," Mrs. Scheinberg reminded.

"You know, I have an old elephant costume that Junior wore when he was young," Candice offered, perking up a bit. She turned toward Emily. "George would fit in it, I think."

"That would be adorable!" Emily agreed.

"It's too dangerous," Yvonne shot from across the table. "I don't trust the Junior Rifle League not to use our little animals for target practice, and they're marching behind us in the parade. I know. I saw the lineup yesterday on my Kayla's counter."

"You really think the boys'll be carrying rifles?" Rebecca asked, skeptical.

"I wouldn't put *anything* past a league run by the likes of Mort Lohenssohn," Yvonne pulled at her pearls authoritatively.

"It's a parade, not a safari, Yvonne," Mrs. Scheinberg contested. "Though I suppose we can't be too careful. Besides," her nostrils flared ever so slightly, "I don't think Noah's ark is going to work."

"Why?" Bev looked disappointed.

"There's no rain in the forecast."

Yvonne was the one to stretch her eyeballs this time.

Bev only frowned, her brain too literal to catch most jokes in the moment. "Well, I don't think sunshine'll be a problem, Arlene. In fact, that's what we want, right? And I don't think those boys'll shoot any rifles. Maybe at a funeral, but not at a parade, surely. I say we stick with Noah's ark. Everyone'll love it, and we can hand out animal crackers *along* with catechisms. Harold can be Noah and the kids can be the animals and—let me see—what else do we need?"

"A rainbow," Emily said. She looked invitingly across the table, extending the proverbial olive branch. "Would you sew a rainbow banner for us, Yvonne?"

"You mean Arlene doesn't already have one flying over her front door?" Yvonne openly scoffed. "I thought for sure she'd have hoisted all of the colors, what with Blaine Maler back in town."

That killed the joy faster than a shot from the Junior Rifle League. Everyone held her breath as Mrs. Scheinberg turned a hot eye toward the mouthy matron.

"Why, Yvonne," she seethed, "you sad, sad woman. And here I was just about to suggest that you wear a costume on the float too, but then I remembered. There was no witch on the ark."

Bev gasped and covered her mouth.

Yvonne didn't even flinch. "Oh, Arlene. I hurt for you. I do. No children, and your only consolation is, well, not quite a man."

Decorum, completely shattered, lay in dangerous shards at the women's feet.

"Blaine is more of a man than either of your delinquent sons will ever be." Mrs. Scheinberg's voice shook. "What girl is Gerry on, now? Number four or five? I've lost count over the years."

Yvonne actually flushed. "At least Gerry is with a *woman*."

"That's enough," Emily intervened, her voice quiet.

Mrs. Scheinberg immediately closed her mouth, properly shamed, but Yvonne turned toward the little pastor's wife and openly gaped. "Excuse me?"

Emily's cheeks burned even brighter, but she held her ground. "Stop slandering Blaine. Please. He is your brother in Christ."

"He is no brother of mine. He is—"

"All of our brother," Emily interrupted, trying to keep Yvonne from ruining her own reputation as well. "You were there for his Baptism. We all were."

Yvonne practically spit, "And what about my Gerry? Doesn't he get any support from the pastor's wife? Oh, wait. Of course not. You're a *Fletcher*."

Emily didn't know what that meant, but she gathered it was not a compliment. "I have never met Gerry."

It was true. In her six years at Zion, she had never once seen the man—nor Yvonne's other son, for that matter. She had met only Yvonne's daughter, Kayla, and of course, her daughter's husband, Lance.

"The reason you've never met my son," Yvonne hissed, "is because he won't step foot in a church run by *your husband*."

"I think we should—" Rebecca tried to stave off the oncoming deluge, but Yvonne's mud had already begun to slide.

"There are *many* people in this town who won't step foot in our church, thanks to your husband," Yvonne sneered, her teeth vibrating with hate. "We've been bleeding members ever since he came to Bradbury. He is singlehandedly destroying our church, and I've been saying it for years. Did he tell you that he chased both of my boys away? And after decades of my serving on the altar guild!"

"I don't know what you're talking about, Yvonne." Emily really didn't.

"Of course not," she clucked. "Your husband doesn't make a habit of trumpeting his failures around the church, does he?"

Emily was pretty sure Yvonne had it backwards. It was other people's sin that her husband made a point of keeping silent about in the church. And as for his own faults, well, he wasn't perfect, but she had never met another person more ready to apologize whenever convicted of wrongdoing. That was part of why she had married him.

"Both of my sons came to church every Sunday before *your husband* started pestering them," Yvonne made clear. "They were boys. They did what boys do. But your husband kept insisting they be angels, or else. Gene stopped going to church altogether, but Gerry—at least he tried to marry his girl Felicia. He tried to do the right thing by her. But do you know what *your husband* said to them in premarital counseling? He told them he wouldn't marry them in the church as long as they were living together."

Yvonne stopped and stared piercingly at Emily, obviously waiting for a grand reaction. Emily merely blinked, confused. Had she missed something? She risked a glance at the other women. They were all red-faced and staring into their laps. She looked back at Yvonne, trying to understand. Did the woman think her son should have kept on living in sin until marriage? Surely not.

"If he had just married them," Yvonne explained, "it would've fixed the whole problem."

Would it have? Emily tried to wrap her mind around the situation, but her heart was pounding in her ears and she honestly couldn't think of who this Felicia woman was. She had thought Gerry Roe was married to a woman named Quinn, but she must be remembering it wrong. "Have I met Felicia?"

Yvonne narrowed her eyes. "What's that supposed to mean?"

"Nothing, I was just—"

"Mocking my son is a family tradition, I see."

"No. I just thought that Gerry's wife's name was—"

"What do you know about the matter anyway?"

"Nothing!" Emily's temper sparked into flame. "Obviously, I know nothing, because my husband has told me *nothing* about it."

A new, delicious feeling of power—or was it hate?—began to pull at her shoulders and chin. This was definitely not a fruit of the Holy Spirit. Emily tried to shrug it off, but it resisted. It clung to her comfortably, like a well-tailored jacket. "Who is Felicia, then?"

"It doesn't matter."

"Sure it does. *You* brought her up."

Yvonne frowned. "You just want to judge my son."

"I'm pretty sure the only person judging anyone right now is you." Emily knew that wasn't exactly true, and the disdain in her own voice proved it. *Be angry and do not sin, be angry and do not sin, be angry and do not . . .*

"She's the mother of my eldest granddaughter, if you must know, but it's your husband's fault I never see them."

"Really? Did my husband put a restraining order on them or something?" She felt Mrs. Scheinberg's hand rest warningly on her arm under the table.

"Your husband shamed her."

"Did he, now?" Emily asked, her confidence way too high to be holy. She really needed to stop. Now. But it felt so good to finally vomit all of the emotion she had been holding in for months. No, years. She shook off Mrs. Scheinberg's hand. "Because I'm pretty sure the man who shamed this Felicia is the one who bedded her out of wedlock. That's how shame works, see? It tends to follow people's sin."

"They wanted to get married!"

"Then why didn't they?"

"Because *your husband* wouldn't let them."

"But Yvonne"—it felt so good to say her name out loud in this way, like pouring water on that witch of a woman and watching her shrink—"you said *my husband* wouldn't marry them unless they stopped living in sin. Well, it sounds to me like he was trying to protect Felicia from further shame. It's *your son* who treated her like a whore."

She had gone too far too fast, and Yvonne's face showed it. Emily did her best to backpedal.

"What I mean is—"

"*Don't,*" Yvonne spat, "preach to me, young lady."

"Yvonne . . ." Emily started. She lowered her eyes in contrition, floundering under the weight of the woman's name. Saying it out loud now felt very different than before. "I hurt you just now. I'm sorry."

"Shut up."

Emily's breath caught short in her throat. Yvonne was gathering her purse and walking toward the parish hall door. This was not how they should part from each other. They should be reconciled. Emily began to panic. She rose from her chair and followed the woman. "Please, Yvonne. Forgive me. I shouldn't assume anything, and I certainly shouldn't have said those things about your son. Not now. Not in front of others, especially. I'm sorry."

Yvonne was shaking her head. "You're just like your husband."

"What do you mean?"

Her white head turned at the door. "You assume the worst of people."

Emily conceded only what was true. "I may have done that just now, but my husband only speaks of you in the kindest way."

"He chases people from the church with his hate."

"Right now," Emily was crying, "it is not the pastor I see chasing people away with hate."

Yvonne's face and tone reclaimed the sickeningly sweet expression she had given Emily in the sacristy two months before. "Oh, now, dear. Are you talking about yourself? Because thanks to you, I will never step foot in this church again."

# Chapter Thirty-Two: Saturday Night Fever

Emily was inconsolable.

"You apologized to her?" Pastor asked, standing over her arm-chair in the parsonage like a sentinel.

"Yes," Emily sobbed. All three of their children were standing in the middle of the room, mouths agape at their quickly disintegrating mother. "I apologized to her in the parish hall and then again in the parking lot. She wouldn't listen to me, so I called her phone and left a message. Twice. Was that bad?"

"No." Pastor held her hand. "I think that was nice."

"What do I do?"

He shrugged. "You apologized. There's not much more to do. Pray for her."

It couldn't be that simple. Yvonne was leaving the church, and it was her fault.

"I lost my temper, Michael."

"And you apologized. You are forgiven."

"I told her," Emily hid her face against his arm, shuddering, "that her son treated women like whores. I shouldn't have said that."

"Well," Pastor's voice was grim, "there are kinder ways of saying it, but it's not a sin to speak the truth."

"I said it in hate," Emily moaned.

"Listen to me." Pastor knelt on the floor to better look her in the eye. "You are baptized into Christ. 'There is therefore now no condemnation for those who are in Christ Jesus.'[4] Your sins are washed away, Emily. God remembers them no more."

"But Yvonne remembers them!"

"Yes, but she doesn't have to. She's the one who chooses to enshrine her hurts. Pray for her, Emily."

She clung to his hand. "I'm afraid."

"Of what?"

She could barely whisper her deepest fear. "Of being the reason Yvonne leaves."

"Honey," Pastor tenderly kissed her head, "Yvonne has been leaving for years."

"But she said—"

"I think it's best to forget everything that was said today, don't you?"

Emily nodded, but there was still something bothering her. "Yvonne said you're chasing people from the church."

Pastor sighed and lowered his head. "I sure don't mean to. God help me."

"She said you're a hateful man," Emily heaved the words into his ear, unable to stop herself. She felt out of control. "She said you are the reason her family won't come to church anymore."

Pastor's hand suddenly disappeared from her grasp. Emily looked up to find him rising to his feet.

"Why would she say that, Michael?" She kept pushing, even though it felt dangerous. Yvonne's accusations had unleashed a pernicious doubt in her, and it was anesthetizing her sense of trust in her husband. "Is there something I need to know?"

"No."

---

4   Romans 8:1

"Don't put me off like that, Michael. I just want to understand."

"And some things aren't for your understanding, Emily." He turned away and reached for his keys on the cluttered end table.

"What does that mean?"

"It means," he was keeping his back to her, "that Yvonne's troubles with me are not your business."

"Aren't they?"

"No."

"But I'm your wife."

"And I'm your pastor." He turned to look at her then, his face guarded. "Please don't tempt me with idle gossip."

"But what if Yvonne is right? What if you are doing something—"

"That's enough." He effectively shut down the conversation with three quick strides to the front door. Emily rose from her chair to follow him, and the children followed her.

"Where are you going?" she asked.

"To check on Yvonne."

That wounded her. "But I need you."

"Do you?" Pastor suddenly turned on her, his dark eyes uncharacteristically cold. Emily shivered. "It seems to me that all you want to do is memorize and repeat everything Yvonne tells you."

"Michael, if you're hurting people—"

"Woman," he snapped, "if you're going to stand there and tempt me to speak something other than the truth from God's Word to these people," he threw open the door and blocked her from following him, "then get behind me, Satan!"

The sharp slap of his words stung more than if he had physically struck her. Emily stood, stunned and winded, unable to do anything but watch openmouthed as the wooden door swung resolutely shut in her face.

George, ever sensitive to changes in atmospheric pressure, both physical and spiritual, began to cry, but Julia was steelier than her brother.

"Mommy," she asked evenly, her tone more curious than afraid, "is Satan in the room?"

Emily's compunction was already at toxic levels. What was one more indignity? She put her cold hands to her burning cheeks, closed her eyes, and acknowledged the truth.

"Yes, sweetheart, he is."

⎯⎯⎯⎯⎯⎯⎯⎯⎯⎯⎯⎯⎯⎯⎯⎯⎯

The spiritual battle in the parsonage was real. It often was on Saturday nights. Whether it was the devil and his minions sabotaging the upcoming Sabbath with attacks against Pastor's peace of mind or simply the sinful humans in the house indulging their nefarious natures, there was no doubt that powers and principalities and even people—small and tall—were opposed to God's servant of the Word having a good night's sleep before preaching in the pulpit. And this evening was no exception.

Julia, empowered by her mother's show of apparent weakness, launched an immediate and vigorous campaign to be alpha in the house. She talked back to her mother and tore choice toys out of Becky's soft hands, replacing them with her brother's preferred action figures, effecting enraged shrieks from both parent and siblings. She sweetly offered to "read" books to George but then torturously changed the stories until they were unrecognizable, working her brother into an unholy fit. And when Becky's lovey came up missing at bedtime, Julia adamantly denied any participation in its disappearance, but Emily found the blanket hidden under Julia's pillow exactly one hour after Becky had cried herself to sleep.

George, who had never fully recovered from his initial distress at his father's unsatisfying departure, accompanied the climax of each of his sister's devious plots with wails of ever increasing volume and frequency. And in the unhappy moment when he discovered that the shredding of his own larynx failed to satisfy his magnanimous grief, he resorted to pushing Becky down onto the floor and wrenching Julia's ponytail with his sweaty, little fist.

Emily spent the remainder of the evening vacillating between naked contrition for her sins and guarded anger for her husband's swift dismissal. One hour, she penitently baked Pastor his favorite chocolate chip cookies, and the next—when he did not immediately come home from visiting Yvonne—she spitefully threw them in the trash. The children's raucous misbehavior and belligerent cries underscored her shapeshifting thoughts, and when Pastor finally stepped through the front door at nine o'clock, the church carillon was ringing its swan song for the evening, "Now Rest beneath Night's Shadow."

"I'm going to bed" was all he said, walking past her armchair without even a glance.

Emily, hot in a flash, slammed her book shut and jumped to her feet. That man was going to bed without reconciling to her! The hypocrite! She stomped off to the kitchen, removed a piece of chalk from a drawer, and dragged a dining room chair underneath the front door. Stepping onto the seat, she removed the small chalkboard from the nail on the wall and rubbed it clean with her elbow.

"'Joy comes in the morning,'" she muttered, spitting out an ironic laugh. "Not in this house." She scribbled a few hasty words on the board with a shaky hand, rehung it on the wall, dragged the chair back to the table, threw the piece of chalk in the kitchen sink, and made for the bathroom. There would be no resting beneath night's shadow in the Fletcher home tonight.

## Chapter Thirty-Three: The Harvest Raise

"Grace, mercy, and peace to you from God the Father," Pastor began his sermon, making the sign of the cross from the pulpit, "and our Lord Jesus Christ."

He looked out over his congregation, pained. There, just seven pews back from the Communion rail, was an empty seat, the one Yvonne Roe had occupied for years, long before he had ever arrived on the scene. The woman was conspicuously AWOL this morning, no doubt a clear message to him and everyone else in the nave that the entreaties of the Fletcher family went unappreciated. Kayla, Lance, and their children were missing as well, but it was the half-empty pew on the lectern side that threatened to break Pastor's concentration and heart. Curt, Kathryn, and the Jones family were blinking back at him as usual from their seats in the third pew from the front, but his own wife and children were agonizingly absent.

Pastor was shaken by the sight but not entirely surprised. Emily was still upset with him—that much he had ascertained from the admonition she had left for him above the parsonage door that morning: "Do not let the sun go down on your anger." But apparently, he had not quite realized the depth of her agitation. Never before had any of their marital misgivings kept her from bringing their children to church. Emily felt too keenly her motherly responsibility to answer Christ's call, "Let the little children come to Me." His wife's present affliction—whether of mind, body, spirit, or all of the above—must be severe indeed.

Pastor stood in the pulpit and wished that he had woken Emily this morning before leaving the house. He had risen long before her or the children or even the sun, and his valiant efforts to noiselessly pull on his clothes in the dark and slip out of the house unnoticed hadn't been motivated by some chivalrous desire to preserve his family's sleep. No, he had simply been afraid to look Emily in the eye. He could bear a lot of things as a pastor—Yvonne's hate, the scorn of unbelievers, the loneliness of his vocation—but he couldn't stomach his wife's suspicion.

How he got through the sermon and the rest of the service that morning, Pastor didn't know, and the walk to the parish hall for Sunday School proved equally excruciating. No one bothered to inquire after Yvonne and her family—the gossip train had obviously tooted its horn all around Bradbury the night before—but every woman stopped him to ask after Emily and the kids. The only answer he could muster on the spot was some incoherent half-truth about hard days and difficult nights and poor sleep and pregnancy hormones. They all nodded understandingly if a bit skeptically and offered him various home remedies for first trimester trials and insomnia and asked him to pass along their well-wishes to the homebound.

Sunday School was also a bust, and when Pastor finally crossed the street to the parsonage in the middle of the day, the guilt over the starring role he had played in his family's absence from church piled onto his conscience with ever increasing speed and threatened to bury him alive.

"Emily, I am so sorry." The words spilled from his lips before he had even fully stepped across the threshold.

His wife, puffy-eyed and red in the nose, was in his arms the very next second, burrowing her face against his chest. "Me too, Michael."

"You needed me, and I abandoned you," he confessed.

"I accused you of things I know nothing about," she acknowledged.

"I didn't take care of you."

"I filled our home with hate."

"I thought only of myself."

"I kept the children from church."

"I forgive you."

"I forgive you."

And like that, it was all over. The pain, the confusion, the division, the guilt of the past twenty-four hours—all of it—forever absolved, buried, and gone, though they all felt a bit worse for the wear. Pastor held Emily tight, breathing in the familiar scent of her hair and remembering all that he loved about her: her gentleness, her compassion, her intensity, her vulnerability, her readiness to forgive, her determination, even her stubbornness. He would better care for her and protect her and preserve her from now on, God help him!

A sound in the hallway caught his attention, and he looked over Emily's head to find Julia and George curiously staring at them.

"Come here," he smiled, keeping one arm firmly around Emily's waist and gesturing to the twins with the other. They burst into motion, running with abandon and smashing up against his legs. George giggled in the middle of the family hug, but the second Julia made contact with him, she began to cry. Pastor released from the embrace and knelt down to tend to his daughter's tears.

"Honeybee, what's wrong?"

"You left, Daddy."

He nodded. "I did. I'm sorry, Julia."

"You didn't come back."

"I did come back, but . . ." He was about to explain that he had needed to leave again before she woke up this morning, but what was the point? To her, he had been gone at all of the wrong times, and she was right. He let his wrong remain undefended.

"You left us here with Satan."

That pierced him through like a sword, slicing him open from nave to chops. He reached out and pulled Julia to him, crushing her against his heart. "I am so sorry, Julia. You are right. I left you alone with Satan last night, but I will try *never* to do that again. Will you please forgive me?"

Julia was wounded, but she was also well catechized. "I forgive you, Daddy."

"But we weren't really alone, Julia, were we?" Emily reminded their daughter, touching her golden head with her hand. "Who was with us?"

"Jesus."

"That's right. And even when Daddy has to leave the house because of work, he is never leaving us alone. Jesus is always with us, so we don't need to be afraid of Satan or anything else."

Pastor looked up at his wife, grateful for her best construction put on the situation. He loved this woman.

"Mommy was too sad for church this morning," Julia explained.

"She cwied," George added.

"Did you take care of her?" Pastor asked.

George nodded soberly. "I hugged her. So did Caw-wots."

"How about," Emily suggested, "the two of you sit with Daddy for a bit while I wake Becky and get lunch on the table? He can share with us what we missed in church today."

"Doughnuts?" George asked eagerly.

"No," Emily tittered, half amused, half exasperated. "I was thinking more along the lines of what we missed in the service."

Pastor sat on the couch with the twins and read the day's assigned readings from the Bible, taking Becky from Emily's arms when they entered the living room and snuggling her on his lap. Emily listened in as she set the table, and over lunch, Pastor relayed points from his sermon to the entire family, questioning Julia and George afterward like he would on any other Sunday. It never failed to amaze him just how much the two of them absorbed and understood of what he said about God, even at the tender age of three. But then, they were baptized. They had been given God's Holy Spirit, and they had ears to hear and mouths to speak. Why wouldn't they be able to confess the faith?

After returning thanks to the Lord and singing through the hymn of the day, Pastor soundly defeated each of his children in a wild wrestling match on the living room floor. Then, as Emily sat in her armchair and rubbed essential oils into her hands and wrists, he carried the squealing children to their bedrooms, put them down for naps, and quietly escaped to the kitchen to make hot chocolate for his bride and for himself.

"Thank you, Michael," Emily beamed up at him from her chair, taking a steaming mug from his hand.

"I know what my girl likes," he winked and settled onto the nearby couch.

They sat in amicable silence for a few moments, sipping at their mugs. Eventually, Emily asked, "Is this the week confirmation starts?"

"Next week."

"That's right. But you still need to head back over to church this afternoon, don't you?"

Pastor nodded. "Jeremy handed me some new applications for the secretary position to review, and I have a few calls to make before supper. You get me all to yourself tomorrow, though."

Emily graciously didn't complain. Instead, she leaned her head back against the chair, closing her eyes. She looked tired, but her face still glowed with a youthful vitality. Pastor openly admired his wife while she rested. He had always been partial to her brown eyes, but her perpetually pink cheeks were a close second. One time, before they were married, he had tried to tell her just how much he liked them, but Emily had shut him down faster than a bank on a holiday.

"Don't stare at me, Michael!" she had said, covering her face bashfully with her hands. "I have rosacea. That's why I'm red all of the time. The blood vessels in my face are broken."

Well, he had never beheld such a beautiful brokenness, and as he studied Emily now, he knew that he would never grow weary of looking at this woman. His eyes wandered down to her slightly distended middle, and he thrilled. Baby was growing bigger every day. It would be just a little over five months before they would get to meet him or her.

"Emily?" he asked, interrupting her repose.

"Hm?" She opened her eyes.

"How are your hands?"

She smiled at him, obviously pleased that he had noticed, and he immediately felt embarrassed. He hadn't thought to ask her about her hands this entire pregnancy, and she always developed carpal tunnel when pregnant.

"Same as usual," she shrugged.

"And the fatigue?"

"Worse today."

That made sense. Emily was being considerately undemonstrative—no doubt for his benefit—but he wanted his wife to have a chance to talk about yesterday's ills. Wasn't that what she had tried to do with him before he had selfishly left, simply talk?

"Why did you stay home this morning?"

Emily thought for a moment before answering. "We weren't reconciled."

He nodded, keeping silent. She would say more if he gave her enough room.

"And," she added slowly, "I suppose I was afraid of seeing Yvonne—or *not* seeing Yvonne, either way." She suddenly looked at him questioningly, and he shook his head.

"She wasn't there."

Emily's rosy complexion deepened to crimson. "Michael, can I tell you something awful?"

Here it came. The words she most likely had been trying to say to him last night, but he hadn't given her the chance.

"I think a part of me has been wanting Yvonne to leave for a long time. Isn't that terrible? I shouldn't feel like that. I mean, she's my sister in Christ. I should want her to be in church, right? Why couldn't I make it work with her? I feel like the biggest failure in the world."

"It takes two to make it work."

"But I hate it that I'm so weak! And you haven't even heard the worst of it." Emily suddenly leaned forward, setting down her mug on the coffee table. "I had been planning to bring Charlene with me to church today. I invited her two days ago, and she said yes. And then I called her this morning to cancel! Isn't that horrible? I not only kept our children from hearing the Word of God, I kept Charlene from it too."

"Next week, okay?" he suggested, concerned that Emily was going to dwell in the past long enough to set up house there. "Invite her again next week."

Emily nodded, but she didn't look appeased. "I didn't realize how hard this was going to be."

"What?"

"Being a pastor's wife."

He felt that familiar pang of guilt again, the one that had plagued him ever since he had asked Emily to join him in this life.

"Or maybe," Emily pondered, "it's that I didn't realize how bad I was going to be at it. I'm the worst pastor's wife in the world, Michael! I just can't quite figure it out. How am I supposed to love and respect these people when they hate and disrespect you? I'm not sure I can do it."

"You are doing it."

"But look at what I did to Yvonne yesterday! And then today—well, today was an all-time low. I *knew* I should be in church—I *knew* it was sinful to stop our children from keeping the Sabbath—but all I could think about was those things Yvonne said about you. 'What if she is right?' I thought. 'What if you really are tearing the church apart?' But then, well, I guess I finally came to my senses. I mean, I *know* you, Michael. I sit in the pew and listen to your sermons just like everyone else, and you preach the truth. You speak to us what God says in His Word, and it hit me this morning, right around the time the service was wrapping up, that Yvonne probably accuses you of being unfaithful because she wants to hurt you. She doesn't want to listen to what you have to say."

"What *God* has to say," Pastor amended. "Pray for her, Emily."

"I do," she confirmed, "but how can I go to church when there are people there who openly despise you and God's Word?"

Pastor knew the answer to this, because he had been asking himself the same question for years. "Jesus is there too, remember. We go to church because He bids us to come and hear, to take and eat, to take and drink, and to rest from our labors in Him. So in faith, we do. Even in the face of persecution."

Emily knew the truth when she heard it—he could see it on her face—but her eyes were still pained. This life in ministry was not for the weakhearted. He stood and walked over to a low shelf lining the southern wall and pulled out Luther's Large Catechism. He quickly turned to a familiar passage in the explanation of the Eighth Commandment and read aloud, "'Wherever there are godly preachers and Christians, they must bear the sentence before the world that calls them heretics, apostates, and indeed, instigators and desperately wicked unbelievers. Besides, God's Word must suffer in the most shameful and hateful manner, being persecuted, blasphemed, contradicted, perverted, and falsely quoted and interpreted. But let this go. For this is the way of the blind world, which condemns and persecutes the truth and God's children, and yet considers it no sin.'"

Emily smiled ironically. "I guess I wasn't prepared to find the world in our church."

"It hurts, doesn't it?"

"Yeah, it does." Emily stood and walked to the dining table, pulling a chair toward the front door, conspicuously hooking her forearms underneath a rung rather than using her hands. Pastor anticipated her intent and quickly closed the book, walking over to the door and lifting the chalkboard from its nail.

"Here," he said. "Let me. What do you want to write on it this time?"

"Something a little more encouraging," she said ruefully, her eyes relaying repentance. "Is it okay to quote Luther?"

"Sure."

"Then," she said, taking a deep breath and exhaling slowly, "I'd like to write, 'But let this go.'"

Pastor sat at his study desk, his *Treasury of Daily Prayer* open before him at the commemoration of St. James of Jerusalem. It was a bit early in the calendar year for this particular reading, but he often turned to it in times of fear and uncertainty. This pastor was in need of hearing a good sermon, and the sainted Dietrich Bonhoeffer was the one to do it.

"'It is not we who build,'" Pastor read aloud, that his own ears might hear. "'Christ builds the church. No man builds the church but Christ alone. Whoever is minded to build the church is surely well on the way to destroying it; for he will build a temple to idols without wishing or knowing it. We must confess—he builds. We must proclaim—he builds. We must pray to him—that he may build.'"

Yvonne had turned a deaf ear to his petitions last night, and while her leaving the church had hit Emily hard, it had left him effectually slain. For ten years, he had been preaching and teaching God's Word in its truth and purity for the benefit of Yvonne and her family. How he wanted her to believe it—how he wanted everyone to believe it!—but not every seed fell on good soil. And the thorns of this world continually threatened to choke the good grain.

"'We do not know his plan,'" Pastor continued. "'We cannot see whether he is building or pulling down. It may be that the times which by human standards are times of collapse are for him the great times of construction. It may be that the times which from a human point of view are great times for the church are times when it is pulled down.'"

Pastor had witnessed several people leaving the church over the years—some because they simply moved out of town, others because they wanted a "happier" church service, and others still because Zion "wasn't meeting their needs"—but Yvonne's leaving was particularly painful. Her leaving was being blamed solely on him. He was the thorn which was choking her faith, so she said.

Her leaving was personal and, sadly, appeared to be accompanied by unbelief. *Lord, help!*

"'It is a great comfort which Christ gives to his church: you confess, preach, bear witness to me and I alone will build where it pleases me. Do not meddle in what is my province. Do what is given to you to do well and you have done enough. But do it well. Pay no heed to views and opinions. Don't ask for judgments. Don't always be calculating what will happen. Don't always be on the lookout for another refuge! Church, stay a church! But church, confess, confess, confess! Christ alone is your Lord; from his grace alone can you live as you are. Christ builds.'"

Pastor shut the book and stood, walking out of his study and down the long hall to the darkened sanctuary. He was alone, but he wasn't alone. He knelt at the rail before the Builder of the church, the Shepherd of the flock, the Lord of the harvest. And burying his face in his hands, he prayed, "Search me and know me, Lord Jesus. If I have not done well for Your kingdom, forgive me. Create in me a new heart, O Lord, and help me to do what it is that You have given for me to do. Help me to confess, preach, and bear witness to You alone. Build and pull down Your Church, Lord, according to Your will, and give Yvonne and Emily and all of us faith which trusts in Your Word. Amen."

## CHAPTER THIRTY-FOUR: BEFORE THE PARADE PASSES BY

Blaine was sleeping in this morning, and Mrs. Scheinberg let him. She covered the bowl of readied apple pancake batter with a towel and pulled the bubbling cider sauce off of the stovetop. It would be easy enough to heat it back up whenever Blaine awoke. She silently motioned for Ceci to follow her, and the two slipped out the back door to feed the chickens. She had already managed to walk two miles, chore the cows, and harvest the last of her late summer tomatoes and squash from the garden before the sun had even stretched its delinquent arms above the eastern horizon. Personally, she thought the sun was growing rather slothful in September, and it would persist in behaving like a self-centered teenager for the rest of the year, hiding away in its room after supper and sleeping in every morning well past any hour that was decent.

"You're no better than the sun," she fondly ribbed her prized partridge-colored Italian rooster, emptying her small kitchen pail onto the ground before him in the southern chicken pen. Cogburn strutted cockily before the booty of chopped apple cores, melon rinds, carrot peels, and potato skins—her and Blaine's spoils from yesterday. "Save some for the ladies, now."

Ceci planted herself directly across the fence from the flirty fowl while Mrs. Scheinberg shouldered open a barn door just to the right of the pen. She reached for a plastic cup sitting on a nearby shelf and filled it from the large garbage can of scratch feed in the corner of the stall. "Coo, coo, coo, coo!" she called out, shaking the pellets in the cup and stepping back out into the sunshine. "Coo, coo, coo, coo!"

Cogburn's harem promptly scurried from the safety of the coop out into the open air, trotting toward the edge of the pen where Mrs. Scheinberg was scattering feed. They scratched and pecked enthusiastically at the ground, a feathery pandemonium.

"Slow down, now, Madge. Don't be such a hog. You're a chicken, not a pig, remember. And share with Beatrice for once."

Mrs. Scheinberg had named all twelve of her laying hens. It was something she and Dean had done for fun their first year of marriage, and even after his sudden death she had continued the tradition every year without him. She sighed and rolled her shoulders, suddenly tense. This Friday was the forty-third anniversary of Dean's accident, and she was feeling anxious. She usually did this time of year. Emily Fletcher had noticed and asked her about it once, but all Mrs. Scheinberg had been able to say was that the month of September always made her shoulders tight and her stomach loose. Emily had understood. The younger woman felt the same way every April whenever the anniversary of Peter Duke's death rolled around.

*Oh, crawfish!* Now she was thinking about it. She expelled the bad air from her lungs, returned the empty cup to the barn, latched the door shut, and made her way toward the northeast corner of the property. It had been awhile since she had visited the old corncrib, and she supposed now was as good a time as any to pay her respects.

Dean's father had built the corncrib in the 1950s, back when the family had needed to store ear corn year round to grind into feed for the milk cows. As time passed, however, the farm's storage needs shifted more from feed to seed, and the corncrib fell into disrepair. It wasn't by any means decrepit like The Offense—Mrs. Scheinberg never would have allowed for a building on her property to injure the landscape in such a way—but the red paint on its wooden slats was peeling and entire patches of shingles were missing from the roof. Even now as she rounded the stone silo at the southeast corner of the barn and beheld the corncrib's gaping roof, she wondered if she shouldn't have the building pulled down once and for all. But it was yawning charmingly in the morning light and smiled back at her like a favorite, toothless uncle. She could no more tear down this building than she could her new house. At least, not as long as the corncrib entombed her last physical link to Dean.

Mrs. Scheinberg grabbed the handle of the heavy wooden door and, pulling at it with all of her body weight, slid it open on its rail. The musky smell of corn dust greeted her nose, and something small and furry on four legs skittered noisily out of sight. Ceci, fancying herself a hound dog, immediately barked and chased after the unidentifiable critter, but Mrs. Scheinberg stayed rooted to the spot. There, resting in the center tunnel of the crib, basking in the dusty, golden beams of sunlight shining through the gaps in the widely spaced slats of the eastern wall, was the Ford 8N "Redbelly" tractor, Dean's pride and joy. Her husband had loved that old machine—inherited it from his granddaddy—but she would never be able to harbor such affection for the engine which motored the auger that took her husband's life. In fact, she could barely stand to look at it now, even as she could barely stand not to look at it. She reached out a remarkably steady hand to touch a shoulder-high rear wheel, carefully avoiding eye contact with the murderous driveshaft. Then, her heart racing, she ran her fingers along a gray tire guard, scooted alongside the tractor in the narrow crib, and lifted a green Slogger onto the footrest. Rust was beginning to show through the vibrant red paint, but otherwise, the tractor still looked as it had forty-three years before.

In one swift motion, Mrs. Scheinberg reached up to take hold of the spindly steering wheel and pulled herself onto the shovel-shaped seat, letting out the breath she had been holding. It had been a long time since she had been fit enough to pull herself up onto any tractor, but thanks to the hundreds of step-ups Candice had been making her do every week, mounting this metal horse was relatively easy. A small feeling of quiet satisfaction softened the sting of her present sadness.

"Going for a drive?"

Mrs. Scheinberg almost jumped out of her seat at the sound of Blaine's voice. She hadn't heard him approaching the corncrib, and her joke of a guard dog was somewhere off in the north pasture pretending to be Daniel Boone.

"Sorry," Blaine apologized, stepping into the crib and looking around. "I didn't mean to scare you. I thought maybe you'd need some help with the chores."

"I finished the chores an hour ago, sleepyhead."

"What are you doing out here?" He impulsively reached out to touch one of the Ford's wheels, just as she had done. "Is this . . . ?" his voice trailed off knowingly. He automatically glanced down at the driveshaft, and Mrs. Scheinberg felt her stomach loosen all over again. "It's September, isn't it?"

He had remembered. She closed her eyes and sat, comforted, in the warm embrace of Blaine's knowing. It got lonely in her memories sometimes. She reached out a grieving hand to him, and he met it with his own.

"I've loved three men in my life, Blaine." She was having trouble getting the words out. "My father, Dean, and you. Two of those men are dead and gone, so it means the world to me that you came home this week."

"Well," Blaine's voice was sincere, "I wanted to see my new bathroom."

The laugh gave her no warning but erupted from her throat before she could account for it. The force of its motion threw her unsuspecting head back against her shoulders and shook the dust out of the golden air. Only Blaine could save her with a laugh like that. Well, and Dean.

"I didn't know you still had this thing," Blaine marveled, releasing her hand and circling the Ford to get a full view of its mid-century character.

She shook her head, wiping at her eyes. "I can't bring myself to get rid of it."

"You mean it's been parked in here this whole time?"

"Not the *whole* time. Dean's brothers have used it off and on over the years."

"And you?"

Her face pinched defiantly against the threat of tears. She bit her lips and shook her head.

Blaine was watching her evenly over the tractor's hood. Sometimes, she wished he couldn't read her quite so well. "Does it still run?"

"Of course it does," she snapped. "It's a Ford."

He gave her a tolerant look. He usually did whenever she indulged in what he liked to call farmspeak. "Well, it sure seems a shame to keep an old beauty like this cooped up in a shed—"

"It's a corncrib," she corrected.

"—in a *whatever!*" He threw his arms wide. "It's been parked in here long enough, don't you think?"

"What are you saying?"

His eyes were mischievous. "Let's take her for a ride."

"What?"

"Let's take old Henry Ford for a ride!"

"Where?"

"Down Main Street, of course."

She gave him a perplexed look.

"The parade. It's this afternoon." Blaine's eyebrows were doing cartwheels now. "You said the ladies never decided on a float. We can make a couple of signs with the church's name, hang them on the front and back of this glorious hunk of metal, and drive it in the parade!"

"It's not exactly a two-seater."

"Well, then, I'll walk beside you and throw candy!" His boyish grin reminded her of a young Robbie Jones. "C'mon, Arlene. Let's do it. Dean's not here, I know, but you said he loved this old Ford. It's a tractor, not a tomb. Why keep it hidden away in some corncob?"

"Corncrib," she corrected again, a small smile playing at her lips.

"Are you or are you not Mrs. Dean Scheinberg?"

"I am."

"Then drive your husband's tractor in the parade!"

She put both hands on the steering wheel, remembering. Something hidden—something that had lain dormant behind her heart for years—began to animate. "Dean would love it," she admitted, more to herself than to Blaine.

"And so would you."

"And so would *you*." She frowned and sighed irritatedly, a final, grand show of resistance to Blaine's slick maneuvering. "I see what you're doing."

"What's that?"

"You're trying to keep me from moping."

He didn't seem threatened by her in the least. "It's what we do for each other, Arlene. Now, c'mon. How do you turn this thing on?"

⁓⁓⁓⁓⁓⁓⁓⁓⁓⁓⁓⁓⁓

Mary was sitting on the steps of her front porch when Blaine drove up to the Mulberry property later that evening.

"Hey," he said, hopping down from the truck and walking up the sidewalk to sit next to her on the top step. The sun had bid adieu to the sky, and a heap of cumulus clouds stacked directly overhead waved good-bye in romantic shades of pink, purple, and blue. Mary wasn't feeling the romance, however.

"Hey."

They sat in silence for a few moments, she staring at a crack in the old, winding walkway and he watching the labored progress of an ant carrying a small leaf across the sidewalk's edge. The weight of all that remained unspoken between them strained at Mary's neck.

"How was the parade?" she finally asked.

Blaine spontaneously smiled. She liked how his dark eyes glinted whenever he did that. "It was fun," he said, chuckling at some memory she didn't share. "Did you see it?"

"No." She had helped put together the library board's float earlier that morning, but her head had begun to hurt by lunchtime. The only thing she had seen all afternoon long was her bedroom ceiling.

"Arlene was in rare form today. You should have seen her, Mar. Any time one of the boys from the rifle league got even with one of her rear tires, she braked to a full stop in the middle of the street and refused to drive any further until the boys got fully behind her. I don't know," he shook his head, his voice curving upward along with his smile, "I think I may have unleashed a monster in her with that tractor."

Mary smiled politely in return, but her heart wasn't in it. She had been looking forward to watching the parade with Blaine—they had made plans after church on Sunday to see it together the next day—but he had called her early that morning to cancel. "Arlene needs me today" was all he had said. Well, she needed him too. "When do you get to see your mom?"

"Tomorrow." Hope dawned on his features like a golden sunrise. "Did I tell you? She's started painting."

"Has she?" Mary was pleased by this news. Ellen Maler had been suffering from severe depression for years, ever since Blaine's father had divorced her, and her doing anything was a victory. "Will you see your dad too?"

"I'll take the train up to Chicago on Wednesday morning. He wants to grab lunch before I fly to Fort Wayne."

Mary had met Tony Maler only a few times. She had found the man to be incredibly charming but also selfish. No one's needs were ever as great as his own, and she found that mindset baffling in a father. Her own dad was so attentive and selfless, always calling her every Sunday afternoon and driving into Bradbury on Tuesday nights to take her grocery shopping and then to Koelster's Kitchen for supper. Blaine had never known that kind of altruistic love and devotion from his own father. "Are you all packed?"

"Yep."

"Good."

Silence reigned once again, and Mary squeezed her arms tightly around her middle. She was usually comfortable in the silence, especially Blaine's silence, but this one echoed with all of the awkward things the two of them had said—and not said—to each other the Thursday before. She honestly didn't know what to do. They had never talked about their relationship status before. Were they supposed to keep talking about it? Was she supposed to bring it up again and ask him to better explain himself, or was that something she should wait for him to do? But why would Blaine ever bring it up again? She had pretty much shut down the—

"Mar?"

"Yes?" She snapped to immediate attention. Blaine was looking at her, his eyes protective, just like her father's. For some reason, that disappointed her.

"You are my best friend."

She really wanted him to look at her in a different way, a softer way.

"But I won't be your friend if it hurts you."

Why couldn't he look at her the way Pastor Fletcher looked at Emily? Why did he never look at her as if he *needed* her?

"I've been thinking about what you said, you know, about people talking about us. And maybe it's not possible for a man and a woman to be such good friends for so long. Maybe it causes . . . confusion."

Was it her epilepsy? Or was it the color of her skin? Maybe it was because she couldn't drive. Maybe she was too much of a deadweight to be wanted and needed by someone who could go anywhere at any time.

"I just don't want to hurt you, Mary."

Her sight was blurring.

"I'll stay away if you want me to."

She shook her head furiously, panicked. She definitely didn't want him to do that.

"What would you like me to do, then? I can't keep people from talking, but I'm not . . . able to give you more."

She was crying now. Her glasses were fogging up, and her throat was making ugly hiccuping noises.

"Oh, Mary, I'm so sorry. Please don't cry."

She stood up and turned toward the door, embarrassed.

"Mary, please talk to me."

She couldn't. She just couldn't.

"I do like you, Mary. It's just—"

She fumbled at the doorknob, unable to look him in the eye.

"Mary, please. Let's not leave it like this."

Her shoulders slumped in defeat. She didn't want to leave it like this either, but she couldn't tell him what she was thinking. Her thoughts were all too deep, too personal, and too impossible to be helpful now. What good would come of telling a man who merely liked her that she actually loved him? that she needed him? that her life was so small without him? What kind of friend would she be to burden Blaine in such a way? And he was already so burdened by so many people in his life.

"What do you want me to say?" she finally asked, her voice crumbling.

"I don't know." Blaine was standing right behind her, but his voice sounded completely lost.

She took a deep, shaky breath, turning around. There was at least one truth she could tell him. It wasn't the whole truth, but it might appease him for the moment. "I'm jealous, all right?"

"Jealous? Of what?"

"Of your going off to school for the *third* time, while I'm still stuck here in Bradbury!"

His face flickered through about seven different emotions, relief winning out in the end. "Well, you can always come visit me, you know."

"Oh, really? How?"

He frowned again and then acquiesced a timid smile. "I don't know."

"My point exactly."

Blaine looked as if he were keeping guard over a few private truths of his own. "Well, then, I'll keep coming home to visit you."

Mary's throat threatened to close on her again. How could he misunderstand her so? She didn't want him to come home for a visit. She wanted him to take her away from here and make her his home.

Blaine opened his long arms to receive her, and she meekly tucked herself into his brotherly embrace. It was easier to hide from him this way.

When Blaine got back to the farm that night, Mrs. Scheinberg was using a piece of floss to cut individual cinnamon rolls from a log of raw dough on the kitchen counter.

"How'd it go?" she asked.

Blaine shrugged and slowly returned her truck keys to a rack hanging by the back door. "She didn't slam the door in my face, at least."

Mrs. Scheinberg nodded thoughtfully, returning to her task at hand without pressing any further. She was already privy to Blaine's feelings on the subject of Mary, but she felt a desire to respect the privacy of that dear girl. She must be hurting right now. *Lord, help her.*

"What's this?" Blaine asked, fingering a slip of paper lying on the kitchen table.

She kept her eyes averted. "It's your paycheck."

"My what?" She heard him pick up the check, and she could feel his eyes bulging.

"It's for school," she hastily explained. "You'll get one like it in the mail each month until you are done with seminary."

"Absolutely not!" He dropped it on the table. "It's too much, Arlene."

"It's not enough if you ask me," she replied hotly, "*which* I know you never will." She pointed an accusing finger at the boy, not because he had done anything wrong but because there was no one else to point at. "I looked up what seminary is costing you boys these days. What with boarding and insurance and books and everything else, you're going to have to take out tens of thousands of dollars each year just to get by. And we both know your father isn't going to give you a *penny* to help with this degree." She lowered her finger but maintained her frown. "Besides, as it turns out, a widow can save quite a bit of money if she orders a two-bedroom home instead of three."

He shook his head emphatically. "Nope. I can't take it."

"You most certainly will, young man!" She picked up a nearby wooden spatula and waved it in the air. "Are you going to deny me the blessing of taking care of the pastors of my church?"

"I'm not a pastor yet."

"Past, present, future pastor—what does it matter? They're all mine to care for, and God has given me much so that I can give much."

"You should be putting this money away for a nursing home or something."

Her eyes were the ones that bulged this time. "You did not just say that."

He impulsively grinned, and so did she.

"The way I see it is," she said, lowering her spatula and returning to her rolls, "your job for the next four years is to study and practice." She couldn't keep the self-satisfied tone from her voice. She was enjoying this so, so much. "I'm simply paying you for doing your job."

Blaine shook his head, giving one last show of resistance to her slick maneuvering. "I see what you're doing."

"Oh? And what's that?"

"You're taking care of me."

"Yes, well," she positively crowed, "it's what you and I do for each other."

# Chapter Thirty-Five: Good Order

It was a tradition in the Fletcher home to invite Pastor Otto Weaver and his wife, Esther, over for supper every Labor Day. The elderly couple lived just seven miles north of Bradbury on two wooded acres Esther's brother had given them upon the clergyman's retirement.

"How's retirement treating you, Otto?" Pastor liked to ask. It was an ongoing joke between the two of them. Since Pastor Weaver's retirement at the age of sixty-five, he had been serving Grace Lutheran Church in Fancy Grove as vacancy pastor. The man was now eighty-two years old.

"Retirement?" the white-haired man usually replied with a wink. "You mean I retired?"

This evening was no different. Pastor Fletcher and Pastor Weaver recited their customary litany, laughed good-naturedly, clapped each other's shoulders affectionately, and then settled on the couch before a tray of black olives—Pastor Weaver's favorite— and bourbon.

Pastor Fletcher trusted Pastor Weaver implicitly. The older cleric had befriended and supported him in his ministry from the very first moment he had stepped foot in Bradbury, and the faithful man had also served as his father confessor for years, even offering premarital counseling to both him and Emily and officiating at their wedding.

And Emily simply adored Esther. The round woman was soft and tender in all of the right places, inside and out. She had birthed eleven children in her sixty-four years of marriage, eight of whom were still alive today but none of whom lived within a hundred miles of Illinois, and Emily gladly took on the role of surrogate daughter with this warmhearted woman.

"Well, hello, cupcake!" Esther cooed at the front door, leaning in to caress both of Becky's porcelain cheeks with her wrinkled hands. The two-year-old was shyly clinging to her mother's neck. "You look like your daddy with those dark curls."

"I Beck-ee."

"Listen to you!" Esther praised. "You're talking like a big girl now, aren't you?"

Becky nodded solemnly.

"If she can ever get a word in edgewise," Emily wryly informed. "The twins hardly give her a chance to speak most days."

"Where are my two honeycombs?"

"In their bedroom." Emily let her daughter slip down to the floor. "Becky, take Tante's hand, and show her George and Julia's bedroom."

Becky obediently complied, and the three of them made a slow procession down the hall. Emily couldn't wait to show her friend how perfectly the quilts she had lovingly sewn the twins last Christmas fit on their beds. It wasn't meant to be, however.

"Julia!" Emily cried, mortified at the sight of the tangled mess on the floor. Her daughter had managed to pull all of their clean bedding—Esther's beautiful quilts included—onto the old carpet and arranged it in a twisted pile at the center of the room. Emily threw an embarrassed glance at her elderly friend, but Esther's facial expression remained graciously neutral.

"What are you doing?" Emily hissed.

"We're playing crack babies, Mommy!" Julia explained.

"What?" Emily's heart skipped a beat. Crack babies? What did her children know about crack babies? Sure, they had held meth in their little, innocent hands, but they were none the wiser. Or weren't they? She wracked her brain over the last two weeks, searching for some slip of the tongue, some precarious moment she had mentioned hard drugs in front of them and not realized it. She couldn't remember ever talking about cocaine, but with her pregnancy hormones and fatigue and general frustration over all that had happened across the driveway and then across the street, well, she couldn't be too sure.

"It's a game, Mommy. Look! George is a crack baby!"

Emily hid her flushed cheeks behind her hands in horror as her downy son proceeded to jump up from the middle of the pile, discarding sheets and blankets with his teeth and clucking like a chicken. Becky clapped and cackled appreciatively.

"See? George is a baby chick! He cracked his egg!" Julia clapped merrily for a moment before pushing her brother aside to take his place. "Now it's my turn. Cover me up, George."

Comprehension was pokey in making its way across her hormone-washed brain, but when it finally arrived and dismounted before her eyes, Emily found herself giggling with subsequent relief. Esther, too, indulged in a few snickers as George threw the covers over his sister and then stood back to watch, eagerly hopping up and down on both of his socked feet. Becky shrieked wildly in anticipation.

"Cr-aa-ck!" Julia called, standing straight up, shedding the bedding, and looking around at everyone, obviously pleased to have an audience.

They all clapped appreciatively, and then Emily ordered her little chicks to return the quilts to their beds.

"But Becky hasn't had a turn, Mommy," Julia shrewdly pointed out.

Emily sighed. Her eldest daughter was growing into quite the negotiator. Heaven help the prosecutor who came up against this little snip of a defense lawyer in court someday! *Or heaven help her husband and children*, Emily thought with a knowing smile. "One turn for Becky, and then the quilts go back on the beds. Then I want you to come out to the kitchen. It's time to set the table for dinner. George, you've got the forks. Julia, spoons."

"I hep!" Becky insisted.

"You can help Daddy with his olives."

Emily turned and offered her arm to Esther, and the two made their way back down the hall.

"How are you feeling?" Esther asked.

"Tired," she admitted. It didn't work to be anything but honest with this woman. She had tried that with her first pregnancy, but Esther was the queen of mothers. She could see through every blinder. "My hands hurt."

Esther patted her arm sympathetically. "This too shall pass. Baby is due in . . . ?"

"February."

"Oh, a valentine!"

Emily couldn't help but smile. Esther found the bright spot in every moment.

Dinner was joyous. The rainbow chicken was baked to colorful perfection, the apple pie crust flaked under Esther's attentive fork, and Pastor Weaver entertained the children from first bite to last with stories of a family of raccoons that had made their home in the Weavers' burn barrel.

"I want a wa-coon!" George decided at the end of the meal.

"Well, honey," Emily declared, "Carrots doesn't. Rabbits and raccoons don't mix. Now, why don't you, Julia, and Becky show Pastor Weaver your pumpkin out in the garden?"

As the men and the children emptied the house, the two women stayed behind to clear the table.

"Has the church board hired a new secretary yet?" Esther inquired, following Emily into the kitchen with a plate full of used silverware.

"Not yet."

"Let me guess. They want you to do it."

Emily laughed. It felt so good to talk to another pastor's wife. "I don't know about that, but I'm holding out for the janitor's position anyway. It opened up this week."

Esther frowned. "Not with the baby coming, surely."

"I'm joking!" Emily assured. "Well, not about the position opening up. That really happened. A longtime member of our congregation left and took the janitor with her."

"Did they get married?"

"No, no. The woman who left is the janitor's mother-in-law."

"Oh dear." Esther's eyes grew wide with alarm. "How terrible! The poor daughter! Did the janitor leave her behind with any children?"

Emily quickly saw the misunderstanding and explained what she could of Yvonne's situation before Esther recreated the entire plot of *The Graduate* with Bradbury as the backdrop.

"I see," Esther nodded, running hot water in the sink. "That's quite a different story, isn't it? Though I'm so sorry for you, Emily. And your husband. Is this woman older?"

Emily shrugged noncommittally. "She's older than Michael, younger than you."

"I figured."

"What?"

"Well," Esther lowered the silverware into the foamy water, "she probably had trouble with her pastor being younger than her. Some people do, you know."

Emily frowned, considering this. Really? Was that a problem? She had never minded having a—well, come to think of it, she had never had a pastor younger than herself. She supposed she hadn't yet hit that season of life.

"A pastor is a father of sorts," Esther explained, "and it's a hard thing for some people—in fact, most, I would venture to say—that a father be younger than them."

Emily nodded, somewhat astounded. She had never thought of this before. Had her husband?

"Think about it this way. Our sinful flesh is already opposed to being obedient to authority of any kind, but having to be obedient to a father—a spiritual father, no doubt—who is younger than us? That's hard. It tests our faith, that's for sure. I know Otto was pained early on in his ministry when people in the congregation despised him for his age. That kind of derision is not a fruit of faith, as you know, and it hurt him to see people not believing in God's promises for them." Esther turned off the water. "But not all is lost. There are those who are able to listen to their pastor regardless of his age, because they trust in God. They have faith in His Word which says, 'This man is the one called to speak God's Word to me.'"

Did Yvonne have trouble living under the authority of a younger man? Was that part of why she had left? Emily hoped not, and since only Yvonne could tell for sure, she yielded to her chalkboard once again. *But let this go.*

"It's a great shame—that's what Luther calls it—when Christians don't value and honor the ones whom God has sent,"

Esther continued, turning to give Emily a tender smile. "And it hurts to be married to the one who is being shamed, doesn't it?"

Emily nodded, her eyes filling with tears.

"Come here, dear."

Emily's breath caught in her throat at that last word. Years had passed since anyone had called her by that particular term of affection. She had assumed the word had died with Alice. No one at church used it anymore, that much was certain, and hearing it again unleashed a flood of emotion. She walked toward the soft arms extended to her and buried her head against Esther's shoulder.

"Now, listen to me, Emily. Your Michael has been called to be a father to these people, whether they want him to or not. Pray for him, all right? And comfort him. Take care of his needs. That's your special job as his wife. You and I both know that he has a paternal heart toward this congregation—we've both seen it—so help him not to grow hard toward his more unruly children."

Emily nodded, and as she pulled away to wipe at her face, Esther's face was radiating a certain joy.

"Did I ever tell you about the gift Otto gave to me on the anniversary of his ordination? No? Well, it was the thirteenth year of his ministry—I remember it better than most of my own birthdays—and it was so sweet of him. He had never done anything like that before. But then, we had just lost Isaac and I was having a particularly hard time with a couple of feisty women at the church and, well, he was trying to encourage me, I guess. That," she gave Emily an ornery look over the sink, "or he was trying to bribe me into not leaving him. Ha! Anyway, those two peahens kept complaining to everyone in the church about the way I handled my children. They even went to the elders about it, the old coots. Oh yes, Emily! They did. They made such a fuss, but not once did they ever come sit next to me in the pew and offer to help. No, they remained on their high perches Sunday after Sunday and watched me wrangle my children all by myself and then broadcasted a report as if they were critics in the newspaper. They even tried to bar me from a women's mission society meeting once, but a sweet woman named Gladys Stremming—God rest her soul!—brought me to the meeting herself and showed her teeth any time those women stepped out of line."

Emily thought of the time Mrs. Scheinberg had picked her up and taken her to church one Sunday after the women at Zion had publicly shamed her. "What happened then?"

Esther shrugged her delicate shoulders. "Nothing. Time passed is all. Eventually, those birds cooled their beaks, and my children grew up."

"Did they never apologize?"

"Not once. Well, that's not true. One of them complimented my Angie on her manners years later. I like to think of that as an apology, of sorts. Anyway, the gift! I almost forgot to tell you about the gift. That's what I get for focusing on the negative. Well, Otto gave me the most beautifully embroidered cloth for his ordination anniversary. He didn't make it himself, of course. Heaven's no! That man can barely weave a belt through his own pants without some help let alone thread a needle. He paid a local woman to do it. But he told her what to embroider."

"What?"

"Otto called it the 'Order of the Pastor's Wife.'"

"Is that a seal or emblem of some sort?"

"No, dear," Esther gave Emily a meaningful look. "It's the text from Colossians 3:12–17. Anyway, I had it framed. It's perfectly comforting and convicting, all at the same time. I hung it in our bedroom where I could read it every morning. It really is wonderful. Read it tonight before you go to bed. You'll see what I mean."

Emily did read it, as soon as her head hit the pillow, first to herself, and then again aloud to her husband.

"Michael, listen to this." She shifted on her side, so he could better hear. "'Put on then, as God's chosen ones, holy and beloved, compassionate hearts, kindness, humility, meekness, and patience, bearing with one another and, if one has a complaint against another, forgiving each other; as the Lord has forgiven you, so you also must forgive. And above all these put on love, which binds everything together in perfect harmony. And let the peace of Christ rule in your hearts, to which indeed you were called in one body. And be thankful. Let the word of Christ dwell in you richly, teaching and admonishing one another in all wisdom, singing psalms and hymns and spiritual songs, with thankfulness in your hearts to God. And whatever you do, in word or deed, do everything in the name of the Lord Jesus, giving thanks to God the Father through Him.'"

"Colossians?"

"Mmhm." She stared at the text, thinking. "Esther suggested I read it."

"Why?"

"Because . . ." She closed her Bible and set it on her nightstand, making a mental note to begin learning how to embroider the very next morning. She needed a wall hanging of her own. "It's the 'Order of the Pastor's Wife.'"

# CHAPTER THIRTY-SIX: ANTHEM OF ZION

Emily set the plate of peanut butter cookies on the floorboards between them.

"Thanks, Miss Emily."

She watched with delight as the lanky boy sitting on her front porch steps downed a cookie in two bites and tossed back a glass of lemonade in three gulps. He reached for another cookie. *Just like Ben.*

"I kind of miss the old mower," she confided.

"Me too," Robbie Jones agreed, his mouth around another cookie. "This one self-propels, though. Sure makes pushing that fourth yard at the end of the day easier."

"How's Ben's rider?"

Robbie's grin parted his freckles like the Red Sea. "It'll do."

Emily laughed. Ben Schmidt would always be the golden boy in a John Deere shirt who captured her heart, but Robbie Jones could charm the ears off of a rabbit. The two of them together? They were pure, small-town magic—Bradbury's own Bing Crosby and Danny Kaye—and it made her sad to think of the ruddy, young sidekick being without his lead for the entire school year. The two boys were more than friends. They were business partners too, mowing an average of twenty-nine lawns a week between them every summer, one of which was the parsonage.

"Are you going to let me pay you this time?"

Robbie shook his head and wiped his hands on his jeans. "Already been paid for, Miss Emily."

He had been giving her the exact same answer for the past four years. Ever since she had married his pastor, Robbie refused money from her hand. She once asked him who was paying to have the parsonage lawn mowed, and all he did was flash her one of his winsome grins and shrug. Whether it was Rebecca or Mrs. Scheinberg or the Davises or the Schmidts, she didn't know, but she had a sneaking suspicion it was the hardworking mower himself.

"Thank you, Robbie," she humbly replied. "Will you at least take some cookies to go?"

The bottomless pit with legs didn't say no, and while he loaded his mower onto a trailer hooked up to the back of his bike—some things in Bradbury never changed—Emily brown-bagged what was left on the plate.

"See you on Sunday?" she asked, walking down the sidewalk and handing him the bag.

"Yes, ma'am."

She smiled appreciatively. Ben may have left Bradbury, but he had thoughtfully left his manners behind with his friend.

"Playing club ball this fall?"

"Nah."

Emily was careful not to overreact. She knew this summer had been tough on Robbie, but dropping club ball was a big change for the boy. But then, it wasn't unprecedented. Ben had let go of summer baseball for bigger and better things. Those two boys were more forward-thinking than most teenagers she knew.

"Don't worry," Robbie assured, seemingly reading her mind. "I'm not done with baseball. Still planning on playing come spring, but I thought I'd try the debate team this fall."

"Debate team?" Her eyebrows raised involuntarily before she could pull them back down. "You like debating?"

Robbie shrugged. "Mom suggested I try it. She said living with Davie my whole life's given me plenty of practice."

Emily laughed at that, and as she waved Robbie on down the street, she pondered how much the boy had grown and matured over the years. He didn't leave her handpicked tiger lilies on her front step like his predecessor—that tradition had ended with Ben—but Robbie left her something profoundly more important. She turned around and eyed her children's noses pressed up against the glass of the front picture window, following the bike with their curious eyes. Robbie Jones left her children a clear example of what it is to help and serve their neighbor.

ıllıllıllıllıllıllıllıllıllıllıllıllıllıllıllıll

This Wednesday evening was quieter than usual. Emily had dropped all three kids off at Mrs. Scheinberg's house after an early supper along with a birch sapling from the nursery in Hamburg. The kids were going to help their godmother plant the new tree in the front yard where the old oak had been, and then Mrs. Scheinberg had promised them popcorn and a movie before coming back home. It was going to be a late night for everyone, but that was okay. This arrangement gave Mrs. Scheinberg a much-needed diversion the week of the anniversary of her husband's death, and it gave Emily a little more flexibility in caring for the altar. In fact, she decided to stay for the entire service that night. It seemed only right after she had unduly missed church the previous Sunday morning.

"You'll lock up?" Pastor asked, popping his head back into the sacristy after having removed his vestments.

"Yep." She didn't even turn to look at him. She was concentrating on holding the chalice between both of her hands. Her fingers had felt particularly numb all day, and she didn't trust her grip.

"I'll head on over to Arlene's, then, and pick up the kids."

"Thank you, honey. Tell her hello for me." She suddenly turned her head. "Oh, and Michael? Be sure to invite her over for supper Friday night. She's going to try to tell you no, but insist on it, okay?"

Pastor stepped in to give her a quick kiss on the cheek before leaving, and Emily turned back around to resume rinsing the chalice. It was an exquisitely ornate piece, its silver circumference decorated with detailed filigrees of Christ and his twelve disciples sitting at the table for the Last Supper. It was a work of art, donated by the Schmidt family in loving memory of Harold's brother Herman, and ever since, it had been the centerpiece of the church's Communionware. Unfortunately, it also had been the catalyst for Gloria Eisentraut's leaving the altar guild five years before. The persnickety woman had declared the "gaudy cup" to be a nuisance, and she wouldn't tolerate the inconvenience of polishing it every Christmas and Easter. No one had told Emily as much, but she suspected Gloria's dismissal had more to do with the Schmidt's chalice replacing the stainless steel one her father had donated fifty years before than any extra bit of buffing. Emily sighed now, remembering Nettie's tears of confusion and hurt about the whole ordeal. Emily hadn't been a member of the altar guild at the time, but she had lingered late in the balcony one Sunday morning to put away some music and had witnessed Gloria's dramatic and final exit from the sacristy. Life together in Christ was so complicated.

*That was it!* Emily thought to herself as she dried the chalice and wrapped it in silver cloth. *That was what made being a pastor's wife so hard!* All of the holy things in and around the church that normally inspired reverence and comfort in believing hearts were now dirtied with the fingerprints of people's brokenness and sin. They were tarnished from the erosive residue of Church Stress. These precious objects of devotion—these icons of Christ's own goodness and mercy—were now stripped of their consolation. Regard and affection were replaced with anger and pain, and it wasn't just the chalice. The painting hanging on the narthex wall of Jesus preaching to His disciples had been painted and donated to the church by Joseph Curry in honor of Pastor Fletcher's ordination, but the local artist no longer attended Zion. One month into the new pastor's tenure, Joseph had decided that his young cleric's chanting of the liturgy was "too churchy" for him. He left in search of more reformed pastures.

There was also the marriage kneeler stored behind the sacristy door. Darin Weber had made it three years before in honor of his daughter's wedding, but the bride was now divorced and pregnant with another man's child. So much sin in every direction! So much pain at every glance! Even the sacristy itself was now tainted for Emily. The sacred space set aside for preparing the Lord's Meal and tending to His body and blood now stank of discord. Yvonne was gone, but she had left behind accusations that sat rotting in the corner.

But Emily knew she should let this go. "'Whatever is true, whatever is honorable,'" she spoke aloud, disciplining herself as she put away the chalice in an upper cabinet. She turned toward the slip of paper pinned to the corkboard above the sink and read, "'Whatever is just, whatever is pure, whatever is lovely, whatever is commendable, if there is any excellence, if there is anything worthy of praise, think on these things.'"

Thankfully, however much Church Stress threatened to disturb the peace at Zion, there was not an absence of commendable things on which to think. She smiled, remembering Ben Schmidt's firm handshake five years before when he first had promised to start attending church with his grandma. And—oh!—the sight of

Blaine's dark head bending toward those baptismal waters. And nothing could compare to the joy of receiving Michael Fletcher's proposal of marriage and then God's good gift of children. And just this evening, as she had opened the cabinet to the right of the sink to pull out hosts for the service, Emily had discovered twelve Ziploc baggies filled with already-counted hosts—enough to serve her for the next three months of Wednesday nights—accompanied by a handwritten note from Irene: "Hear you've had a rough summer. Here's to hoping for a better fall." No, the darkness of Church Stress could never dampen the light of Christ, which burned brightly through this tiny, seemingly inconsequential congregation tucked away behind a nameless cornfield in Illinois.

||||||||||||||||||||||||||||||||||||||||||

When Emily finally crossed the street that night and opened the front door of the parsonage, she found the living room dark. Her husband must have put the kids to bed by himself, but the man was nowhere to be found. The light above the dining table was still burning, however, and there, casting the tiniest of shadows in the middle of the table, was a lone brown paper bag. Emily immediately grinned. It had been a long time since she had received one of those, and she tore into it as quietly as she could, drawing out a scroll of paper tied with a red ribbon. Her smile threatened to break her cheeks as she untied the ribbon and unrolled the paper. A smaller piece of paper fell from the scroll to the table. She quickly picked it up and read:

> *To my favorite pastor's wife:*
> *Every Order needs a good anthem.*
> *All my love, Michael*

Emily's tears were already falling as she set aside the note to unroll the scroll in its entirety. Her husband's careful, measured script read:

> The Word of Christ in me does dwell.
> No earthly siren song can quell
> This pure pleasure.
> Though devils taunt and fiends assail,
> Though allies turn and princes fail,
> Christ's my treasure
> In full measure.
> Alleluia!
>
> The Word of Christ in me does reign.
> All passions, lusts, and worldly gain—
> No more living!
> I am a new creation blessed,
> Marked with the Lamb's baptismal crest.
> Now forgiving.
> Sin outliving.
> Alleluia!
>
> The Word of Christ in me does bind
> My reborn self to all mankind,
> Love perfecting.
> Beloved, holy, chosen ones,
> Together, living as God's sons,
> Grace reflecting,
> Joy effecting.
> Alleluia!

*The Word of Christ in me does sing
Songs of the highest heav'nly King.
Raise a glad psalm!
With wisdom, teaching from above,
Admonishing in truth and love.
Join the vast throng
In an old song:
Alleluia!*

*The Word of Christ in me endures,
Eternal life my Lord procures.
High endeavor!
Beginning, Ending, God's own Son,
Before His throne we sing as one
All together,
Now, forever:
Alleluia!*

*That man!* Emily hugged the anthem to her chest and turned to find her husband standing in the darkened hallway, leaning against the doorpost with his arms crossed. He had shaved his beard, and his eyes were glistening. He must have been watching her read the poem.

"Think you could set it to music?"

She nodded her head, fumbling awkwardly with the scroll. Her fingers were still numb. She looked back up and opened her mouth to tell him how wonderful and thoughtful and talented he was, how much she appreciated his tender care and attention, how earnestly she needed him—but emotion had rendered her mute. Thankfully, her feet still worked, so when he opened wide his arms, she ran across the room to fill them.

## Chapter Thirty-Seven: The Evangelist

The entire congregation, young and old, gathered in the parish hall following the Divine Service on Sunday morning for a special presentation.

"As you all know," Pastor Fletcher said, addressing the entire assembly, "Nettie Schmidt has been volunteering in the church office all summer long. She's been covering the phones and generally keeping us afloat while we look to hire a new secretary."

Everyone politely patted the backs of their hands in appreciation. Their fingers were already gripped around Styrofoam cups of steaming coffee.

"What you may not know is that today marks the forty-fifth year in a row that Nettie has taught the third-grade Sunday School class here at Zion."

The gentle patter exploded into genuine applause, and Nettie, completely mystified by the unsolicited attention, covered her mouth with both of her hands and spontaneously dropped at the waist in a sudden, solemn bow. When she rounded back up, her eyes were watery.

"Robbie?" Pastor prodded.

Robbie Jones nodded and stepped forward, holding both of the flower arrangements from the altar in his hands. "These are for you, Mrs. Schmidt. Curt and I arranged them for you last night."

"Iiiee peek dah woh-zez!" Curt proclaimed.

"What?" Harold Schmidt hollered, his face crumpled in senile aggravation. "I can never understand that man. Tell him to speak up."

"Curt picked out the yellow roses," Robbie repeated evenly, setting the arrangements on a nearby table and standing protectively next to his friend, "and I chose the purple asters."

"Oh, how lovely!" Nettie beamed, taking one of Curt's hands between both of her own and putting it to her face. "Thank you, boys! I do love yellow, and purple is a holy color, of course."

Mrs. Scheinberg made a face that begged to differ, but Candice's gratuitous smile communicated only ardent approval.

"Purple *is* divine, Nettie," she agreed, sweeping onto the scene from the kitchen—Mrs. Scheinberg was relieved to see that, for once at least, the fitness queen was fully covered in a modest, be it lavender, skirt and blouse—"and in honor of this happy occasion, I baked twinkie cakes!"

Joyous cheers erupted from the crowd, and even Mrs. Scheinberg indulged in a pleased nod of her head, elbowing Max in merry anticipation. This was perfect. She couldn't think of a better first impression for Zion to make on the heathen hermit than a thick slice of twinkie cake.

"And don't worry!" Candice called out over the noise. "I made the batter with Sucanat instead of sugar and the frosting with tofu instead of cream."

Every individual cheer spun despondently through the air and fizzled to the ground like a balloon leaking air, and Max's eyes grew wide with honest concern. Mrs. Scheinberg sighed and set down her coffee, shaking her head. She was all for eating better, but some things—like parish hall cuisine—were not to be messed with for the sake of the Gospel. She promptly abandoned Max at the drink station to go lecture Candice on the finer points of evangelism.

"Speech!" Bev cried.

And she immediately spun back around, mumbling under her breath, "For the love of propriety," and resuming her post beside her guest. Remonstrating Candice would have to wait. Who knew what kind of nonsense was about to spill out of Nettie's mouth, and she didn't want Max thinking all Lutherans were certifiable.

"I still remember my first day teaching Sunday School," Nettie began, both of her hands reinterpreting everything she said in waves and loops and flutters. "Why, Lois Rincker was in that class. Where are you, Lois honey? Oh, there you are! Do you remember what you said to me that first day of Sunday School?"

Lois Kull, obviously mortified to be pointed out so unexpectedly, blushed and shook her head with the ferocity of a pup with a chew toy between its teeth.

"I asked the class who died on the cross for their sins, and you, Lois honey, raised your little hand in the air and answered, 'Mr. Christ!'"

Everyone chuckled, Max included, and Mrs. Scheinberg felt her shoulders ease a bit in their race to touch her ears. She didn't let her guard down entirely, though. Nettie's mouth was still moving.

"And you were in my class too, Donald," Nettie said, pointing an expressive finger toward Lois's husband, who was refreshing his empty cup from the ancient percolator.

"Me an' ever'body else in this room, Nettie!" Don hollered back good-naturedly.

That brought another chortle from the crowd.

"Well, you said the cutest thing one Easter," Nettie sang, throwing her hands up in the air for emphasis. "I asked you, 'Donald, who is Jesus?' and you answered, plain as a penny, 'Jesus is a raisin.'"

Everyone hooted loudly at that one, and Don tipped his head and lifted his cup in the air in friendly obeisance.

"And you, David," Nettie pointed to the eldest Jones boy who promptly tried to tuck his head between his shoulder blades like a turtle, "I'll never forget that Wednesday night Advent service when you asked for a doughnut after church."

Davie looked like he would like her to forget.

"I told you," Nettie continued, "'Well, David, it's not Sunday, so there are no doughnuts.' 'What day is it, Mrs. Schmidt?' you asked. 'It's Wednesday, David,' I answered, to which you crinkled your freckled nose and asked, 'Is there Wednesday school?' It was so darling, I almost cried. Your grandmother was the one who asked me to teach Sunday School, you know," Nettie reminisced, and everyone's gaze fell to their steaming cups in sober remembrance. "It doesn't seem so long ago to me, but then forty-five years is over half of my life, isn't it Harold?"

"What?" he yelled.

"Over half of my life!" Nettie raised her voice.

"Of course you're my wife," Harold nodded.

Nettie smiled tenderly at her husband, not seeming to care that he had misunderstood her. She, at least, had understood him. "You know," she continued, looking around the room, her voice beginning to waver, "I've had most of you in my classroom over the years—you and your children—and there's not much else a Sunday School teacher wants than to see her students all grown up and still going to church. It doesn't always work out that way. Most of my former students are missing here today, including my son," her voice strained painfully. "Hank's got himself convinced that farming's more important than faith come Sunday morning, but I remind God every night that Hank was trained up in the way he should go, and I pray that, even when he's old, he won't depart from what he was taught here at Zion."

Max suddenly sniffed loudly, and Mrs. Scheinberg, awed by his unexpected show of emotion, watched out of the corner of her eye as the blubbering man wiped at his nose with the back of his hand. Was he a Hank—a prodigal son—returning to the way of his raising? She fished in her bag for a tissue.

Pastor Fletcher stepped forward then, putting a comforting arm around Nettie's shoulders and pointing everyone's attention toward the north wall where the door to the third-grade Sunday School room stood ajar. "Nettie, we thank God for the gift of you, and in honor of your forty-five years of faithful teaching, the congregation has hung a plaque above your classroom door. Can you read it from here?"

Nettie, tears streaming down the riverbeds that her wrinkles had cut deep into her cheeks, shook her head. "I sure can't, Pastor."

"Then," he squeezed her affectionately, "allow me to read it for you: 'Nettie Schmidt's Room, forty-five years and counting . . .'"

Everyone clapped once again and moved in to hug the elderly woman, some laughing and some wiping at their eyes. Candice and Bev began to lay out celebratory slices of cake on a nearby table, but there were very few takers of the apostate confection. Max hung outside the rim of the group, shyly sipping at his coffee and watching from a safe distance, and Charlene, also visiting Zion for the first time that morning, stood near the kitchen door fielding nosy questions from a few well-meaning women of the church.

"Are you married, Charlene?" Marge Johnson asked pointedly.

The young woman shook her head.

"Well, that's all right. We support a seminarian who's coming back to preach over Thanksgiving. He's single. We'll set you up with him."

"No, Marge," Candice scolded mildly from behind the table. "Blaine's reserved for Mary."

Mary, who was standing nearby against the wall, blushed miserably, but no one noticed.

"Well, Dr. Brandt's still available," Janet Koelster offered, pointing a thumb across the parish hall toward the tall, handsome man with sandy hair leaning down to congratulate Nettie. "He goes off to England every summer to read books, but he just got back in town. C'mon, we'll introduce you to him."

"No," Marge hooked a confident hand around Janet's elbow, effectively stopping her. "He's too old for her."

"Says who?" Janet asked.

"Says decency," Marge replied, as if Charlene weren't standing there to answer for herself. "But I declare, Janet! Joe Pike's been taking his sweet time with you all of these years. Why don't you up and marry Dr. Brandt yourself?"

"Because," Janet instantly grinned and wiggled her left ring finger meaningfully, "*I'm* no longer available."

Marge shrieked as only a first soprano could and grabbed at Janet's hand to get a closer look at the dime-sized cubic zirconia. "Janet Koelster, you sneaky little devil! Joe finally proposed? Why didn't you tell me?"

"Because he only just asked me last night!" Janet squealed loudly like a teenager.

"Asked you what?" Emily inquired, suddenly appearing on the scene. She linked a protective arm through Charlene's. In all of the hubbub surrounding Nettie's celebration, the pastor's wife seemed to have lost track of her neighbor. Janet flashed her ring afresh, and the happy, feminine squalling started all over again.

Mary leaned against the wall, wishing it would swallow her whole. She watched as the noisy cluster of women swarmed around Janet's sparkling hand like bees around a raspberry bush. She bit her lip, fighting down a surprising wave of jealousy. Blaine was back at the seminary, and her own left hand was embarrassingly naked.

"Ah yoo meh-weed?" Curt asked.

Mary jumped, surprised. She hadn't noticed Curt scooting along the wall toward her for the raucous scene playing out before them. She took a deep breath and tried to smile at the man. "No, I'm not married. Are you?"

"No," Curt sighed. "Iiiee wanna fwam-lee."

Mary stared at him, unexpectedly touched by the man's confession. Of course Curt wanted a family. Why shouldn't he? He was sweet and gentle and gregarious and, well, human. Mary suddenly felt ashamed that she had never bothered to consider that Curt would understand exactly how she felt. "I want a family too."

"Iiiee yook for ma wiieef."

"You do? Have you found her?"

"No."

"How will you know when you find her?" Mary was genuinely curious. She felt that she could use all of the advice she could get. Her own skills in spouse-finding seemed to be lacking, presently.

"See muss haa mun-eee," Curt nodded, "an a how-suh!"

"Money, house. That makes sense."

"An see muss dwive!"

"That is an absolute must!" Mary smiled. "You know what, Curt? Your checklist isn't so different from mine."

Curt's eyes grew wide. "Can Iiiee meh-wee-oo?"

Mary shook her head. "I'm sorry, Curt. I've got a house, but I can't drive."

Curt's face fell, but only a little. "Aww, dat too bad. Iiiee yike-oo, Meh-wee."

That seemed to be the way most men related to her, apparently. Mary felt her eyes fill with tears. "I like you too, Curt." She took his hand in hers and squeezed it once before excusing herself. She couldn't take all of this marriage talk any longer. She snuck out of the parish hall, through the narthex, and into the darkened nave, tucking herself into a corner of a back pew where she could listen to the quiet in private. Before long, her shoulders began to shake, and she leaned forward to bury her head in her arms on the pew before her.

"Mary?" Pastor Fletcher asked.

She started, sitting up and wiping shamefully at her face. What was it with men creeping up on her unawares this morning? She hadn't heard Pastor opening the sanctuary door, but then, she hadn't exactly been listening. She leaned respectfully back against the pew, stiff as a statue, but she avoided meeting his eyes.

Pastor lowered himself onto the pew in front of her and sat sideways, thoughtfully showing her only his profile. He stared at the sunlight shining through a stained glass window picturing Jesus welcoming the little children. She knew that he was giving her a moment to compose herself.

"Did Blaine get back to the seminary all right?" he eventually asked.

Mary shrugged.

"Have you heard from him?"

Mary waited to answer until she could trust her voice. "No."

Pastor nodded, seeming to require no further explanation. "Well, how's work going?"

"Fine."

"And the Mulberry house?"

"It's fine."

"How do you like living in Bradbury?"

"Fine." But Mary's face melted into her hands.

Pastor waited for this wave of tears to pass, and then he said, "Mary, will you wait here for a second?"

She looked up at him then, confused. It was a strange request. Pastor rose from his seat and left through the center aisle door, returning a minute later with a book in hand. It was a slim volume with three swans pictured on the front, and the cover was outlined in a familiar blue.

"Emily found this book of poetry at the library a month or so ago," he explained. "It's written by a woman—a sister in Christ—who daily wakes to face demanding genetic predispositions and serious mental and physical challenges. Her voice is forthright yet gentle, poignant yet cheerful. Anyway, Emily and I both fell in love with her poems, so we ended up buying a copy of our own." He handed it to Mary. "It's yours now. I think, maybe, it's always been yours."

Mary took the book in her hands and looked at the cover: *Through Time's Looking Glass* by Michelle Lynn Swope. She recognized it immediately. Emily had checked it out that morning in July when the twins had been especially precocious. Her lips twitched at the memory. She opened the book to a random page. *Under the shadows, Just one girl*, she read silently, her eyes immediately smarting. This Michelle Swope apparently understood her particular kind of suffering. Her eyes wandered further down the page.

*She has not life's helpmeet,*
*Compensation life's only woe.*
*Her friends have gone,*
*To where does she turn?*
*Nowhere but alone,*
*Under the shadow*
*Where no one wishes to be . . .*
*Though years and years go by,*
*Still she remains.*
*Alone,*

*And I only know*
*She'd wish otherwise.*

Mary immediately shut the book and wiped at her eyes. She could tell that it would be best to read this in the privacy of her own home. "Thank you," she whispered.

"You're welcome."

"I think I'll go home now."

Pastor nodded. "Would you like a ride?"

Mary actually smiled. "I don't have very far to walk."

"That's right," Pastor chuckled. "How could I forget? I've walked that route more times than I can count. Well, good-bye, Mary. And God bless you."

⁙⁙⁙⁙⁙⁙⁙⁙⁙⁙⁙⁙⁙⁙⁙⁙⁙⁙⁙⁙⁙

As Pastor stood on the front church steps, watching Mary walk away, he wondered if this was how Pastor Gardner had felt so many years ago, looking down upon a young, widowed Mrs. Scheinberg, grieving and alone and in need of blessed occupation, a job which would serve her needs while giving her a chance to serve the needs of others. Wasn't the church secretary position at Zion birthed in such a moment? Well, to him, the answer for Mary was just as plain and clear forty-two years later. She wasn't a young widow, but she was a woman with special needs who, in spite of having a big heart ready to love and be loved, had not been given the gift of a husband. Mary needed the people of Zion, and the people of Zion—whether they knew it or not—needed her.

"Hey, Mary!" Pastor suddenly called out, running across the parking lot to catch up with her on the sidewalk.

Mary turned around, giving him a bewildered look. "Yes?"

He grinned then, unable to help himself. "I wonder if you might consider something for me."

# CHAPTER THIRTY-EIGHT: THE END

It wasn't her first day on the job, but there were moments when Mary seriously considered making it her last. This secretary gig was impossible. For starters, the computer squatting on her desk was a Dell dating from the prehistoric era. It might as well have been a typewriter for all it contributed to the design and layout of the bulletin, and the petrified copier stuck in the corner of the office jammed with every fifth sheet of paper. How Mrs. Scheinberg managed to produce multiple-paged bulletins week after week using these two fossils, Mary didn't know. She suspected the older woman had resorted to heterodox measures to get the job done, seeing as there were multiple files of hard-copy clip art hidden in the bottom drawer of the tall filing cabinet pushed up against the back wall. It seemed the former secretary literally had cut and pasted images—using actual glue, no doubt, based off of the gummy residue still clinging to the copier glass—onto the proof before sending it through the copier.

The clerical work was baffling, as well, and it was the garrulous phone's fault. It rang every five minutes of the day, and whoever was on the other end of the line—farmer, female, friend, or foe—ended up trying to tell her their life's story. She hadn't realized Lutherans could be so chatty. Their Sunday morning stoicism was feigned, apparently, for the moment they picked up a phone, they confabulated like spirited Pentecostals. The only way Mary could ever get any work done was to sneak back to the office in the evenings for an hour or two of uninterrupted labor, and even then she rarely succeeded in clearing her desk.

This morning, Mary was busy logging everyone's church attendance onto an ancient Excel spreadsheet, but the registries pulled from the pews were almost entirely unreadable. From the looks of it, handwriting had never been taught in the Bradbury school district. Several of the names—at least, she assumed they were names—had been chicken-scratched onto the forms, and she couldn't decipher male from female, child from adult, person from animal. She sighed. This job was so much worse than working at the library. There, at least, she had been able to enforce quiet zones. And read books.

"Who in the congregation has a last name starting with B?" Mary called aloud from her seat behind the cherry wood desk.

"Bradbury?" Pastor guessed, his faceless voice floating out of his open study.

"No."

"Bingley?"

"No." Mary took off her glasses and rubbed at her tired eyes. "Maybe it's an R instead of a B."

"Rincker, then? Irene and her husband, Phil—"

"That's it."

Mary quickly slid her glasses back onto her nose and hastily checked the appropriate box in the appropriate column before her brain lost hold of this precious information.

Working with Pastor Fletcher was easy enough. He was kind and attentive and helpful, though the man was forgetful. Four times over the last week she had reminded him to return the books he'd ordered over interlibrary loan—they were due today, and she was a stickler about such things—but the books were still sitting on his study table when she arrived this morning. She had resolved to walk them over to the library herself over lunch that day and just be done with it. Pastor also misplaced his keys at least once a day, and he usually forgot to give her his mileage. He never missed a meeting with a congregant, though. It seemed that he forgot only things, not people. Mary supposed she would rather have it that way than the reverse.

Pastor was also quick to come to her defense. Last week, when Candice Bradbury had fluttered into the office with concerns about the recent drop in weekly attendance, she suggested that Mary make phone calls to all of the delinquents.

"That's more a job for the elders than for Mary," Pastor had revised.

"Well, I mean no offense, Pastor, but I think most people would rather hear from a pretty woman in her twenties than an old farmer. I'm thinking of the good of the church, of course."

"Of course." Mary had been able to hear Pastor's voice stretching wide with a smile from within his study. "Then why don't you call them yourself, Candice? I bet everyone would love to hear from the first lady of Bradbury."

"Oh, now, Pastor," Candice had laughed lightly, "you flatter me. I don't have time for such things, of course, what with the gym expanding and Thomas's case load increasing by the hour. Besides, Mary is the one on salary here. I'd hate for her to run out of things to do, is all. Perhaps it would be better if she spent her energies organizing a young adults program for the community."

"She already does. It's called the church choir."

"No, no, Pastor. Something different. Something specifically designed to target young people. You know, to grow the church."

"The church is grown when people encounter the Word of God, Candice, not some program."

"Well, of course. That's why we should design a program where people can come here to Zion to encounter the Word of God."

"But we already have one. It's called the Divine Service, and we offer it two different days a week."

Mary had smiled at that. Pastor Fletcher had a tendency to be absentminded, but he was no idiot when it came to God and His Word.

"Besides," he had continued, "Mary's job description does not include organizing and executing new church programs. She has too much on her plate already."

Amen to that!

Candice was assertive to a fault, however, and hadn't stopped there. On her way out the study door, she discreetly handed Mary the Ladies Aid Society's handwritten secretarial notes for typing, "Double-spaced, not single, please." Thankfully, Pastor had been just two steps behind her, and in between courteously inquiring after Caroline and Thomas Jr. and the weather and Candice's health, he picked up the handwritten notes from Mary's desk and genially handed them back to the persistent woman, suggesting that the task of typing such notes was better suited for the society's secretary than the congregation's.

Pastor had then shut the door behind Candice and swung around toward Mary. "The people at Zion are some of the most caring, generous, faithful, stubborn, and opinionated people you will ever meet, and they will absolutely eat you alive if given the chance. You are the church secretary, nothing more. You are not the personal assistant to Candice and the Ladies Aid nor the church maid nor the groundskeeper nor the live-in babysitter. Do you understand?"

Mary had looked up at him with unblinking eyes and soberly nodded.

"You look scared," he had said.

"That's because I am."

"You don't need to be afraid of Candice."

"I'm not."

"Then what is it?"

She had been careful to maintain respectful eye contact but simultaneously lifted her left hand to point toward the table in his study. "I'm afraid you're going to forget to return those books."

At first, Pastor had given her a peculiar look—almost as if she had shape-shifted into someone else before his eyes—but then his face had relaxed into a familiar laugh that sounded as if they had shared a thousand such interactions and not just one. "Mary, you are a Godsend. You are the perfect person to be sitting behind that desk. And I'll return those books tomorrow."

His forgetfulness aside, Pastor did have one particularly annoying habit. He persisted in bugging her about developing a protocol for the church staff—namely, him—should she have a seizure. Mary had tried telling him that he would rarely know when she was having one, but that wasn't exactly true and they both knew it. And if she ever did go down with a full-blown tonic-clonic, she supposed it would be best if her boss knew what to do. She finally, with eyes downcast and cheeks hot, explained to him that it would help if he would remove any obstructions that might prove dangerous, time her seizure, and roll her onto her side should she vomit.

Mary flushed again, remembering the conversation. It was mortifying to have to talk about such personal things with an employer. She hated epilepsy. It forced its way into all of her relationships—even the professional ones—stealing everyone's attention away from her and forcing it on her condition. It was hovering over her desk even now, threatening to betray her at any moment, and it had no concern for her feelings of propriety. It would shame her in the end. It would make her convulse and drool and wet herself in front of this man she respected, and there wasn't a single thing she could do to stop it.

The phone rang just then, her heart skipping a beat. She couldn't help but hope that it was Blaine. He hadn't called her once since leaving for seminary.

"Zion Lutheran Church, this is Mary."

"Oh, Mary, your voice is pure moonshine! This is Nettie Schmidt."

She pushed down her disappointment with one tight swallow.

"Isn't it a beautiful day?" Nettie continued. "I woke this morning and thought, 'I should check on our new secretary and see how she's getting along.' Did you find the chair I left for you?"

Mary's hand involuntarily flew to her nose. "I did. Thank you, Nettie."

"You're so welcome, honey. Harold and I found it at an estate auction outside of Fancy Grove. I thought it smelled a bit smoky, but Harold said it was just the pork burgers at a nearby food stand."

The chair didn't smell "a bit smoky." It smelled as if its cushion had been stuffed with a bag of old cigarettes instead of foam.

"Thank you, Nettie. It was kind of you and Harold to think of me."

"Would you also like a footstool, honey?"

"Excuse me?"

"A footstool. To rest your feet. I wasn't sure if your legs were long enough to reach the floor on that chair. It seemed a bit tall to me."

"No, thank you. The seat is adjustable. My feet are firmly on the ground."

"Exactly as they should be! We once had a chair that was too tall for my feet, but I kept a stack of books nearby for a footrest."

Mary winced. Books were for reading, not for treading.

"Anyway, Harold is out in his truck this morning, poking about the country. He likes watching the harvest. It reminds him of his childhood, I think. A man never escapes his childhood, Mary. Don't let the wrinkles and the white hair fool you. Harold is still a boy at heart, and he'll never stop caring about his father's land. I told him that Hank's got everything under control, but he still wants to see the grain safely put in the bins. Every boy is born a farmer, you know. Or a fisherman."

Mary smiled. Nettie said the strangest things.

"Well, I'll let you go now, honey. I just wanted to make sure you heard a friendly voice today. Not everyone who called the church this summer was friendly."

But no sooner had Mary set down the receiver than the phone rang again.

"Zion Lutheran Church, this is Mary."

"Mary honey, it's me again. Nettie Schmidt."

She was never going to finish logging attendance.

"I am such a loony tuney! I forgot the reason I called earlier. I wanted to ask if you've seen my slip."

Mary frowned. "Your what?"

"My half-slip. It's white. No, it's more of a gray color now. Have you seen it?"

"Um. No."

"Are you sure?"

"Yes, Nettie. I've never seen any of your undergarments."

"Oh no, honey. Not those. This one's an outergarment."

Mary dropped her face into her free hand and wondered if there were any possible way this conversation could go on without her. She just couldn't take it at the moment. It already had been such a long day, and it was only ten fifteen in the morning.

"I wear this one on my head. It's for my hair, you see? Harold used up all of my scarves, and I can't exactly put a rug on my head, now, can I? And hats don't work right. They're too tight, but my slip breathes like a caterpillar. That's why I need to find it. My curls won't set right without it. Could you look in the women's restroom for me?"

"For your slip?"

"Yes, honey. Try the drawer to the right of the far sink."

Mary set down the receiver and set off down the hall on what she knew was a fool's errand, though she immediately repented of thinking Nettie a fool. Her parents had raised her to be more respectful of her elders than that. Nettie was simply imaginative. Yes, that was it. The sweet lady was probably recalling some repressed childhood memory—but there was the slip! And just like Nettie had said, tucked away in the far right drawer of the women's restroom. Mary, mystified, picked it up by the elastic band, using just a thumb and index finger, and quickly returned to her desk.

"It's here," she breathed into the receiver, lowering herself into her stinky chair. "You were right, Nettie."

"Oh, I'm so relieved! Thank you, honey. I was afraid my curls were going to have to go it alone this time."

"What shall I do with it?"

"Just drape it on one of the bushes out front."

"Excuse me?"

"Hang it on one of the bushes. The sun'll be good for it. I'll drive by and pick it up in a minute. Oh, wait till I tell Harold! He'll be so happy to hear that he doesn't have to go to Walmart this morning. I can't thank you enough, Mary. You're a gym!"

"A what? Oh, never mind. You're welcome, Nettie. Good-bye."

Mary did as she was told, but she didn't relish it. Respecting her elders was one thing, but decorating a boxwood with someone else's underwear was another.

"Just another day in the office, huh?"

Mary looked up, startled, her hand still on Nettie's half-slip. Mrs. Scheinberg was stepping down from the driver's side of her truck. Max Mauer unloaded his booted feet from the passenger side.

"Oh," Mary stumbled over her tongue, accidentally releasing the slip before it had properly caught on one of the limbs. It fell conspicuously to the ground. She quickly bent over to pick it up and spread it out evenly on a boxwood. "I was just . . ."

"Doing your laundry?"

"No." Mary's cheeks felt hot, and not from the sun. "I'm . . . helping Nettie."

"Ah," Mrs. Scheinberg nodded, seeming to understand automatically. "Of course. Well, while you're out here, can you give us a hand?"

Mary stalled for a moment, thinking of what Pastor had said to her last week.

"It's something for the office."

Mary gave in and walked toward the truck bed, slowing as she realized what it was they wanted to unload. There, wrapped in blankets and anchored by several bungee cords, were what appeared to be two waist-high bookshelves. Mrs. Scheinberg was watching with delight as the realization dawned on Mary's face.

"What's the good of hiring a librarian as the church secretary if we don't actually have a church library? Max here made some shelves for the south wall of the office, and the Jones family is bringing over Pastor Gardner's old books this afternoon. It'll take some time to catalog everything, but," Mrs. Scheinberg winked, "I think you're up to the task."

Mary's heart quickened along with her step. A library? Just across from her desk? She couldn't help but smile.

"It was all Pastor and Emily's idea, just so you know," Mrs. Scheinberg explained. "Two shelves is a small start, but the library should grow over time. Maybe we'll have the entire south wall and the whole length of the hallway lined with bookshelves by the time you retire."

They enlisted Pastor Fletcher's help as well, and the four of them—mostly three, as Mrs. Scheinberg stepped aside to open doors and direct traffic—carried one shelf at a time into the office. The older woman had lost a lot of weight over the summer, but Mary noticed that she still sometimes moved with a telling stiffness. The heavy bookcases were made of solid oak—too substantial for Mrs. Scheinberg's arthritic hands to grip—but they fit perfectly against each other along the south wall. Just the smell of them revived the entire scene.

"And don't forget this!"

Mrs. Scheinberg walked through the front door once again, wheeling into the office a new, coffee-brown executive leather chair. "Here, now. Every secretary needs her own chair."

Mary, hopeful, felt her eyes growing large as dates, but they shrank back to baby almonds the second she remembered her smoky pleather monstrosity. "The Schmidts already gave me a chair."

"Oh no, Mary Hopf," Mrs. Scheinberg shook her head resolutely, pulling the little gray economy seat away from the cherry wood desk and replacing it with the luxury vehicle. "Emily called me yesterday afternoon to warn me about this heinous chair, and—I'm sorry—we all know the Schmidts are sweet, but we can't have you and Pastor dying of lung cancer from breathing in secondhand smoke every day. Besides," she gave Mary a no-nonsense look, "*you* are everyone's first impression when they walk into Zion, and you can't be sitting behind this Cadillac of a desk in a Kia. No, your chair needs to be a Lexus."

Mary was sorely tempted to comply. She looked at Pastor, and he nodded his consent.

"Go ahead," Mrs. Scheinberg urged. "Sit in it."

Mary lowered herself onto the leather cushion and closed her eyes with sheer pleasure.

"That's memory foam you're feeling." Mrs. Scheinberg was practically giddy. "It provides optimal firmness and support for your back. And look! The chair has ergonomic controls too. I'm telling you, Mary, these things have gotten *so* much better since I was a secretary."

Mary laughed at that, hardly believing this was *her* chair. She ran her hands along the sleek arm components with the marble mocha finish but immediately halted at a miserable thought. "What do I tell the Schmidts?"

Mrs. Scheinberg silently questioned Pastor Fletcher with her eyebrows, and the man answered with a resolute nod of his head.

"I'll talk to the Schmidts," Pastor explained, turning to Mary, "but if they happen to ask you about it, tell them the truth: the church gave the chair away to someone in need, and Mrs. Scheinberg generously replaced it."

Mrs. Scheinberg nodded and pushed the ashen chair toward Max. "We were headed to Hamburg for lunch anyway. What do you say, Max? Shall we drop this beauty off at Goodwill on the way?"

Max grinned, approving of the plan.

"How's the harvest going, Max?" Pastor asked, expertly changing the subject.

"I's got all ma corn in day 'fore yesterday. Lost 'bout three acres total from Abigail, but I's gonna still come out in tha black."

"Glad to hear it," Pastor nodded. "And next year? Did you make a decision yet?"

"I's leasing ma land to Don."

"You're staying, then?"

"Both him and the hogs," Mrs. Scheinberg sighed. "God help me."

Max seemed anything but put off by his companion's drama. "New double-wide's comin' day after t'morra."

As Pastor and Max chatted some more about his land, Mrs. Scheinberg not-so-subtly leaned over Mary's shoulder to peer at her desk. She ran an experienced finger down the list of names on the top attendance sheet.

"Phil and Irene Rincker, the Plueth family, Penny Holley," she rattled off faster than an auctioneer, lifting a corner of the page to peek at the form underneath, "and the Jones family, the Fletchers, Charlene Nordheimer, Kathryn, and—oh, yes. This here is Curt's name. See how he presses so hard on the pen?"

Mary sat there, stunned. "How—?"

"I know it looks like hieroglyphics now, but you'll get used to everyone's handwriting, I promise. That, and everyone always sits in the same spot on Sundays. Learn the names by pew."

"Yes," Mary nodded, understanding.

"Just give yourself some time. You'll get the hang of it."

Mary sank back in her chair, more to be closer to this motherly woman than to get comfortable. She had thought Mrs. Scheinberg would be critical of her sitting behind this desk, but the woman was clearly rooting for her success.

"You're coming back to the office to work in the evenings, aren't you?" Mrs. Scheinberg's tone held a distinct note of criticism.

Mary held her breath.

"Your desk is too clean," Mrs. Scheinberg nodded, eyeing the near-empty desk and building her case sentence by sentence. "There's no way your desk can look this clean unless you're working overtime." She suddenly turned Mary's chair around and wagged her finger in her face. "Listen to me, young lady. Don't come back tonight. I mean it. Everything can wait until the morning, and anything that can't? Well, that usually falls under Pastor's domain anyway. You'll make yourself sick working day and night, and what good would you be to us then?"

The retired secretary was trying to make that last statement sound like a joke—Mary could tell—but it carried way too much truth to come across as funny. They looked at each other, one concerned and the other convicted.

"Now," Mrs. Scheinberg let go of the chair and stepped back, giving her some space, "have you heard from Blaine?"

Mary shook her head.

"Well," the older woman smoothly kept talking, "did I tell you that he left a crucifix hanging on my living room wall? Yes, he did. He must have hung it as I was gassing up the car to take him to Lincoln, the sneaky boy, and I found it when I got back home that afternoon. It's beautiful—an icon of Christ painted on a wooden cross—but I fear it's going to give Bev an early stroke. She may never come to my house ever again."

Mary laughed in response to the teasing twinkle in Mrs. Scheinberg's eye, and Pastor and Max quieted at the musical sound.

"Well," Mrs. Scheinberg motioned to Max, "our job is done here. We best let these two get back to work."

Max shook Pastor's hand, Mary stood to hug her benefactress, and Mrs. Scheinberg whispered in her ear, "Remember. You make him possible."

Mary knew she was talking about Pastor Fletcher.

"And don't let him lean against the wall all of the time," she groused more loudly as she pulled away, giving Pastor Fletcher a warning look. "It'll ruin his back, and it stains the walls."

Pastor didn't seem upset by the woman's accusation in the least. In fact, he looked surprisingly sentimental all of a sudden. The two exchanged a long, meaningful look, and then the good reverend quietly stepped into his study.

Max walked out the office door, pushing the rejected chair ahead of him, and Mrs. Scheinberg turned to follow. The second her hand touched the door, however, she doubled back and marched straight to the desk, cupping both of Mary's cheeks in her warm hands and surprising both of them.

"Child," she said, her voice breaking, "I was your age when I started this job. I didn't want it. I wanted something very different. I wanted to be home with Dean, cooking his meals and washing his clothes and milking his cows—definitely not typing bulletins and answering phones, that's for sure. But looking back, I realize this job was good for me, and I was good for it. I think you're good for it too."

Tears slipped down Mrs. Scheinberg's cheeks unchecked.

"Now, I don't know what God has in store for you or for Blaine or for any of us, but I can tell you this. Sitting in that chair, taking care of Pastor and looking after all of these dreadful, wonderful people . . . it's a good life. Okay? If God gives you nothing more than this all of your days, it'll be a good life." She kissed Mary sweetly on the cheek. "It'll be a *blessed* life."

Then, Mrs. Scheinberg turned and walked out the church door, leaving Mary behind with wide, seeing eyes.

# FROM ME TO YOU

TO THOSE WHO LIVE IN BRADBURY AND TO THOSE WHO
WISH THEY DID:

I suppose we could say that it is all my husband's fault.

Eight years ago, after punctuating the final sentence of my
first nonfiction book with a dramatically decisive period, I turned
around and put the following question to my beloved: "What
should I write next?"

"Write something you want to read," he responded, and I remember an immediate, pleasurable warmth spreading across my
shoulders as an Avonlea-esque island town with an Anne Shirley-
ish heroine wearing puffed sleeves came to mind.

"And write about what you know," he added.

Well, that nixed Prince Edward Island—and all green ga-
bles were out—but a small-town church balcony somewhere in
Cornfield, Illinois, began to take shape in my mind. You see, I had
just finished writing on the heavy topic of barrenness, and I was
hungry for a little humor and happiness on the page. That's how
Bradbury was born.

The imaginary town itself lies somewhere in the nutrient-rich soil of Illinois's glacier belt, not far from where I was raised. And Bradbury's unique shape, character, and commerce are closest to those of Strasburg, Greenville, and Auburn, Illinois—three small towns of which I am ever fond and whose setting in the story of my own life provided the perfect combination of toil and triumph for a daydreaming girl to grow, mature, and I pray, bear good fruit. There is no better place for a writer to plant her adult feet than in the fertile field of nostalgia.

The people of Bradbury? You probably already know that Mrs. Scheinberg—particularly the opening chapter of *House of Living Stones*—was shaped by my favorite, principled meddler, Mrs. Rachel Lynde, and rumor has it that Pastor Fletcher was born from a second cousin once removed of a particular Dr. Gilbert Blythe. But what you may not know is that Emily Duke and Candice Bradbury and the Jones family and everyone else living in Bradbury County are nothing more than figments of my imagination (and, most likely, my subconscious).

I've never met Emily Duke in real life, though I modeled her face and stature from a girl I met in college whose natural, quiet, rosy beauty radiated across time and space and, now, pages. Frankly, it brought me pleasure to think on her face more than any other, and thus, in accordance with many such trivial whims, a fictional character began to take shape. Emily's personality most resembles that of a dearest and best of friend's, whose faithfulness and patience amidst adversity remain the objects of my deepest admiration, and our musical heroine's particular kind of suffering, however different in specifics from that of my own or that of my friends and family, is universal in its essence to that of every Christian. Or so I believe.

The Rev. Michael Fletcher bears the same first name as my own husband, but that is merely coincidence. I wanted God's messenger to Zion Lutheran Church to be named after an angel, and who else but the archangel Michael could bear the "arrow" of God's Word, the very meaning of the surname "Fletcher"? Evan Ebner is the musical maestro I've always wanted to please, and I spent an entire book trying to earn that man's respect just to sit with him in the balcony for one chapter and talk shop. Blaine Maler is every student I didn't love enough, Ben Schmidt is my hardworking, self-sacrificing father, Robbie Jones is the son I've never had, and Alice Gardner-Ebner is the best in every churchwoman I've ever met.

Many of you have asked me, "Which character in Bradbury are you?" My closest friends tell me that I am an odd combination of Rebecca Jones, Alice Gardner-Ebner, Emily Duke, and Mrs. Scheinberg. But honestly, everyone is me, and no one is me. I gave Emily my music and my vocation (and my tears), but her shyness and hesitancy in life are as far from me as the east is from the west. Alice's instincts and feelings are more like my own, but her thoughts and words are wiser than anything I've ever produced in real time. Rebecca Jones has my personality, Beverly Davis has my values, Evan Ebner has my stubbornness, Candice Bradbury has my tenacity, and Mrs. Scheinberg has my principles and sins, but otherwise, these characters—these people, in my mind—departed from my hearth long ago. They are their own selves, through and through, and I love them. It blesses me that you have loved them too.

I tried my best to heed my husband's advice to write about what I know, but the truth is that I don't know enough to fill an entire book let alone a trilogy. And not everything I do know is good for sharing. Writing about church life is tricky that way, but thankfully, a little discernment, scholarship, observation, empathy, dreaming, God-given creativity, and good editors go a long way in securing a solid, edifying story. It has always been my intention to serve you, the Church, in writing fiction, and it is my hope and prayer that I have served you well.

I wrote these books because I wanted to ponder—no, dwell in—the miraculous beauty of the holy ordinary in the Christian life. Thank you for dwelling in that holy ordinary with me in Bradbury, and may God bless you in the towns and times ahead.

Gratefully yours,
Katie

## "IN THE HARVEST" BY MICHELLE LYNN SWOPE

AN ORIGINAL POEM CREATED FOR *THE HARVEST RAISE*

*Wisdom is God given, God breathed;*
*God's Word is issued, heard in a pew.*
*The harvest is large,*
*The workers few.*
*Oh, how much there is to do.*

*In the town of Bradbury we see,*
*Uniformed for you, for me,*
*The Word of God in state professed,*
*Jesus, God's own righteousness.*

*The years have come,*
*The years will go,*
*And still the Word is taught aflow;*
*Sacraments taken—water; bread and body,*
*Jesus' blood and wine.*
*People gather*
*God's Word to find.*

*From near and far, uphill and down.*
*They travel here and yon.*
*God's Word is preached,*
*His Word confessed,*
*Jesus our own righteousness.*

*Inaugurated at Creation's birth,*
*past the flood,*
*Christ's death on the cross . . .*

*In this little town of friends*
*with joy and sorrow, tears galore*
*Peace is given without end.*

*Pastors preached*
*The Word to know,*
*And in the town God comes to call,*
*A little Baby born to all.*

*Harvest time brings gifts again.*
*Thanks be to God who sent His Son,*
*Who taught the Word, Amen, Amen . . .*
*Lord, please come in.*


Michelle Lynn Swope is the author of *Through Time's Looking Glass: A Book of Poetry*. A Missouri native and a young woman with disabilities, Michelle has a twin brother with whom she shares a close friendship, an adoptive family, and a love of words.

# ALTAR GUILD 101

## ALTAR, LECTERN, AND PULPIT PARAMENTS

### Superfrontal

A parament that covers the front of the altar. It is shorter than the frontal, hanging down only 8 to 12 inches from the mensa.

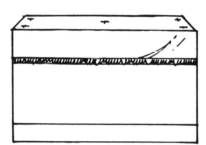

### Fair linen

A cloth of fine linen that is placed on top of the mensa of the altar. It is the last of the three cloths placed on the altar, on top of the cerecloth and the frontal linen.

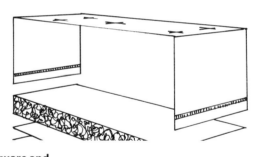

### Square and band antependium

A parament that hangs from the pulpit or lectern and displays the liturgical color of the season. Also known as a pulpit or lectern fall, or a pulpit or lectern frontal. The plural is antependia.

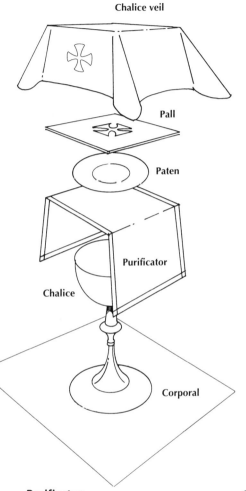

**Chalice veil**

**Pall**

**Paten**

**Purificator**

**Chalice**

**Corporal**

## SACRAMENTAL LINENS AND VESSELS

### Chalice veil

An 18- to 24-inch square cloth of the same material and of the same color as the paraments. It is the last item draped.

### Chalice pall

A 7- to 9-inch square of glass, metal, or plastic covered with white material. It fits over the paten when the chalice is vested.

### Paten

A round plate to hold the sacramental hosts of the service of Holy Communion. Normally it is the sacramental vessel on which the Communion breads are consecrated and from which they are distributed. The size of the paten should allow it to sit on top of the chalice when the chalice is vested.

### Purificator

This sacramental linen is used to wipe the rim of the chalice after use. In setting up the sacramental vessels, the purificator is placed over the chalice and under the paten when the chalice is being vested. Usually several additional purificators are put in the burse or laid on the corporal next to the vested chalice.

### Chalice

A cup with a bowl, stem, and foot that is used to distribute the Lord's blood. Also referred to as the common cup.

### Corporal

An 18- to 21-inch square white sacramental linen. It is placed in the center of the altar and on it the vessels for Holy Communion are set.

## Cruet

A container of glass or precious metal for wine or water in the service of Holy Communion. It is often smaller than the flagon.

## Ciborium

A sacramental vessel shaped like a chalice but with a cover. It was used originally as a container for consecrated hosts. It now can function either as a pyx or a paten.

## Pyx

A small round or rectangular container with a cover that is used to hold hosts. See also ciborium.

Information and images taken from *The Altar Guild Manual: Lutheran Service Book Edition,* © 2008 Concordia Publishing House. All rights reserved. Used by permission.

Cruet

Ciborium

Pyx

# DISCUSSION QUESTIONS

The title of this book is taken from the hymn "On What Has Now Been Sown" (*LSB* 921). Who raises the harvest in the Church?

Emily is most comfortable living within the boundaries she creates for herself. How does Charlene keep crossing those boundaries?

Should pastors be married or not? Why?

There are several examples of male-female relationships in this book. Which ones succeed, and which ones don't? Why?

What is the cause of Pastor and Emily's "Church Stress"?

Life in Christ is not a solitary experience. We are all members of one Body, and we live to serve the other members even as they live to serve us. Who at Zion Lutheran Church understands this truth? Who does not?

How are Mrs. Scheinberg and Mary similar? How are they different?

What are some ways children and adults with special needs can be better integrated into the life of your church?

Everything we do teaches children something. What does it teach children when we forgo church in order to attend programs, clubs, and camps?

Who is the evangelist in chapter 37?

Aging is often accompanied by physical, emotional, and spiritual trials. Which of these trials are hardest for Mrs. Scheinberg? for Beverly?

Are Yvonne's feelings and behaviors justified? Are Pastor's and Emily's?

Emily and Mrs. Scheinberg are given opportunities to serve their neighbors amidst extraordinary circumstances. How do they rise to the challenge? How do they fall short?

What do you hope for Mary in life?

## ACKNOWLEDGMENTS

Thank you to . . .

Peggy Kuethe for advocating for this trilogy from its conception as a story worthy of taking risks—I am forever grateful; Concordia Publishing House for choosing the Anthems of Zion series as the right product for launching a new Christian fiction line; Elizabeth Pittman, Holli Rolfes, and Lindsey Martie for cheerfully seeing this series to its completion; Lisa Clark for naming this series and for being a rock-star editor and an even better friend; Jamie and Emily for polishing this book to a happy shine; Dad for making maps out of my sketches and facts out of my dreams; Mom for being my favorite English teacher and sounding board; Jenny and Crissy for encouraging and supporting me in all things; Lucy for repeatedly reminding me for whom I am writing; Becky for counseling me to write what's right, not what's expected; Vicki for teaching me to be a better listener; Crissy for her professional advice as a speech pathologist; Grandma for instructing me in the finer points of farmin' ugly; Carol for baby doll baptisms; Lisa for helping me find the humor in Penny Holley's hygiene; Elizabeth for telling me the truth about trash; Joan for creatively using an electric knife; Tony and Jesse for having great chancel conversations; Cris for teaching me about personable issues; Jenny for braving the hallway critics in assisted living homes; Mona for encouraging and comforting me in the sacristy; Barb for duly warning me about Saturday nights; JT for Christological dried fruits; Evelyn for Friday school; Heather, Cris, Tad, Andrea, and Kahra for cheering on my Olympic lifts; Michelle Swope for dignifying my book with her beautiful poetry; Mona Fuerstenau for teaching me how to better care for and respect Curt,

Kathryn, and everyone in the church with intellectual and developmental disabilities; Officer Tad Stalets for coming to my rescue on a very scary porch and giving authority to the law in Bradbury; the Rev. Dr. Jon Vieker for encouraging me to write about the real conversations had between a pastor and his wife; Pastor Nus for faithfully reminding me and the church that men should serve and protect their families even unto death; Pastor Mohr for preaching Christ on the cross for the forgiveness of our sins; Pastor Wilken for instructing Pastor Fletcher, Blaine, and me through the "Same-Sex Marriage" tract; Pastor Oliphant for pointing me to Loehe for sound advice regarding pastors and their wives; Kelly Schumacher for asking me, "What about those who are heartbroken over being single?"; Mia, Mary, Charlotte, Lily, Lydia, and Eva Maria for giving Julia and George their charm; my focus group readers: Mom, Dad, Michael, Lucy, Becky, Becca, Crissy, Julia, Elizabeth, Cheryl, Michelle, Grandma, Rebekah, Emily, Lauren, Kristi, Nora, Steve, Jo, Jane, Amanda, Karin, Heather, and Vanessa—thank you for going into the writing vault with me; the saints of Good Shepherd Lutheran Church in Sherman, Illinois, for taking in loving stride all that comes with having an author for a pastor's wife; every one of you who joined me on this trip to Bradbury and delighted in the people found there: your companionship made every challenge and difficulty experienced in the writing process worth it; Michael, my beloved husband and pastor, for being Bradbury's faithful first responder as well as my own: I was able to write these books because of your love, support, and generous benefaction; and God the Father, Son, and Holy Spirit for creating, redeeming, comforting, and preserving the Church as promised unto life everlasting and for graciously giving me every good and perfect gift, including these words.

*Soli Deo gloria.*